My mother sits next to me in the parked car. . . .

"What's this one?" she asks.

I don't even look to see what tape she's holding but I say, "I don't know, Mom. They're just mix tapes. Mostly from years ago."

She turns and looks at me, tucks a bunch of my hair behind my ear.

"Laney," she says, "give me a break. I know they're tapes."

"What do you want to know about them?" I ask, watching the blink of streetlights on the empty roadway. "You might not like them."

"I don't need to like the songs. It just seems to me like these are more than tapes, almost like they are love letters or bits of your past I don't know about."

"And?" I ask. But I know what she wants.

"And I want to know the stories."

"I can try to explain them, the tapes," I say.

"Start with this one, tell me everything. And tomorrow, we'll do more."

I put the key in the ignition and the tape into the player. Side A starts.

"*Liner Notes* tells the story of two simultaneous journeys—a cross-country road trip and a musical voyage down memory lane—that both end up in the same happy place. Like one of the narrator's prize mix tapes, Emily Franklin's charming debut novel is a grab bag of delights."

—Tom Perrotta,
author of *Election* and *Joe College*

LINER
notes

EMILY FRANKLIN

Thanks for coming to my reading!

E

doWn
tOwn
press

New York   London   Toronto·   Sydney   Singapore

DOWNTOWN PRESS
1230 Avenue of the Americas
New York, NY 10020

ISBN: 0-7434-6983-6

First Downtown Press trade paperback printing October 2003

10 9 8 7 6 5 4 3 2 1

DOWNTOWN PRESS and colophon are registered trademarks of
Simon & Schuster, Inc.

Printed in the U.S.A.

For information regarding special discounts for bulk purchases,
please contact Simon & Schuster Special Sales at 1-800-456-6798
or business@simonandschuster.com

For Nathan and Sam
and most especially
for Adam—forever my unexpected song

acknowledgments

SIDE A: To my parents—who were certain this was possible. Your support and love make this a reality. To my brothers—my first friends and original music and memory-sharers. To my grandparents—for reading, believing in, and inspiring me. I love you all.

SIDE B: To Tracy Fisher—champion agent; Amy Pierpont for seeing the whole as more than just the sum of its parts; and Jenny Meyer for answering a million questions and believing in this book from the beginning. I am grateful for Heather Woodcock and Greer Hendricks who gave early readings and valuable comments. Many thanks to friends who graciously lent mixes and the tales behind them or provided help in the making of this book: Pic-Boy, Jocelyn, Taylor, Maria, Tania, Jules, Nicole, Becca, Jer, Christian, and Marty. To the Strauss family—you are better than the best bagels. And, of course, to JFC, as promised from (and for) the beginning.

LINER
notes

CHAPTER
one

Moons and Junes and Ferris Wheels

SIDE A

Blue Sky
  —Tom Waits
C'mon, C'mon
  —Sheryl Crow
Fountain of Sorrow
  —Jackson Browne
The Gambler
  —Kenny Rogers
No Sleep Till Brooklyn
  —Beastie Boys
Summer Breeze
  —Seals and Crofts
The Piña Colada Song
  —Rupert Holmes
Gardening at Night
  —R.E.M.

SIDE B

Both Sides Now
  —Judy Collins
Isn't She Lovely
  —Stevie Wonder
Play Me
  —Neil Diamond
I Will Be in Love with You
  —L. Taylor
Empty Pages
  —Traffic
Sister Golden Hair
  —America
Taxi
  —Harry Chapin
Whenever I Call You Friend
  —Loggins

Paris, Texas
    —Ry Cooder
Carefree Highway
    —Gordon Lightfoot
Sneaking Sally (Through
    the Alley)—Palmer
Glory Bound
    —Martin Sexton

I Saw Her Again
    —The Mamas and the Papas
Remember the Feeling
    —Chicago
For You
    —Bruce Springsteen
Can't Let Go
    —Lucinda Williams

These are the two cross-country driving scenarios I have pictured:

One :

My best girlfriends and I drive through random states and pick up crappy souvenirs from each place—pens that undress women when you turn them upside down, glass balls filled with snow that flutters over some landmark, shot glasses from saloons called things like the Dirt Cowboy. With the windows rolled down, we listen to seventies favorites like "Summer Breeze," "Hot Child in the City," and "Right Down the Line."

We say things like, "Gerry Rafferty? I always forget he sings that. I love that song!" And when "Same Auld Lang Syne" comes on, and it's late and dark and the lights of Vegas or Tahoe are just appearing over the dash, we cry a little, since it's such a sad song. But then, we gamble and eat steak dinners for $1.99 and stay in a plush hotel and win big. Or, we go to some run-down bar and play pinball and check in at the Blue Bell Inn, roadside, where we meet handsome, smart guys who are also doing the cross-country thing, but with eighties tunes. Together, we're our own not-sold-in-stores CD.

Two:

Without a shirt and while holding my hand, my boyfriend is a safe, confident driver. Past all the tourist spots like Myrtle Beach, Virginia Beach, even Savannah, we drive for hours a day and sleep at bed and breakfasts with rich cultural histories. At night, there are no televisions, so we read our books out loud to each other. We aren't sure of our destination, only that we'll know when we get there. The landscape will reach out to us and we will be sure that this spot is where we are meant to be. Also, the boyfriend is very good-looking and an excellent mechanic.

But what happens is:

Neither the friends nor the Road Trip Guy—who has never actually existed—can make it. Sure, my girlfriends and I had always talked about a cross-country trip, but the reality of hovering at thirty years old didn't leave us the time to do it. Somehow we'd missed our opportunity at music video-style driving. Now we're simply too old or too busy to sling a backpack into the trunk and get our tank-topped selves into a convertible. Or maybe that's just my excuse.

At the very least, we're all scattered: Red-haired Casey, my college friend, is in London working as a professional puppeteer. Tall, glamorous Maggie's off in Hollywood—her role of being lifelong friend to me is tempered with her role as Superstar Wife to *People* magazine's "Sexiest Man Ever." Completing my group of friends-as-seen-in-a-hair-care-advertisement is Shana, whose brown hair is perpetually a different shade. Shana who is meant for a road trip like this. Shana, my funny, irreverent summer camp friend, who isn't here because—well, that's another issue altogether.

What I do know is that my girlfriends and I would have made the perfect shampoo copy—you know, the glossy photo spread ones where each woman has different hair so you can tell them apart, or identify with the one who's most like you. "Oh—that's me! I'm the curly brunette!" or "She's got a ponytail just like mine."

And as for my Imaginary Road Trip Man—he might be out there, somewhere. But if I've ever met him—my ideal—I probably didn't recognize him. Sometimes I think the greatest guy around could be right in front of me and I'd pick the guy next to him. Or maybe I'd pick the right guy, but manage somehow to mess it up.

So, since I am alone—please not forever, but at this point who knows—I've looked at the road trip as time to myself. Or maybe that's just my rationalizing why I'm making the three-thousand-mile drive by myself, unkissed, unadored in the pit of Southwest canyons. Unappreciated in some revolting motel that, unlike in fantasy, really is disgusting with mothy sheets and someone's forgotten underwear in the shower.

Of course this isn't how I planned this trip. But here's what I figure:

If I can't have Fantasy Guy along for the trip, I'll be the heroine of my own never-filmed John Hughes movie, cute and perky with a sound track to boot, or—moody, quirky, half filmed in black and white to the tune of Ry Cooder's eerie melodies following me as I drive through the rock and sand west. To make like a camera and film myself—instead of being a part of it and feeling my way. But it's hard—how do you know why you do what you do? And even when you figure it out, what to do with the knowledge?

My artistic motives professor made us start our final year of graduate school training with our backs to him. Each of us stood in the bright hall facing huge empty canvases. He instructed us to start even though we had no oils, no watercolors, no charcoal, just a dry brush.

"I want you to create here," the professor said. He'd been there since the late fifties and rumor had it that he'd smoked pot with beat poets and had his share of undergrads visit his tapestried office, but we all listened to him as he paced back and forth, his paint-splattered shoes echoing on the linoleum. "When you can't make something work, when you can't figure out your motivation, you become paralyzed. Start with all the images of paintings, of art, of creating something whole, and then stop the fragmenting process . . ."

I don't remember everything else he said. I just remember standing, looking at the plain white sheet ahead of me and thinking, *This is what I have to do—not just on the canvas, but in my life.*

When I'd started my advanced degree in art restoration, when I'd taken chemistry and memorized cleaning calculations, I felt like I was accomplishing something—fixing paintings, degriming unappreciated sculptures, helping. But now I'd finished my degree, earned my papers, and lined up a job back in Boston and I wasn't sure I could do it—make the art or my life whole.

Maybe the hippie-professor guy was right, maybe I've patched up enough items—myself included—and now I'm ready to move forward, not distancing myself, making my past into vignettes, but cohering my memories so where I've been and where I'm heading fit together.

So this was my plan. I would pack up my things, ship them back east with the ease of hot sweaty moving men, and I would hit the road with my coffee and snacks, with my music, and try somehow to figure out where I came up empty—and how to fix it.

And I wouldn't be truly alone—I had my mix tapes. Each one signified a piece of my life—two summer months, a year in high school, a boy I no longer knew, a friendship that had crumbled—and this made for excellent time travel. I could listen to each one and be right back there, and maybe regain whatever it was I left behind. In traipsing back into these memories, these specific periods in time, maybe I could sort out how I came to be here—three thousand miles away from where I started, and no real idea either how to get back or what exactly I hoped to find once I did.

Of course, I could fly back to Boston where my new job lies in wait. Where I know I have to face facts—get an apartment (alone), live at my parents' (with them) until I find a place, and go to a wedding (also alone) where Marcus (call him my Backup Guy) is the groom, and possibly reconcile the fact that I might never speak to Shana again (more me alone, but as a withered old woman with no other old granny—we planned on aging together—to dance with). So, sure. I could fly back to Boston and get it over with. But I think it's time I took this trip—alone or otherwise.

Of course, like my Road Trip Guy, or my fabulous girlfriends who could magically drop their lives to join me on my journey, my alone time vanished, too. But not in the way I imagined, not when I got the phone call that my parents were in town, not when they announced they were coming over. Something in my father's tone let me know they had something to tell me—something that I knew meant a major change in my plans.

CHAPTER

two

You know that catalogue that arrives every other week in your mailbox? The one you want to throw out but end up inevitably paging through just in case there's some new desk or table lamp or wonderful ceramic mugs? That's my dad's company. Ceramics Shack. While he does the design and mock-ups in Boston still, the headquarters are in the Bay Area, so he comes out here regularly. During graduate school, I'd meet him for a drink or a movie when he came to town, or watch the catalogue layout while assistants pecked at him, and then he'd go back home to Mom and I'd return to life as normal. Dad could come into town, exchange some loose banter about consumerism (which he benefited from) and Mom's illness (which he didn't), and leave me with a mug he'd just designed or a platter that would never be sold in the catalogue, and I could go home with something new, but not remarkably different myself.

But this June, while he's supervising the photo shoot for the Ceramics Shack holiday catalogue, my father decides he needs to have one of his old original pottery pieces brought out to him in San Francisco for inspiration. Back in Boston, my mother has been working furiously to finish the designs for the collection of "antiqued farm furniture" which will be sold through the catalogue in the spring. My father calls my mother, frustrated that the shoot's not perfect. He feels the cover looks bland. He questions whether he should have ever allowed his pottery to become mass-produced, unnumbered things. My mother tells him to relax. This is when he decides he needs to put his Giant Old Blue Bowl on the cover of the catalogue. My mother thinks this is a wonderful idea and says she'll FedEx it the next day. This is met with a groan as my father envisions his art arriving in a mess of jumbled fragments suitable only for mosaic tiling.

Even though she's supposed to have stowed it underneath her seat or above her in the overhead compartment, my mother flies to San Francisco with the Giant Old Blue Bowl strapped into the seat next to her. Kisses and thanks from my father, a jolly couple of days in the swanky hotel there, and a stunning catalogue are the results of her trip. The Giant Old Blue Bowl, as it has been known in our family for twenty-six years since the first one was made and I was small enough to sit in it, is renamed the Moroccan Entertaining Dish. It's destined to become a Ceramics Shack "classic"; it sells for $189 plus shipping.

When the shoot's finished, and my parents are scheduled to fly home the next morning, they call me and inform me they're coming over for brunch. My graduate school days are finished, I'm half packed into cardboard boxes and suitcases for the drive back east, and have no eggs, no bread, nothing that constitutes a snack, let alone the spread they've probably envisioned. Plus, my mother's never come out here before, so why bother now?

"I don't have any food," I say to my mother before she's even up the front stoop.

"We didn't come for a meal," she says and reaches out to hug me.

I move toward her and let her, and then pat her back. I remember how my friend Marcus always told me that when people pat you during a hug, they don't want to be touching you in the first place. Then I feel terrible that I'm potentially sending this message to my mom, despite the fact that I'm not sure I want to be hugging her. We do better when we're seated facing each other, but not necessarily hugging.

"I brought the goods," my father says.

He holds up a bag from the Bagel Basement and takes my mother's arm. She pretends to pull him up the steps, which they find very funny and I show them inside to where the boxes are stacked and labeled. This is my biggest move as an adult. Somehow I'd acquired kitchen utensils and linens, towels—albeit a mixture of junky threadbare castoffs plus two plush white ones my mother had shipped out to me in one of her bizarre Valentine's Day packages (each year she sent a card and books with titles like *Doors to Hearts: How to Open Up and Let Love In* or some similarly crappy one like *Why Does the Lonely Bird Still Sing*—in the hopes that somehow this would make my life sunny and simple, but that only emphasized that it wasn't).

And to make it worse—I couldn't get rid of those lame books. I'd packed them with the rest of my things: lamps and papers, my canvases, some rolled up—some stretched onto frames. I'd moved cross-country before when I'd left New York and my live-in situation with Crappy Jeremy—a name Marcus called him that seemed to stick—and moved out of the dorm at college, out of my parents' house, too, but this feels larger. I don't want to think about what and where I'm leaving, I want to concentrate on where I'll live next, which sink my toothbrush will rest on, which view I might have from my kitchen.

Packing up this time, I realized how much effort moving requires. Growing up I'd only moved once. My parents had packed up the house in Vermont while my brother, Danny, and I had created a pathetic kid yard sale out front. We lined up half-broken toys, decks of cards that were missing an ace or king, withered stuffed animals we'd outgrown and marked each one five cents or ten in the hopes of making candy money while our parents ended one part of our lives and readied for the next. Surrounded by boxes and roles of bubble wrap now, I realize I am about to do the same thing. A whole segment of my life is done now, but unlike my parents when they moved us from Vermont to Boston, I'm making this trip by myself.

My mother opens a flap of one of the boxes and before she can even peer inside, I find myself rushing to the box as if I'm protecting it.

"That's just art stuff," I say. "Nothing interesting."

My mother sits at the kitchen table where I've left the final phone bill to be paid. I know she's looking around at things—not so much being nosy, just making herself at home and looking for evidence, I think, of the Daughter Creature she hardly knew. I know part of her must view me as an unknown entity—she'd been around for the previews and the first bit of my life movie, but then suddenly left the theater for the middle section and now was unable to follow my plot.

I show my father a couple of slides of my work from the art show in town, holding the small squares of film up to the light. He studies each one and makes comments.

"This one's amazing!" He holds it up to my mother as if she can see it across the room.

"Thanks," I say to him and go sit at the table with my mom, who looks at the photographs I have stacked up. The pictures are not in any sort of order, just ones I've kept around from scattered times. My mother looks at an old one—my days of summer camp gone by—and points to Shana.

"She always had such a nice smile," my mother says, tracing Shana's grin with her pinky. I nod. "How is Shana these days?"

"Fine," I say. Really, I have no idea how she is, since I haven't returned her calls and she hasn't responded to my emails. I make up excuses as to why—maybe I have the wrong email address or maybe she's annoyed that I won't call her. Email just seems easier, less emotional, more rational.

My mother studies me, able to tell I'm faking. "What's she up to?"

"So," I say, pretending I didn't hear her. "How's the catalogue coming?" Deflecting questions back to my father's business was a fallback, a simple way of showing interest and not having to delve into my own issues.

I collect the pile of photographs from my mother before she can press me for more information and listen to my father's rambling about pottery. I put the phone bill on top of my stack, noticing briefly how many itemized calls there are to Marcus back in the 617 area code. He's in Massachusetts, engaged. Engaged! If Shana were here, I'd tell her how I've managed to misplace the wedding invitation and we'd come up with dozens of meanings for this action. But neither Shana nor Marcus are around, so I pretend not to know when the wedding date is, even though I'm fully aware that come Labor Day I'll be perspiring with the rest of the guests, under an oceanside tent, decidedly not standing next to the groom.

I lead my parents to the porch for our brown bag brunch. My father hands me the latest catalogue—I like to see the thing with only photos, no text, since it makes me feel like an insider to the trade, like I have one up on everyone's mail.

"Quite a view," my father says, looking at the slope of the driveway, the mountains behind. He wraps a piece of lox around a wedge of red tomato. He has a smile spilling out from behind his mouthful—I assume due to the catalogue's success.

"Yes," I say, "I used to hike up there with friends." I don't mention Jeremy, even though during his last visit—our last attempt at togethering—he almost left me up there on the mountain. I shake the memory of that off and focus on my bagel, peeling the outer layer off in glossy strips.

"You can hike in Boston, too," my mother says. "I'd like to do that some time with you."

"Oh, yeah?" I have that slightly false-positive tone of a math teacher trying for patience with a student who can't figure out the equation. My mother hasn't hiked in years, not since after her first remission. Post-relapse, she'd saved her strength and made it partway up Blue Hill, the only mountainlike place near us. In the cacophony of late fall—airplanes overhead, school tour groups learning about nature by collecting leaves, cars cluttering the parking lot—we'd spread out the Hudson Bay blanket on the stubbled grass and pretended we were far off, in another land, looking past the highway out to sea or safari land. So the idea of hiking with my mother seems unlikely at best.

"Yes," my mother continues, "the only hiking I've done, really recently, is up a flight of stairs." She makes a joke of some kind that doesn't quite fly. I get the first part of a laugh out when my father gives me a look and I stop.

"I'm almost done packing," I say and pile our paper plates and plastic knives into the brown bag. "I'm leaving tomorrow after the moving van comes."

My father leans on the porch railing and rubs his temples with his hands in a circular motion. Used to be, he'd have wet clay on his hands that would dry in his hair and crumble out at dinner or when he was tucking us in. I was always brushing clay dust from my clothes and sheets like I'd been to the beach and returned with pockets full of sand.

My mother mouths something to my father. He does some secret gesture back to her and then she flaps at him with her hands. I look from my mother and back to my father several times—at their indecipherable marital Ping-Pong.

"What's going on?" I ask.

"Well . . ." my father begins and turns around so he's addressing both my mother and me. He gives my mother a married look, a knowing exchange I simultaneously long for with another person and loathe the idea of—my parents almost always know what the other is thinking.

"What your father means is," my mother jumps in, "is that I'm all better." She stands up as if this will show me.

All better. Two words that seem to come from a Band-Aid advertisement—a simple flat sticky brown strip plastered over a playground abrasion and a television mother saying, "All better."

They are not the words I associate with hearing my mother's recurrent and resistant non-Hodgkin's lymphoma is no longer control-
ling and destroying her small frame, the treatment no longer making her alternate between throwing up and falling asleep, slumped,
her mouth slack and mellow, sometimes even in midsentence.

"It's just fantastic," my father says softly to my mother. And
then, louder, less privately to me, "Isn't it?" He looks to me.
"Laney? Isn't it?"

They are waiting for my After-School Special response, the
sobbing and hugging and complete release of more than a decade
of being the daughter of an ill mother. In the Norman Rockwell
cancer painting that doesn't exist, we are cartooned, rosy red
cheeks and grins as wide as watermelon slices, the happy tears
stuck oil-painted in our eyes as the caption reads "Mom's All
Better" or "The Doctor Fixed Annie's Boo-Boo."

I remember finding out, hearing the word *lymphoma* for the
first time. It was early summer. We were on the way to Logan
Airport to collect my English cousin Jamie and his friend Ben who
were to spend the summer with us. The vinyl of the car stuck to
my thigh and I'd peeled myself off from one spot and tried to get
into the shade. My brother, Danny, had used his elbow to guard
his side of the backseat and a shoving match ensued. Soon, my
parents had pulled the car over to the dirt-edge shoulder and
turned around to face us. Danny and I thought we'd get the usual
get-along-and-share talk, even though we were too old for it. I'd
put my Walkman headphones on and listened to nothing until my
father had started to cry. The yellow plastic U slid down onto my
neck and Danny removed his elbow from my rib cage.

Then we listened to my father's explanation, how it started
with the simple "Mom's sick" and moved on to "lymphoma, radiation therapy, possible memory loss, fatigue." I remember thinking—even then—how movies had ruined any hope of gentleness,
of picturing Mom lying in bed calmly. *Terms of Endearment* and
that movie with Mary Tyler Moore and the sick daughter who has
only the six weeks of the film to live had implanted terror-

inducing hospital scenes of shrieking for more medication and begging paper-capped, clipboard-wielding nurses for statistics.

And the statistics had been good. Whatever "good cancer" was, that's what Mom had. Everyone said, "Of all the ones to get, it's not bad." She'd weathered her first round of treatment well, diving right into her role as high-spirited patient, the one who never complained as the intern missed her vein and had to restick the needle until her thin wrist was as bruised as aubergine skin. If she'd ever felt lonely in the odd, quiet hum of the radiology lab, she'd never said anything.

Not until the non-Hodgkin's lymphoma had come back, when we learned to call it resistant, recurrent—like it was an emotion that wouldn't change or a song somehow persisting through her body, unable to find another tune—did she seem to give in, allow the exhaustion to hover and cling, the fog of it stretching out between us, mapping us away from each other.

I longed back then for the movie scene I'd create again and again in my head: I'd come home from college, or from my job at the museum in New York, from anywhere, the supermarket even, and Mom would be standing in the doorway, greeting me with an embrace that needed no words—I, we, we'd all just know that she was in the clear.

Now, more than a decade later, I have my movie scene right in front of me. Past the porch-lined bushes, crickets make their summer sounds, the leaves unfurl into the morning sun, and far up and above the sloped and shaded side of the mountain, a plane arcs noiselessly away from us.

"Are you sure?" I ask.

"Laney, I've been free and clear for nearly twenty-two months. I just had a PET scan and have another one scheduled for August back in Boston." My mother grins and breathes deeply and I go kiss her cheek. I feel immediately that the cheek kiss is inadequate and half imagine a scene where a brass band comes out with posters and a parade with me leading and cheering.

"Of course, my immune system is always going to be a bit

weaker, but the CT scans, everything, show it's behind us now."

I'd spoken with my brother two days before and he'd obviously been hiding this information from me, which is doubly annoying because we'd been allies in the whole mess. We'd slept in hospital lobbies together, made middle-of-the-night phone calls, wondered if Mom would make it long enough to see us graduate, get jobs or licenses, if she'd ever live to be a grandma.

"What's up?" Danny had said into the phone, his keyboard clicking away in the background. "How're you doing these days?"

"You're the med student," I'd said. "I'm fine. How's Mom?" He was emailing while talking to me and I was painting while talking to him. The long, narrow canvas—a skyline, a marsh, stretched out in front of me, angled toward the bay windows—and I was distracted since I hardly ever take the time just to paint for myself.

"Mom's . . . well—you'll see her soon enough when you get back here . . . but just so you know, she might be acting a bit weird."

"Well," I said, "she is weird. That's what we love about her."

At the time, I thought he might be preparing me for more bad news. We were all used to the cycles of health and sick, sicker, sickest, but we still tried to protect each other from the shock that still came when tests came back positive when they should have been negative or negative when they should have been positive. All told, there'd been three rounds of it; the initial diagnosis followed by radiation, then remission. Then, just as we'd begun to relax into that, and Mom had started quilting again, creating a bunch of sample designs for potential retail sale, she'd relapsed. The half-stitched squares of starred and swirled patterns stayed stuck under the Singer's needle collecting pollen dust from the open windows in her room as she underwent a heavy dose of chemotherapy that made her muscles weak, made her stomach intolerant of almost everything, made her wither under the heat of summer and go into hibernation.

My father explains, as he finishes the lox, that my mother is not only well, but since the third segment of her treatment, the bone marrow transplant, the doctors at Massachusetts General are "thrilled." Her oncologist doesn't say "see you soon" at the end of her appointments now. I don't ask more, because all I can do is feel my breathing increase and watch my mother look at me and my father like we are mimes, like we're talking about someone else.

My father says to my mother, "Annie, now you say something."

"Laney, my love," says my mother and she sounds normal, "I hope you understand my waiting to tell you in person. I just didn't want another situation where we all got disappointed again. I wanted it to be real."

"Oh, Mom," I say while I hug her, "I'm so happy for you."

"I'm happy for all of us," my father says. My mother nods.

We all look at different things—my mother slides the seeds from her wedge of tomato using her slender thumb. The guts of it go out in one fine stream onto a paper plate. I watch the seeds like they are yellowed ants, rowed and organized for action. My father watches my mother nibble on the fruit-as-vegetable and hums a Neil Young song, the one about going back to something or someplace. I look at my parked car and wonder if I should make reservations at some hotels on my trip or just wing it.

"What time do you guys leave for the airport?" I ask.

Another parental-married look. My mother stands up, straightens her linen shirt, and says, "I don't want to fly back to Boston. I decided I don't like flying, and so I should drive back there with you. If you don't mind."

What I think is: But I do mind. I mind very much.

CHAPTER
three

So my mother doesn't want to fly? This from the woman who would be so excited to get on planes that she would make us pre-board even though we didn't need extra time. My mother loved the organization on planes; the small trays, how the used dinner dishes fit together in stacks, how the music was chosen and headphones in plastic wrappers were handed out wordlessly. My mother spoke with the flight attendants and cleaned the bathroom sink as a courtesy to the next passenger like the sign asked. More than anything, my mother loved the bags of toiletries and socks that were distributed on long flights. When we'd flown to London, my mother had looked at everything carefully: the mini-toothbrush and paste, the flimsy comb, mints, slippers, and then carefully tucked the whole package away and stored it in the linen closet at home.

"You love to fly," I say. It comes out almost desperate, like I'm the failing airline economy and she's my last passenger attempt.

"No, I really don't. The trip here was the last one I want to take on a plane. I am ready to see this country by car. I want to drink Hurricanes in New Orleans, sit in the Giant Chair in a Cornfield somewhere. I want my picture taken on an oversize cowboy hat. The real Americana."

"Laney," my father says and puts his hands on my shoulders while he stands behind me, "your mom doesn't want to fly, she wants to drive home with you, okay?"

"Oh, Mom, I really . . ." I say and stop before I say something I'll regret. I breathe deeply. "This is important to me. I just want some space."

"All you ever want is space," my mother says stonily and looks right into my eyes.

"What do you mean?" I ask, wishing I had some bagel left to chew, to distract my parents with as I try to avoid this whole conversation.

"You know what I mean, Laney," my mother says.

"Annie," my father says and steps toward my mother, "maybe we should let Laney finish packing and come back later."

"No!" my mother shouts. "It's always later, isn't it?" She takes my hands. "We're always saying we'll talk about it later or deal with it later, and maybe that was what we had to do." She doesn't say *when I was sick* but I know that's what she's talking about—how our whole family could shove past an issue or just tuck it away without talking, just so we could face her illness.

"What can I say to you?" I ask. "Obviously, I'm glad you're not sick anymore. But I don't understand what this has to do with interrupting my road trip."

"I'm sorry you see it as an interruption," my mother says, stretching out the last word so I see it hurt her. "I see it as a chance for us to spend time together before you move back and get so busy with museum work and dating—or whatever you call it these days—that we don't have any mother-daughter quality time."

I cringe at the expression. Mother-daughter time growing up barely existed and when it did, it ended with my mother correcting my hairstyle or choice of friends, trying to squeeze in any motherly advice in the few minutes she had between treatments or appointments. Sometimes the years before the sickness seem nonexistent. But then I think about Vermont, and the family we were, the girl I was before I lived with a mother who was likely to slip away while we watched, helpless.

I try to find the warmth from back then, the surety of the time when we'd lived in Vermont. Looking at my mother's open face on the porch I can see her younger, the way she was back then. On weekend mornings I'd wake to the sound of the record needle sliding onto the vinyl. The stereo sat on top of a farmhouse hutch and the only thing separating me from the music was a thin, makeshift wall my parents had constructed from salvaged plywood. The house was a converted barn, big enough to keep us all—my mother, father, brother, and me—and the rows of records that lined the main room.

We all sang back then. Music swirled in my mind, through an open window, under the door cracks, seeping in like water. As he potted, my dad would go through entire albums, early James Taylor, *Mud Slide Slim*, or Odetta, *Go In and Out Your Window*. Danny would poke his small fingers into the wet clay as my dad turned the wheel around and back, checking for symmetry. My mom and I mixed up glaze for the pots and plates Dad had already made. Not everyone wanted to live in Vermont, though. Maggie's parents were moving to Boston, where academics flourished and creative types like my dad could find both artistic peace and room to grow a business.

For the life of me, I couldn't figure out why someone wouldn't want to live in a giant barn like we did then. My mother did most of the interior painting herself. She'd always been good with colors and fabric and knitting. Not that we had knitted curtains or anything, but she could sew a vest or make a blanket in a day, even Irish chain quilts, their complex lines and loops melding into each other.

When I turned ten, my dad had me wait all day before he gave me my birthday present. He stood around with Mom and Danny and watched me open it. Danny played with the leather fringe that hung loose from Dad's vest and I watched my mother's eyes for a hint as to what the gift was. All I'd wanted was Mom's old tape recorder. After I undid the wrapping paper and found I had it, Danny said, "Guess which hand?"

"Left," I said.

When he brought the hand in front, Danny was holding tightly to a blank tape. In the other hand, there was a tape, *Annie,* my favorite musical, and coincidentally my mother's name. I'd dance around singing her name over and over like it was a prayer of some kind.

"What's the blank one for?" I asked.

"It's for recording music, or talking, or anything that you'd like," my mother said. "It's for remembering."

Later on, I'd taken some records from the crates that held them upright and filed in no particular order and one by one chosen songs to record on my new machine. Some beginnings were cut off since I'd forget to press the record button, and the sound quality is only fair, because my arm grew tired from holding the recorder up to the speakers. Once in a while, I'd catch myself singing along to the music, but no matter what the final product, that tape was the start of something.

Early On

SIDE A	SIDE B
Carolina in my Mind	The Circle Game
—James Taylor	—Joni Mitchell
Go In and Out Your Window	BSUR
—Odetta	—James Taylor
Annie's Song	Red Pajamas
—John Denver	—Pete Seeger
Andy's Gone	Loch Lomond
—Bok, Muir, and Trickett	—Acapella
America	Octopus's Garden
—Simon and Garfunkel	—The Beatles

Something—
  The Beatles
Plant a Radish
  —from *The Fantastiks*
Love and Affection
  —Joan Armatrading
The Right Thing to Do
  —Carly Simon
Forever in Blue Jeans
  —Neil Diamond

Let the Sun Shine In
  —from *Hair*
Proud Mary
  —Ike and Tina Turner
Suite: Judy Blue Eyes
  —CSN
The Weight
  —The Band
The Rainbow Connection
  —Kermit from *The Muppet
    Show*

I'd played the tape for Maggie when we sat in my room. Maggie grew up with a series of "helpers"—the last was Marlene, who'd been fired by Maggie's dad when he realized she was using her days off to be a "lady of the evening." After Marlene's departure, a package arrived addressed to her and it had sat in Maggie's attic until one afternoon when she'd lugged it over to my house. Wondering what the contents could be, we stared at the box until we couldn't take it anymore. Upstairs with scissors, we sliced along the edge and looked at each other before opening the flaps.

"You do it," Maggie said. Her parents taught at the local college and were planning to move soon. I couldn't imagine not living where I was.

"Okay," I said. I hummed the words to "Suite: Judy Blue Eyes," making up the Spanish part as I went along, hums turning to mumbles, not realizing then that it was *Suite*, instead of *Sweet*.

"Why make a tape?" Maggie said. "Why not just play the whole record?" She'd feel the same her whole life, even when she ended up marrying a man who still liked to make her tapes.

I didn't know what the answer was, only that it felt good, right somehow, that all the feelings of listening to the records could be summed up in one small cassette. That you'd have a marker of some sort to show where you'd been and what you'd listened to, and who or what it all meant.

Up in the attic, Maggie and I readied ourselves for the package contents.

"Come on, let's see." Maggie perched on her knees for a better view. We hadn't been friends for that long; she was new that year. When Kelly, the mean girl in our class, had decided Maggie was too conceited about her child modeling—Maggie always had that self-assuredness all girls long for—and wanted to switch desks, I traded. Kelly had made a similar decision about me when I was new, only she'd said, "Laney's new. A new Jew, isn't that right? She thinks she's special." But I wasn't really new to the school, only to the class, so I wasn't looking for Kelly's friendship. "I'm not a new Jew," I had said, unaware of Kelly's intent to slur, "I've always been one." Kelly raised her eyebrows and shook her head, then went back to her own desk.

I'd casually mentioned the incident to my mother, who told me to ignore the mean things people say, that not everyone would understand or welcome you, but that it was my job in life to know where I stood.

"Here we go," I said to Maggie and began to reach inside. I pulled out a long necklace chain made from blue stones and jewels.

"Are they real?" Maggie asked.

"I don't know. Oh, there's more." In her excitement, Maggie reached into the box, too, and grabbed some bangles, which she put on her wrist. More things: pink lipstick, faux diamond hair clips, hatpins, a macramé belt with green beads woven in, too much to count. Maggie and I could not believe our good fortune. We sat with the heaps of jewelry draped over us until we emptied the box of its last contents, a pink satin robe with butterflies embroidered onto the sleeves, slippers with feathers on the front, and diamonds lining the edges.

"We can take turns," we said to each other slightly out of unison.

Maggie wanted to keep the stuff a secret, but I showed my mother, wanting to share my found treasures with her. She held the necklaces just as we had, like a foreign thing that might come alive any minute.

"You girls are really growing up," she'd said and it never occurred to me that this might be sad for her. That in her plaid shirt she wore all the time, the soft one that I like to put my cheek to, she might already miss the part of me that was growing away from her.

We brought the piles of clothing outside and unpacked it on the surface of a large, flat rock that had warmed in the afternoon sun. My mother watched as Maggie slinked around between the apple blossom trees wearing the shiny robe. I moved the boa I had around my neck against my cheek and thought about the baby chicks that hatched at the next-door farm the week before.

"Come on," Maggie yelled to me. The metal bangle bracelets clinked together. We swung each other around and around until I was sure my head would come off or Maggie would go flying against one of the orchard trees. The spring ground was spattered with apple blossom petals and we were new spring birds. Chicks, even.

I think now of my mother then, how healthy she was, how normal it all seemed—pre-sickness, pre-growing up, pre-everything.

Unaware of my thoughts of Vermont and the past, my mother looks out at my car and says, "Please, Laney." She motions to the road with her open palms, asking me again to let her come with me.

I'm not sure whether I'm defeated, too tired to argue, or if maybe part of me, that part I hardly recognize, wants to have her there. Wants her to be the passenger on my journey back. I think again about my tapes and how they were each a time capsule I wanted to revisit.

"I listen to music you might not like," I say. She nods. "I like to eat gross food when I drive—really gross—like fluorescent Cheetos and corn nuts and drive-through delights." My mother smiles.

"It's okay," she says. "I will, too."

"Sorry to be missing it," my father says, and laughs. He buttons his jacket and crumples the brunch remains, taking them with him and leaving us—my mother and myself—alone together, staring at the mountains in front of us.

That night I give my mom the futon and I sleep on a camping pad curled up in an old shirt, sheets wound up around my legs.

"We should leave early," I say.

"Whenever you want," she says. I can hear the shift in her breathing as she gives in to sleep. "I'm really looking forward to it."

"Yeah," I say. I picture the roadway, the tarmac ahead like the canvas in class, open, ready, uncontrolled—and I pull the sheets tighter around me, tightening myself against whatever's ahead. When I can't sleep and the clock reads two, I go to the basement where suitcases filled with off-season clothes are piled up. I shove a final sweater inside—its wool brings up the swell of winter, of other places I've lived and visited, of kissed lips and jokes I can't quite recall. The last of my tapes to be packed are crated by my duffel bag and my lousy paint-splattered double-cassette stereo box waits to be put into a packing container. I fish out a couple of old tapes and finish the tape I'd started for my road trip. When I'm finished making it, I title it Moons and Junes and Ferris Wheels since my mother is joining me. She used to sing the lyrics to me, and I know she'll want to be part of the tape, just like the music is part of me.

"I slept so well—even on that old thing," my mother says, and points to the futon with her take-out raspberry smoothie cup as she slides into sandals. I can't help but notice the sags in the mattress, the odd wine stain, unidentified streaks of don't-want-to-even-know, and think about the fun and crappy nights spent on that bed. Thankfully, it will remain here, donated to the frat down at the university.

"Are you ready?" I ask, tying my hair back with a rubber band from the newspaper.

"If you are," my mother answers, and waits to see if I hug her or high-five her, if I want to celebrate our starting out.

When the movers slide the rolling door closed, they rev and drive off with thirteen feet of truck filled to the roof with my things. On the porch steps, my mother and I sit and watch as the truck shrinks to toy size in the distance. My mother waves to the miniature moving van and I watch her hand move up and down, side to side, flapping like a small, near boneless wing.

CHAPTER
four

Several days later, my camera has film in it—photographs as of yet undeveloped—of the first days of the cross-country drive. Snapshots: my mother, sitting cross-legged in a linen shorts outfit and wide-brimmed hat in Carmel, the two of us in Los Angeles, in front of that movie theater everyone stands in front of, pretending they're someone famous. I'd wanted to stay at the Madonna Inn in San Luis Obispo, California—the ultimate in theme hotels where I knew I'd have spent one night with Maggie or Shana, just for a laugh. In college, Casey and I used to joke about taking dates to cheesy places like that, but we never did. Now if she went she'd be taking an entirely different sort of date—I realize I should tell my mother about Casey's new life, about my trip to London this past winter and what it revealed, but not today. Maybe if we'd been in the Safari Room with its fake green jungle plants and zebra-striped cushions or the Caveman Suite, described as having Neanderthal-style décor, whatever that meant. But my mother didn't even look inside the inn; she bought postcards next door and then took a photograph of our personless car while I looked at the hotel brochure.

One picture from the roll is of me standing with my hands in my pockets, biting my lip, while the ocean rolls back onto itself behind me.

When I ask my mother why she chose to snap the shot just then, she says, "I like to see you that way, thinking."

"I was looking at you," I say.

"You were looking at me looking at you," she replies.

She's right. In my Red Sox cap and one of Danny's well-loved sweatshirts, she looks elegant and crisp, toned even. Her weight had plummeted during the various courses of treatment and she was always sipping those cans of Ensure or Boost, protein shakes that contained a billion calories that never amounted to anything on her. Her collarbone jutted up through her turtlenecks, her arms lost their tone, and she took to layering her cottons and draping a cardigan over her shoulders, even in the heat, so no one would see the protrusion of shoulder bone from under her T-shirts.

"You know what I like even more than seeing you think?" she asks as we're back in the car. "Hearing what it is you're thinking."

"I'm thinking about what tape to listen to, if you must know," I say, but I'm sure it's clear by my tone that that's not all. I'm thinking about early days in families, how they seem so easy. "Vermont was so easy," I blurt out.

"What?" my mother asks, but I don't repeat myself. Then she clicks her seat belt into place and says, "It wasn't, really. You see it that way because you were little."

"And how was it, really?" I ask.

"Not as easy as you think," my mother answers without looking at me. She leaves it at that, with me wondering what she means.

My mother's wearing a shirt she's had since way back when I wore overalls and napped because I had to, not because I stayed up too late the night before chasing a boy or seeing the midnight showing of a scary movie. I brush against her sleeve as I go to put the radio on and feel the fabric between my fingers and smile at her.

"It's very soft," I say, hoping to ease the silence between us.

When we'd moved from Vermont to Boston, way before she got sick, my mother's style had hardly changed. While my dad traded in his faded, clay-caked jeans for corduroys and blazers with patches on the elbows, my mother kept to her button-down shirts and pressed khakis. Always, I could picture her in a Fair Isle sweater, crouching to show me the fallen leaves on a trail I couldn't name, a still photo in my mind of her healthy and me with her, holding her hand and not wanting to let go.

We'd sort-of traded trails for towns when we moved. In Cambridge, my dad's potting shed was bigger, fancier. My mother sewed cushions for his built-in benches, covered them with antiqued tapestry material. People were already noticing my father's work. He was a local celebrity of sorts. It seemed that everyone had a David Jeeks piece in the house, a trumpet vase, an orange serving plate, mugs in crackled blues, violets, and soft creams. The glaze was one my mother still loved—its color hovered between white and yellow, a lost ring of opened egg.

In the car, I find myself studying her, memorizing her now as I try to get the images of her unwell out of my head. It's as if I want to remold her into the present. I wonder if, as her health becomes greater, clearer, and surer, she will regain her gestures, hug a bit more loosely, one hand in my hair, the other on my back. Sometimes, or at least the whole time she was sick, she'd hug with such abandon it made me feel so sorry for her, for myself, that I'd have to push her back.

"Not long," my mother says and points to the green road sign that heads us to Arizona. "I thought you were going to put on a tape."

"The radio's fine." I sip at the dregs of iced coffee, crunching sugar granules through the straw.

"Why don't you put on one of your famous mixers?" she says and reaches to the compartment on the door side to find a tape.

"Mixes, Mom. Mixes, not mixers. Those were dances—like a sock-hop," I say.

"Fine," she shrugs, "Mixes—put one on, will you? I can't take much more of this static."

She reaches forward and fiddles with the radio knobs, hoping this will somehow give us better reception even though we're in the middle of craggy rocky nowhere. When I don't put a tape on, she switches the radio off and it's quickly apparent how little we're saying. I try to think of words or stories or questions, but I'm so used to asking how she's feeling and what the treatment plan is that, in the absence of these questions, I can't think of another thing to say. We sit. Landscape slides by and hot wind seeps in through the car's old windows.

"This is ridiculous," my mother says. "I came here to be with you."

"You are with me." I stare ahead, afraid to look over at her in case she's near tears.

"I'm next to you," she says.

My mother slips her hand past the gears, touches my cheek, her nonverbal *please*.

I do nothing. The truth is, I don't want to listen to old tapes with her. They are mine, my memories, all safely tucked down where only I can get at them, where only they can get at me.

By the time we've driven past Flagstaff, I have learned that my mother is still my mother, but not. I feel the way you do when you learn that "Ring Around the Rosy" is actually about the bubonic plague or that "Shoo Fly Don't Bother Me" is a slave narrative, the same but altered. She is the supercheerful counterpart to my straight face. When she orders coffee, regular now, not decaf, I wonder if I should tell her to try half-caf, since she nearly flits around the diner. She rips a sugar packet in half and then decides against it, leaving the tiny granules to stick to our palms or slide along the Formica tabletop. Midway through a sentence, she leaps up and announces her bathroom intentions. Before I can say something sophomoric like, "Great, Mom, now everyone knows about your need to pee," I think about how she'd fallen once in the bathroom at home, bruising her cheek on the tubside, and then, too weak to stand back up, how she'd had to call for one of us. Danny had gotten there first, scooped her up like folded linens, and pushed past me in the hallway. I'd brought tea that sat untouched on her bedside table and my father had held a bag of frozen peas against the swelling.

Now she's the vision of health, her face is kid-caramel colored, despite constant slatherings of sunblock. Her newfound lust for everything swells around us like steam in a tight space, threatening to overtake any visibility of what she had been.

"Aren't diners great?" she beams, tucking into her egg white-and-spinach omelet. "And the service here—so friendly!"

So far, my mother has raved about everything—using *wonderful, fantastic, lovely,* and even *cool* to describe the lines of palm trees in Santa Monica, California, the brochures of tourist activities at a rest stop on the Arizona border, even the car after its journey through Melvin's Suds n' Duds, the combination car wash/dry cleaners we'd gone through before breakfast. I tried to remember how she used to talk; was she always this annoyingly positive all the time?

On the long stretch of blank highway that leads us closer to Utah, my mother sings the entire Rodgers and Hammerstein score from *Oklahoma*—the overture to the finale.

"You know we're nowhere near that state, right, Mom?" I say. She continues, acting both the male and female leads.

"That's incredible that you remember so much of it," I say.

"Because of the radiation, you mean?" she asks, taking a pause during "I'm Just a Girl Who Can't Say No." One of the side effects of her many series of radiation therapies was a blurred, patchy memory. Maybe she'd forget the name of a college friend, knowing it began with a C, but unable to think *Casey*. Or she'd have to retrace her steps in dialogue in an attempt to verbalize what had been so clear moments before. She minded that less than the nausea, or the sore throat. "At least I fit in with my age demographic," she'd laughed at a dinner party once when she wanted truffle oil for the pasta but had to call it "mushrooms those pigs like" instead.

"No, actually. That didn't even occur to me. You always mess up songs." And then I add, "I mean, even before, you could hardly . . ."

"I've always loved this show. 'Corn as high as an elephant's eye.' How funny!" she says. "I doubt any one of those characters had ever seen an elephant before."

"Maybe a circus passed through town once," I say.

"Of course, you'd find a way to make it plausible," my mother says like she's proud.

Soon I'm sorry she has such recall for the musical genre, since she hums her way through the wordless sections and sings all the vocal sections.

On the outskirts of Lake Powell, after checking into a small hotel, we eat a lousy fried fish dinner and walk around a strip mall built into the concave side of a mass of rocks until I am saturated with the red moonscaped nothingness and soft-serve ice cream. I can't help but wish I had my camp friend, Shana, with me. She'd be the perfect person for this. We'd sit on the car's roof, looking at people we felt no connection to, wonder at the details of their lives. I think about calling her from the payphone outside the motel later, but I doubt I will. She's call-screening now, and probably wouldn't pick up since we're both still mad at each other.

The sun slips behind the man-made lakes. Some rocks are loops, hollowed by years of water lappings; some are towering points piled up, like frozen dribbles of dark, wet sand. I look again at the pamphlets my mother has acquired at each gas station, tourist area, or restaurant—one for the Hole 'N' the Rock, located in Moab, Utah, which appeared to be just what it was titled, an enormous hole in an even larger rock. Fascinating! At least according to the brochure, which bragged of its "toilet in a tomb." Sign me up. I hand the leaflet to my mom, who smiles knowingly and puts it into the cave of her purse.

"There's a drive-in up there." My mother points to a glowing sign behind the copy center, a few crazy U-turns up the hill. We'd already encountered Antelope Pass; a highway sign pointed out the steep incline and narrow lanes by showing a car careening off its black lines, falling into the nothing of its yellow sign—a warning to all.

Wordlessly, we get in the car and drive the twenty yards to the entrance of the drive-in. There's a *No Pedestrians* sign on the fence. A twenty-foot-tall neon cowboy, precariously perched, electric holster and red-embered cigarette aglow, marks the way in.

The film's about a couple who are so meant to be that hurricanes, lost addresses, and the passage of time can't keep them apart. I wonder briefly if there's someone like that for me. My mother is sucked into the plot before I have even tuned the radio so we can hear the words. I'm more interested in looking around and imagining when the place thrived. The screen's torn in one corner, so whenever there's a blue sky in the movie part of it looks like rain, a solitary ripped-screen cloud that hovers in the background.

At the intermission, when hot dogs and candy Dots dance across the screen, I say, "Oh, I like this."

I am Sandy in *Grease,* about to swat away John Travolta for putting his arm around me or touching my perky breasts. For my mother, the cartoon images are not at all unusual, not retro, just real, even though it's probably been twenty years since she's seen the footage. Now I wish my Fifties Movie Star Boyfriend would appear in his appropriately worn-in leather jacket, or at least a local cowboy wanting to rescue me from my mother, from retro oddity.

At night, in the motel, my mother lies flat on her back and falls easily to sleep. Hands resting on her hips, she looks as if she could launch into conversation any minute, but she doesn't. On a television station that doesn't exist on either coast, there's a made-for-TV movie about a group of high school kids who get lost on a mountain and learn to do things like collect rainwater from tarps and drink it. Meanwhile, there are lots of opportunities for kissing in the wilderness and a surprisingly good sound track.

I could sleep if I tried, but instead I go and sit on the hood of the car. Outside, the bug hum is indistinguishable from the buzz of neon signs—*Laundry Land, Marge's Motel N' Mart,* one set of letters simply spells *BAR,* but in a shade of violet that brings to mind the lavenders of my old Laura Ashley skirts from school, a mottled garden of pale purples and blue. Then I remember my mix tapes and decide they are just the company I want.

I move to the driver's seat and rifle through the box of tapes, undecided about which one I want to play. I'm going nowhere, but gripping the wheel regardless when my mom is suddenly in view out the window. I roll down the glass as if she's a gas station attendant.

"What are you doing out here?" she asks.

"I'm not sure," I say. "Just sitting."

"What's that on the seat?" she leans in my window and looks next to me.

There's a large crate filled with old tapes that I had put under the seat back when I thought I'd be driving alone. I wanted them on the passenger seat now, allowing me to revisit my past simply by pressing play. I figured I could listen to mixes, moments that were still so vivid for me, by sneaking one or two at night when I couldn't sleep. I loved sliding a cassette in with little idea of what song came next. During the day I could keep them stashed away, out of my mother's sight, tucked away just for me.

My mother comes to the car and sits next to me, the dark night and haze of dewy fog coming in close. I'm just about to put the box of tapes in the backseat when she stops me.

"Could I look at those?" she asks, trying again.

"Why don't you look at this instead," I say and hand her Moons and Junes and Ferris Wheels, the tape I made for her before we left. She takes the tape, looks down at its title, and smiles.

"That's so nice of you, Laney." She sighs. Then she puts it on the dashboard and sneaks a glance at the older tapes that sit in my lap. "What about those?"

I give up. Or give in, whichever makes it okay for me to heft the whole box onto her nightgowned lap, her thin legs visible through the cotton. Carefully, like she's thumbing through glossy photos, she picks up one tape at a time and examines it. I figure if I let her look through here, she'll leave me alone.

"What's this one?" she asks.

I don't even look at which one she's holding but I say, "I don't know, Mom. They're all just tapes. Mostly from years ago."

She turns and looks at me and tucks a bunch of my hair behind my ear and then the rest back from my shoulders.

"Laney," she says, "I know these are tapes. Give me a break." She looks out the window at something—the empty roadway? The rusted camper van parked nearby? The blink of the laundromat sign? I can't tell what it is she wants or what she's looking for, but I have the feeling she's finally going to tell me.

CHAPTER
five

"What do you want to know about them?" I ask and gesture to the tapes as if they'll spring to life like the popcorn and hot dog animation in the drive-in. Then I let my voice soften. "I think there's at least one you'd like in there. Aside from the one I made for this trip, I mean."

"I don't need to like the tapes. It's not the music I need to know about, it's my daughter, about you and why you're like this."

"Like what?" I ask.

"Why you'd be making a trip like this by yourself, why you're receiving wedding invites but don't have any prospects yourself, why you can't seem to find a relationship that gels."

"I'm not by myself. You're here," I say.

"But I wasn't supposed to be," she says.

"That's the story of my life right there," I say before I can edit.

"I see," my mother nods. For a minute I think she's going to leave the car, go inside, and call my dad to tell him she's flying home the rest of the way. Instead she goes on. "I don't need to like the songs. It just seems to me like these are more than tapes, almost like they are love letters or bits of your past I don't know about."

"And?" I ask. But I know what she wants.

"And I want to know the stories—unless they are too private. I'm worried . . ." She stops as her voice dips the way it does before she cries. "I'm worried that I don't know enough about you. That I never did." She opens and closes the small cassette case over and over. "I saw the pictures from your college graduation. Do you know what that's like? Looking at photographs of an event I was sure I'd see firsthand?"

"I wanted you there, too," I say.

"So fill me in," she says. "Tell me what I missed. I know you, Laney, the core of you. I just want to know more."

"We never talked," I say into my hands, "why start now?"

"Because we can," she says. And then almost angrily, "I'm not sick anymore!"

Tears slide down my mother's angled face, roll off the gentle sweep of her jaw, and land on the tapes in the box.

The distance between us was caused by more than just her physical absence from my life. As my mother's illness waxed and waned, grew and sank back into itself, the rest of her world, our family, kept moving forward. The cells in her that divided and attacked pushed us in our own directions—my father kept potting, focusing less on the art and more on the business, though he would always say, "I just love getting mucky in the clay. I need to do that more." But being with glazes and moist blocks of unformed clay made my dad think of being with my mother, and it was easier somehow for him to think about numbers and sales and a countrywide pottery takeover of sorts. Even though we'd joked about it then, it had happened. He and his small-town hippie art form had become a household name, a household need. "Perceived need," he'd told me once.

Danny, of course, studied and joked and was the best at being with her. No one was surprised with his acceptance into medical school. Even though he was pretty sure he wouldn't end up focusing on oncology, he loved the science of it. He distanced himself, made it all okay by learning and teaching. He'd show her what her cells looked like under a microscope, treating his histology home-work like artwork, her sickness on display.

"Kind of pretty," she'd said, her eyes still looking into the focus. "Even though they're attacking me."

"Isn't it?" Danny said, his hand on her back.

For me, there was very little pretty about it. My father had taken me shopping for my prom dress the spring of my mother's diagnosis and I'd wound up wearing some drop-waist dress with unnaturally colored flowers set against a moss-green background. The skirt bubbled up at the hem and made me feel as if I were hid-ing small children in there or that I could puncture at any moment. My mother had looked at me all dressed up, her fatigue from her first series of radiation making her appear years older, and nodded without saying anything.

Since then, I'd been odd girl out. I didn't live at home and wasn't a part of her everyday life, treatment, remissions. Danny was home for most of her sickness and my father, despite his best attempts at being a businessman, loved being home more than anywhere else.

Now that my mother is cancer free, there's a part of me that feels I owe it to her to explain myself. Maybe more than I would if she'd been well, if she'd never thought she'd leave me too soon, if I had never had to live every day with the knowledge that the cells within her might resist the treatment and leave her to fully disappear.

In the car, my mother looks at the liner notes from various tape cases. She wants to read the writing on the covers, to ask me: Why this song? What did it mean? Is there an order to the music? To know what I know about myself when I hear these time capsules.

"I can try to explain them, the tapes," I say. Picking out a cou-ple and instantly putting them back, thinking, college, Italy, the mix I never finished for Jeremy, and on and on.

"This one?" My mother holds up a well-preserved tape case that is decorated with colored-pencil drawings. "Start with this one. Tell me everything. And tomorrow, we'll do more."

I put the key in the ignition and the tape into the player. Side A starts. Despite where I am, and even though my mother is my listening companion, I can't help but think of the various songs that went with early high school. I am amazed and relieved at being transported back.

Freshman year was linked somehow to middle school, or camp, summers and school dances. But this was the sum of sophomore year—the tape that held that time for me. It is the clarity, the incredible focus of those days—no sickness, no what did I want to do with my life—just lyrics, finger-picked guitar, the fast-beating longing of waiting to be chosen. I tell my mother the first of many stories, prefacing this one with, "Just so you know, you're way off base with the nongelling relationship talk. I have had good relationships. Very good, in fact."

And I play her this one to prove it.

Eric's Mix, for Laney and Marcus

SIDE A

Into White
   —Cat Stevens
Warm Ways
   —Fleetwood Mac
Badge
   —Cream
Lemon Song
   —Led Zep
He Comes for Conversation
   —Joni Mitchell
Sweet Jane
   —Velvet Underground
Farther On Down the Road
   —Taj Mahal
Thick as a Brick
   —Jethro Tull

SIDE B

Three of a Perfect Pair
   —King Crimson
Mother Nature's Son
   —Beatles
Rondo, Klavierquartett G-moll
   —Wolfgang
Allegro Con Brio, No. 5 in C
   Minor—Ludwig
Good Lovin'
   —Dead
One Thing Leads to Another
   —Fixx
Harvest Moon
   —Neil Young
Good Morning, Little School
   Girl—Yardbirds

Take This Longing   Woods/Moon/Autumn
  —Leonard Cohen   —George Winston
                              Apology Accepted
                                —The Go-Betweens

Eric is the boy in high school girls couldn't decide about wanting
to kiss. Now they'd want him to propose. People would remember
him as smart, if anything. Some wouldn't remember him at all,
certainly not the pretty, shiny girls, who weren't even sure if he was
a senior or a young teacher. Bulky sweater, doe-haired, guitar-
playing, the writer. Put that together with an MBA from Wharton
and a law degree from Yale, and all of a sudden he's not a mushy
hippie, he's the catch. But, of course, it's too late. It's always that
way, right?

Eric and I become friends when he's the senior, I'm the sophomore. Together with his friend Marcus we have math together.
They aren't dumb, I'm just advanced, and Eric likes that. The class
is just the three of us and one other guy, Joe Something, a total
stoner with a gift for numbers. In class, he calculates his pot-selling
profits from the weekend.

Eric, Marcus, and I don't smoke pot. We keep our lungs clear
for singing and sports and our notebooks organized, save for the
lyrics that wind up written on the inside covers. Almost all the
songs were written between when he was born and when I was. We
don't think about this at the time.

One modern song that makes it on his mix is "One Thing
Leads to Another." This is not yet ironic. It's not even that great a
song. Not like CSN doing "Blackbird" or "At the Zoo," the Simon
and Garfunkel tune we whistle during the math final. Mr. Banks,
the teacher, is in his sixties and can't hear well, so he doesn't mind.
Plus, his wife, the funky English teacher, has just left him for the
much younger ethics teacher, so he's distracted.

One Saturday, Eric and I meet in Harvard Square and head to the
used-record stores. This is back when records were still the main

form of recorded music, so there's much more to choose from. Record shopping has not yet become a statement.

"*Tea for the Tillerman.*" Eric holds it out to me. "Great." We thumb through bin after bin, buy a Leon Russell album, and then leave.

Outside, the cool breeze makes me forget that it's still summer. I say this to Eric. We picture walking, sometimes arms linked, often alone, down streets littered with musicians, coffeehouses, and bookstores. In the image, it occurs to me it's always fall and I ask about this.

"I don't know why," Eric says, adding more sugar to his mug. "I guess it's my least favorite time of year."

"Your least favorite? It's the one I like best!" I say, very aware of the exclamation point in my tone.

"But since I don't like autumn—it seems better to picture it with you."

And this is how I know he likes me. In *that way.* I begin to panic. Is this a date, then? If you don't know it's a date to begin with, does it count? Do I like him? His lips are so thin, I don't know if that's good. I wonder about kissing him. The thought doesn't excite me. Then I question that response and decide that I don't want to kiss him because I'm scared.

Eric's oblivious to all of this and proves it by saying, "I need to get a new pair of sneakers. Want to come with me?" He's been sys-tematically going through his list of things to do before leaving for Cornell in a month. Briefly, it occurs to me that I may be on that list in some way.

At the Foot Locker the next day, I watch him try on regular sneakers, cleats, high tops. He settles on a basic blue pair and goes to pay. The girl who waited on us is on her knees putting the unchosen shoes back in their cardboard boxes. I know her name is Candi because Eric and I are in a phase of calling everyone in the service industry by the names on their nametags. We feel this is more humane than not addressing them by anything. Part of me wonders if this is just obnoxious.

Candi looks up at me through her spiral-permed bangs. "Your boyfriend's really cute."

It takes me a minute to register that she means Eric. At this point, I have never been able to use the word *boyfriend* in reference to myself—boys, yes, but not boyfriend.

In light of this, I say to Candi, "Thanks." And then, "He's really smart, too." This seems not to interest her in the least, but Eric's back with his purchase, so we leave. Candi stays, grounded in her fake referee outfit, and gives me a small wave.

Eric and I have no idea what to do at the mall, so we go into the one crummy bookstore and look at calendars.

"Why do people care what's on these pages?" I ask, paging through Twelve Months of Dogs. I annoy myself by hoping there's a cute dog for my birthday month, and further when I register some mark of letdown upon finding schnauzers for September.

Eric asks what I said, but I shrug off the question. He wanders over and lifts my hair up off my back, leaving my neck bare. His T-shirt grazes my shoulder. Eric's clothes are always in the perfect state of worn-in-ness, faded and soft without being torn or stained.

"You can hardly even see these hairs," Eric muses, touching the short, ungatherable wisps. I wait for him to keep talking. He doesn't. *Please, kiss me,* is what I'm thinking. *But not in B. Dalton's Books,* is my afterthought.

I am mature and interesting with my mother's old wrap skirt, plain Hanes V-neck T, and thoughts of summer's end when I meet Eric and his friend Marcus at a Thai restaurant near Harvard Square. Eric and Marcus will leave for college the next day, so this dinner is our dramatic good-bye.

After we order, we play a game where you get to ask questions like, "If I were a color, what color would I be?" to find out how the other people perceive you. Eric's answers match what I decide about myself, that I'm green, I'm a scarf, the moon, and, for a drink, a Kalhua and milk. Marcus's answers couldn't be more wrong—well, not wrong, but skewed, since all he wants to do is get in my pants. He's like, "You are definitely red. A tiger, a Corvette." Eric smirks at me. He knows Marcus's game.

Later, when "Lay Lady Lay" is on the radio, and Eric's gone back in to leave our forgotten tip, Marcus will ask me, "Laney, are you in love with Eric?" I won't know what to say, so I will sing instead, and Marcus will join in.

Marcus is attractive, athletic, Jewish. There's no reason not to let him in your pants, and maybe I would have, except that for most of the year he dated some girl named Sarah from Connecticut. In high school, anyone from off-campus seems made up. Inevitably, they are from Connecticut. Maybe sometimes from Princeton. But Sarah was real, and came up to watch Marcus receive the Community Service Award. Everyone in the assembly room watched her hug Marcus. Sister? Friend? they wondered, until Sarah put her hands on the back of Marcus's head and opened her mouth to kiss him. Then in May, right around when Eric made that mix, Sarah called Marcus and told him she wanted to break up. He hadn't been upset, really, but he hadn't made any motions toward me, either.

Eric walks out from the Thai place and gets in the backseat. Through the rain and the windshield, the lights outside are mottled red and white, echoes of a festive holiday season that's months away. By then, I think, Eric will be done with his first semester of college. I will be doing the same old thing.

Inside my house, it's totally dark. Thinking I know where the lamp switch is, I rush to the living room, only to bash into the side of the writing desk that wasn't there this morning. Now there's a Meissen lamp base on the sea trunk, and I switch the light on.

My father moved twenty-three times before he was nineteen years old. The son of a diplomat and an aggressively social wife, my dad found himself uprooted and relocated everywhere from Sweden to Ecuador, Dominica to Greece. One day he'd come home from school to find everything in boxes, or he'd be woken in the night and shuttled out on a small plane not knowing where he'd be in the daylight. As a result, we have incredible furniture and decorative objects from all over the world: an 1850 Fruitwood Bureau plate from France, Welsh country colored pottery, a Sevre porcelain platter, a cherry- and walnut-inlayed bench from some cabin in Scandinavia. My favorite is a Scottish Whemesware inkwell in the shape of a heart, even though it's in the shape of a heart.

And because of his upbringing, my father, upon becoming a parent himself, vowed never to move after that first time. But he allows himself this: Every time he gets restless and thinks of packing it in—when he spends too long looking at the back of his Ivy League alumni newsletter at houses for sale in Tuscany, San Francisco, Saint Marten—he clears his mind of such thoughts and clears each room of the house of its furniture. He rearranges so that every couple of months everything's different, but not. The couch that was by the arched entryway now freestands with the Indonesian mending table in back of it.

Eric sits in the still-dark far corner of the room and Marcus leans on the doorframe. Wondering what the silence is for, I all of a sudden remember that this is when we're supposed to say good-bye. That this is it for *us* as we know it. And then I get sad. And nudgy, because I won't be getting in any car tomorrow to go to my new college and meet my new roommate. I'll just be waking up to go buy school supplies.

I go over to Marcus and say, "Well, thanks for driving. And I guess I'll see you soon."

Marcus nods. "Yeah, I'll be back up for Head of the Charles. Not too long."

We hug for a while. His windbreaker rustles and slides around. Marcus catches it between his knees just before it falls onto the floor. Backing up, Marcus says, " 'Bye, Laney. I'll miss you." And to Eric, "I'll be in the car."

I feel dramatic and sad in my skirt and bare arms. Eric pulls me over to the love seat. I know what will happen now. He will kiss me and I will like it, love it, melt. Eric's hand on my thigh, the other on my face, he says, "Please write to me." I wait.

"I'll be back up in a couple of months. But obviously, we'll talk before then. And, Laney, don't wish you weren't here. That's not a good thing."

"Eric," I start but can't say any more because I start to cry. He puts his arms around me with his palms pressed back against my shoulders. We're in that position you learn to do as a kid when you want to imitate two people making out, so you wrap your arms around your own self and move your hands all over. But none of that happens. Eric kisses my cheek and pulls away.

"God, this sucks," he says. I nod and brush away the hairs that have stuck to tears on my face. And then, he leaves. I look around for an unseen thing, the kiss I never got. The door closes with a small click. Alone in the rearranged room, I miss him already. I miss the way he laughs under his breath. I miss his hair falling in his eyes, the way he'd slip me a note before class and watch me read it during. And his sweaters. Always the baggy, knitted kind that leave bits of fluff on everything. And then I see he has left one for me by the door—the Irish fisherman's sweater with the stretched-out cuffs.

I pick it up and put it on my shoulder like a beach towel. I cock my head to the left to hold the sweater like I am talking on the phone. Suddenly I'm less sad, more curious. Before I go upstairs, I turn out the light in the living room, and it occurs to me I can't remember how the furniture was before—it all seems to have been put in its natural order.

Halfway up the stairs, there's a soft tap on the front door. Eric's back to claim what's his—the sweater, I figure—and open up to find him leaning on the doorframe. Rainwater drips from his hair. Marcus is in shadow form in the car with the headlights illuminating the stormy night. Without saying anything, Eric takes my face into his hands and kisses me. I put my hands around his neck, then on his waist, feeling the wet cotton of his T-shirt. When we pull back, I am not just looking at Eric, I know I'm looking at my first real boyfriend. The one I'll remember forever, the one whose sweater I'll wear, the one who is leaving tomorrow.

"But you're leaving tomorrow," I say as Eric goes to kiss me again.

"I'll be back," he says. "And you'll come down to visit, right?"

Marcus leans on the horn to break the spell and Eric takes my hand, tracing invisible patterns on my palm with his wet finger. Then he kisses my hand and puts one to his cheek, the other to where his heart should be.

And then he leaves. Kisses and good-byes. Somehow they are linked, but Eric and I date almost all year. He comes back at holidays, I visit him twice—once for a whole week when I went to classes like I was really a college student with a college boyfriend, living in a dorm, kissing him whenever I want.

Just as spring approaches and I think I'm headed for the Most Romantic Summer Ever, when I'll sleep with Eric for the first time, when we'll swim and see each other every day, my mother is diagnosed with non-Hodgkin's lymphoma. When Eric comes over and I tell him, I feel myself back up out of the whole scene, like I'm watching the hologram me tell the sticker Eric that my mom might die. We sit in the shade of the copper beech tree out back and he puts his arms around me.

"I'm so psyched to be back," he says. "With you," he adds in case I couldn't figure it out.

"Yeah," I say and can barely feel his arms on me, barely feel breeze or presummer heat. He talks about some funny something that happened at college and I nod in the right places so he thinks I'm listening. But really, I'm gone from him. Really, I want to be alone.

So instead of kissing him to welcome him back for the summer, I leave him slightly agog in the just-blooming tulips and go check on what's happening in my house. And that's the way it went—first I'd be busy or we'd meet up and not talk much, or Marcus would join us and we'd see a movie, but there's no clear end point to my relationship with Eric, just a soft fading.

Of course, part of me regrets this. When summer ends and it's nearly a year to the day since Eric first kissed me, I think maybe I should try to get him back. But how to tell him this? I plan to make him a mix, the teenage way of communicating. The next day I sit down and make a partial list of songs for the tape I plan to send Eric. Eric, my ex-boyfriend who is back at college. The list looks like this:

Can't Find My Way Home—Blind Faith
Long Distance Run Around—Yes
Tupelo Honey—Van Morrison
Jennifer Juniper—Donovan
Stretch Out and Wait—The Smiths
Cold Snow—Jonathan Edwards
Sad Lisa—Cat Stevens
When We Grow Up—from *Free to Be You and Me*

I cross out "Long Distance Run Around," afraid that Eric will overinterpret its place, even though it's partly what I feel. Looking at my albums and tapes, I add some songs and put them in order on the carpet and make the tape. At the end of each side, I talk into the microphone and say hi to Eric. Then, I fast-dub a copy for myself and mail Eric's to him.

The following Saturday it's Head of the Charles—the rowing regatta. I wear an old sweater of Eric's and have the surface confidence of a girl wearing an article of clothing that belongs to her once-boyfriend. But when I meet Eric at Au Bon Pain, he's got a girl with him. She's wearing his Peruvian sweater with the blue snowflake pattern.

"Laney, this is Sarah," Eric says. For a second I make a joke with myself that Eric and Marcus have made some pact to only date girls named Sarah. My private laugh makes me smile and appear thrilled to meet her.

The bathrooms are only for customers and I have to pee so badly that I order an orange juice I don't want just to qualify for standing in line. Advertised as fresh squeezed, all I can taste is thawed, diluted Tropicana. Sarah asks if she can cut in front. I let her and then have to deal with all the other women who are mad at being one more person farther from relief.

"Oh," Sarah says like she's remembered the one thing she has to say to me, "everyone in our dorm loves that tape you made."

"Which tape?" I say, knowing exactly what she's talking about. I count the people ahead of me and focus on the door to the bathroom, willing it to open.

"You know, that tape you made after you guys broke up—I really don't remember what it's called. I've never seen a tape with a title," Sarah says.

"Really."

"Yeah—no one does that where I'm from." Sarah waves to Eric, who leans against the glass outside and points to his watch.

"Well, it's your turn," I say.

"No, you go first," Sarah offers.

The bathroom floor is wet with leaking water. I try to flush, but nothing happens. The bowl stays yellow and papery. For some reason, this makes me nervous because Sarah's due to come in next. I try again to flush. I jiggle the handle, but nothing works.

"Go in if you want," I say to Sarah when I'm out, "but it's really gross in there."

Sarah goes in and I head outside, wishing Marcus were with us to make the day balanced. Eric's watching two old guys play chess on boards that are built into the concrete tables. One guy moves his rook. Then nothing happens.

"Can you believe this is Sarah's first time here?" Eric says.

"Where's she from?" I ask.

"Connecticut," Eric says.

What I think is: *You've got to be kidding me.* But what I say is, "Well, probably they don't drive that far to watch boat races. I mean, we only went because we were local, right?"

Eric shrugs and says without looking at me, "The sweater still looks good on you."

"Your sweater looks good on Sarah," I say and it comes out a little angry.

Eric turns to me. "Sarah is my girlfriend now, Laney," he says. "Something you didn't want to be, remember?"

"That's pretty obvious," I say. But what's maybe not obvious, especially since I don't come right out and say it, is that I miss him, that I'm sorry for pushing him away, that I needed him this year when my mom started her treatments. Instead, I'd called Marcus, who'd come back from Brown and hung out with me, renting all the dumb movies I'd wanted to, and took me for ice cream I didn't want to eat. With Marcus around, my life felt vaguely normal. Somehow he was able to make me relax even when things were miserable.

Watching Eric watch the chess guys, watching him wait for his New Girlfriend Sarah, I think about what would happen if I swept the chess pieces to the ground, how they'd sound on the pavement, how mad the men would be, how cold the inlayed tile of the board would feel.

"What I mean is—Sarah and I are having a relationship. But I don't kid myself. It's not like—well, this isn't such a big deal . . ." he trails off.

"What's she like?" I ask.

"She's like you, but not as smart or as pretty or as into music."

"Oh," I say and look right into his eyes.

"I'm kidding," Eric says as Sarah waves to us and motions to her watch.

"I know that," I say. But I didn't think he was joking at all.

We walk over to her with Eric pointing to his watch again.

"What's with all the watch stuff?" I ask.

Sarah and Eric do that couple exchange with small smiles and head tilts.

"It's our thing," Sarah says, "like you say, time to kiss me, or time to give me a hug before class, or time to tell me you love me."

"Time to go," I say. They don't get my joke.

"Oh, sorry, that's too bad," says Sarah. "I thought we were spending the day with you."

I look at Eric. "I'm so glad you shared that tape with your whole dorm," I say, sugarcoating so only Eric knows I'm pissed.

"Um . . . yeah," Eric says.

I cross the street before they do, so there's no need for hugging.

"See you later!" Eric calls to me, using his hands like a megaphone.

I wave.

"By the way!" shouts Sarah. "I like your sweater!"

I don't see Eric until two falls later, when we're both back for the same weekend. We wrote a couple times—a postcard and two short letters—but they're mainly of the "What's up?" collection on High School's Greatest Hits.

Marcus's party is in full swing and I have had two beers already. I'm in the living room looking for a way out of the conversation I'm supposedly having with Katie Something, in the year below me, who I don't remember. She's talking about how she thinks maybe Middlebury was the wrong choice and maybe she should have picked her backup. I nod until I see Marcus pumping the keg.

"Excuse me," I say.

Marcus spills beer on his shoes when we're hugging. He's the same, but even broader, like he is actually a rectangle in pants and a rugby shirt. It's the first time I've seen him in almost a year.

"Laney, Laney, Laney," Marcus says and pulls me up the stairs to look for a dry pair of shoes. I think I know where we're headed, but I don't say anything except, "Marcus, Marcus, Marcus," right back at him.

By the fish tank in his room, we kiss and it feels good. He's strong and smiling. Downstairs, "I Want Your Sex" is playing on the stereo and I can't not think about how funny it is to kiss to that song, whereas, in high school, Eric and I might have kissed only to Crosby, Stills, and Nash, or maybe Van Morrison.

"God, it's good to see you, Laney," says Marcus. We're lying on his bed with our shoes off and our feet are rubbing. And then, "How come we never did this before?"

"Sarah," I say. Marcus looks confused. "From Connecticut," I add and he nods. We kiss some more and then Marcus pulls away and says, "It wasn't Sarah. It was Eric. That's why we didn't do this before."

I move so I can see Marcus's face better. "What do you mean?" I ask.

"You liked Eric," Marcus tells me. "Even before you went out with him."

"So?" I ask. "I thought about you, too."

"I'm sure you did. Who doesn't think about me?" He cracks up. "I thought about you. Even when I was with Sarah," he says. I wonder whether to be flattered or feel bad for Sarah. "Even when you and Eric got together."

"Well, nothing's ever going to happen with me and Eric. I'm not even sure anything would have happened back then . . ." I sit up and look around the room. I stare at the bubbles poking their way to the surface of the fish tank.

"Yeah, but that's just because you were, you know . . ." Marcus sits up, too.

"I was what?" I ask.

"A virgin," Marcus says like I already know. And when it's clear I didn't he says, "Eric didn't want to be your first."

"My first what?" I ask.

"Your first boyfriend, or sex. Your first anything." And then, "Besides, just when you got close to it, you broke up with him. Then you were definitely off-limits for me."

"I don't know what was up with me and Eric." I watch the fish tank as if it will give me answers.

"I know," Marcus says.

I stand up and go to the tank. Small yellow fish swim in circles and the angelfish lurks by a fake treasure chest. "I see," I say. But all I really see is fish and bubbles, air popping into more air. From downstairs, R.E.M. comes on and I listen to the words: *Swan swan hummingbird* and then something about being free.

"What's this song about, anyway?" asks Marcus.

"I have no idea," I say and exit.

When I see Eric he's talking to some girl in a red sweaterdress. He spots me and leaves her standing there, mouth open in midtalk. After bounding over, he asks where I've been.

"Upstairs with Marcus," I say. I picture the Yaz album *Upstairs at Eric's* and how it always seemed like a cool title, and how now I knew what it meant.

"Really?" Eric says and makes the word have three syllables instead of two.

"Yup," I say. I reach for a cigarette from the pack someone's left on the stairs. I light it and lean on the banister, one step above Eric. Across the room, Marcus flirts with some red-haired girl we don't know. I think how the triangle of us—me, Eric, and Marcus—has been dissipated. How now we were just random pairings.

"Want to go see some fish?" Eric asks.

"Blub, blub," I say. I want not to have feelings left for him, to hate him even, and to think he's crude and mean and not the sensitive guy I thought for not wanting to first-sex me. But then I remember that he's not the senior anymore and I am not what he thought.

Eric taps in some food for the fish. It looks like pepper flakes and floats on the top of the water until the fish dart for it or until it gets weighted down and sinks.

"I can't believe you," I say.

"My fish finesse or that I didn't want to be your first?" he asks, still looking at the fish. "I assume when you were up here doing whatever you two were doing that Marcus the Mouth told you."

I'm swiveling in Marcus's desk chair, in my own version of a business meeting. I prop my feet up on the desk and try not to tilt so far back as to wind up on the floor.

"So you have a thing about dating virgins," I say.

"Had a thing, maybe. Not all virgins, just you as a virgin," Eric says and turns the chair around so it's facing him as he sits on the bed.

"Explain," I say. To my surprise, he does.

He says, "Laney. Do you know how much I liked you in high school?" I shake my head. "Too much. So much I took that math class to be with you. I had already taken it before."

"No wonder you did so well," I say.

"Yeah, well, I'm also brilliant," Eric throws in. "But when I really liked you and thought you liked me, you vanished. I just thought it was for the best, that I should be able to enjoy college and not worry about when and if I'd see you. And you were young. Plus, I thought you liked Marcus. So then I rationalized the whole thing—like maybe it would be good if you got together with him, and, you know . . ."

"Got hurt?" I ask.

"Something like that," he says. "I don't want to be the bad guy. And if I ever am, I hope you'll forget me. That's why, not your first."

"So I was the bad guy," I say.

"Yes," Eric says. "You were. That I didn't count on. But I got over it, right?"

I go and sit next to him on the bed and hold my hands in my lap. "Eric, just because you are or aren't someone's first or last anything doesn't guarantee you immunity to or from being remembered." *That came out well*, I think, and feel good.

"I know that now," Eric says. "So, can I kiss you?"

"Sure," I say and it comes out smooth, distant, and done, and I wonder if he can sense the relief I feel at the disconnect.

I turn to him. I turn to him and know that he will always be remembered. But the kiss is not very good. Our kiss is thin and empty, since it turns out Eric doesn't use his tongue now—some college thing, maybe. It's obvious that Eric thinks that we're a fit, though, because he has that guy look where he looks to the door to ask if he should close it.

The door stays open and we end up downstairs, not really talking about much. Before Eric gets in his car, he gives me a hug and tells Marcus he'll call him.

"Does this mean we're back in touch?" I ask him.

"Of course," he says.

But we're not. Every once in a while, he will call, and one other time we meet up in New York and we try kissing to the same result, and then he asks to sleep with me, tells me he loves me. I say no, have no words to give back, and that's the end of it. Almost. The real end is years later, when he calls from Japan and says he's coming back to the States and needs to see me. We plan to meet in Harvard Square at Cafe Pamplona and all I can do is envision and hope he has changed, that he kisses with his whole mouth, that he turns out to be that long-lost friend you end up falling for like in the movies. But he's not. So when he tells me he's engaged, I am actually happy for him. And when we leave the cafe, that's it. And it's okay. It's okay because when I think back on it, I left first. I left before we ever broke up. I left when the shock that someone can leave you or get sick or go to college and never come back hit me, when without my even deciding to do it, I just pressed stop.

Meanwhile, back at the party, I'm the one who stays and helps Marcus clean up. We mop up puddles of beer with butt ends put out in them and clear away the bottles of Sam Adams.

"You okay?" Marcus calls to me.

I say, "I sure am." I hope that Marcus will leave the bag of garbage he's holding in the bright lights of the kitchen and that he will come over to where I'm sitting in the den. This is what he does. It's what he does before he leads me upstairs to see how one of the fish glows in the dark.

After the last song on Eric's Mix ends, I wait to see if my mother has any response before I eject it. But when she doesn't say anything, I pop the cassette out so it doesn't flip back around to side A. Who wants to repeat what they've just heard? Certainly not me. In fact, in the spreading silence, I wonder if I should have said any of this.

"I feel guilty," my mother finally says.

"About what?" I put the tape back in the box with its mute friends, my other years.

"If we hadn't told you right away, maybe you wouldn't have felt so fragile," she says.

"I don't know what you mean," I say. "I was the strong one in that scenario."

"Well, not from what I just heard. You told me that you broke up with Eric because I was sick," she says.

"No." I shake my head. "That wasn't why—you're reading too much into things. Eric wasn't right for me. We just grew apart— you know, college, high school, that sort of thing."

"Laney, first of all, you talk much more about your friendship with Marcus than whatever happened with Eric," my mother says.

"So?" I shrug. "That's because he's the one I'm close with now."

"Right," she says as if she'd proved her point.

"But Eric . . ." I don't finish my thought because I don't know what else to say.

"That relationship was fifteen years ago," my mother sighs, "so if that's your example of a good one, don't you think that maybe you're missing something here?"

I shake my head and smooth my hair, trying to show my mother, my traveling companion, that I'm tired of sitting here. That I want to go inside and try to sleep, something I can do all by myself.

CHAPTER
six

In Santa Fe, my mother and I spend the first evening having dinner outside. The restaurant's garden is lighted by tiny bulbs strung onto wires. Miniature spheres reflect in my gazpacho, show up twinkling in our sangria. Nearby, a chamber music concert floats half-eerie, half-lovely sounds as a backdrop to our conversation.

"I hope I'm not imposing too much on your trip," my mother says, spreading green chili paste onto bread and eating each bite delicately. At camp and then later on, Shana and I had gone though containers of Easy Cheese, sandwiching the admittedly disgusting stuff onto crackers or even a bare finger while we talked about boys. If she were here, or if magically, Maggie—fresh from some Hollywood awards show or whatever fantabulous thing she's doing—were with me, we'd be crunching shared nachos, cutting the spice with limed beer, swapping *which would you rather* questions, and afterward, wandering the darkened town in search of desserts or boys, or neither, or both.

"Well," I say to my mother, "it's okay, I guess. Did you ever picture something happening in a certain way and then it doesn't?"

"Of course," my mother says and signals the waiter for the bill.

"Well, let's just say I never thought about driving cross-country with my mother."

"What did you picture doing with me?" she asks.

And I look right at her and say something I've been holding back.

"Mom, I used to ask myself all the time, *What would I be doing right now if she weren't here?* Like I was practicing for when you wouldn't be."

When I think she's going to say more to me, she just fixes her scarf and wipes her mouth with her napkin, listening to the music from nearby.

"Isn't that incredible," she says. "Music from another country, from another era, here in this magical place."

She is the kind of woman who can say words like *magical* and not sound like she needs to be hit over the head with a large bag of crystals. I want to see things like she sees them, so I try. I look at the lights, let the music fade in and out of earshot, think about the mountains around me.

"Don't you have anything to say about that?" I ask and want to stand up and run. I link my feet and ankles around the bottom of my chair to make me stay.

"It's okay." She laughs. "I know maybe it's not that way for you, seeing beauty everywhere."

"I see plenty of goddamn beauty," I say.

"That's enough, Laney," she warns, like I'm fourteen.

My mother pays the bill and we stand up. She stretches her arms skyward, as if the open air itself could reach down and scoop her up.

Our hotel is situated at the end of the Santa Fe Trail, near the Sangre de Cristo mountains. The slope of terracotta buildings, the odd shapes and shades of brown, beige, and mochas blend together and are soothing. After we take a quick walk around the grounds, I tell my mother I am going to get something in the car when, in reality, I just need to be away from her. She heads for the room, to call my dad and do yoga. I will find her later, in the downward-facing dog pose, her thin purple yoga mat unfurled like an animal's tongue.

I lie on my back outside, trying to ignore the itch of earth underneath my bare legs. I pull on my skirt so it covers my knees in the dark, cool air. When I can't take it anymore, I walk to the hotel lobby. In one of those cavelike phone booths, I call Danny.

"It's late, Laney," he says as his hello. First, I think proudly how psychically brother-sister connected we are, then I remember he has caller ID.

"Hi, doofus," I say.

"Hey, lovable loser. What's up? How's the desert? Or the dessert? Ha-ha."

"How better is Mom?" I ask.

"All better."

"God, Danny, don't say *all better*. I'm not eight."

"Look, Laney. She is better. Cured. Healthy. Obviously, after it recurred, she was more at risk, but now her percentages are good—it's been a couple of years since the bone marrow transplant, and each year that passes with nothing showing up makes it less likely that she'd relapse again. Could she? Sure. But she has a relatively normal adult female prognosis."

I don't say anything. I just let my brother listen to my breathing. I hear him yawn.

"I'm doing surgery right now," he says.

"As we speak?"

"Ha—yeah. No, that's my rotation now. Another week. I gotta go, Lane. I need to be up in five hours."

"Sure," I say.

"Kiss Mom for me. Get me something revolting out there— you know, like a rabbit's foot key chain dyed blue or a giant pencil that says Texas on it that I could take to lectures or something."

This is as close as Danny ever gets to saying, *Mom is not going to die.* I go to bed that night fantasizing ugly souvenirs that I can send to him.

*   *   *

My mother adores the adobe style. We wake up refreshed, not addressing any tension from the night before, and spend a day wandering the center of town, browsing through galleries. In the main square, we kneel and look at silver jewelry and frames, showing each other what we like. My mother lifts up a belt made of silver disks with lapis set into the center of each one.

"Always check for the nine twenty-five," she tells me. She points out the mark I already know is there, the small stamp that means sterling.

"Are you going to get that?" I ask.

"What do you think of it?" my mother asks. She tries it on over her jeans and white blouse.

"It's great," I say. My mother can pull off just about anything—headbands, smocks, heels with shorts, whatever she wants.

"Why don't you choose a pair of earrings," she says. She points to a cluster of silver ones. I look at them, hold some up to my ears, shake my head.

"They won't look good," I say.

"Okay," my mother says to me, and then, to the saleswoman, "just this belt then."

We separate and I go into the Open Studio, to look at a local artist's work. The colors are electric and take up all the space on the canvases. No borders, no elaborate frames. I think about art and landscape, about color with the smooth, tan adobe. I picture working full-time again instead of being in school. The smell of museums, of cleaner fluid, and the dripping sounds of wet brushes.

My first job in art restoration had been in New York. Almost the whole time I'd worked on a painting titled *Angel Mourning*. Big as a lap pool and in bad repair, the canvas was rippled, paint flaked at the edges, cracked to show the true tones of the color underneath the grime. I'd lived with Jeremy then, the post-college boyfriend, the one who nearly left me stranded with a broken foot while hiking, the one who'd nearly left me stranded, period.

After breakfast, my mother hasn't asked for another mix tape explanation, and I haven't volunteered. In the car again, heading out of Santa Fe, I am Radio Hog. I switch channels midsong and often until my mother pleads, "Laney, stop it. Find something and leave it."

I remember a friend once asking, "Are you looking for a particular song or just trying to make me get out of the car?" It's a bad habit. Sometimes I even switch stations during songs I like, just to see if there's a better one out there. I feel like I am constantly missing the songs that play elsewhere, and I worry they might be ones I've almost forgotten about, that I long to remember, to revisit.

"Can you find that tape I made you? The Moons and Junes and Ferris Wheels one?" I ask. There's no story to go with this one, so I figure I'm safe. Out of the case and in the cassette deck, the tape cues and we listen. I calculate my driving speed by running time and figure on crossing state lines by the last song.

After each song or during, my mother gives feedback, as if I not only chose the song, but wrote it.

"Feathered canyons, everywhere," my mother says while Judy Collins sings. "How lovely."

"Jesus, Mom, you're so positive about everything," I say and realize maybe I need more coffee.

"I am," my mother concedes and then looks at me with her "I birthed you" eyes, "and it's a luxury."

"Do you know what this song is about?" my mother asks about Stevie Wonder's "Isn't She Lovely."

"Yes," I say.

"I'll bet you don't," she says.

"It's about his daughter, Meredith, and how lovely she is," I say.

"How did you know that?" my mother wonders.

"You've told me a million times."

We harmonize Neil Diamond's "Play Me" as we always did; she's the sun and I'm the moon. Together, we're a full twenty-four hours. I think about why I chose these songs for the tape, for us, and what they might later signify.

"Neil, Barbra, Carly, Barry," my mother lists.

"Yeah?" I ask. "What's your point? Oh—are we gathering names for our Jews on Tour concerts?"

"Something like that," my mother says.

"I need a snack," I say.

"I'd like a salad," my mother says.

"Mom, we're not going to get a salad at a convenience store. We're in New Mexico, not San Francisco."

By now, my fingers are gross orange with Cheetos cheese and I feel disgusting. The empty Big Gulp has perspired all over the dash from its inconvenient convenient cup-holder position.

"Oh, Livingston," my mother sighs when Livingston Taylor's song comes on. Even though its grammar bugged me, I liked the melody. I'd included it on the mix just to hear my mother swoon a little, maybe to make her think about her own past.

I am Sister Golden Hair, I think, when we drive over the causeway and are sheathed on both sides by the stillest blue water I've ever seen. My window is open, my hair is blowing, I imagine I am the one someone can't stop thinking about.

"What do they mean, 'one more correspondent'?" asks my mother when she listens to the lyrics of America's "Sister Golden Hair."

I shake my head and shrug. I don't want to pick the song apart until it makes no sense, I just want to sing it, sing it, sing it until I am somewhere with radio reception.

"You loved the song 'Taxi' when you were little," my mother smiles. "You and Maggie would dance around the kitchen, twirling around that pole—"

"That was during 'Hopelessly Devoted to You,' " I correct her.

"No, this song, too," she says. "You wanted hair all the way down your back like Crystal Gayle. And sometimes, I think you even acted out the song—you know, you'd be the taxi driver and Maggie would be the long-lost woman who goes for a ride."

"How do you remember that?" I ask.

"You're my girl," she says and tilts her head back and to the side, staring at the rush of landscape.

My mother sleeps, head back on the seat rest. I eject the tape, saving it for her. On the radio, static fuzz is interrupted by the occasional weather update and then a Tom Petty song. It's midway through by the time I find it and then the drum kicks in. Suddenly, I am back to where the song takes me. Back when I knew the song so well I could mouth the instrumental bits.

I could let my mother sleep, flashback to the moments of this song by myself, but now I kind of want to tell her about it. I fish around in the shoebox for a certain tape and when I've found it, I wake her up.

"I have another tape for you," I say quickly before I change my mind.

"For me?" she asks, raising her shoulders and stretching her hands like a concert pianist in cartoon.

"For me to tell you about," I say. "It's called Red Coats and Blue and White Stars."

"I know when this was made," my mother says. I nod. The summer she was diagnosed, where she watched us all outside from her bedroom window as we reeled from the news.

"Here we go," I say, "but don't feel the need to comment afterward."

"We'll see," she says and I take this to mean that of course she will.

It's the summer my London cousin Jamie comes to stay with us in Cambridge, Massachusetts, and brings his friend Ben with him. All Ben brings with him are two large bags full of clothes that are way too warm and an expression: "gutted."

"Oh, an import," I say when Jamie announces he's got a friend stuck in baggage claim. Turns out, Ben's the best tennis player I've ever met. By July, he's beaten my dad every game but one, and by Labor Day he's aced even the country club pros.

"Did I forget to tell them I'm nationally ranked at home?" Ben whispers to me as we exit the club's front gate.

"Gutted," Jamie says. At first, the expression annoyed the crap out of me. Then it was just strange. I couldn't believe it was really a thing to say. It felt funny coming out of my mouth—like the way it feels weird to part your hair on the other side. Now it's just part of our summer, like the greenery—the court, the trees, the school shirt Ben's lent me with his initials written in permanent ink on the inside tag.

Ben's brought two rolls of film for every week he's here and we're always miming goofy dances to use up the last snaps in a roll. Or my father drives us to the amusement park where Ben, Jamie, and I get stuck at the top of Finnegan's Wake, the flume ride. We sit in the fake log that acts as our seat and wait for the fix-it guys. Ben sings the song "Kayleigh" from our mix and tells me about being in Belsize Park and tells me he'll take me there sometime. Jamie drags his hands through the water, splashing me, and I suddenly feel bad that I'm here having so much fun while my mother is curtained off in her room. Then I also feel guilty that I've been avoiding Eric's phone calls. But Ben's around so much that eventually he's the focus of the summer. He is the foreign Marcus—and part of me wishes he would do more than just teach me pub songs.

At night, Ben and Jamie and I listen to *The Hissing of Summer Lawns* because it's the right album for us. They've never heard Joni Mitchell before, which I find strange. Then we sit on the roof and listen to Tom Petty sing what we're doing; sitting on the roof, sharing a cigarette, staring at the moon.

Ben chimes in with Petty, messing up the lyrics. "Don't let it be so easy to forget about me . . . I'm a lucky loser."

"Even you," I say, not bothering to correct him.

"Even you," Ben says back.

Upstairs, my father puts night-lights in the hallway so he can find his way to the study when thoughts of my mom keep him awake. My mother barely emerges from the house, except to sit in the umbrella shade to watch us all play outside and to pick at a bunless burger during a cookout.

To mark their time in the States coming to a close, Jamie, Ben, and I make a tape. We dub three copies and alternate who writes the song titles and artists so that each tape will have something of all of us on it.

Red Coats and Blue and White Stars

FIRST SIDE

Kayleigh
 —Marillion
Summer Nights
 —from *Grease*
Little Red Corvette
 —Prince
Letter from America
 —The Proclaimers
Boogie on, Reggae Woman
 —Stevie Wonder
Telephone Line
 —ELO
Condition of the Heart
 —Prince
That's Entertainment
 —The Jam
Oh Yeah
 —Roxy Music
Jennifer She Said
 —Lloyd Cole

SECOND SIDE

Life on Mars
 —David Bowie
Paper Late
 —Genesis
What Is Love?
 —Howard Jones
Wuthering Heights
 —Kate Bush
Dream in Rio
 —James Taylor
Even the Losers
 —Tom Petty
Stars
 —George Winston
Souvenir
 —OMD
Around the Girl (in 80 Ways)
 —Big Audio Dynamite

The boys teach me and Danny the rules of the Most Boring Game Ever, cricket, to pass the time while my mother is at the hospital for treatments. They humor me by calling it by my name.

After I'd come back from baby-sitting, Jamie and Ben would be out on the lawn, white shirts and trousers, bright against the green. I'd watch them hit singles, twos, threes, fours by getting the ball to run over the boundary rope and sixes, which they did by getting the ball to clear the boundary rope without bouncing. It was like a homer in baseball.

As my mother appears silent in the window upstairs, looking down at us, I try not to focus on her and instead watch my father with his sister, Jemima. They look like adults, but when my aunt walks by and my father swats her on the arm with a dish towel and she says, "Grow up, and get rid of those shoes. It's not 1969," I think that they are really still trying to share the backseat of the car on a long trip.

Danny likes to watch them, too, and I wonder if he pictures us like this when we're older. If Mom will be around to witness.

"I'll have you know these shoes have never gone out of style," my father says and displays his purple-strapped Birkenstock for all of us.

"Not in your mind, anyway," Aunt Jemima says. She's got a half lilt in her accent and sounds like she's from somewhere in the middle of the Atlantic.

"Iceland?" she asks when I mention this to her.

One night, Ben and Jamie and I are all lying on the lawn, waiting for nothing.

"Grand," Jamie says like it's a normal teenage thing to say when we're looking up at the blank sky.

"I thought there were meant to be stars in this country," Ben says.

"There are stars," I say. "Just not on cloudy nights." We lie there waiting for the rain to start and when it does, we stay there, still. Like a photograph taken from above, I can see the three of us, flat as gingerbread cutouts, looking up.

"I wish you lived in London," Ben says.

"I do, too," Jamie says. They are on either side of me, so I roll my head back and forth, looking from one to the other and back.

"I'd rather you guys lived here," I say.

"That'd be okay, too," Ben says.

I think and say out loud to Ben, "This is how I will always picture you."

And I do. Even after we visit in London over Thanksgiving break and I see him sit with Jamie on one of the big lions in Trafalgar Square, even when he sends me a photograph of himself looking dashing in black tie, even when he's diagnosed with osteosarcoma in December and dies in the spring.

When I find out, I think one word: *gutted.* I think of going fishing once with my dad's dad on the cape. How we'd used a simple drop line and pulled up some fish neither of us could identify. Using the knife he kept in a leather case looped to his belt, Grandpa showed me how to clean the fish. It's a swift motion, really. One deep, long incision, a tug, and then rinsing until the white meat inside is bloodless.

I feel it, too, sliced and open, empty of insides and sad. Since I never see Ben sick, either at home or at St. Mary's Hospital, where he writes to me from his nonprivate, crappy room, I have no image of him that way. In my mind, he is in shorts, standing, bouncing from one foot to the other, ready to play tennis. Or, when I let myself really go there, we're sitting on the night-wet lawn out back, the fireflies blinking like indicator lights around us.

The last song ends and my mother starts in right away with her analysis:

"You know, I always wondered if something had happened with you and Ben."

I do my half laugh. "No. Nothing did."

"For someone so bright you aren't able to look at yourself much, are you?" she asks. Before the tape can flip again, I eject it. On the radio there's commercials for stores I'll never see, lawn equipment on sale, banks offering special rates on loans for farmers.

"I mean, obviously, something happened. Ben died and that was sad and I miss him—missed him, I mean."

"It was more than that," my mother says. "I could see it then. You were so at ease with him, just the way it should be. You kept that shirt of his for years. I'd find it every now and then when we'd go through your closet and drawers. Your face—it looked the same each time."

"I still have it," I admit. "It's in my bag as we speak. But that doesn't mean anything except—"

"Except that Ben appeared right after I was diagnosed, right as things fizzled with you and Eric. And then—boom—Ben died. And my treatments progressed."

"I never really thought about the time line of it all," I say.

"But it's all connected!" she insists. "Your life isn't little fragments," she gestures with the tape. "It's continuous."

We sit still a minute and I swallow hard, the way you do when you realize that your mother might be right.

CHAPTER
seven

In Tulsa, Oklahoma, where I am spared another rendition of the Broadway hit, my mother and I decide to pose in front of Healing Hands, the sixty-foot statue that points skyward near the City of Faith Hospital. The hands are rather gross, actually, since they are not only huge, but detailed with veins the size of fire hoses and a slight sheen as if the hands and forearms, like us, are hot in the afternoon haze. We laugh as we sit at the base of the giant wrists. The clear broad sky is empty, save for the oversize fingertips above us. We laugh quietly, then louder, as we attempt to get a self-timed picture. My mother balances the camera on a rock and gets back in time to sit down next to me, but the camera never goes off. Then, just as we are about to stand up, the camera clicks into action, capturing on film only our feet. I think ahead to how tiny our shoes will seem against the backdrop of enlarged prayer. Being near disgusting landmarks makes me miss Shana again—she has always appreciated all things gaudy and tacky.

"Mom, wait up," I say as she hurries down the healing steps. I feel like a seventh grader trailing after her, but I want to tell her how much I miss Shana.

"Whatever happened with you two?" she asks.

I can feel my forehead burning in the sun and my cheeks flush with embarrassment as I try to explain.

"It's stupid, really," I say. "It's about a boy—not even a boy . . ."

"An infant?" my mother cracks.

"No, a full-grown man—at least he probably is by now. Just this guy, Josh, and being Jewish and Shana overreacting to everything."

"You're arguing about a boy? That's why you're not talking?"

"Not exactly. It's not a recent thing—it's a boy from way far back. And it's not just him, it's what happened last fall when I went to her sister's stupid wedding in Ohio."

"I'm totally confused." My mother shakes her head. "And what does being Jewish have to do with anything?"

"It's not being Jewish exactly, it's just about being honest, I guess." I glance up at the oversize hand statue and wonder what they're asking for. "Maybe this would make more sense if you knew the whole story," I say and know I have to explain way back. "I'll tell you soon, over tapes," I say, like the cassettes are martinis.

The next day stopping for lunch, we laugh while "The Gambler" plays.

"Remember how Grandma Zadie used to sing along to Kenny Rogers?" My mother smiles. Not all of her memories of Zadie are positive—I think my mother wishes Zadie had been more cultured, refined, less Old World Jewish, but to me she was pure grandma, a baker and a hugger who lived life very simply, comfortably.

"She always did like a good country song," I say and think about her.

Zadie wore gingham housedresses and smelled always of lemon icing and hand cream. Around the house, she'd sing lonesome tunes of whiskey and prairies, her Lithuanian accent jumbling the words, hyphenating some, confusing others, but always in the correct key.

"And she loved lemon pies," I say.

"That she did. Sometimes, when I really miss her," my mother says, "I realize I've been near a lemon, a slice of it in my water, even some detergents!" My mother is quiet for a minute and then says, "She loved your visits."

"I did, too."

"When you or Danny used to go to stay with her, I used to wonder about having grandchildren visit me," my mother says. She says this matter-of-factly and waits for me to say something.

"I bet my kids will love coming to you," I say. "You'll be like Project Grandma, always teaching them how to make things. They can come home with quilts and collages, and mobiles made of fallen leaves and waxed paper."

My mother smiles at the thought. "I already have a file of ideas put away," she says.

"You have to meet the guy first, don't you?" my mother jabs.

It hits me wrong and I say to her, "I only hope you can be the grandma that Zadie was. You're not exactly up on all her recipes."

My mother doesn't register the dig, but says, "I'll have to grow into it. I spent a good deal of time trying to not be like her, but you wind up just following your instincts. You can't control the future, only what you do today." The last bit sounds every bit like Zadie.

I do not allow myself to calculate the years ahead, of the time it would take to produce the grandchild, to get the kid to an age where projects are possible, and how my mother might be at that time—well, ill again, no—healthy and vibrant, the grandma who bakes and sews and never tires. Instead, I take a tape from the shoebox and get ready to put it in the player. I think about my mother's mother, and my visits there, and the way it felt to hug her, the gentle sag of bosom and smell of lemons.

One Memorial Day weekend in junior high I had gone to visit Zadie by myself. She still lived in New York then, and I'd taken a Peter Pan bus to get to her. She insisted on meeting me at Port

Authority, and when I'd retrieved my bag from the mysterious cavern of luggage beneath the seating area onboard, I saw Zadie. Purse clutched in her hands, she spoke with a scraggly man dressed in an outfit that appeared to be a costume party giveaway, Napoleon meets *The Love Boat;* admiral's hat, marching band jacket, and bright white flares.

"Lovely speaking with you," Zadie said to him and she led me to the curbside cab line. "That man is fantastic. He knows all of the bus schedules and names and information without so much as looking at the boards! He stood with me the whole time I waited for you."

Back in her apartment, Zadie sliced a piece of cake for me, set it on a flowered plate, and poured cold orange blossom tea. She would heat water the night before and let the tea bags float and sink, cooling in the refrigerator until the next morning. If ever she ran out of the special bags that came in a wooden box, she would fashion her own from cheesecloth and loose leaves. I kept one of these, dried, in the top drawer of my desk at home, even though it was old and left a fine dust on everything it touched.

Zadie kept a glass pot of honey on the table and slid it toward me so I could let some drip into my glass. The cake was an original recipe she'd created by mistake when she had first moved to America. The details were unclear, but we knew this; she had clipped a recipe from a magazine or newspaper and had my grandfather translate it for her. Of course, being new to English himself, and totally unfamiliar with all kitchen language, he'd substituted his own word, *cake,* when the recipe was Iced Lemon Pie. The results were wonderful, though. The cake was in many ways like a lemon meringue pie, but from cake plate to the top was an easy ten inches. One wedge seemed to take an hour to eat, and Zadie would watch until you'd finished it all. When I gathered the last crumbs with my fingertip and deposited them into my mouth, I noticed the plate on which the cake was served was really a tea saucer. I looked at the indents where the tea cup base was supposed to sit and felt bad for my grandmother. Did she not have side plates? Dessert plates? Did she not know the difference? It never really occurred to me that she didn't care.

After the snack, Zadie led me into her bedroom, my grandfather's empty bed still made, the fabric tucked in, the coverlet ironed and ready. Zadie's bed had yellow sheets on it, and looked the way hotel beds did after the turndown service had come, the sheet and blanket pulled back in an open V. It was inviting, having the linens that way, and I wondered if maybe my grandmother needed that to lure her toward sleep when she was alone at night. From her dresser, Zadie took out a box and handed it to me. I stared at what was inside.

"You might not want to wear it just now," Zadie said, "but it's good to have."

I tried on the star of David necklace and looked at myself in Zadie's faded mirror until I was a sepia-toned image of myself. I tried to imagine myself as a part of a family portrait taken in black and white, back when men wore hats and children seemed to be forever clad in sailor-suit tops. With the star on, I could almost see it.

That summer and the next, I took the necklace with me to overnight camp in the Berkshires. The camp was large, green-and-white painted cabins perched along the lakebank housed all the girls, and, across the lake, similar bunks marked the boys' camp. The third-generation owners, Bill and Phyllis Jaffe, had gone to the camp themselves, around the same time as my mother had. They kept the grounds clipped and clean, updating every year; a soda machine in the snack shack, boom boxes in the main lodge—little things that made the experience seem less dated than other places.

The camp songs were still clear in my mind. You'd start singing them as soon as you got on the bus at whatever your pickup spot was—the airport, the Newton Marriott, or the Howard Johnson's that marked the halfway point in the drive to Lenox. My mother had taught them to me before I'd even gone to camp, and when I sang them, I felt she was there alongside.

*   *   *

I show my mother Shana's writing on the tape cover.

"It's funny how different you and your friends are," she says. "I guess I know Maggie the best since you've known her forever. She's always been eccentric. Shana seems fun—the one who'd be up for anything."

"And what about my other friends? What about Casey from college?" I ask.

"I never really got to know Casey." My mother shakes her head. "I was so sick. I'm so sorry."

"Mom," I say and feel my shoulders slump. "You will know Casey, someday. And for now, you have the chance to learn more about my friends than you even want to. Seriously."

"So this is a camp tape?" my mother asks. She looks at the songs and I can see her nod at the ones she vaguely recognizes. "And this will explain the Shana situation?"

"It's *the* camp tape," I say and feel the giddy rush of being about to arrive somewhere. "And it might help explain how Shana and I got in this mess to begin with."

Having secrets was a part of all girlhood friendships. You kissed someone you weren't supposed to, or you betrayed a confidence. But you weren't meant to mess with fate—somehow good friends were supposed to know, to intuit what meant something, who mattered, and those were the things that were off-limits. And maybe Shana and I had been so close that we'd forgotten those rules. Maybe that's what she and I had done to each other that we couldn't undo.

Camp Mix—from Shana

MORE US	MORE YOU
Cuts Like a Knife —Bryan Adams	Love Cats —The Cure

Along Comes a Woman
　—Chicago

Careless Whisper
　—Wham!

The Search Is Over
　—Survivor

One Lonely Night
　—REO Speedwagon

Walking on Sunshine
　—K. and Waves

Things Can Only Get Better
　—H. Jones

Against All Odds
　—Phil Collins

Raspberry Beret
　—Prince

Praying Mantis
　—?

Glory Days
　—Bruce

Head Over Heels
　—Tears for Fears

Paisley Park
　—Prince

Hot You're Cool
　—General Public

Your Love
　—The Outfield

Perfect Way
　—Scritti Politti

See You
　—Depeche Mode

Take on Me
　—A-ha

Always Something There . . .
　—Naked Eyes

65 Love Affair
　—Paul Jones

Rio
　—Duran Duran

She's a Beauty
　—The Tubes

There is the cutest guy sitting near us and Shana actually took a picture of him. She pretended to want to take a picture of me, but she stood up and pressed the button on her Kodak Disk camera and got the guy instead. I think he knows. He must be a counselor. We are blushing and listening to her Walkman with double headphones.

This summer we are not really campers and not yet full counselors-in-training, we're just sort of there, sleeping in the bunks, only going to the activities we want. *Pre-CIT* is the official term. Shana jokes about doing nothing but hanging out with the kitchen boys. They are all locals who wash dishes to make money for the rest of the year. One guy, Kyle, has the hots for Shana because she has long legs and he thinks she's not Jewish. I wish I could say that she lied and told him she was Christian or something, but the truth of it is that he just assumed she wasn't Jewish because she hangs out with me, and no one thinks I am. Part of the problem is my hair—it doesn't help being blonde and pale—but there's something else, too. People just feel they can launch into asking about Christmas, or even about Jesus, and I'll know what they mean.

"You just don't seem like a Jew," Shana had explained more than once.

"Jesus!" Shana nudges me when the bus stops in front of Howard Johnson's and Carrie Lowenstein cuts ahead of us in the line to get off. Shana thinks Carrie's mean, and worse, that she's going to purposefully sabotage Shana's chances for water-skiing helper. Carrie doesn't really like water sports, she just likes to look good in her noncamp-regulation bikini and flirt with the lifeguards.

It's only late June so the heat hasn't reached western Massachusetts yet. The sunlight bounces from Hojo's angled orange roof.

"Why orange?" I say to Shana.

"What are you talking about?" she asks.

We're waiting in line at the outside ice cream window. Again, Carrie's in front of us.

"These are CP Shades," Carrie says pointing out her baggy, pink shorts to some girl who is impressed. They tally up how many similar articles of clothing they have stored in their trunks.

Carrie orders pink bubble gum ice cream and then pivots so she faces me. I never liked that flavor because I'd forget about the bubble gum and end up swallowing it. Carrie takes licks and spits the pieces out into a cup so she can chew it later.

She says, "Laney, are those Esprit shoes?" I look down. The shoes are blue with flowers woven into the fabric.

"They're just sort-of espadrilles," I explain.

"What do you care?" Shana asks Carrie.

"Well, I think they're Esprit," Carrie says as Shana and I step up to order, "and they are awesome. Can I borrow them?"

I don't think I want Carrie in my shoes, but I say, "Okay," and step up to order.

"You and your mint chocolate chip." Shana shakes her head when we're in the shade and on a bench. I watch what seems like hundreds of girls and counselors eating ice cream in just-out-of-sync time, heads dipping to the cones and swirling around to catch the drips.

"I like mint chocolate chip," I say.

"I know," Shana says, "but only the green kind and only with chocolate jimmies."

Shana giggles. She's from Ohio and she says that out there, jimmies aren't sprinkles, they're slang for blow jobs. I find this hard to believe, but so many people don't know what jimmies are outside of Boston, I don't question it. Plus, Shana would know.

"So," Shana says while shoving the last piece of her ice cream in her mouth, "no star of David this summer?" She looks at my bare neck.

"Nope," I say, "it didn't work, anyway." I thought of the summer before when my grandmother had given me a necklace she wore as a young girl.

I didn't wear the necklace at home. It seemed like my mother tried not to be like Zadie, not be Old World or too Jewish, that she didn't want me wearing something Zadie felt made a statement. Part of me thought about keeping it on, about possibly being a Jew who wore jewelry that announced itself. But that didn't really feel right. But keeping the necklace in its box didn't, either. I didn't know what to make of it all.

I didn't have a bat mitzvah. I was the only Jewish girl in seventh grade who didn't. I went to friends' celebrations, the one with the piano theme, and the all-purple one with those string barrettes in lavender and purple for the girls and skinny purple ties for the guys. Shana's bat mitzvah was over the top. Everyone got a Swatch and two 45s that they picked from the DJ's collection. I got to go because my mother had some design conference near Cleveland. She called it a "fabric symposium" and brought back a whole carry-on full of samples.

"See," she said, "we both got Swatches."

I laughed. I was glad to have a mom that knew about toile and chintz and raw silk. But I watched Shana's mother and father and how they seemed to know everything about all her friends and their families, how interconnected it all was, how Jewish it all seemed, and part of that made me feel like I was missing out. My parents knew some of my friends or what the school play was, but they were more detached than Shana's. They had their world and I had mine and I wasn't quite sure where we overlapped. And part of me longed to be included—longed for assumed connection—the ease that came by oversimplifying; we both like Wham! and this means we could be friends, we're both better at math than history and we could be friends, we're both Jewish and we could be friends.

But when I wore my necklace at camp, people thought I had borrowed it from Shana. Or that I was wearing it as some kind of statement. I don't know what kind of statement that might be since all I really was doing was trying to show my Jewishness. I ended up proving it to Janelle and Kim, the ringleaders of a sort of is-she-or-isn't-she? hunt. I said the only two prayers I know, the one over the bread and the one over the candles. It worked. I had visions of asking my parents to come for parents' weekend with kugel instead of the usual cookies. I hoped my dad would use words like *schlumpy* to describe our disheveled counselor, or *shmata* for my old T-shirt that was falling to bits.

Anyway, I have no plans this summer for proving anything to do with being Jewish. The only group I want to fall into now is the category of girls who have been kissed. Not that I have no kissing experience. I do have some. In the social studies room on the fifth floor of the main building at school, my friend Chris kissed me while everyone danced to "Purple Rain" in the courtyard below.

Also, the summer before, at one of the camp dances, I had gone
for a walk with Brian, from the boys' camp, and he had given me a
dry, quick press of his lips. We also both got poison ivy. Finally, I
had kissed my next-door neighbor the night before he moved
away. That kiss was really an excuse to grope, which we did until
his dog started to throw up. The kisses were strays; they belonged
nowhere in the romance department. And they were one-offs, so I
never felt like I knew if they were good or not or if they meant
anything more than just lips. Lips with no embrace.

In bunk twelve, Shana puts her mix tape into her portable
boom box and presses play. Before orientation meetings, we all
unpack to Wham! and Prince. I know all the words to "Raspberry
Beret," so I sing along and watch Shana unpack her nonuniform
clothes—there are tons.

"This song is so good," she says.

"I know, but I'm glad you put 'Paisley Park' on for me," I say.

"Well, it's like, so you, you know?"

"What do you mean?" I ask, but Shana rolls her eyes.

I know what she means. She's suburban and loves it. She is a
cassingle girl—she likes the songs that make it on the Top 40 and
buys them. I like the ones hidden on side B of the whole tape that
people fast-forward over. I am urban-suburban, which is different.
I don't go to malls or identify with the lockers that all the John
Hughes characters have in the movies. We don't have study hall at
my school and the homework takes forever, so the idea of going on
dates on a weeknight is totally foreign. Dates are actually pretty
foreign, but I get the idea.

"Bruce is so rad!" Shana exclaims suddenly.

"I like the stuff before *Born in the USA* better. *Greetings from
Asbury Park,*" I say to her.

"Asbury, Paisley, it's all the same to me," she says.

"But this is good, too," I say.

At dinner, Shana offers to clear plates. The little kids think
she's the coolest for it, but I know she's headed for the kitchen
where the crew of townie boys work, including Kyle, the one she

has a crush on. That night, I get the scoop. Shana says Kyle's going to be a junior in high school and has a definite thing for her.

"But he can't find out I'm Jewish," she says quietly to me. In front of us, the "welcome" campfire glows bright against the cool night and helps keep away the mosquitoes.

"Why?" I ask. I don't want to hear what she has to say, so I sing along with the camp songs, "When the m-m-moon shines, over the cow shed, I'll be waiting for you at the kitchen door. K-K-K-Katie . . ."

Shana leans in. "I know, it's like, really bad, but he doesn't like Jews. He thinks they're kind of mean—I think about the money stuff."

"What do you mean, *they?*" I ask and then motion for Shana to be quiet. She knows we're supposed to set an example for the junior camp and so she halfheartedly sings. I know she's busy thinking about Kyle.

"I'm going to kiss a townie!" she whispers.

At swimming tests the next day, Carrie struts down the dock in her fluorescent pink bikini and does a perfect dive into the lake. She's the captain of her swim team at home, so she should be a good swimmer, but when she not only passes all the tests but has the best times, Shana's pissed off. I feel glad for Carrie. That she has swimming *and* clothes. When Shana's doing her three minutes of treading water, I sit with my legs dangling in.

Carrie comes by and sits next to me, dripping still, but with her towel expertly wrapped around her waist in a special knot.

"It's called a French bow," Carrie tells me when I ask how she can run and have her towel still not fall off. I look at her and think how easy high school will be for her, how she's so pretty and well-dressed and full of silly confidence. She knows her Guess jeans will always be the right thing to wear with the light green sweater, or how everyone knows her at Temple Israel, and how she says, "Homework? I don't even think about it. It's so easy. You should go to public school, Laney, really."

Carrie is a glider. She glides through band practice and horseback riding and malls like they are all hers. I always feel like the visitor. Nothing seems to faze Carrie, she's a solid B student, the boys she likes like her back, and if her parents bug her, she shrugs off the annoyance. Part of me wishes I could be like that—that I wouldn't overthink everything. But another part of me feels like maybe if nothing bothers you, if nothing is upsetting or makes you wonder *what if,* that it's kind of like it happened to someone else. But when I watch Carrie and try to imagine her in the future—not grown up, but in college—I wish we could trade just for a day, she could feel half-in and half-out like I do, and I could not think at all. I could glide.

As I do my treading in the lake, I think how good the water feels. It's cool, but not cold and there are patches of warmth. Not pee, I think to myself, sun-warmed. I'm sure I'm right. I am standing still and moving at the same time. My feet churn and rotate and my hands do their own dance moves, half dog paddle, half bunny hop.

Right when I hoist myself onto the dock, the cute guy that Shana and I saw on the bus up to camp walks by and says hi to me and Carrie.

"He's the owner's son," Carrie says. She knows everyone, and, if she doesn't, she makes a point of finding out before anyone else. She sees my face as he walks by, so when she says, "Uh-oh, I see a crush!" I can't say anything. I just sit my wet butt down on the warm, dry dock and push my hair away from my face.

Shana walks over and says, "Laney, I want to talk to you during rest hour." She says it like she's announcing detentions, so Carrie and I exchange a look.

"You know," Shana says as we lean on the boulder behind our bunk, "just because Carrie's really Jewish, doesn't mean she's going to rub off on you or something."

"What's that supposed to mean?" I ask. I straighten my uniform shorts out. They're polyester, one hundred percent, so they twist and ride up constantly.

"How come you were talking to her before?"

"You know what, Shana? I'm allowed to have other friends besides you," I say.

Shana doesn't say anything for a minute. I scratch my bug-bitten thigh and Shana redoes her bandanna. "Why Carrie?" Shana asks.

"I don't know," I say. "Maybe she'll be a friend, maybe not. But it doesn't mean anything. It's not against you. She's just different."

"Is this all about Carrie?" I ask as Shana looks at her wavy reflection in the bunkhouse mirror.

"Not just," she says and puts her hands on her hips. "I saw him first."

"What? Who do you mean?"

"You know I got on the bus before you and saw that hot guy, Josh, or whoever, and now you're all telling Carrie how much *you* like him."

"First of all," I say and try to talk softly enough not to be overheard, but loud enough to make a point, "you're busy running off to see the Third Reich Kitchen Crew. Second of all, nothing would happen with that guy anyway. He's the owner's son." What I mean but don't say is, *He feels way out of my league, even though I'm not quite sure I know what league I'm in.*

"Like being the owner's son matters." Shana sighs. Then, tilting her head at me, she adds, "Okay. Just swear you won't do anything with him anyway, just to make me feel better."

"Fine," I say and scratch my bug-bitten shin.

Shana switches gears and says, "Oh my God, I forgot to show you the note I got from Kyle!" From her pocket she hands me a folded piece of white lined paper, the kind with the frayed edges still clinging in bits to the side. The note reads:

Dear Sharon,
   You are cool. I like that headband thing. It kinda looks like that David Lee Roth guy. Not that you are like a head-banger or something. I just mean it's cool. My buddy

*Warren is having a cookout on Sunday. Do you want to go
with me?*

From Kyle
*PS If you want you can bring a friend! Even better if she's
hot!*

What I want to say to Shana is, *You've got to be kidding me.* But
what I say is, "You have got to be fucking kidding me." And then,
"Hey—David Lee Roth is Jewish!"

Shana takes the note back and says, "Why is it such a big deal
to you if I tell him I'm not Jewish?"

"Because you're lying," I say.

"Like you never lie. Like you didn't totally tell Carrie you liked
her ugly pants last night."

"That's different," I say. "You're lying about who you are, about
stuff that's really important."

"Well," Shana says, "it's not like I'm going to marry the guy or
anything. So, will you go with me?" she asks. "Please?"

"Whoa—wait a minute," my mother interjects from the passenger
seat, stopping the tape and putting a pause in the Camp Story and
my musical time travel.

"What? What's wrong?" I ask.

"Don't ruin my vision of you at camp—your father and I paid
for archery and macramé necklace making, not sneaking off with
Shana to drink beers with the kitchen boys."

"So you just assume I went with her?" I shake my head.

"Did you?" she asks.

"You'll just have to find out," I say to my mother, opening a
bag of corn nuts and eating them one at a time, enjoying the
crunch even more as I see my mother cringe each time I lick the
salt off my fingers and go back for more.

CHAPTER
eight

"Well, do tell," my mother says.

"Where was I?" I ask. "God, now I sound like you."

"Very funny," she smirks. "Shana the hidden Jew was just asking you to go to that boy's—Kyle's—party."

"Wow—you actually remembered his name! I'm impressed."

"You'd be surprised at how many things I can remember," she says.

I press play, listen to the artist formerly known as Prince back when he was more than a symbol, and go on:

"First of all," I say to Shana, "Kyle's party is off grounds, so you can't go. Second, it's not a good idea. You don't know much about him—it might be a bad scene."

"Okay, Mom." Shana laughs. "If the kids are smoking or doing drugs, I'll call you and come home." Shana's already been felt up, so she feels immune to being uncomfortable at a party. And she's already been drunk on stale beer at Dale Hoffman's birthday party last winter, so the drinking part isn't a worry, either.

"If you go, just be careful," I say.

"So, you really won't go with me?" Shana asks. "You are less fun than I thought." It occurs to me for the first time that I am less fun than I thought, too, but I feel okay about it.

When Sunday—the day of the party and of the welcome camp-fire—rolls around and we are supposed to be enjoying our one morning to sleep until eight, I wake up at six-thirty and can't fall back asleep. The bunk's shutters are closed, so it's dark inside, but I can see the light around the window edges. Slipping into my shorts and T-shirt from the day before, I go through the bathroom and out the back door.

By the dark line of wet sand at the lake's edge, I go barefoot. What if I fell into the lake and needed help? I wonder and then it occurs to me why campers aren't allowed down here alone. Then again, I am not really a camper, more a counselor, I remind myself.

"You're not supposed to be down here." The voice comes from the boathouse doorway. I turn around and Cute Guy from the Bus is standing there.

"I know," I say, and instead of trying to defend myself I add, "I was just thinking that!"

He walks over and puts out a hand for me to shake. "I'm Josh," he says.

"Laney," I say and point to myself. Even though Shana wants Josh to be off-limits, it's not like I asked him to find me here while the whole rest of camp is in their bunks, so it's not really my fault we're talking. And it's just being friendly, anyway.

"I couldn't sleep," he says. "What's your excuse?"

"Same thing. I am not good at it."

"Like it's a skill?" He laughs.

"Yeah," I say, "I should get better with all the practice, but I don't."

We sit in a canoe that's sand-banked and going nowhere. I rest my feet on a wet orange life preserver. It's a morning like I've never seen—maybe because I'm not usually up this early, or, I realize with a slight shiver—the whole day could seem different because of Josh.

"Mind if I fake-paddle over this way?" Josh asks and mimes the J stroke.

"Good choice," I say and then, "So, do you like it up here?"

"I'm the owner's son," Josh says.

"I know," I say and wonder if I should have played that game where I said I didn't know. Since I didn't, I wonder if maybe that means something.

"Oh," he says and turns around. "Word gets around fast up here. I'm just here taking a break from my college tours." I quickly try to calculate his age.

"Are you going to be a senior then?" I ask.

"Yeah," he says. "Just getting it over with early." *Two years older,* I think.

We pretend capsize and lie on the sand with the canoe on its side. I prop my head up by putting my chin in my palm.

"Don't take this the wrong way," Josh says, "but you seem kind of different than most of the girls here."

"Really?" I ask.

"I mean, yeah—you're Jewish, though, right?" he asks. I nod, trying not to be too emphatic.

"What I mean is," Josh digs his fingers into the sand, "I mean you're different because you're not dressed up, for starters. Also, you seem not to be an idiot—"

"What?" I interrupt. "On behalf of all the girls here, I am offended." But I am not. I am just glad to be a nonidiot.

"That came out wrong," Josh says. "I mean, you seem comfortable."

Comfortable with you, I want to tell him, but I don't. We laugh and keep lying in the sand until we are all first-talked-out and the recorded trumpet sounds out over the loudspeaker.

I get up and brush myself off. Josh flips the canoe.

"Well, Laney, it was good talking to you," he says.

"And to you," I say, sorry that the trumpet sounded, sorry that time moves at all.

"Hey," Josh says as we walk up to main camp, "want to meet here tomorrow morning?"

Beyond thrilled, I say, "Sure!"

On the way back to my bunk I think, *This is it. This is what people mean when they say you just know when you've just met Mr. Right.*

Shana only asks me one more time to go with her to the cookout before she asks some girl named Mandy from Bunk 14. I almost said I'd go because I felt guilty about my time on the beach with Josh, and even worse when I realized I couldn't even tell Shana about how I was reeling inside. Even though I wore the same uniform, spoke the same way, and ate the slimy tuna sandwiches at lunch, I was different now. I had met a boy I really liked—and he liked me back.

Shana says Kyle will meet her and Mandy at the end of the dirt road by the sign that marks the camp entrance and off they'll go. They plan to sneak out when we're all around the flagpole singing and taking the flag down to fold in the way that you're supposed to, triangle over cloth triangle.

On the way to the mess hall for dinner, Carrie finds me and we decide to sit together. Sunday dinners are fun at camp because there's music played on the speakers and there's "revolving" dessert, so you can swap places as much as you want.

"Gross," says Carrie, "cabbage."

"I like it," I say, thinking about Grandma Zadie's cabbage and her advice about love: "Pick it when it's in front of you—you might never get another chance." Who knew if this was Old World farming wisdom, or Zadie trying to explain how World War II shaped her whole world, but either way I wanted to get out there and find Josh and harvest him. According to Zadie, things could be taken away from you at a moment's notice—a heavy wind could wreck your crop of lettuces or Nazis could round you up—and you had to be prepared. I think about this as I smell the swirl of scents in the dining hall.

"Cabbage makes you fart," says Carrie.

"No, it makes *you* fart," I say back, being immature on purpose. Carrie gets it and we link arms on our way to the table.

In the middle of eating the cabbage, I think about Shana going off with Kyle. Then all I can think is that Kyle and his friends work in the kitchen and probably prepared the meal. I picture them touching the cabbage and feel sick.

"Are you okay?" asks Carrie.

"Yeah, I'm fine," I assure her. "Did you ever feel like no matter what you choose, like being with a friend when she needs you—or doing what you really want to do, maybe being with some guy you like—that no matter which choice you go with, you're going to feel like you missed out? Like you did the wrong thing?"

Carrie gives me her look like she does when someone wears a fake Ralph Lauren polo shirt that has a rhinoceros or something instead of a horse and rider. She raises her eyebrows and says, "No—I mean, you just do what you want and it's all the same in the end, right?"

"Maybe you're right." I nod. But I don't believe it.

After dessert, but before lights out, Carrie and I have a Ping-Pong match in the senior lounge. I make a point and Carrie says, "Good shot." We have been complimenting each other all game for no good reason. She's a good player, a bit better than I am, so I have to pay attention.

Carrie wants to know all about life at home, what kind of pottery my dad makes, if my mom has made curtains or anything for famous people, who I like at school, what my room looks like. Carrie tells me about Brad, the soon-to-be-senior she likes at home in Connecticut. "Basically," she says, "he's perfect. He's gorgeous, with sort-of Rob Lowe hair, but lighter, and he dresses great." She waits for my reaction.

"Sounds like your type," I say. "He sounds cute."

"Like, I know you're not into what cars people have and stuff, which is totally fine, but in my school it's a big deal. And Brad's got a nine-eleven. Pretty ritzy for a kid, I know, but it's so nice." I like that Carrie has no apologies for being into clothes and cars. She just is who she is.

Between games, we sit in the plastic chairs by the soda machine. I drink my Orange Crush and she has a Tab. We trade off imagining what it'd be like if I went to her school and she went to mine.

"The hair would have to go," she says and picks up the end of my ponytail.

"What, is everyone bald or something?"

"No," she says, "just stylish." We dish it out to each other a bit and then she goes on. "You'd get it cut into a more feathery kind of style and a little shorter. Also, it's really flat, so you'd spray it more. You'd realize that mousse is your friend."

"I tried mousse, the glittery kind."

"Rad!" Carries says.

"But it's too sticky. I liked the glitter. Maybe I should just stick to doing the art projects I like and leave my hair alone."

Before I can tell Carrie what she'd do with her hair at my school, we're done with our drinks and playing again. That's when Shana comes in. She opens the screen door and the hinges are so tight that it closes with a loud bang, even though the green-painted frame is light. Shana has blue eyeliner on that's smudged and her lipstick had worn off.

"I have to go," I say to Carrie.

Carrie looks at Shana and says, "Of course, sure."

We sit on Shana's empty bunk. You have to sit on the edge because otherwise you sink into the middle of it.

"He's such a dickhead," Shana says and then starts to cry.

"Kyle?" I ask.

"No, Warren, Kyle's friend," she says.

"Kyle and I were making out near the badminton net at the party and then Warren came over and called me a skank."

"So then what happened?" I ask.

"So then Kyle looks at me and says he bets that Warren's just jealous because I'm so pretty and Warren doesn't have a girlfriend. That part was nice. But then Mandy wouldn't kiss anyone, so we had to leave."

"So why are you crying?" I try to be nice, but it comes out frustrated.

"Don't be mad at me, Laney."

"Sorry," I say, "I'm not mad."

Then I think how mad Shana will be if she finds out about me and Josh. If there is a me-and-Josh.

"Kyle dropped us off and he and I made out more—no one was doing drugs or anything, by the way. Kyle only had a beer. Anyway, Mandy went back to her bunk."

"Don't tell me he asked you to . . . do anything?" I say.

"No, it wasn't that," Shana says. "Kyle calls me Sharon, you know, like on his note, because he doesn't know what Shana is. I don't care about that. I can't exactly tell him it's Yiddish, you know. But then, when Kyle and I were leaving, I got this." She hands me a folded piece of paper. "It's from Warren," she explains.

Warren's note says in all capitals:

SHARON

LEAVE US ALONE YOU STUPID KITE.

For a second, I'm confused and then I look at Shana. The tears are drying on her face, so I think it's okay to laugh.

"What a total idiot!" I say.

"I know, it's like, not only am I a bigot, I'm a bad speller, too. Bet he doesn't even know it's supposed to have a *k* instead of a *t*. Fuckface."

Shana and I hug. My heart pounds like she can tell I broke my word to her and spent the morning with Josh. I say, "So what did Kyle say about the note?"

"He didn't read it."

"What are you going to do?" I ask.

"I'm going to tell Kyle I'm not Jewish, and make sure he tells Warren," Shana says and covers her face with her hands.

That night it's all I can do to make myself get in bed without setting my alarm. I tell myself that I wake up early every morning and that if I actually do set my clock, Josh won't show. But I set it anyway and am out the door at 6:00 A.M. and by the lake three minutes later. I creep by sleeping Shana and think about what it means to lie—about being Jewish, or liking a certain song, or falling for the guy your friend told you not to—about what it means to tell the truth.

"I was wondering when you'd get here," Josh says.

"Don't you mean if?" I ask.

"Nah." Josh shakes his head. "I knew you'd be back." We laugh at his overplayed macho man.

We eat cold waffles with maple syrup, the fake kind from those little plastic containers that are usually filled with jelly. Josh took them from the kitchen and filled his old canteen with orange juice. The juice is sweet and cold with the taste of tin.

With some juice still in my mouth, I blurt out, "I wish you went here." And then feel like a complete loser. But at least I said it. At least I'm honest. Josh looks at me with a funny expression. "What?" I ask.

"I don't," he says and then, when he registers that I take this to mean he wouldn't want to be here with me, he quickly adds, "Can you imagine being at the camp that your parents run? How lame would that be?"

I laugh to let him know I get what he means.

"But it would be cool to, you know, be around . . ." His voice trails off. We swish our hands through the lake water and let them air dry. On the dock, we let our legs go loose and kick the water up so it glints in the sun.

"Did you make that?" Josh asks about my rope bracelet.

"I did, actually," I say.

"Most people just buy them," he says and studies my tan line.

"Well, I didn't. I can show you how to make one if you want." I tell him, "My mom taught me."

So I get some thin line from the post on the boathouse door and come back. I show him how to weave the rope between his fingers and tell him the real name of the knot is a Turk's head.

"Your mom's a sailor?" Josh asks.

"She was," I say. "Her dad even had a boat back in the old days. So she learned on that. But we don't really do much sailing now."

Josh shrugs and slips the end of the knot through the tight weave.

"We live in Cambridge, Mass," I explain.

"I might move there if I go to Harvard," he says.

"Is that your first choice?" I ask.

"Nope. Brown or maybe Stanford," he says.

"California," I say and can't think of anything else to add.

Josh whistles. I recognize the tune. " 'California,' " he says. "My favorite Joni Mitchell song."

"*Blue* is such a great album," I say, too scared to say much more for fear of what will come out. Josh nods. We sit in that moment without saying anything else. Across the lake, a sailfish does loops around one of those big floating platforms.

Finally, Josh says, "Laney?" I turn to him. "I feel funny about telling you this, but just so you know . . ."

My heart speeds up, wondering what he's going to tell me. I look at him, "What is it?"

"I have to leave tomorrow," he says and pulls his wet feet up onto the dock.

"Oh," I say, so softly I wonder if it counts.

"And the other thing is—" Josh breaks off midsentence. He looks me right in the eye and then we lean in. He wraps both arms around me and we kiss for so long. The sun is hot, but there's wind, and when the trumpet sounds and the rest of camp is slowly rising, we are so awake I can feel the blood swooshing around my arms, legs, toes.

"Wow," I say when we pull back and look at each other.

"I know," he says. "Isn't this what you always pictured?" I nod.

"Always," I add and I don't feel silly, just real. Not half here and part somewhere else, just completely present.

At breakfast, Shana dashes into the kitchen and tells Kyle she's Christian as he's sopping up the spilled juice by the industrial refrigerators. Kyle nods and then wipes his brow in an exaggerated way like he's superrelieved.

"Do you think I did the right thing?" Shana asks when we're checking our mailboxes after eating our pancakes.

"No," I say and I can tell she's surprised. "I can't believe you."

"You know what, Laney? If you found someone you liked a lot, I bet you'd lie, too," Shana says before walking off in a huff. And I can't call out to her, because she's right. I'm not lying to Josh, but I like him so much I'm lying to Shana.

For the rest of the day, I flit around like a nectar-drunk butterfly with overlapping worries of Josh leaving and knowing I have to tell Shana about him.

I find her in the arts and crafts hut and while we weave waxy gimp into key chains our parents won't use, I say, "Shana, I have to be honest with you."

"Oh, okay, Queen of Reality, what do you have to say?" She raises her eyebrows.

"Josh and I are together," I say.

"Who?" she asks and then when she thinks about it she says, "You bitch!"

"At least I'm telling the truth!" I say and stand up. "And he's leaving today, anyway, so what does it matter?" I start to cry and Shana does, too.

"I'm a terrible Jew," she says and we cry at each other over the tabletop. "And a crappy friend." After a minute, when we girl-fight-hug each other and rock back and forth, she says, "I want to tell Kyle the truth, but I can't."

Back at our bunk we complain to each other instead of talking about the jealousy and meanness girls make each other go through, about our friendship.

"What if I never see Josh again?" I ask.

"Kyle might not ever talk to me if I tell him." Shana moans and stares up at the musty beams in our bunk. All the ceiling space and upper parts of the walls are covered in graffiti. You're allowed to write on the beams since campers have been doing it since the 1920s when the camp first opened. Some of the writing is dated and funny like, "I like coffee, I like tea, I like the boys and the boys are sweet on me—Rose P. '33" and some is more recent like, "Bunk 12 rocks!!!—The Green Girls '83."

Supposedly, my mother wrote in her bunk when she was here, but in my three summers I hadn't found her signature. It could have burned in the fire of '77 that ruined a bunch of the old cabins or maybe it's just mushed in with all the red and blue paint, the carved-out initials, and I can't see it.

When she was here, the camp was Jewish "one hundred percent," she said. "Even the counselors." In the photograph we have of her in senior camp, she's in a starched white shirt tucked into jeans that are rolled up at the bottom. "Dungarees, they were called then," my mother would tell me as I would look at her young face and try to picture her singing in the musicals, climbing the old oak tree that's gone now, or talking to her friends about boys. She has one friend left from her camp days, Jean Reitz, even though everyone signed the back of her camp photo. Even though we didn't see Jean all that much, when we did, she seemed soft and familiar; hugging her was like hugging family somehow.

"Do you think Kyle would still like me?" Shana asks again.

"I don't know!" I say and fish around my backpack for some Wite-Out. "But if he doesn't, he's not worth it, anyway."

"What are you doing, Laney?" Shana asks and sits up.

"Signing in," I say and stand on my bed. I can't reach to a clear spot, so I go to Sheila Monahan's top bunk and stand on that. My head is in a cloud of names and marks. I outline a small square and in that I write my initials.

"Are you going to write in Josh's name, too?" Shana says, and it comes out bitchy. I consider it, but then decide that I won't. She writes her name and then Kyle's and then makes parentheses in which she writes *maybe*. "Sorry Josh has to leave," Shana says, but something in her voice tells me she's lying about this, too.

I'm mad at Shana and since I can't figure out why—if it's because she's not happy for me about Josh, or if it's because she's lying about her religion for some stupid kitchen boy, or both. Suddenly I decide I can fix things. If Shana can't tell Kyle about herself, maybe I could. Then she'd be honest with him and happy, so then she could relax enough to accept that Josh and I are together—at least for the remainder of the day until he leaves for his tour of Brown University. It seems like lying about one thing seeped into the rest of your life, making it hard to smile, just in case you suddenly forgot your lie and were found out.

I pull out Shana's notebook and purple pen and write:

Kyle—

In case you don't know, I am Jewish. If this bothers you, too bad, because it's just the way it is. I liked the cookout but Warren is dumb and anti-Semitic, which means he doesn't like Jews. My name isn't Sharon, it's Shana, which means "pretty" in Jewish, which you probably didn't know. If you want your sweatshirt back, just tell me and I will give it to you at dinner.

Yours truly, Shana

I picture Kyle finding out and making some speech in front of his kitchen buddies, that Shana is amazing, that religion doesn't matter. I envision Kyle kissing Shana and her thanking me later when

I tell her I gave up her secret. But later, Kyle risks his job to come out in the dining hall and talk to Shana. He asks for his sweatshirt back and she's stunned like she's been hit with the tether ball in the face. All she can do is nod while the junior camp watches and giggles. Then some administrator points to the kitchen and Kyle leaves. Seeing Shana run out of the room, I know I can't tell her about what I did. Not now. Maybe never.

In the lower parking lot, I'm in those thin flip-flops that cut into your skin and only barely protect from the rocks underneath, getting ready to say good-bye. Josh's mom is in the car, slightly farther down the drive, waiting for him.

"Good luck," I say.

"Thanks," he says and we link fingers and hands. His thumbs rub my palms.

"I know!" Josh says. "Let's not say good-bye or anything."

"Okay." I nod.

"We'll just stay together," he explains. We have not exchanged addresses or numbers, or tapes, just kisses and words. I can't figure out which I love more.

"I'll be back," he promises. I believe him.

Back in the bunk, I am alone in the muggy afternoon. I climb to the top of the bed again and look at the names. With my tiny Wite-Out brush, I write my mother's initials next to mine. Then I realize that I've put in her married name, not her maiden one, like she would have had when she was here. But then I think, *Well, that's the way I know her.*

Later, I wait while the water-ski instructor readies the boat. I check my life preserver. There weren't any dry ones, so I had to put on a just-used one, which feels gross, like sharing a towel with someone you don't know plus sitting in a wet bathing suit. I give the thumbs-up and we are off. Over the wake, cutting back, I tense my arms more and look ahead at the boat. I'm better than I was last year, that's for sure. I'm up for at least five minutes before my arms ache and my eyes are watering so much it's like I'm crying, which is what part of me feels like doing because of Josh. But I am whizzing past the beach, the trees are a blur, and the campers are dots of red and white. Even when I give the thumbs-down and the boat slows, and my legs start to buckle, I have the sensation of going, going, into the next lane of water, of not stopping.

CHAPTER
nine

By the time the camp tape is finished dark seeps into the sky.

"So that's what your problem is with Shana?" my mother asks. With the doors open, we sit in the car and listen to the whir of trucks going by on the freeway.

"Well, that's the old stuff that we never really dealt with." I sigh. "But I never heard from Josh again. He promised he'd come back, but as far as I knew he never did."

"And did Shana find out about the note you wrote Kyle?" my mother asks. My heart beats fast when I think of telling Shana; even as an adult when you acknowledge you did something wrong, even with good intentions, it's hard. Then I say to my mother, "I'm so glad you're here. It's kind of a relief to talk about all this."

She smiles at me, thankful for my honesty, I think, and says, "When did you tell her? And why?"

"This fall," I say, "when she made me go to Ohio for her sister's wedding."

"Don't tell me there's a tape for that, too?" My mother shakes her head.

"Actually, there is." My mother looks in the tape box.

"No," I say. "It's not in there." I open the glove compartment, pushing aside maps and manuals, noting that Marcus's wedding invitation is tucked in there, too, right where I'd put it—out of sight. I take the mix out.

"Hmmm, interesting—" my mother says like a television detective. "A tape so special it needs to be kept in another place."

The tape is titled Depressing Underwear. Before I put the mix into the tape deck, I eat. My dinner is a bag of trail mix, plump sweet raisins, peanuts salty and halved, and shredded bits of unidentifiable things labeled as healthy. My mother, able to find produce anywhere, even at Katy's Roadside Nibbles, slices tomato with a plastic knife and uses the red rounds as a sort of bread, with lettuce and cheese layered in between. Were I to eat that, the seeds and slime would slick my bare legs and dot my shirt, but my mother, tidy as a television cook, manages to keep everything together.

I sit on the roadside with my healthy mom and just breathe a minute before telling her more.

Depressing Underwear

ONE

Looking for Clues
  —Robert Palmer
Turn to the Sky
  —March Violets
I Will
  —The Beatles
Dance Away
  —Roxy Music
Song for You Far Away
  —J.T.
Secret—OMD
Leather and Lace
  —Nicks and Henley

TWO

Heart Like a Wheel
  —Kate and Anna McGarrigle
On the Radio
  —Emmylou Harris
Ohio
  —The Pretenders
Bring on the Dancing Horses
  —Echo and the Bunnymen
I Get Along Without You Very Well (Except Sometimes)
  — Nina Simone
The Muppet Theme
  —The Muppets

We don't know whose tape this is and Shana doesn't much care. The cassette's a sixty-minute one that we just let flip over and over as we sit, parked, in our formal wear. It's the first time I've ever eaten at Wacko Taco and already I feel ill.

"Don't worry," Shana says, "that feeling passes. It's like getting drunk, really, you have to work through the gross part to fully appreciate it."

I slide fried cinnamon-sugar twists into my mouth and feel a bit better. Out the windshield, the fast-food signs cover all the cars with a purple light.

"How do I look?" Shana asks.

"Great," I say. I am Shana's date for her sister, Rebby's, wedding. Rebby is only eleven months older than Shana and she's stayed in Shaker Heights her whole life.

"Not my whole life," Rebby has said to Shana. "I mean, I went to Kenyon for college, right?"

"They say the gates of Kenyon are the gates to hell," is what Shana used to say to me after her visits there.

Rebby is marrying the right Jewish boy from the right accounting firm. They are in the process of moving their engagement gifts and two terriers into their new split-level house.

"How weird would it be to live in a whole house before you're thirty?" Shana asks when we pull into the driveway for the last of the bridal showers.

"You're just saying that because of New York. You're used to apartments," I say and look at the big, white columns and clipped bushes that point skyward, as if trying to grow up and escape.

"I'm saying that because it's weird. By the way, don't expect a fun time, like at my bat mitzvah. This is serious Ohio shit here. You will be expected to discuss things like the merits of carpet over rugs. And you won't be going home with a Swatch."

"I still have that one. Mine was a smelly Swatch. Strawberry. Pink. Or maybe that was yours."

"It was mine," Shana says as we get out of the car and she pulls up her stocking and fluffs her hair. "Yours was blue."

"Blue?" I ask. "What does blue smell like?"

"You tell me," Shana says and we head inside.

Within the walls of the house, we are part of a small carnival of sorts. A blender full of Laura Ashley, the scent of new leather pumps, and flower vases filled with gourmet jelly beans we're supposed to count and guess the quantity. I stare at the piles of them and imagine they are little rainbow creatures, burrowing their way to the bottom or sides, hoping to dig free.

Rebby sits on a high-backed chair, ankles crossed, and waits for the next gift.

"Wait!" says a woman with starched hair and a pleated skirt. "Let's have a game first." Nods and yeses from all around.

Blindfolded, Rebby has to reach into a silk-lined basket, pick one of the engagement rings from inside, and guess on whose finger it belongs.

"Pear cut, gypsy band . . . oh, it's Janey's!"

Shana has put her own ring, a red plastic spider ring, in the box, too.

"I left my decoder ring at home," I say to Shana.

To Rebby I say, "Congratulations, and here." I hand her a box wrapped in cream-colored thick paper, filled with the cake slicer from her registry. She slides the ribbon off from the box and hands it to the woman who is making her a ribbon bouquet for the rehearsal.

"Thank you, Laney, it's just what I wanted," Rebby says, and she means it.

Looking at Rebby and her friends and their mothers, I think that I have entered a small globe, a semipermeable cell, only they don't know it. They never consider that any one of them could move away, become ill. Even if they divorce, they stay in town and remarry each other.

"You only have two choices if you're from the Midwest," Shana told me once. "You leave or you stay. And if you leave, it's for good. It's not like the East, where you can go to California for ten years and then come back to raise your family—the space closes up."

Back at Shana's parents' house, her Nana Rose has hand-washed various garments and hung them to dry on every available hook, doorknob, or railing. The elderly versions of Peter Pan's undone shadows, hosiery and bras, silky control-top items, are draped and empty.

"Gross," Shana says and picks up a giant pair of black underwear with her fingernails and deposits it into the sink. "Well, at least they're black. Not beige or gray."

"Yeah," I say, "they're downright racy. But now I can't wash my face because you left them in the sink."

Shana and I stand and look down at the underwear.

"It's sort of like she went down the drain," Shana says.

"That's something I would say," I tell her.

"I know," Shana says, "that's why I said it."

"Thanks."

"Laney, I don't want depressing underwear. Make sure that never happens to me, okay?"

"Sure," I say and hug her. "We can go on lingerie outings when we're eighty years old and I'll tell you what looks good."

"Yeah," Shana says, "at least I know you'll always be honest with me."

During the ceremony, Shana is matched with Bill, the bald groomsman.

"I'd like to say he's got another defining characteristic," she says right before they go down the aisle, "but he doesn't."

The wedding itself is fine—draped white fabric everywhere, bright floral arrangements that are already assigned to go home with certain people, a nice Rilke poem, and a huppa made from Shana's grandfather's tallis. I watch Shana standing there, single, and suddenly think about camp and how long we've known each other. I go through all the guys she's dated in my head, counting them on my hands and then toes. I think about Kyle and how I was the SS—or more the LP, the love police—turning her in for being Jewish. When I think of how honest she thinks we are, I decide to tell her later about Kyle, even though I doubt it will matter.

"I love all the dancing," Shana says when she's finished complaining about the ceremony.

"What a lovely affair," Nana Rose says when Rebby and her accountant husband bundle themselves and the billowing wedding dress into the limousine. Rose balances herself by clutching my arm too hard with one hand, her beaded purse drops to the ground. Shana picks it up and gives it to her.

"I wouldn't wish my bunions on anyone," Nana Rose says to no one in particular.

"No, of course," I say and look at her feet. She wears a pair of sandals, clear plastic at the front and a strap at the back.

"The secret to these," she says and points down, "is that you heat them with a hairdryer, and then slip them on. Then they're molded to your feet, see?"

"Brilliant." I nod.

"And the sad thing is," Shana whispers to me, "is that you mean it."

Shana never liked older people. Not their stories of iceboxes or scrap metal businesses, not their elasticized waistbands or the loose hand skin that, once tugged, did not go back into place over the bulging vein. Most of all, Shana did not enjoy knowing that she would most likely become an old person with her own grandchild who thought she was wrinkled and possibly icky. She never wanted to reuse a tea bag, or have her fork shake on its journey to her mouth. But these things just happen.

It was one of the ways we were really different. I loved the stories, how the icebox would be filled with a giant block and drip, drip, drip into a metal pan at the bottom until a delivery truck would come with a new block. Twice a week, in the window, you'd put a white card, vertically for a whole block, horizontally for half of one, and a man with thick gloves would slide it in the icebox for you. My Grandma Zadie had had soft skin, deeply veined, the blue lines perfect for tracing with my small fingers on long car rides or waiting for food to be set on the table at a restaurant. Near her small pool, Zadie would paint my toenails whatever color I wanted, even a different one on each toe if I couldn't decide. She'd never learned to swim herself, but Zadie wore bright orange water wings and stood in waist-high water with her arms stretched out, a slow-moving windmill.

I longed to think of my mother growing old, of lines creeping out from around her smile, of her earlobes somehow growing larger, of her stories of years ago seeming impossibly distant to the children I had yet to birth.

When I thought of being old myself, I drew a blank. I figured on the white-blonde hair that yellows and then fades like smoke, but it was strange to think of singing not just Ella and Louis tunes to my grandchildren, but Ben Folds Five or the Rolling Stones. It was easier to envision being led to the dance floor at a grandchild's wedding and slow waltzing while the band played Count Basie.

This is what I do for Nana Rose while Shana says her good-byes to the wedding guests. Shana smiles at me, both thankful and edgy that it's not she who is leaving for a honeymoon in Acapulco. She gives her bouquet to her mother before we head out.

"So, who made this tape?" I ask Shana when we're back in her car. The car lives at her parents' house in Ohio and is therefore frozen in time with her graduation tassel hanging from the rearview mirror and parking stickers from when Echo and the Bunnymen were on the radio.

"I don't know, Laney." Shana tries to shake off the question. "Let's listen to something else." She ejects it and then I push it back in. We do this a couple times until she gives up.

We pull into the Wacko Taco drive-through and she asks what I want to eat.

"I can't do it again," I say. "Where's the tape case to this mix, anyway?" I try to find it and Shana looks at me and says loudly, "Just pick something to eat!"

She's overemotional as the unmarried sister on her sister's wedding day, I figure.

Shana says, "I only eat this crap when I'm here, maybe twice a year. Call it a fair trade for schlepping back to the Midwest." We pick up the order at the next window and park.

She bites her three-cent burrito and says, "You know what? I do know where this tape is from. But just out of curiosity, why do you want to know?"

"It seems like one I would have made, but I know it's not. So I was thinking, since I've been here, about whoever made it. How I can tell I'd probably like them."

"Well, I don't know if that's true. I've met plenty of assholes with good taste in music." I can tell she's thinking about telling me something—maybe she slept with the bald groomsman.

The car windows fog with faux Mexican food while "Ohio" plays.

"I'll tell you this," Shana says with her mouth full. "No one who is from here puts this song on."

"Makes sense," I say. "So you didn't make this tape?"

"No." Shana licks the drip of sauce from the side of her hand before it slips to her forearm and says, "When we were back for camp reunions, we got to look through the lost and found crates from all the years past. I guess the owners keep them as sort of time capsules things."

"That sounds so fun! So that's where you got this? You just took it from the lost and found?"

"Um, not exactly," Shana says, "but that was fun—looking though all the stuff that's collected over the years. Just your type of thing, which was why I wished you could have been there. But you weren't." This comes out like I've never been anywhere for her. Shana's never given me much sympathy for not going to camp or reunions while my mother was sick. I never wanted to go up for those kinds of weekends in case something bad happened at home—Mom fell or suddenly got admitted to the hospital. She crumples her wrapper and plays a miniature game of catch with herself, hand to hand, passing the paper ball.

"Shana—don't tell me you're mad about that? I stopped going to camp—to reunions and whatever—because I grew up," I say.

"What're you saying, that I didn't?" she says.

"No," I say, but when her tone is shrill I reconsider. "Maybe you didn't. Maybe that's why you liked it there so much. You didn't have to grow up. You could just keep being a teenager who bends herself to fit what any guy wants. Did you ever date a Buddhist? I hear you can fake that just like you learned to fake being Christian."

"That is such bullshit," Shana says and sips her soda. "And you're one to talk."

Shana will probably use expression like "one to talk," "so didn't I," and "you should know" until she's ninety. "Hey—I stopped going to camp at a normal time," I say. "And besides, you know my mom got sick. I couldn't keep going."

Shana shakes her head and starts to talk, then stops.

"What?" I ask. "Just say what you want to say."

"Fine. You stopped doing everything when your mom got sick."

I don't say anything. I cram all the wrappers and half-chewed tacos and open the car door to throw them out. When I get back in, Shana's gripping the wheel with both hands.

"I can't believe you said that," I say when I'm buckled back in.

"At least I'm honest." Shana plays with her hair.

"You want honesty? Good," I say. "You know how Kyle dumped you right in the middle of the dining hall?" Shana's mouth twists like it just happened last week. "Well," I say, "that's because I told him about you. About being Jewish."

"Yeah?" Shana tries not to be shocked. "Well, Miss Honesty, you want to know whose tape this is?" I nod, despite the rhetorical nature of the question. "It's yours. Your lover boy Josh—who I asked you not to get together with and you promised not to—made it for you that summer."

"How come I never got this tape?" I say and it comes out small.

"You were water-skiing," Shana says and then, very dramatically, like she's doing voice-over for a soap opera, "Josh made his mother drive all the way back to camp after his tour of Brown or whatever. He came running back to camp and tried to find you. But he found me instead. I said I'd give it you—but I guess I never did."

"So you stole this tape?"

"Basically, yes," Shana says and hands me the cover.

"Oh my God," I say when I look at it. I read the cover aloud: "To Laney from Josh, Songs for the Sunrise."

"Is that what it's called?" Shana asks. "How sappy. I've been calling it Depressing Underwear—you know, in honor of Nana Rose and coming back to the land of crap."

"He wrote in his phone number!" I'm shocked, amazed, pissed.

I can't think of anything to say. I think about my morning on the lake with Josh so many years before, how his hands felt, the way he'd kissed me in the calm of prerevelry.

"So, you've had this since then and never gave it me?" I ask.

"Maybe I would have eventually, but I left it at home, with my yearbooks and old stuff, so I forgot."

"If I got it back in college or something, maybe I would have called. Now it's way too late."

"Look, Laney, you never would have called him anyway," Shana says as if this justifies everything. "Especially not once your mom got sick. That would have been your excuse. Just like it is for everything you don't do."

I hold the tape like it's Josh's hand.

"Now I'll never know what could have happened," I say.

"Yeah, well, maybe Kyle and I would be married by now," says Shana.

"What, and raising an army of skinheads?" I ask. "Don't compare your torrid lie-affair with Kyle to me and Josh."

"Look at where honesty gets you," Shana says. We look ahead at the blank midwestern night. I look at the songs and come up with the letter Josh was meaning to imply and am happy at least that the songs are good, that I can keep something from back then. I pick apart a couple of the songs and think that this is just the kind of tape you want to get from a boy. It's lovey, but not so mushy you feel less attracted to him.

We turn up the volume so we don't have to talk and drive down the wide streets with the windows down and feel the new fall air as it whips our hair around. Shana's still in her bridesmaid dress with flowers in her hair, the pins loose. When she shakes her head, buds fall out and onto her lap. I know we won't talk for a while after this. I wonder if we ever will.

On the tape the Muppets sing about getting things started. I imagine a thick, red velvet curtain parting, revealing the next act. Somewhere, those two old-guy puppets are in their balcony, cracking jokes, maybe at my expense.

I show my mother the cassette cover, pointing to songs to tell her what Josh might have been trying to tell me.

"If it's such a love-filled tape, what is 'Ohio' doing on it?" she asks.

"Mom, I'm impressed!" I say. "That's the one song that is sort of out of place."

My mother smoothes her hair in the rearview mirror and waits for me to continue. "My theory," I explain, "is that it's a kind of bluff. A song that's different from all the others and has nothing to do with the whole theme or feel of the tape."

"I see."

"Because this way, if the feelings aren't mutual, you always have a way of saying, 'Love tape? Are you nuts? I mean, "Ohio" was on it for Christ's sake—you think I'd put that on a mix for someone I was interested in?'"

"Good thinking," my mother says. "These are all codes—ways to express yourself." She pulls her old plaid shirt tightly closed around her like she's caught a chill. "I think you and Shana will get past this. Now that you've started to talk about how you feel without needing a tape to do the work for you."

This annoys me, so I say, "Oh, Mom, give me a break. Don't make me regret telling you stuff, please."

"Fine," my mother says. "I have something I need to tell you, too."

Then just as I think she's going to reveal a secret, we get a flat tire.

CHAPTER
ten

While we wait for the tire to be patched, my mother and I sit on ripped vinyl chairs in the lobby of Hal's Automart USA. We watch the mechanic spin the tire on some machine and I think maybe I won't press my mom for her secrets. That way maybe she won't press me for mine.

"So would you ever call Josh?" she asks.

"I wouldn't even know where to find him now," I say.

"You don't get what you want in life just by sitting there." My mom puts a quarter into a vending machine and opens her palm to cup a handful of dusty cashews.

"I know that, Mom," I say. Outside the service sign flicks and dims.

"You have to find a way to make it happen," she says chewing the nuts. "I want to help you any way I can."

"You can't just make everything all right for me. It's not like when I was a kid and wanted a sweater with a rainbow on it and you knit it for me in a matter of hours." Before she got sick my mother had a habit of trying to solve my problems before I'd even identified them—to keep me from wanting—but in doing that she made me unsure what it was I was looking for.

"You mean like the dream house?" my mother says, remembering the same things I am.

"Just like that," I say. "Just like Barbie's Dream House."

We talk about that time and since I don't have the tape anymore, I tell my mother the songs that went with the time before she was sick, before I knew about boys, when Maggie and I had moved from Vermont and were both the new kids. It was so simple—she was my new best friend and I hadn't met Shana or Josh or even crappy Jeremy—before I had any secrets worth keeping.

Laney's Mix for Maggie

SIDE 1	SIDE 2
Let the Music Play —Shannon	All Out of Love —Air Supply
Baby, Give It Up —K.C. and the Sunshine Band	Love on the Rocks —Neil Diamond
Human Nature —Michael Jackson	The Best of Times —Styx
Abracadabra —?	No Gettin' Over Me —R. Milsap
The Look of Love —ABC	Black Cars —Gino Vannelli
Eye in the Sky —Alan Parsons Project	Acrobat —Elton John
The Morning Train —Sheena Easton	Magic —Olivia Newton-John
Queen of Hearts —Juice Newton	Sweetheart —Frankie and the Knockouts

We listen to the tape when Maggie invites me over to her new house to play. We've both just moved to Boston—the big city—from our middle of nowhere houses in Vermont. Her dad got a new job at the college here and my dad's selling his pottery every-where and needs to be more centrally located for travel.

The songs on the tape are ones we listen to when we go to Spin Central, the disco roller-skating place. Almost all the girls in our class will have birthday parties there at one point during grade school. The only bad thing about going is the gross guy we nick-named Slimer. He always dresses in white pants that are way too tight and a white, silky shirt that's open so you can see his chest hair. We try to ignore him and work on our form. Maggie can do shoot-the-moon, where you go down on one leg and keep the other one straight in front of you. It's really hard.

Maggie's dad teaches languages at the college and likes modern writers. He tells me to call him Hank. Maggie's mom, Harriet, sends us out of the kitchen after I arrive so she can make lunch.

To get to Maggie's bedroom we climb a spiral staircase, the first of its kind I have seen on the inside of a house, so it seems special, and dangerous in just socks, so I make a note to be barefooted or in shoes. Maggie gives me the grand tour of her room, twin beds, walls lined with books, green silk comforters on each twin bed.

"Let's listen," I say and hand her the cassette. "Sorry if the songs are kind of cut off, I taped some of them from the radio."

"Far out," Maggie says. Her expressions are all dated since her parents left the States in the late sixties and she imitates them. "You can sit if you want," Maggie says. She hands me a worn paperback, "Have you read it?" It's a copy of *Catch-22.*

"No," I say, "have you?" Maggie takes the book back and thumbs through the yellowed pages. "My dad's teaching it this year. It's supposed to be hard. But I'll read it." She shelves the book back without even taking note of where it's placed, a corner of its thin cover tacked down. My own books have their special spots, out of alphabetical order, not by genre, but it's a system I've worked out so that the characters of one book might get to know ones in the book next door, or the neighboring rabbit in one pic-ture can leap to the field on the cover of the next book. The way Maggie's done it, the Major Major Major guy's next to *The Shaun*

Cassidy Fan Book, and who knows how that relationship would work.

"Let's play Barbies," Maggie decides and I agree, even though I don't like dolls and still don't own any Barbies despite the fact that Maggie hoped my transition to city life would change my interest in dolls. I figure if I go along with her plan, then we can go outside and climb the giant oak tree in her yard. Maggie drags a wooden wine crate out from her closet and slides it in front of me.

"Here, open it," she says.

"What is it?" I ask. My parents have the same crates in the living room, but ours are filled with albums, Jacques Brel, James Taylor, Odetta.

"Clothes, obviously. You still don't play Barbies?" Maggie looks suspicious.

"Nope," I say. "I never had a Barbie."

"That's sad."

"I don't think so," I say. Maggie waits for me to say more. "But I want to play."

Maggie smiles. "I'll teach you." She sighs.

I open the crate and display the small clothes on the thick blue of the carpet. I carefully arrange the tiny beret, the pants suit; Barbie's boa lies limply near the fancy blue shimmer dress and some other evening wear. Maggie sorts out the activity clothes from the rest of the wardrobe.

"In case the Barbies decide to play tennis or go cruising or something," Maggie explains as she piles the terrycloth sports slacks into the trunk of the pink Corvette that Barbie drives. Since she was born abroad and speaks fluent Swedish, Maggie sometimes mutters words I don't even know are words. She does this as she makes an example of herself for me for next time, lowering the cut of Barbie's V-neck velour jumpsuit to show more of what's underneath.

The dolls lie on their backs staring up at the blank ceiling as we finish preparing their activities. First, Barbie needs to shower. Her friends, one with shorter blonde hair and one with auburn hair kept back in a ponytail, are not as dirty, so they stay still as Maggie undresses Real Barbie. Nippleless, Barbie's breasts are as smooth as the rest of her tan body. We help Barbie into the small plastic shower stall. Maggie connects the small spray hose to the rest of the Barbie plumbing mechanisms.

"She had a rough night last night," Maggie says and sprays Barbie in the face.

"Did she and Ken have a fight?" I ask.

"Yeah. But she doesn't even like him. Baby, give it up! Still, she was up really late, talking on the phone, trying to let him down easy. And she has an important meeting today."

"Really?"

"Yes." Maggie looks at me until I realize she wants me to come up with the story behind the important meeting. Barbie's matted hair leaks water onto the carpet. "Shit," Maggie says, "hurry up."

"Okay. Okay," I say and look around the room. The floor-to-ceiling windows let in the light of early fall. Smoke rises into the sky from the chimneys of the nearby campus houses. "So, maybe Barbie should call Ken back or meet him for tennis or something."

"No, that's dumb. The tennis part is good. She can meet him and the girls for a match after she takes care of business."

An idea. "Yeah," I say, "she has to meet with the broker so she can sign the house papers."

Maggie looks impressed. "Why?" she asks.

"So she can buy a house. One with a better shower. And more rooms than this one." I point to the shoebox Barbie rents at present.

"Good one!" Maggie says. "You mean the dream house, right? I knew you were only kidding about not having any Barbie stuff!"

"Right," I say. I have no idea what I'm talking about.

"That is so cool you have it! Did you get it as a moving present or something?" she asks and then, "Where do we have to go to get the papers?"

It occurs to me that Barbie's Dream House is a real thing. One I don't have but Maggie wants and thinks I can lend her. I don't know why I don't explain myself right away, but now that we're not in Vermont everything is different. My world is bigger now than just our house barn, school, and Dad's potting shed. In the city, it feels like anything can happen.

I delay with, "It takes a long time. You have to get Barbie a meeting with a real estate guy and sign papers. Plus, how does Barbie have enough money? And then there's more meetings."

Maggie looks annoyed. "It's going to take forever."

"It'll work out," I say.

We take a break and go downstairs for lunch.

When it's time to leave Maggie's house, I have that Sunday feeling of having to go back to school, back to routine. The feeling that stays with you your whole life even though you're not in school anymore, but working, or leaving the place you've gone for the weekend. The vague knowledge that the emptiness kicking around inside you will meet with slim anxiety about whatever's coming Monday, or whatever might not come at all. At the doorway, my mother and Maggie's exchange bits of information as Maggie and I kick at the leaves on the porch. From her back pocket Maggie pulls a Barbie out and hands her to me. I take it and look at Maggie.

"So you can practice," she says.

"Thanks," I say. My mother herds me to the car as Harriet drags Maggie back inside to where Hank sits smoking Parliament cigarettes and listening to his recorded lecture ideas.

In the car, before the talking starts, I inspect the doll. It's the Barbie with the pushed-in boob, the one Maggie tried to restyle so the hair is cut at an angle and the bathing suit is borrowed from another doll so it keeps riding up Barbie's butt.

"That suit doesn't seem to fit too well," my mother points out.

"Tell me about it," I say. "The whole thing is weird. But I guess it's better than nothing."

At home, I reread *Thimble Summer,* about a girl on a wheat farm in the thirties. It's a book that's too easy for me, but I find the hay and descriptions of farm food comforting. I read it while eating vegetable soup with my legs tucked under my butt. Barbie sits on the edge of my desk, looking like she'll jump any minute, so I go get her and bring her into the bathroom. The house we live in now looks like a house on the outside, but inside I still imagine we live in a barn. It's not hard, since this house was built a long time ago when people were a lot shorter, so the ceilings are low and the beams show. I feel taller than my four feet, ten inches as I sit on the rounded porcelain of the tub and run a bath.

From the hallway, my mother peeks her head in. "Didn't you just take a shower this morning?" she asks.

"It's not for me, it's for Barbie," I say, aware of how stupid that sounds. My mother smiles and secretly, I think, she might be pleased that I am showing interest in a doll or in hygiene. My dad's working in the potting shed still and I am glad he doesn't see me attempting this sort of play.

Barbie floats on her back in the water. First, I pretend she is on vacation in an exotic locale, the running water from the tap is a waterfall and she lets her bathing suit straps slip off her shoulders. Who is around to see her, after all? Then Barbie is in charge of diving for marbles and other treasures that I place on the bottom surface of the tub. She's a competent swimmer, thanks to my teachings, and wins a medal for her heroic save of valuable historic artifacts like the soap stone box she dragged up from the deepest part of the bath. It occurs to me as I award her a prize that the box weighs way more than she does, but I decide it can't all make sense. Then I'm out of things for Barbie to do. I resort to holding her high above the water and seeing how she lands or what she'll splash if I let her free-fall. She high-dives recklessly from the shampoo holder that hangs from the shower neck and almost misses the tub.

As the drain sucks in the bathwater, Barbie sits in the sink dripping until I find a washcloth and dry her off. I towel her wet suit and rub her hair as gently as my father did to me when I was young enough not to be able to dry myself, the way Danny still gets dried today.

After dinner, Barbie's hair is still damp, so I get the hairdryer from the linen closet. I can't stand the heat for my own hair, but my mother straightens her ringlets into flat strands twice a week, so I know how to blow-dry. I fluff Barbie's locks up, try to fix the botched cut job Maggie's done by making Barbie have bangs and a side part before turning the hairdryer on. Then, with a flick of the red button, the heat's out in a steady stream and seems to be working. I watch myself perform this task in the mirror and try to navigate in backward image until I notice the disturbing fact that Barbie's hair is not so much getting dry as it is melting.

I turn the switch to off, but it's too late. Half of Barbie's golden waves are stuck to the side of her head in a plastic blob. One side of her face has melted, too. I trace her drooping cheek and forehead and remember a person we saw at the hospital once when I got stitches and had to wait for a long time in the emergency room.

I bring the doll to my parents' room where my dad has turned on *Masterpiece Theatre* and is trying to stay awake.

"Hi, pumpkin," Dad says and pats the bed where I should sit.

I sit down and show him Barbie.

"Oh, dear." Dad smiles. "What happened?"

"I tried blow-drying her hair," I say. "Now she looks like she's had a stroke."

Dad nods. "Yes, she's not looking well. She's not yours, is she?"

"Nope."

"We'll think of something," he says and touches Barbie's sagging face. "It could be worse."

Dad and I watch the English people in their costumes act out a story about a pirate and a shipwreck. All the women have breasts that rise above their frilly shirts and the men have beards. Just as the action gets good and the cast washes up on the shore of some distant land, the music comes on, signaling the end of this week's program and also bedtime for me. The moon is distant outside my window. Under the covers, my flannel nightgown and moving legs create green sparks of static, and when I tire of that I let my eyes close with the light from under my parents' door as a night-light, a marking point.

When I tell my mother the situation with Maggie and Barbie's Dream House, she knows just what to do. We cut up a moving box and tape two shoeboxes onto the sides. We cover the walls with wrapping paper and mom leads me to her closet to choose special fabrics from her sample books to make rugs and drapes. Soon, it's a perfect house for Barbie if she ever did *Masterpiece Theatre* and wore less terrycloth and more petticoats.

"Gosh," Maggie says when she sees it, "this is like a castle. It makes me miss Sweden." Turns out I never knew Maggie lived in a castle back there. She shows me a photograph of their turret and the left wing, which is where they lived. They shared a music room with the five other families that lived in the other sections and Maggie played the harpsichord.

"You could have been a queen or something," I say when I find out.

"That's like saying you could have been a cow or something in Vermont," she says. "The house doesn't make the kid inside, you know." And then she giggles and tosses her big head of curly hair. I do the same with my fine, blonde ponytail and we sway like that, looking at the empty box house in front of us. From upstairs, my mother calls out that we have ten minutes until we need to be ready.

When Maggie and I are picked up after school, we tell my mother everything that happened at school, even about which boys we like and girls who are mean. Then while we're washing our hands with foaming purple soap, my mother shrieks from the other room. Without drying, we rush to the next room where Moo, the golden retriever, props herself up on her front paws and whines for attention. My mother stands up to her knees in dried kibble, the small morsels of dog food pebblelike around her. Unsure if she will keep screaming or laugh, she points to the open back door. "They went into the garage," my mother says.

"Who is they?" I ask.

Maggie and I start scooping up the dog food with empty coffee cans and put it into a big storage container.

"Giant raccoons!" my mother says, brushing the kibble dust from her pants. "I came in to get Moo's food and there they were, just nibbling away. They managed to rip open the bags."

"How big were they?" Maggie wants to know. Nothing with animals ever happens in faculty housing, so she's wide-eyed.

"So big that they stood up to here." She points to an invisible mark on the doorframe.

"But you're okay?" I ask. It's the first time in my kid life that I fully understand that even your parents—who are supposed to be there to take care of you—can find danger, can get in trouble.

My mother looks me over. "I'm fine, honey. Just surprised, that's all."

"I was worried about you," I say, like I'm the mom.

"It's not your job to worry about me," my mother says. "You leave the worrying to me."

On my bed, my father has left a gift box that's smeared with dry clay. Inside, there's a set of the tiniest plates and cups I've ever seen. All of them fit into my palm at once. I arrange the pottery on the small table in the box house kitchen. Then I realize that no one lives in the house yet, that despite its perfect build and design, the thing is empty.

Back in the fix-it shop, our car is released from the hydraulic lift.

"Tire's all set," the mechanic says to my mother. We stand up to pay the bill. As my mother reaches into her handbag for the credit card, she shows me something.

"What is that?" I ask. She holds in her palm a tiny square of a pillow attached to her key ring.

"Does it look familiar?" she asks and laughs a little.

"Yes," I say. I take it in my hands and turn it over and over, feeling the soft squish of green paisley fabric between my fingers. We walk to the car to head to the next state.

"Now smell it!" my mother says. I rub the pillow on my cheek. "That's just what you used to do!" My mother smiles as she watches me. I close my eyes because it seems that's what you're supposed to do when smelling and remembering. It works.

"Hints of aged rose and pine—"

"And citrus!" my mother adds.

The tiny pillow is one of the couch cushions from my Barbie Dream House. Even after I'd stopped playing with it, my mother would sometimes take her scraps of leftover fabric and sew them into pillows or rugs for the house, simply not wanting the project ever to be completed. I never knew whether to be happy about that, or feel bad. I tell her this now.

"Why would you feel bad?" she asks.

"Because it was like you couldn't let go," I say. "I mean, I outgrew it. That happens. I didn't want you to be one of those moms that kept looking back on when we were small. It made me feel bad for growing up." And as I say it, I let myself tear up, just a little.

"That's not just me as a mother," she says, "that's all mothers. And I didn't add a cushion now and then to make you feel bad. And I certainly never meant to have you play with something like a dollhouse when you outgrew it. I just kept it—maybe for grandchildren or maybe just for me. Each time I'd add a little something, even years later, I could still feel your small palm on my face the way you used to place it there to thank me. It's funny—that was such an old gesture for a young child."

We don't touch each other now, we just look and look, and I pass the pillow back to her after I smell it again. She tucks it away into the dark of her purse, nestles it among all the other unseen things.

CHAPTER
eleven

We're heading out of town on Broken Arrow Expressway. I'm passengering for the first time, so it takes a couple of minutes for me to realize we're not heading south, toward Texas like we'd planned.

"Mom, you're going the wrong way," I say, craning my neck to see what the last exit number was so I can look on a map and try to direct us.

"No, we're fine," she says, a bit smug with her eyebrows raised and lips pressed together.

"What're you doing?" I ask.

In the reflection of the dash, my mother's mouth widens to a smile. "I'm not going to say 'guess what,'" she says, "but guess what?"

Sounding increasingly like a high schooler with *likes, you knows,* and *cools,* my mother proceeds to tell me we're detouring to Vegas. The tickets are nonrefundable; we'll leave the car here and come back for it, and the side road trip is just for two days. She turns on the directional, signaling to me and to everyone driving behind us that we are going to the airport.

"The tickets are in the glove compartment, Laney. I hear there's even gambling in the terminals!"

Momentarily, I pause over the word *terminal*. It's suddenly nice to think about the different twists the words and roads can take, but still, I wish we were heading forward, heading home.

"All the way back there?" it comes out whinier than I want it to. Ahead, small aircraft are parked on the tarmac, ready to fly out. Somehow Vegas, despite the whir of possible fortunes and slots, and girl time with Mom, makes me feel like I'm sliding, back-treading, when what I want to do is drive into the blankness ahead.

Out on the runway, I think about landing in Las Vegas: how the lights will halo into the rush of evening, Rat Pack music will blur from my mother who never can sing "Fly Me to the Moon," and how I will wish I were with my sexy imaginary boyfriend who can pull off wearing a fedora, or at least knows the rules for craps.

But I am not with him, Imaginary Road Trip Guy. I am with my mother, so it comes as no surprise that, as we land, she hands me a tube of moisturizer and says, "Air travel can really dry you out, Lane. Put some on."

"No, thanks," I say and push it gently back to her. She uses Kiehl's Creme de Corps, a thick and silky lotion that I can neither afford nor turn down when offered in free sample form, but here I am beginning to prickle.

"Why not?" she asks. "Look at my skin."

She takes my hand and makes me feel her cheek. I start to laugh half out of annoyance and half to keep from crying out, *This is not what I want to be doing right now!* My mother laughs back and continues as we get closer to the airport gate and the metal accordion thing comes to connect us to land.

"You know why my skin looks this way? Even though I'm not in my twenties? Even though I had radiation and chemo?" she asks. I want to mention that she is not in her thirties or forties, either, but I keep quiet, watching the heat rise from the tarmac in waves of nothing that I know are really something. Her face glows with moisture while my skin stays flaky and parched.

"I think I know how to take care of myself," I say. Some random passenger overhears me and raises her eyebrows, like even she's not sure this is true.

We have to choose hotels before we get to the strip—my mother has made reservations at two. She asks the cabdriver to wait while I run inside and check out the first hotel, Circus Circus. Inside, the high pitch of children's screams competes with the jingle of slots and, from somewhere, the vague smell of manure—maybe elephant manure, I muse, and then head back out into the blast of oven air and onto the sticky vinyl cab seats.

"No way," I say to my mom, who is busy chatting with the cabdriver. From the bits of conversation I hear, he has a sister in stage four lymphoma. He keeps his wide hands on the wheel and doesn't bother to wipe away the tears that drip down the stubbled rise of his cheeks. My mother reaches out and touches his shoulder.

We head to the other end of the strip and round the drop-off circle at the Golden Nugget. My mother has chosen two hotels I wouldn't—both extremes of her personality, maybe. The circus one is her whirled childish self and the Golden Nugget, removed from the other hotels by its downtown location and historic by Vegas standards and subdued, is slightly un-Vegas. With Travel Boyfriend, we'd be at the Hilton, or even the Sands.

Our room overlooks the strip as the sky tries for darkness and fails against the shocks of light that burst from everywhere. My mother peels back the floral bedspreads on both our beds and then takes off her shoes. She lies down on the bed closest to the window, staring half-lidded at the roadway and glitter.

Outside, the slight hiss of a plane overhead. In her hospital room once, I'd come at night, after hours and Lily, the head nurse, had let me in even though it was late. My mother's arms were folded one on the other, her breathing so slim and regular I thought she was sleeping. I stayed only a minute or so, my Walkman headphones awkwardly half in one ear, half around my neck. This was a sicker time, a time where she stayed in the bed, didn't try for walks around the cool linoleum of the corridors, didn't come, complete with IV tubing, out to the family area for frozen yogurt. The pink plastic pitcher of water was set to one side of the rolling dinner cart where her food sat untouched. I stared at the Jell-O, at the way the cellophane wrap reflected the fluorescent overhead lights and felt myself sway, the way my mother and I moved when she hugged me.

I left the room then, and wanted very much to cry. I thought about being one of those people who sat, bawling outside of Massachusetts General Hospital, or who smoked and let the quiet tears go. But I wasn't. I put my headphones on, went to the elevator, reread the sign stating a patient's right to privacy for the hundredth time, and pressed play on whatever tape I'd selected for the journey.

I listened to the college tape a lot back then. It was unlabeled and I hadn't yet memorized the song order, so I felt loose, no connection to the music, to anything.

"Mom," I say now, and it comes out a bit panicked, the way it could have back then looking at her thinness under the hospital's sickly glow.

"Ready for dinner?" she asks.

The Lucky Sevens buffet is the same as every buffet we've seen so far, but the neon sign by the doorway blinks $1.99, compared to the other ones that are a full penny less.

"What could possibly make this one cent better?" I ask, sliding the fake wood tray along the metal rail of the counter.

"Maybe two Jell-Os—lime *and* cherry?" my mother says.

"Maybe curly fries instead of straight?" I say.

"Could be the rice—pilaf versus plain?"

We continue like this the whole way around the buffet line, racking up foodstuffs like we haven't eaten in days. There's so many items on my tray they look foreign to me when I sit and ponder them. My mother goes to get extra napkins and a knife I won't use for the squishy white rolls.

In mock horror, she watches me spread the butter onto my bread using the square paper pat of it as the tool itself. In similar fashion, I make a point of actually licking the tiny white wax of paper before I eat the roll, just to show I can, even though plain butter makes me feel ill.

"We're in Vegas, Mom," I say, as if that explains everything.

"Right, of course," she says, and to show me she's game, she plucks a lime Jell-O cube from its fake crystal plastic flute and eats it from her fingers. Then she uses a wet wipe and calls her own bluff.

Standing by the nickel slots, I slide in one coin after another, fairly joyless over the hollow *clink,* over the way you can avoid the slot's arm-pull mechanism and just press a button. What's the point, then, I wonder. Two rows over, seated on a plush red swivel stool, my mother gives a little shriek.

"I won! I won!" She claps her hands and looks for me. When I go to her she is still scooping dollar chips into a plastic cup. Two other already-filled cups balance on the edge of the coin return. I smile at her.

"See?" she says. "You really should play the dollar ones, not the nickels—low risk, low return, right?"

"I guess."

"Well, this is about it for me tonight," she says. I watch her as she rests on the side of her chair. Absentmindedly she touches the small keloid scar that formed where her surgically placed port was, just under her collarbone. She lets out a sigh.

"Are you okay?" I ask and take the coin cup from her.

"I'm fine, Laney. Just tired," she says. "Regular tired," she clarifies and stands up, taking the cup back. I help her carry the coins to the cash-out booth. After the lady counts out the crisp money and slides it out to my mother, we walk to the elevator.

"Will you be up soon?" she asks.

"Yeah. Soonish."

The big rollers' table is encircled by velvet ropes, as if political dignitaries or rock stars are expected any moment. Maybe rock stars do frequent Vegas, but not in this hotel. The big spenders tonight are polyester-clad or tracksuit-wearing folk who smoke cigars and give nods to the dealers, signaling something I don't know about. I go back to the nickel slots and stand there, nursing the free watery drink the cocktail waitress has thoughtfully brought over to me, and for which I had to thoughtfully thank her with three of my mother's dollar chips.

I somehow find my way out of the gambling labyrinth and feel like I'm in the "Streets Have No Name" video as I come out of the hotel and realize there's nowhere to go but another casino. Across the street, a fake volcano erupts, the gooey lava spilling down its sides to the *oohs* and *ahhs* of bystanders. I breathe the night-hot air into my lungs and lift the hair up off the back of my neck. I could go off, explore more, since it's only midnight, the beginning of Vegas time, but I let my hair fall back down and turn around to go get my mother.

"Mom," I whisper to her. I'm excited, I realize, since I can wake her up and not feel badly about it. All she'll be come sunup is regular tired. Not sick tired. She doesn't respond at first.

"Mom? Annie!" I say, wondering when I will wake her and not feel the slim panic of wondering if she is able to be woken. She bolts upright.

"What? Laney, are you okay?"

I pull her out of bed and onto the balcony. Her long, white T-shirt billows out in the breeze. She stands and looks at the strip lights, then sits down on the deck chaise.

"I'll be out in one sec," I say.

"Wow!" she says when she sees what I've brought out. On top of the cocktail tray are two martinis, chocolate for me, raspberry for her. A lime skin curl pokes out of the red liquid in her glass, a Godiva straw sticks up from mine. I hand the drink to my mom and take my first sip. The busy night below us is quiet up here.

"Are you still sorry you're not with one of your girlfriends like Casey? Someone your own age?" my mom asks, reading my mind and mentioning my college friend.

"It's funny you should mention Casey, she's just who I would want in Vegas," I say. "I mean, if I weren't . . ." I try to switch the subject. "She's in a really serious relationship." I think about explaining Casey's love life, but then I'd have to go into my whole trip to London when I last saw Casey, so I shut up.

"Good for her," my mother adds. And then, "It's about time."

"Is that supposed to be a dig of some kind?" I ask and crunch my chocolate straw.

"Not at all." She offers me a sip of her red drink. I shake my head. "I only want you girls to have what you want."

"And what is it you think *I* want?"

"Connection," she says simply. I think about the word and can almost reach out and touch it, as if it hovers in a cartoon bubble in front of my mother's mouth.

She waits for me to comment and when I don't, she tells me, "When I was in college, a couple of my friends and I started out on a road trip like this," she says. "One of the girls still had a thing about Elvis, so we were going to drive south. But just when we'd planned the whole thing, you know, bought some snacks and put our cases in the car, Daddy showed up for a surprise visit. And then he proposed."

"So, no Graceland?"

"No. But . . ." She shows me her engagement ring as if we'd just met. "Definitely worth it."

"I do want to connect with people," I say. "Or—with *a* person." I think about telling her my road trip fantasies, but I don't.

I get the tape player from inside the room and put in the tape I'd thought about earlier tonight.

"This is college," I say as I rewind it, the years spiraling, slipping backward like roadway underneath wheels. And then I say, "I listened to this when I went to the hospital to see you."

"That sounds like an admission," my mother says, not getting her own joke.

"I guess it is," I say. "I think I felt guilty for still trying to live a regular life while you were stuck on the seventeenth floor with an IV. Anyway, this sort of sums up college, even though it's from freshman year."

I press play and think about what Shana said, about how I never acted on what I felt, and how she was right—at least partially—and how I'd repeated that mistake at college, too.

Untitled

SIDE ONE

Any Major Dude
   —Steely Dan
Welcome to the Working
   Week
   —Elvis Costello
Scarred but Smarter
   —Drivin' n' Cryin'
End of the Party
   —English Beat
Hesitation Blues
   —Hot Tuna
Cracking
   —Suzanne Vega
Luck Be a Lady
   —Frank
Some Grand Funk Railroad
   Song
I Say Nothing
   —Voice of the Beehive
What Game Shall We Play
   Today—Corea

SIDE TWO

Sensitive Artist
   —King Missile
She Doesn't Have to Shave
   —Squeeze
Prey
   —Let's Active
Fat Man in the Bathtub
   —Little Feat
It Can Happen
   —Yes
Running to Stand Still
   —U2
Jane Says
   —Jane's Addiction
Hardest Walk
   —Jesus and Mary Chain
? —Butthole Surfers? Not sure
Birdhouse in Your Soul
   —They Might Be Giants

Cheap beer and other people's shoes. This is the way we're spending Friday night: bowling. It's the week before spring break. No one at our college is hitting the sunbeds before heading to Daytona, though. They're doing things like riding trains through former republics, driving to Twitty City in irony, or becoming art. One guy has set up a video camera to record himself living in a box for three weeks—he gets food delivered, but the *St. Elmo's Fire* theme will play constantly; punishment enough.

I don't know what I'm doing for my vacation, but it's my turn to bowl. It's one of those nights that just flows; my jeans are in that perfect state of not being fresh-from-the-dryer tight, but not the stretched-to-baggy-ass stage, either. Tonight, my offhanded remarks are heard as clever, and I am magically granted the ability to bowl a strike on more than one occasion.

I am just about to realize that, with a cigarette or the right boy, I enjoy crappy beer from flimsy plastic cups. Casey's turn to bowl. She knocks a couple of pins down with her first go. After the second, she does her gutterball dance. Clad in a one-piece outfit that looks like a baggy union suit, she lets her red hair out from its clip and shakes her small frame.

"You're like Raggedy Ann," calls Jack from his position as air hockey ref. Jack has a soft spot for Casey that has nothing to do with her reputation for casual, intense sex. He comes over to the scoring table to join her in her loose-limbed shuffle. It's boys against girls, but Jack's on our side, the honorary girl for the evening.

Jack's tall and looks like how I picture one of the Victorian poets looking if they lived now—a modern Keats, hollow cheeks, dark eyes, slightly greasy hair, smoldering. He is the house movie star.

Even though our house is supposed to be segregated by gender, with men on the first floor and women on the second, Jack lives on our turf. Casey and I are the only women left after Arabella, the resident advisor, took a leave of absence ("From her mind!" Casey would add whenever this came up) and Marcia the religious fanatic moved out.

As the only Jews in the house, Casey and I soon found ourselves at odds with Marcia, the born-again, who cornered us every morning at breakfast.

"Have you found the Lord?" Marcia inquired, as if asking about a misplaced shoe.

"Not in this Pop Tart," Casey replied, accepting the coffee mug I handed her and making a quick exit. Casey and I didn't have the unspoken girl rules in our friendship. We were like the guys we knew. We never had to defend our actions to each other if, say, one of us left the Wheel, the local bar, with a finally snagged crush and left the other person sitting there talking to Ned, the weird old drunk guy who lived above the place. So I couldn't blame her for getting out of the breakfast and leaving me behind.

"The Lord is the way of All Good," Marcia continued. "You will come to understand." She suddenly grabbed my hand. "He is with you right now! In that morning nourishment!"

"It's just coffee," I mumbled, and sat down with her at the round, fake wood table. I spread my Italian notebook in front of me. The remnants of the night before stuck to my papers, and I had to hand in vocabulary words with ash and something that looked like toffee in the margins. When good old Marcus had taken the train from Brown to New York to visit me one weekend, I'd lost him to the vacuum of Marcia's soliloquies. They'd sat discussing the virtues of virtue and I'd gone to White Castle with the rest of my housemates.

When Marcia's tirades became too much to handle in the mornings, Casey took to sleeping in or rearranging her schedule so that she never had a class before one in the afternoon. Language classes met at nine and I wanted to be in Italy for my junior year, so I woke at seven, went running, made coffee, put a cup in the microwave for Casey, and sat dealing with Marcia until midway through December, when she left for a spiritual retreat in the South and never came back.

I could have had breakfast elsewhere, but it rained a lot that fall. Leaves slicked to the pavement outside the house, creating a colored path up the steps to the main campus, and the truth was I felt bad. Not guilty, exactly, but bad leaving Marcia alone with her Bread of Life breakfast proselytizing to the contents of the fridge or to one of the senior guys who lived downstairs who were prone to telling her to fuck herself, or Thomas, the white-haired Rasta, who tried baiting her with conversation of Nietzsche or *Hustler.*

Not all of the guys were like that, though. Chapin was always decent, and Jef, who dropped the other *f* somewhere in high school, just smiled without showing his teeth, more like a straight line you might draw on a face to show *fine.* Jef never said anything bad to Marcia. He never said anything to her, in fact, but at least he didn't avoid her.

I liked to watch Jef navigate his noninteractions with Marcia. He'd lean against the fridge and listen while he made his chicken-flavored Pot O' Noodles, but when the meal was ready, Jef would manage to slip away. Full-lipped with thick, dark hair, Jef wore wool crewneck sweaters. When he wore the brown one, I wanted to hug him. The sweater had patches on the elbows that covered up actual holes, the holes weren't there to make a statement. Or, if they were, it was, "This sweater has holes in the elbows." It always struck me as sweet that Jef's khakis were dirty, his sweaters torn, and his shirts buttoned incorrectly. He had been dating a girl whose family owned a large, upscale department store in New York City and I tried hard to picture Jef at their champagne brunches and fashion launch parties.

In late afternoons, Jef came to my room. The last light stretched across the wide floorboards. Jef put his sketchbook out in front of him and lay on his belly. He moved his palm over a spot on the floor, motioning for me to take a place near him.

"Hey," I said.

"Stay right there." Jef fixed his eyes across my shape as I folded my knees against my chest and leaned my back on the edge of my single bed. Jef thought my room had the "best light on campus," so I tried not to kid myself about being the kind of girl people wanted to draw. I'd take comfort in my room's décor. My mother had started to sew drapes and a coverlet for my bed that looked authentic sixties before she'd become too ill to finish. I'd brought what she had done to college as a reminder of her talent, or maybe

I felt like if I used them it would prove she'd be okay enough later to finish them. She'd found an old tapestry and Marimekko fabric, some taken from her maternity clothes, and made circular pillows and square floor cushions that made it through the first semester before they were stained with red wine and streaked with ash. Jef would lean on the same maroon-and-green pillow every time.

"It's so cool your mom made these," he'd said the first time he'd come to draw me. Eventually, he was the one I'd confided in about my mom's illness, about how thin she was, her dry cough that she couldn't tame from the radiation, about how scared I was about how I felt like at any second my life could change forever.

"You think?" I'd asked. I didn't know what was cool or not about parents, whether they were sick or healthy. I only wanted to have Jef want to stay, so I never offered to let him borrow the cushion he liked, even though he'd asked. Looking back, I wonder about his motives, if he'd wanted me to let him take the pillow to his room only to have me come and retrieve it at some odd hour when the house was still. Sometimes, I imagine what could have happened then. Mostly, though, I just remember the events as they did unfold.

"Isn't this shadow incredible?" Jef asked as he worked with his pad and shaded with his thumbs.

"I guess. I don't draw. Or sketch, or do anything that involves charcoal, except, you know, barbecue . . ." I stopped myself before I embarrassed myself more.

Jef flipped his paper over. His hands grazed the rough newsprint, his fingers scuffed with charcoal and ink, and I pictured them holding my face, tracing the outline of my collarbone and leaving a trail of fingerprints and longing on my newly pale winter skin. I let myself momentarily forget about Jef's girlfriend, Leah.

"In high school, I made a whole project of this one girl," Jef said, not looking up.

"It must have been really interesting to get to know one person's form so well."

"Yeah. Well, no, actually. That's the thing, Laney. I feel like the more I draw the less familiar I get with what I'm drawing. Does that make sense?" Jef paused and looked at me as the sun dropped behind the bare trees. "Sometimes I don't even know what I'm looking at. Light around your neckline? Or your hair, or a shadow."

I stretched my legs out so my feet just reached Jef's sweatered arm. Jef looked up for a second and then continued, "Anyway, that girl, the one I drew? She got together with my best friend the night before the senior prom. I haven't spoken with either of them since. I tore up the project, the notes, sketches, whatever."

"But you graduated, right?"

"Sure. Of course I did. I churned out about ninety drawings of fucking trees and put adjectives with them. You know, a big maple tree with a title like *Pensive* or *Indecision,* and got an A."

I couldn't help but think about Jef's word choice, and of trees fucking, and what that might look like, and the fact that there was a joke brewing inside my head and I wanted it to stay hidden because it wouldn't come out right. Accidentally, maybe, Jef's hand touched the bottom of my right foot. He stared at it. Would he touch it? Draw it? Lick it? He did nothing and then stood up quickly, taking his pad and pencils and backing toward the door.

"It's getting dark," he said as if this explained it all. Then I realized it did.

"Sure," I said. I thought then that Jef might leave and I would be left with my own self, my voice, my lecture notes spread across my bed, the slow beat of unidentifiable music piping its way up the wall from downstairs. Or that, somehow, Jef could drop his armful of art supplies, forget his graceful, ringletted girlfriend, and walk to me and hold me.

"Your feet are really cold," Jef said, "put some socks on."

One A.M. that same night. My door opens and Jay the obnoxious but incredibly hot guy from the downstairs triple comes to the foot of my bed.

"Lane? Laney?"

"What?" I turn to the wall.

"There's a Sudden Party, baby. Come on down." Jay's so good-looking that when he me calls *baby*, it's exciting. Jay was always waking me on the nights someone brought cases of beer or some JD into the living room and announced a gathering. As a reformed surfer turned philosopher, Jay was an active social participant in night adventures and sought me out since I was not. He'd show up in a gas station attendant jacket that made me want him, even when he would start ridiculous conversations, typically of the hypothetical, sexual kind.

Downstairs, Casey sits in her nightgown drinking Sam Adams and smoking part of Tom's Marlboro. I smile at her. She has on a Lanz nightgown, white, with tiny blue flowers and a lace ruffle around the neck—an ironic clothing choice given her reputation. But one thing I love about Casey is for all her pretenses, she's pretty grounded.

She'd been so normal when she'd met my mom during parents' weekend, even though I'd explained my mother's situation and Casey could see very well just how bad things were with my mom. But when Mom tried to make it unassisted up the stairs or sat shrunken in her now-oversize clothing, Casey was just herself. Watching her joke with my parents I wished for her ease. I knew she didn't have the baggage—it wasn't her mom after all—but still, I longed to have any nonchalance, any chance at normalcy.

I go and sit on the arm of Casey's chair. "Want some?" She offers her beer to me. I shake my head. "You sketch with Jef today?" she asks. I nod. "You know it's not going to happen, right?"

"I know, Casey, I know. I *think* I know. Sometimes, I get this feeling that all it would take is extreme courage on my part." And when I see Jef and his girlfriend standing near the doorway, I go on to say, "Courage or idiocy, one or the other." Jef makes one of his smooth departures with nobody, except for me, noticing he's gone.

Tom lights another cigarette while he and Casey use her empty beer bottle like a microphone, and lip-sync some Tom Petty and the Heartbreakers song.

"So, Tom," Casey says into the bottle during the guitar solo, "how long have you and the Heartbreakers been together? And if you wrote a song about me, what would you call it?"

In the kitchen, I take a beer and Chapin, better known as Curly-Haired Van Man, opens it for me. I have walked in on four guys talking about women and one guy talking about men and women. Besides Chapin, there's Jack, Jay, Freddy, in his ever-donned blue blazer and button-down, and Big Joe. When Freddy asks Chapin if he thinks some girl is hot, Chapin looks at everyone and sighs. "She's got creepy hands. Her thumbs are gross."

"Damn, dude," says Jay. "Could you be more obscure?"

Practical, Freddy says, "So you don't look at the hands."

Chapin looks at me as I drink my beer. Until now, I've just been part of the background. As if in my honor, Chapin looks at Freddy and says, "Yeah. I don't think I could just block out some part of a girl like that."

It's the first time I've heard men pick apart women. Not comment or say lewd things, but really dissect bodies, voices, accents that annoy or appeal. Thumbs that are "too small with dwarfy palms."

Chapin takes the last two beers and motions for me to follow him. Outside, his van's parked in the driveway, backed in, with the spare tire and ladder almost touching the line of hedge. After he opens our beers, Chapin unlocks the passenger door and we climb inside. The van's from the era when it was the coolest ride around, 1978–'82, somewhere in there, and the décor has not been altered to reflect the passage of time.

The bucket seats are vinyl, red, and noisy as I make my way to the back. Chapin stays up front for a minute and warms up the car. He sees my face when he puts the key in the ignition.

"Relax, will you, I'm not stupid enough to drive anywhere. I just don't want you to be cold," he says. The van's engine churns and Chapin turns on the radio. There's a tape deck, but the radio has buttons for tuning instead of a dial and nothing's programmed in except some talk show.

"Do you have any Steely Dan?" I ask. After he looks through a box of tapes, Chapin pushes one into the stereo.

"*Katy Lied?*" he asks. I pretend it's not my favorite of their albums, but a question.

"Did she?"

"Yup," says Chapin. "She's a no-good liar, that girl."

We continue on like that for a while and then "Rose Darling" comes on and we both have to listen.

"So good," I say, like it's cake.

"I know," Chapin returns, like he's the one who baked it.

I watch Chapin stand up and shake his beanbag out before sitting in it again. Everything he does is with a particular grace. He's fluid and gentle, but sarcastic.

"So," he says halfway through "Your Gold Teeth II." "Does this song make you sad?" All the song's longing—the time that is slipping by too fast makes me curl like a fist inside, but I don't say this. Instead I just nod.

"Me, too," he says.

"So," I say, waiting.

He's got his elbows on his knees and his empty beer bottle cupped between his hands. I move a little closer to him so I'm almost kneeling in front of him and touch one of the tight curls on his forehead. Chapin turns to me and slips an arm around my waist. In one motion, he brings me between his legs so my chest is against his. Kissing me, he lets his hands go through my hair. He holds my face with his thumbs tucked under my jaw.

"You know I've wanted to do that since September?" Chapin says.

I laugh the half laugh of someone who has been complimented, but is still nervous.

"Really," he says, "you were moving in, Freak Show Marcia was lugging that giant cross thing up the stairs, and you just had this look. I don't know . . ."

I kiss him. He's the perfect kisser, slow and then faster, pulling my mouth onto his by palming the back of my head. Soon, we're lying on the green shag carpet and the tape flips over again. By the third time through the "Dr. Wu" lines, we've undressed, rolled around, and are talking about house dynamics.

"You've got to understand, even though Marcia's gone and Jack's up with you and Casey, the second floor feels off-limits in a way." Chapin says this into my neck since I'm positioned between his legs like a bobsledder. The tape Chapin puts in is some random tape he picks up off the floor.

"Off-limits, like you want to come up but don't?" I ask.

"I guess, yeah," he says.

"Too bad it doesn't seem that way to Jay." I reach behind to feel Chapin's cheek. I'm struck by how fun it is that, at least right now, in the van, I can touch Chapin's face, legs, and kiss him, where in the kitchen I would have been careful not to let my fingers linger on his during the beer bottle handoff.

"Oh, Jay, he's something, huh?"

"Which philosophic movement best fits your sexual agenda: Kant, Hegel, or—wait, let me guess—the Socratic method? And don't say Freud, he doesn't count in this," I say, imitating Jay. Chapin laughs.

"So," I say to him, "how come you never asked me out or something?"

"Well," Chapin says at the same time that we unstick ourselves and lean up against opposite sides of the van, "because of Jef."

"What do you mean?" I ask. Caught between blushing and being pissed off, I don't let him answer before I ask again.

"What I mean is, everyone knows you like him. He knows it, we all know it, so . . ." This doesn't come out in a mean way, just matter of fact, gentle, in the Chapin way.

"I don't know . . ." I start.

"Look, Laney," Chapin says and changes the tape. He's in boxers and nothing else and steps on the side of a tape case. "Ouch. Fuck," he says.

"So if you didn't do anything before, why is tonight different?" For a second, I'm in the antithetical memory of Passover dinner and question asking. And then I'm back.

"Well, spring break's only a couple of weeks away, for starters." Chapin thinks this clarifies.

"And that means what, exactly?" I put my turtleneck on and don't fluff my hair out, but instead leave it tucked in, warm.

"Hey," Chapin says, changing his tone, "I don't know . . ." He sits in one of the bucket seats and swivels it back to face me. "What I mean is, people know you've had a thing for Jef. Don't worry about it. But Jef's my best friend, and I liked you, you know."

"So you were protecting me," I say.

"Maybe. But more Jef than you."

"Why Jef?"

"Because he likes you, too." The words come out and Chapin looks at me. The tape plays on, some song I don't know. Chapin says, "I can tell by your expression that you didn't know that." I shake my head.

"I thought everyone knew that, too," says Chapin. "Anyway, tonight, I just thought that it wasn't fair. You know, that Jef gets to be with Leah and go to her room and I got to pine for you from across the kitchen."

Here's what I think: *Someone pines for me. Jef likes me but is off in Leah's room. Chapin pines for me!*

"And when you came into the kitchen and the guys were having that dumb-ass conversation . . ." Chapin trails off.

I go and sit on his lap, feeling very attracted to him and very glad to be in the van and not in the house. Still facing backward, we can see out the tinted rear window. Jay's peeing on the bushes by the side of the house and Tom walks out of the house with his arm around some girl I don't know.

"Check it out," says Chapin, "that's the thumb girl."

Chapin and I kiss a little more and I try to remember his kiss as I feel it. When I pull back, Chapin's eyes are still closed.

"You ready to head inside?" he asks.

"Can I stay here for a little while?"

"Of course," Chapin says and gets dressed.

When he's gone, I slip into the driver's seat and realize I can't even reach the floor pedals. Out the front window, along the line of trees, there's a slim light. The same tape has been playing for what feels like hours and when I look at my watch I realize it has been hours. After I eject the cassette from the steel-rimmed mouth of the player, I look at it. No label, no title. I pocket it and hold the wheel for a minute. I hop down from the driver's seat onto the asphalt. The distance from the van to the ground seems bigger than when I first climbed in. I will keep the tape all through college, slipping it into the cassette player enough times so that even Casey knows what song comes next.

When Jack bowls, he does it backward and through his legs like a kid. He can pull this off. We're all impressed because he gets a spare and is leading. Jay's in second. Tonight is the night, I think, when Jef walks in and rents some shoes to join our game. I'm playing air hockey with Casey and winning. This says little about my ability and lots about the fact that Casey is a distracted, distractible player.

"Do you think Jack would ever want to fuck me?" she asks.

After I cringe, I say, "Not with a mouth like that." Smirking, Casey tries to score, but I block the puck and ram it back to her side. It hits the side and comes back to me. I do this three times before Casey even notices.

"I thought you were like his little sister or something," I say.

"Maybe. Maybe not." Casey smiles and waves at Jack, who's up again, this time doing an under-one-leg shot. "Want to get a couple of cigarettes from Jay?"

"Sure," I say and head over to him. He hands them over wordlessly with his red plastic lighter. The sides of the lighter are scraped and the metal's warped from Jay's neat trick of opening beer bottles with the edge of it. Casey and I go and sit in one of the orange booths.

"This light is so unflattering," Casey says, looking up at the greenish bulbs. The eating/drinking/smoking area is tinted one of those shades that shows every facial flaw, each pore, pimple, scratch magnified and on display. The smoke is thick and calming to me as I watch Jef talk to Jay. They glance toward us.

"Where's Chapin, anyway?" Casey asks me even though she knows I don't know.

"I don't know. God. Just because I got together with him one night doesn't mean I'm privy to his whereabouts."

"Here's a thought," says Casey in sarcastic reporter mode, "you don't use words like *privy* with me and I won't say *fuck* so much. Deal?"

"You bet." I inhale and blow a lame smoke ring that evaporates almost as soon as it's formed.

"I think Jef's coming over here, Laney. I bet you guys finally get together tonight. Oh, the glamour of Fairweather Lanes and Games."

Just then, Jack does some kooky move with his arms flailing and Casey does it back. This is their weird hello and they meet over by the hot chocolate machine. I smoke the butt down to the filter and put it out before it burns my fingers. Jef walks over and slides into the booth. Sitting across from me, the old scar on his cheek seems bigger. He told me about diving for third base and hitting his cheek on a sharp rock and how he scored, but then the home plate had drops of blood on it and he had stitches. I wonder what Jef is focusing on as he looks at me and then I think that it's probably the two pimples I have on my chin. As cover-up, I lean into my hand, propping my elbow up on the table.

"I'd like to draw you like that," Jef says.

"Okay," I say before I realize it's not an offer.

"Laney."

"Jef."

"I broke up with Leah last night," he says.

From the lanes, Jay whoops about getting a strike and Jack tries bowling with Casey on his back. *Jef and I are going to have a big-*

time relationship, I think. *He will reach across the table and take my hand and we will be a couple right away.* I look at Jef. He stares back at me, but doesn't smile.

"That must be hard," I say about breaking up, because it's what I should say. But what I feel is, sucks to be Leah!

"Not really. Well, a little, because Leah's pretty bummed."

"But you're not?" I ask.

"It was never going to happen," he says.

"What wasn't?"

"Leah and I were never, you know, never going to get married or anything. I mean, her parents couldn't deal with my artistic side. Plus, I'm only half Jewish, so that was a problem for her."

"You're Jewish?" I ask and feel more excited than I want to.

"Half. My mom's Jewish."

"So, that was important to Leah," I say.

"Yeah. More than to me, but that's just the way it goes, I guess." He pauses. "I knew you guys were all here, so I came down to find you."

"To find us, the group, or me?" I ask, getting brave and nervous.

"You." Jef pulls a single cigarette out of his pocket. He's in a plaid flannel shirt with a gray T-shirt underneath. His hands are clean. No charcoal.

We share the cigarette and then, as I'm inhaling, Jef says, "I came to find you tonight because I was hoping to spend some time with you, more time with you, I guess."

"Now that you and Leah are broken up?" I ask and then regret saying her name in case it reminds him that he has the right to miss her.

"That was my thought," Jef says. "I had this vision of us, doing something, driving across country or spending spring break together. I even pictured graduating and getting a place in Manhattan with you—you could commute for classes."

"Yes and . . ." is all I can say. I am zipping ahead to warm Sundays spent reading the paper, dog lazing somewhere near the kitchen, a wedding photo of the two of us, flower-wreathed under a huppa.

Jef takes my hand. It feels just like I thought it would. He holds my hand the old-fashioned way, not laced fingers, just hand in hand.

"But I can't see that happening anymore," Jef says, looking down at the table, the flecks of fake gold like ash on the Formica.

"What? Why?" I am afraid to ask more, but I need to know.

"See, I liked you, but I figured you would be scared off by me. You know, senior guy, just out of a long-term thing, so I just decided to get to know you. And keep going out with Leah. But then, that didn't work, because I wanted to hang out with you all the time, which is why I made that thing up about your room being the best room on campus to draw. Really, I'd never been in that room before, so that was a crock."

He sees my face and says, "Sorry. I just had to find some excuse for coming to see you every day."

Jef lets go of my hand and rubs his face like he's just woken up from a nap, "So that's what I wanted to happen."

"So what's the plan now?" I ask, flirting.

"Now, nothing. You hooked up with my best friend." Jef looks right at me, right at the pimples, the green-toned skin, my pale hair, and sad mouth.

"What was I supposed to do?" I say, suddenly a little mad.

"I don't know, maybe not touch Chapin."

"So you get to have whoever you want whenever you want and tell your friends who they can be with, too?"

"I don't see it like that, Laney," Jef says. "What I thought I saw was that you liked me and I liked you and you'd—"

"Wait for you?" I ask and then realize that I would have.

"Yes." Jef sighs and gets up from the table.

From the shoe-rental desk, Casey and Jack yell to me, "Come on, Laney, game's over! The boys won!"

*   *   *

I didn't see the whole group of guys again until they all came back my senior year of college after they'd gone out into the working world, mainly to Brooklyn.

"Wake up, baby," Jay had said, kneeling by my bed and whispering into my ear.

"I don't want to go to a party," I mumbled, not that surprised that he was there, in my room, after three years. Back then there weren't locks on any dorm room doors, and checkered cabs still existed in the city for real, not just in films. Jay drove one, actually, not for the money, he said, but for the experience.

"There's not a party tonight; it's an adventure," Jay said and handed me a coat to put on over my sweats. The name embroidered on the jacket was "Vinny" and I casually considered asking to be called that until I was led outside to the front of the house where Chapin's van was waiting.

We were all in there; Chapin at the wheel, Tom shotgun, Jay on the floor with Jef and Jack, Casey and I were in the swivel seats at the back. Casey was all smiles; she had her group back. She was always game for an adventure and the boys were, too. We were heading to White Castle for crappy burgers cut into tiny squares and then off toward the city where night called. Tom put his face to the radio and messed with the buttons until he found a clear station playing "lite and easy favorites," and I knew all the words. Some flute and keyboards number from 1978, back when the van was new. Casey said, "Sing it, Laney."

I shook my head and looked around the van. With so many people in it, it seemed like a classroom, cluttered and messy. There was the smell of old smoke, of paint, and bad air freshener. One of those little smelly trees dangled from the rearview mirror. Those were all details that I didn't notice before.

CHAPTER
twelve

In the morning, my mother and I have slept off the martinis and late stories from the night before. We go for a swim in the dollar sign–shaped pool. My mother coats herself with SPF 1,000 and then hands the Kiehl's tube to me. This time, unlike on the plane, I accept and slather away before easing myself down the metal ladder and into the water. My mother jumps in. When she surfaces, hair wet and grinning, I say, "That seems so un-you. To dive in like that."

"Really?" She is genuinely surprised. "It's funny how you see yourself differently than other people. I always thought of myself as a run-and-jump-in kind of person."

"Not at all," I say, swishing my arms forward through the warm pool. "What kind am I?"

"I think you're a jumper-inner." Only mothers and third graders can make up words like that and be endearing. She goes on, "You take risks—emotionally, I mean."

"But never enough," I say. "Not all the way. I run toward the pool like I'm going to jump and then I halt right at the edge."

"Like how you waited with that college boy, Jef?" she asks. "He had a girlfriend," she says like this makes it okay.

"Yeah," I say. "But I never even told him how I felt until it was too late. And look where that got me."

"Where did it get you?" my mother water walks to me.

"I'm pretty sure that my whole relationship with Jeremy was one giant reaction to Jef." I watch my mother's face as I bring up Jeremy's name. She frowns and opens her mouth to say something about him, but I preempt and say, "Forget about it, Mom. I don't want to talk about Jeremy." Not now.

Later, my mother and I venture past the casinos. We find the "neon graveyard" we overheard two cashiers talking about. A repository for out-of-use signs, the place is at once beautiful and melancholy. *"Weltschmerz,"* Grandma Zadie would have said if she'd seen it; sentimental sadness. The Hacienda horse and rider that once glittered high above the traffic, the former Golden Nugget sign, damaged and now reading "olden ugget." We walk toward Aladdin's lamp, its teapot shape set off by the blank blue of sky behind it. Dust and sand coat the glass bulbs of the Silver Slipper, cast off by some giant ballerina or nonexistent princess.

"Do you ever think of trying to find that college boy, Jef?" my mother asks, saying it like that's his name *College Boy Jef,* as if that's his whole part in my life. My mother reaches out to touch an unlighted bulb, cupping its smoothness in her palm.

"No, not really," I say and wonder why this is true.

"Maybe that's why you keep these tapes," she says. "So you can think about what bits you want to keep."

"I'm sure that's part of it." I watch her wipe the perspiration from her upper lip and then say, "I guess I think about that camp guy, Josh, that I told you about." I feel sad when I think he, too, might forever be summed up as Camp Boy Josh.

My mother turns to me. "I understand why. He sounded very . . ." She drifts off, wandering among the odd memorabilia. Then she turns back, "Very much like a song you'd rewind to."

"Yeah," I say. I tell her about Road Trip Guy, about how perfect he seems in my mind, how impossible it would be or feels like it would be to find a real version.

"Well," my mother says, like she totally understands the fact that her daughter wants to date a pretend man of her own creation, "Road Trip Guy does sound hard to beat."

"I'll never get him back," I say. And then we're both confused.

"Back? So you mean you've met this Wonderguy before? He's not imaginary, after all?"

"I'm nuts," I say. "Don't listen to me. I meant *find* him. Not get him back."

"Oh." My mother smirks. "Right." Somehow she gets me, knows me, even though she doesn't know all my stories yet. Slowly, this is becoming a comforting thought rather than just annoying.

I watch my mother in this neon graveyard and suddenly picture her being taken away from me. She's standing near the glass slipper sign, its arch unreasonably high, even for a stiletto, and I burst into sobs. My whole body shakes, my nose runs, and I let my bag slide off my shoulder and onto the dusty ground when my mother hugs me. She cries because I cry, even though I am crying over thoughts of her. Of losing her, of needing her, of growing up all over again in my mind, this time with her well. Of course, she has clean tissues in her bag and wipes my face, which annoys and makes me happy at the same time. She kisses my cheeks, my forehead, my closed puffy eyes, and tells me she loves me. I am secure in the halo of her, of the bizarre landmarks around us.

CHAPTER
thirteen

"No Sleep Till Brooklyn" blares out from the car speakers and my mother asks to fast-forward through this part of Moons and Junes and Ferris Wheels, the tape I made for this trip. She flaps her hands around her ears like she's trying to cool them off, when really I know she's just telling me the stereo is too loud.

"Sure," I say and do. "Sorry about that. The first half of this tape is what I made before I knew you were coming with me."

"Oh—so the second side's for me?" she asks.

"I guess," I say. "I just put on some songs I thought you'd like."

"Well, I'm flattered," she says. "It's been a long time since I was the recipient of one of your famous mixes."

What I say is, "I'll make you another when we get home."

But what I think is, *Bad, bad, bad.* I was too busy painting and learning and being quizzed on Dutch artists and flailing at relationships to make a tape for my mother. I picture making loads of mixes when we get home, of lining up my tapes and compact discs and stacking them in the order they'll go in on the Mom Tapes, a whole collection. I reconcile my thoughts as the belts and ribbons of tar wind their way past and under me. At least there's no one tape she took with her to the hospital or listened to only when she was sick, the kind of tape you'd just about want to pack up and forget about.

"Gardening at night," my mother says when the R.E.M. song comes on, "what a lovely idea."

I laugh at her literal interpretation and then picture it: weeding through the dank earth with the stars all around us. As a small girl, she'd woken me one night at a time that seemed then very late. Down the back stairs and out the screen door, we'd gone barefooted and in our nightgowns to watch a meteor shower. From high up, the splotches and remnants of light scattered down onto the barely visible horizon line. I remember looking down only for a minute, not wanting to miss anything, but noticing how the ground felt different at night. I noticed my mother's bigger feet next to my own and watched as we both curled our toes against the cool dirt. Back inside, I'd felt the scratchy granules of sand that clung to my soles and found its way back into my bed. My quilt then was quite plain, cream-colored, with one large blue star on it. I went underneath it after my mother had tucked me in for the second time that night and watched how the moonlight through the window made the quilt star glow.

"I want to paint some of the quilts you made," I say.

"What an interesting idea," my mother says. "I've been waiting for you to talk about your art." I still get embarrassed when people refer to my painting as "my art." I still feel like a kid with a dress-up palette.

"We could do something together," my mother suggests softly. I realize she's afraid I'll say no.

"We could, I guess," I say. But I'm not sure what.

A southern state or two later, we're in a very nice hotel, the kind I couldn't stay in if I weren't traveling with my mother. We have in-room massages, wear plush robes to the pool, where we order cranberry and seltzer, and the drink is the perfect shade of blush.

"I've really enjoyed swimming this trip," my mother calls from the deep end.

"Good," I say back to her. No one else is out with us except for an older man asleep in umbrella shade. I watch my mother's easy sidestroke. With her ear on the top of the water, it looks as though she could go to sleep there. This trip is the first time in ages I've seen my mother swim, even longer without a bathing cap. Her springy curls are usually tucked under a sheath of thick rubber. Today her hair is matted and wet when she climbs out of the pool by way of the side ladder. I imagine her as my father must have seen her for the first time, when she was an undergraduate, working one summer at the pool he walked past to get to his first art internship.

My mother is small-framed with long arms and slim legs. I wonder about her as an old person, in a way I never got to project her before. It seems like there are two kinds of elderly people, the skinny, frail ones and the plump, waddling ones. I figured my mother would be the frail kind, though she is strong.

During our two o'clock lunch, my mother flips through magazines like her mother did, backward. Zadie had read no English, so she never minded which way was back and which way was front.

"What are you stuck on?" she asks when I haven't turned the page of the newspaper in several minutes.

"I'm not stuck," I say. "I was thinking of how Zadie read back to front."

"Stop making me into my mother!" my mother says too loudly. Some guy on a pool chaise looks up at us. "I'm sure there's part of you that hates the thought of turning into me someday. So don't rush to make me into Zadie. I'm my own person."

"Whatever, Mom," I say and hate how teenagey I sound. "I wasn't saying you are Zadie, just that you're like her. Relax."

"How would you like it if every time you turned around your daughter was telling you you're like me?" She looks at me and clutches her damp towel.

I don't know exactly how to respond—but I'm annoyed, so I say, "I don't have a daughter or any children, in fact, so I guess I wouldn't know."

"Well, when you do, then we'll talk about it." Case closed for Mom and she walks away.

I sit there as the clouds move in, watching a young mom with her two kids and thinking about babies, admitting to myself how much I want to be a mom. Then I walk inside to tell my mom something I never have before. Something too important to keep hidden anymore.

There's too much air-conditioning in our room and my mother is already under the covers and nearly asleep by the time I come in. I draw the curtains and lie down on my bed, debating waking her to talk. I remember staying with her at a hotel long ago and how she reached across the gulf between the beds and held my hand. The memory brings up nightgowns and not being allowed to drink Kool-Aid and some song my mother used to sing that probably neither of us could get our mouths to say now. I decide again that now's not the time.

When I'm out of the shower the next day, there's a small box in the middle of the king-size bed. I have a towel around my body and one around my head, the ultimate hotel luxury. Inside are earrings, silver drops with turquoise and lapis set into them. I think of my mother buying them for me in Santa Fe, using her wandering time to get me earrings I'd said I didn't want. I could fight her about the purchase, let annoyance register about her not listening to me, but I'm just relieved she's around and able to think about earrings instead of remissions.

"I never want to take them off," I say, exaggerating to sound like her.

"Lovely, Laney. You're like that girl in that song," my mother says when she sees me near the concierge desk in the lobby.

I don't have to have her clarify what song she means. *Sail on, silver girl,* I think, and then hum her the tune. She smiles and signs her name to our tab and then we're off.

"I didn't get the earrings so you'd wear them forever," she adds when we're in the car. "Just as an extra pair. You're so extreme sometimes—you don't have to adore them or loathe them, just have them."

"I hate automatic drives," I say, my hand resting on the gearshift as if I could choose third or fifth.

"You've always loved driving," my mother says.

"I guess," I say and then, "It runs in the family. Danny likes driving."

"Grandpa loved cars," my mother says, no doubt imagining her father at the wheel of some antique car. "He didn't need to drive in New York, but he still adored them. The shiny new colors, the finger indents on those big wheels—the whole thing. I think that's why he wound up in the Berkshires, he always looked forward to driving."

"You were a really late driver," I say and it comes out a bit accusatory. My mother traces the map veins in front of her, running her finger along some route we aren't taking. She'd waited until Danny and I were almost driving ourselves to get her license. She'd had me test her on road signs and their meanings, on state drunk driving laws while I was longing to learn the stuff myself.

"I was meant to get my license before that road trip I told you about—the one with my college girlfriends. But I guess I never did. Then Daddy was a good driver and I was home so much in Vermont, it didn't really occur to me."

"Didn't you feel stranded up there?" I ask.

My mother looks at me. "I certainly did." The way she looks at me tells me she's not just talking about driving.

We drive in quiet. Then I tell her that I wish she'd been able to teach me to drive instead of my grandfather. She tells me she didn't feel capable. I think about her as the kid, with my grandparents as parents, how you could never really know how it all filtered down to you.

I have few memories of my grandparents' place. I can see the round shape of a cloaked car in the driveway, a circular drive, which was necessary because my grandfather had never mastered the reverse gear. The car was a Nash Rambler, blue with fake wood, no seat belts, nothing to hold you down when the bumps came.

"Why did Zadie and Grandpa get a house in the Berkshires?" I ask.

"Why not? It was lovely, very artistic," my mother explains.

"Didn't everyone go to the Catskills back then?"

"Well, *we* didn't," my mother says. She rubs her legs, palms flat and moving fast. "It's nippy in here."

I turn the air-conditioning down. I remember my grandfather's hands, his wide fingers and manicured nails. He was a dentist, so he kept his hands clean and soft. Even with Parkinson's, he'd kept his business going.

"Grandpa loved that summer place," says my mother. "You remember how he made the swing for you?"

"Yes," I say. He'd rigged a rope and wooden plank up for me, secured it to the copper beech tree in the front of the house, and everyone watched as I tried it out. Making a swing was the kind of thing my dad did all the time, but when Grandpa did it, my mom felt a special kind of pride. She looked at the swing like it was her father's approval over the life she'd chosen.

"Your grandfather had no interest in the Catskills by the time you knew him," my mother says. "It wasn't so much the place as it was the people."

"What do you mean, people?" I ask. "You mean Jews?"

"Don't be ridiculous, Laney. He was very religious. It was just the house, that's all. He loved the house. And the car."

I picture my grandfather in his seersucker jacket, reading the paper in the afternoon at the inn in town.

He was so different from my father's dad, Papa Hen. His real name was Henry, but I'd spoken only the first syllable as a toddler. I would trace my hand with a crayon and turn the image into a drawing of a chicken, the fingers as feathers, the thumb, complete with added smile, was the face and beak. I would write cards to Papa Hen and he would write back. My mother's father was ashamed of his penmanship and hired a woman to write his patient notes for him. He'd never responded to my early letters and had died before I had the nerve to plead with him to answer.

Papa Hen had been the first to teach me to drive. He'd lived all over the world, and when the time came for him to pick a place to retire to, he'd chosen Cape Cod. The long road that led to his house had no name, not even a number; it just wound its way through the pines and fallen leaves. The year I turned eight, I was allowed to sit on his lap and steer the car while he worked the pedals. There were pockets of sand and gravel-filled holes that made for exciting driving. The rule was, you had to practice steering until you were tall enough to reach the pedals. It was height, not age, that announced your readiness for solo navigating. The year I'd gotten my learner's permit, Papa Hen scheduled "driving lessons" each morning for the whole two weeks I visited. My mother was too sick to do much of anything, and my father was preoccupied with caring for her.

"Do you resent me for not being the driver's ed mom?" my mother asks.

"No," I say. "I guess not."

My mother looks wounded and I realize I've managed to insult her and to bring up her other absences without meaning to.

"I do love driving," I say to cover up. "You're right about that. Stick is preferable to automatic now, but when I first started out, it didn't matter." I hand her a tape to play.

"This isn't even your tape," my mother says as she examines it.

"Yes, it is," I say.

"It says 'For Danny.' " My mother shakes her head, trying to prove me wrong.

"Well, it was his. But it's mine now."

*   *   *

Psycho Hose Beast's Crappy Mix

UP HILL—1

The Joker
—Steve Miller Band
Fool in the Rain
—Led Zep
Brown-Eyed Girl
—Van Morrison
Light My Fire
—The Doors
Walk on the Wild Side
—Lou Reed
Feelin' Groovy
—Simon and Garfunkel
Friend of the Devil
—Grateful Dead
Time Warp
—Rocky Horror
Sweet Home, Alabama
—Lynard Skynard
Magic Carpet Ride
—Steppenwolf

DOWN HILL—2

Wild World
—Cat Stevens
Piano Man
—Billy Joel
Blown' in the Wind
—Dylan
You've Got a Friend
—James Taylor
Hotel California
—The Eagles
We've Got Tonight
—Kenny Rogers
Over the Hills and Far Away
—Zep
Wish You Were Here
—Pink Floyd
Wonderful Tonight
—Clapton
Africa
—Toto

The summer Danny goes on a bike trip through the Canadian Rockies, I get my license. Since I've already had my permit for two years, I spend every minute I can driving my father's old Buick. The car's as big as a bulldozer, which means that I am a risky parallel parker since you can't see anything over either shoulder in reverse. The car gets bad mileage and I have to pay for the gas out of my own pocket, but it feels so good to be able to drive that I ask to run errands for my parents.

By this stage, Dad's branching out to the West Coast. A movie was filmed near our old house in Vermont and they used his pottery in the kitchen scenes—and now my dad can't keep up with the orders. He talks about subcontracting and mass-production and other words I recognize but couldn't put in a vocabulary-style sentence. I think my father will go back to potting in our shed when the fuss dies down, but who can say, really. Mom thinks it's wonderful, of course, since she's the one who happened to be carrying the mug when she bumped into the production assistant and he said he liked the look of the stuff. He did call it "stuff."

When Danny comes back, he has made the transition from eighth-grade dork in wide-wale cords to a prefreshman with good hair. When the braces come off two days later, the transition is complete.

Danny's duffel bag and backpack, biking shoes and water bottle, complete with the signatures of his tripmates, are in a heap at the bottom of the stairs. My mother has told him that she's not doing his unpacking for him, that he is old enough now to sort lights from darks. Really we think it's because Mom's too tired from her treatments to even think about laundry, to even be able to lift the big blue carton of Tide.

"It's just as well," he told me and shrugged. "I have a matchbook collection in there, too. Wouldn't want Mom to get any ideas about what they're for." He tells me this and I get ideas about my no-longer-little brother.

"Don't do drugs," I say and try not to smile as he rolls his eyes.

"Shut up," he says and hands me a beer stein.

"What's this?" I ask.

"Your trip present," Danny says. It was a family tradition. If you went anywhere—Europe like my parents had a couple years before, or a truck stop, or the farmers' market near the Cape beach—you'd bring back a token of your trip for everybody.

"Wow," I say and ogle the gift. It's gaudy as new love—gilt-edged, with a red shield and a boar's head that curves around the whole base and a snake for the handle.

"I know—so cool, huh?" Danny says and walks off.

"Hey!" I shout.

"What now?" he asks and turns to face me.

"What's the beer stein/Canada connection?"

"I have no idea," Danny says. "I just thought you could keep your pencils and stuff in it. You know, like on your desk."

My mom and dad have each been given shot glasses with "I Heart Canada" on them, the heart spelled out as some form of Canadian humor that only Danny finds funny. They display the glasses on the kitchen table like topless salt shakers.

"We only stopped in one souvenir place," Danny explains when my dad brings up the all-liquor gift selection.

"A bar?" my mother asks. I laugh. "I'm not trying to be funny," she says.

"Yeah, Mom," I say, "the trip leaders really took a bunch of eighth graders to a bar and told them to buy stuff to bring home."

"Actually," Danny says, "they did."

My parents write a letter of complaint to the bike trip company and for the next several summers Danny will work at Subway, perfecting the art of the shredded-lettuce sub. He throws in extra olives for my mom when she comes in to visit, even though half the time all she can do is pick at food, her appetite gone.

The shot glasses and my beer stein, still empty of pens, rest on my desk upstairs.

"Danny!" I yell from the bottom of the stairs.

"What?" he yells back. My parents are out of earshot in the yard, so we can yell without getting yelled at for yelling.

Ten minutes later, I'm reading a letter from Shana, back at camp for her last summer as a counselor, determined to find a Jewish boyfriend for once, but failing. Similarly, Marcus, who will always be my high-school-friend-Marcus, is trying to find a Jewish girl amid the country club and manicured lawns of Greenwich, Connecticut, where he's assistant tennis instructor. Marcus has sent me a postcard of himself in stick figure, drawn onto a white pillar in front of the country club gates. Danny pads down the stairs and watches me until I look up.

"What?" he asks.

I hand him an envelope that's covered in the artwork of a girl his age, the predictable swirls, vines creeping up the sides of the letter, the stamp somehow incorporated in. Inside, there's a tape. Danny opens it.

"Check it out," he says. He holds out the tape. The insert is a photo of him with his arm around two girls, looking smug.

"And these girls are . . . ?"

"From the trip. That one's Melissa—so cool. She lives in Canada. She's not Canadian, though, it's just her mother is, like, some government official or something. . . ."

"Wouldn't that make at least her mother Canadian?" I ask. "If she's in the government?"

"Look, I don't know what the deal is, but she's so cool," says Danny and he points to her again. Melissa's bangs manage to stay on her forehead even though there's clearly a strong wind—I base this on the fact that Danny's shirt is mostly behind him and his hair is all over the place. Unlike Melissa and her cute bobbed hair, her genuine smile, her worn-in sweatshirt with the bottom hem ripped off, the other girl in the photo seems posed, awkward despite her not-yet-fourteen-year-old beauty.

"And who's this?" I put my thumb near the other girl's face.

"Oh, man, don't get me started on that one." Danny shakes his head.

Up in Danny's room, we go through his pictures from the trip. Melissa is in almost all of them, but Amanda, the other girl, is a close second. Also, there's his group of seemingly interchangeable buddies. Three of the five guys are "Dave," so they called all the guys "Dave."

When I hear this, I say, "So, Dave, tell me about Amanda."

Danny clears his throat and stretches out on the floor. He looks so long, stretching almost the length of one wall.

"Amanda is Psycho Hose Beast," he says, as if this explains something or means anything to me.

"And?"

"And that's it."

But it's not, of course, and that night when I drive the two of us to the movies, he tells me more. He tells how Amanda was the girl everyone thought was so nice in the beginning of the trip, how she brought people together and made them feel less shy. Plus, she really knew a lot about her bike since she started the bike team at her school. Melissa was not even on the radar, except that all the Daves thought she was pretty. So it comes out that Amanda likes Danny and for a day or two, he is psyched. He's biking better, less homesick at the end of the day, and more interested in Amanda than he thought. Then he sits next to Melissa at dinner and she just sits and listens to him talk, so Danny tells about school, soccer, his love of computer games, his family, and Melissa nods and sometimes plays with her hair. That night, he lies in bed and thinks that he is less excited about Amanda. Especially after one of the Daves says he saw Melissa's bra when they did laundry and it was big and lacey.

At breakfast, Amanda hands Danny a note, which tells him all the stuff he already knew. That she *likes* him likes him. And can they ride near each other, and does he like her back. Even though the day before, Danny would have left his cereal and gone to write back, on that day, he just eats and doesn't look at Amanda.

Later, Melissa kisses Danny and they are officially going out, except that there's "no going out" on the trip by law of the trip leaders, so they aren't. Amanda's confused and never gets a straight word out of Danny or the Daves or Melissa, but she keeps asking because she just wants to know what happened, if she did anything wrong. Her questions are distorted and retold and soon she's a crazy girl who harasses Danny and the Daves. Someone, Danny or a Dave, comes up with the name Psycho Hose Beast when Amanda bursts a tire and freaks out when she can't get the air pump to work.

"I feel bad for her," I say as we pull into the movie theater parking lot.

"Why?" Danny seriously has no clue.

"Because you were mean. And you picked the cute girl who said nothing instead of the not-as-cute girl who said stuff and made you laugh."

Danny doesn't answer, but thinks for a minute.

"You can have the tape she sent," he says and opens his door.

I spend the next month driving in the buggy summer dusk, learning to merge while listening to Amanda's tape. Since she had no title on it, Danny wrote in "Psycho Hose Beast's Crappy Mix" and then left it for me on the dashboard.

Truthfully, the tape sucks. It's everything you don't want to get on a mix and more; predictable, best-of songs that you already have on five other tapes. But it's also real. The first time through I laugh and fast-forward. Then after that, I listen to it the way Amanda must have when she made it. I think about it: She came back from the bike trip friendless and still hurting about Danny and yet had the guts to make the tape. I picture her singing "Wonderful Tonight" and brushing her hair at the same point as in the song. I think of her putting "Brown-Eyed Girl" on and wonder if she meant her or Melissa. And I love her for putting "Africa" at the end—I've always liked it, and it has no place being on the tape. It doesn't belong.

CHAPTER
fourteen

"So you identified with the Amanda girl? The, um, what is it—Psycho Hose Beast?" my mother says. I laugh hearing the words come from her grown-up mouth.

"I guess," I say. "Part of me still feels like that."

"Like what?" my mother asks.

"Like that girl who just didn't quite get it." I feel the ridges on the steering wheel. "What if I never act at the right moment or only know what to do in hindsight?"

"Oh, Laney." My mother sighs. "You will. You will." She stops repeating herself before she sounds like the train in *The Little Engine That Could,* the book she read to me over and over again, as a kid. Then when "The Joker" comes on again, I lean in to eject the tape. "Poor Danny," my mother says suddenly, "he was so young."

"What do you mean?" I ask.

"I don't know. He was just such a little boy when I got sick. I always worried about him—that he'd just grow up without a mother or that he'd be so scarred he wouldn't . . ." She doesn't finish.

We look at each other. Up ahead, signs for Columbus, Georgia, point us toward a run-down roadside motel.

Then she goes on, "But now I think the one I should have worried about was you. Danny just accepted life—you were so vulnerable then, such a teenage girl. Daddy and I should have thought more about how or what to tell you."

"Yeah," I say. "I could have used some more support." It comes out like I've asked for a firmer mattress, so I say it a different way. "I needed you guys. It didn't matter that you were sick—well, I mean obviously it mattered—but I just wanted you to still be my mother."

"Do you blame me for everything?" she asks.

I shake my head. I can't blame her for all my mistakes. "No," I say. "I just wish I'd felt you were strong enough to hear my problems, to be bothered with the details of my teenage life. That I didn't feel you were going to die at any moment."

I start to cry and pull over into the parking lot of some ugly modern church that looks more like a Howard Johnson's than a place of worship. I tell my mother the truth. The truth I realized this year—after Shana, after my trip to London I hadn't told her about, after getting Marcus's wedding invitation and coming to the conclusion that my world was carrying on without me—without my emotional connection to it.

"Mom," I say, "I feel like I live my life waiting for the other shoe to drop. I can imagine loss at any minute. I sometimes think I am so busy—so ready for the end of things that I can't even exist during."

Later, as we stand on the bumpy concrete floor of the motel's pool, my mother says, "I'd like to go into that church." She points to the one we'd parked near. Columbus is a military town with beer halls and strip joints and since we've already used the pool, its walls the peeling green-blue of a hospital corridor, there's just not that much else to do. The church's arrowed steeple points to the blue empty sky.

"Okay," I say. I watch her flip-flop her way across the wavy tarmac and into the church doors. After half an hour and another game of solitaire on the poolside concrete, I gather the cards and go to find her.

She sees me and ends her conversation with a priest. Everything seems dark as my eyes adjust from being outside.

"I got a very good recipe for peach cobbler," she says.

We sit in a back pew as primary colors stream in the stained glass and light my fingers, which rest on the side of the bench. Beneath our legs are prayer stools for kneeling. Some are needle-pointed with names, others are simpler, with padded cotton. My mother flips through a book. I think of the word *genuflect.*

"We used to sing this at camp," she says pointing to a hymn. "It's a universal kind of song, I guess, not religious." She means *not Jewish,* but I get her point.

I look at her face. Her brown arms are slightly purple from the cool air. I put my hand on her shoulder.

"Do you like being Jewish?" I ask her.

"Of course I do," she says. "Why on earth would you ask such a thing?" She says *such a thing* like her mother, so it sounds dated and very important.

"Well, we're sitting in a church, for starters," I say. "Sometimes it doesn't seem like you do. With Jean Reitz. You're critical of her, like she's too Jewish. And you didn't want me to wear that star from Zadie."

"First of all—a church is a nice place to sit and think," she says. "Plus, it's cool on a sunny day."

"Maybe it's a good place for your bat mitzvah!" I say.

"You didn't even have a bat mitzvah," she says.

"Exactly my point," I say and realize I have my feet on the prayer stool and blush, taking them off and onto the floor where they echo.

"Did you want one? Is that what this is about?"

"No." I shake my head. "I didn't want one. I just wanted the choice." I look at the oval windows, the colors of glass, and the way my mother tilts her head *sorry.* "And I just wanted to be—I don't know—someone who wanted one. Or have you be a mom who cared about her daughter's bat mitzvah."

"I'm sorry. You're right—I guess I never offered you a chance at the Torah because I didn't want you to feel this obligation. . . ." She stretches out the word. "But saying I don't like being Jewish is like saying I'd rather not be a woman," my mother says and closes the hymn book.

We sit for a minute. In front of us, someone cleans the pulpit. I picture someone vacuuming near the Torah and feel funny. "You're still a good Jew, if that's what you're wondering," she says. "I am, too. If I learned one thing from being sick for so long it's that you are who and what you are, and you need to be true to that. When you're unable to take care of yourself and your own family . . ." She trails off, then starts up again. "Certain situations make you realize who you are, what's important."

I nod. "I know. I guess I want you to know—that I've figured out—from camp or Zadie or maybe just me—that I want to be Jewish, that I feel like it's a real part of who I am as a grown-up, even though I never really knew where you stood about it. You don't even like people to know what radio station you listen to in your car. You never wanted a bumper sticker of any kind. Why?"

"I don't know. It's not me. I just like to keep myself—or my tastes—to myself. Or to people who really know me." My mother nods. We agree.

"You know, Laney, I was raised in a religious household with no sense of spirituality. My father knew every prayer and we had two sets of plates, but if I had ever had the courage to ask him what he believed in, what kept him going, I don't think he would have had an answer. You can't do just to do. You have to understand why and what it—being Jewish, being anything—means to you."

I think about hiking a mountain in New Hampshire with my father one fall after my mother's second relapse. Even though the chemotherapy had hit her hard, she insisted on seeing the foliage, at least through the car and then hotel room windows. Danny had gone to meet a friend and my dad and I had left my mother for some much-needed rest.

We'd brought cheese sandwiches and squirted grape jelly on them in the hiker's lodge. On the wall, there was some quotation about perseverance and heroes. When I'd asked my father about it, he'd said, "I think usually, your kids end up being your heroes."

Up the mountain path, pines jutted into the sky. My father stopped to fix his boot. The tongue had slipped and was rubbing the top of his foot.

"I've got the beginnings of a blister," he said. I took his hand and pulled him up in an exaggerated gesture. We stood, hugging, rocking forward and back on the roundness of a tree root. It was the first time in a long while I'd been able to be with him while he wasn't hovering over my mother. At the top of the mountain, I noticed how we both kept trying to climb higher, as if we could find some special way of extending the peak and the time.

"Mom's been going to temple again," he'd said on the way back down.

"Really?" It was all I said. I didn't want to know then if she had been praying, trying somehow to find a way to correct her health through religion, or if maybe she just missed that part of her past. Or if she'd made peace with dying, a certain knowledge that one day she'd leave this earth. But not now. Maybe accepting who I am as a Jewish person incorporates my faith in my mom. I try to say this to her, but instead I just take her hand and squeeze it. She squeezes back and whispers *l'chaim* in my ear—the Hebrew word for life.

Outside the church, it's warm still. My mother and I make our way back to the motel. We are two Jewish women with bare necks in the bright sunlight. We have shadows twice our size.

CHAPTER
fifteen

Many of the tapes in the box are unlabeled, so after I look again for my sunglasses, which seem to appear and disappear every other state, I try to figure out what the mixes hold, which one is borrowed, which is half made. A couple are of the audio-journal form that make me cringe—sometimes I'd tape myself talking, a verbal letter, and send the tapes to Marcus, who would tape back on the other side. Other tapes in the box are blank. I drive around the edges of the landscaped hotel complex while my mother naps and then park in the shade of a tree that looks like it should live in a swamp. Overgrown and knotted, vines twist up its length, its leaves rest on the windshield.

I decide to indulge myself and listen to a mix or two without my mother present. One tape has a letter folded inside it that I sent to my parents my senior year of college. I have little idea as to how it got into the case. Usually things of this nature got slipped into the pages of my mother's scrapbooks where she'd keep fragments of the kids we'd been—camp letters, second-place red ribbons from spelling bees, pressed flowers we'd given her.

I wrote the letter during one of the first times I stayed in this house without my parents, I think, because my mother was in remission and it felt weird to be in the house without her. I must have collected the letter and the tape once when I'd gone home and found it cast off in a shelf somewhere, unheard once the cancer came back and remission, our peace, ended.

Letter from America

SIDE A

All the Way from America
　—Joan Armatrading
Gypsy
　—Suzanne Vega
Jesse
　—Carly Simon
Ne Me Quitte Pas
　—Jacques Brel
Lemon Tree
　—Peter, Paul, and Mary
A Foggy Day in London Town
　—Ella and Louis
Give a Little Bit
　—Supertramp
And It Stoned Me
　—Van Morrison
Avalon
　—Roxy Music

SIDE B

Graceland
　—Paul Simon
Open Your Heart
　—Madonna
Waltzing Mathilda
　—Tom Waits
House at Pooh Corner
　—Loggins
Stewball
　—The Weavers
Rose Darling
　—Steely Dan
Traveling Prayer
　—Billy Joel
Lonely Boy
　—Andrew Gold
The Chain
　—Fleetwood Mac
Pink Moon
　—Nick Drake

Dear Mom and Dad,

　　By the time this reaches you, you'll probably be on your way back and the snow will have melted here. The house is fine. So's Danny. I'm sitting in the kitchen and the broken clock still says 4:45. When are you guys going to fix it? I guess if you haven't by now, it'll just stay 4:45 forever. I hope you are feeling better, Mom, and that you are eating as many brioches as possible before coming back to the land of the bagel.

I'm glad to be home, even if it's not the most glamorous destination for spring break. Hard to believe there's only six weeks left when I go back—and then graduation! By the way, we're having lunch with Casey's dad after the ceremony. Let me know if this is okay. Casey was accepted into that puppeteering program she told us about. Isn't that great? She could be the next Kermit! Just like how Mom's always saying how she knew that girl in college who became a star on that morning news show, except you'd never know it was Casey. I'll have to tell my kids, "Yes, kids, I was best friends with that big, green squishy creature when I was in school. And that's part of why you go to college, to meet people."

Hi. I'm back. I went out to meet Maggie for lunch. She's going to N.Y.U. Law, in case you haven't heard. Also, I bumped into Mrs. Hancock. She was muttering something about the hydrangeas in the garden and how I should water them through the snow. This seems redundant and possibly a cruel joke, but I will take her advice since her flowers always look so good. For some reason, Mrs. Hancock was under the impression that I borrowed her pruning shears last summer and hadn't returned them. She was pretty insistent, even after I explained I'd been in Italy the whole time. Alora!

Well, I am going to do some required reading. Maybe I'll try you in Vienna. Actually, I just realized it's too late to try you, despite what the broken clock says. By the way, in my Victorian poets class, we read something about how the Victorians were all obsessed with time and symbolism, like in roses (yellow is sweet memory!). Apparently, 4–5 pm is the

*"sad hour," so maybe we should really think about changing
the clock.*

More soon. I love you both,

Laney

*P.S. Hope you like the mix. I thought you could listen to it
on your way home.*

I can't believe how blasé I sound in the letter, as if everything's normal and I'm totally fine. Maybe I needed to have my parents think I was okay just so they could focus on getting Mom healthy. But the truth was, I was floundering.

I'd spent the year before abroad in Italy. The months passed the way most of those group experiences do—there were friends of circumstance, a boy or two, photos of landmarks, of pigeons in piazzas, pink-hued skies cluttered with domes and ancient monuments, and jokes that seemed funnier at the time than in recall. Looking back now, I am able to see how distant I was from the whole year—as if I were videotaping the experience to show to my parents. The "I Am a Regular Girl on a Regular Year Abroad Trip Show." Sure, there were moments I tried to connect—like when I'd met Marco and thought he could be my international answer to the nice Jewish boy I longed for, or when I'd seen cousin Jamie in London, but I let these times slip by me and hadn't connected at all.

Firenze
(Too Cool for School, Too Dumb for the Real World)

UNO	DUE
To the Beat of the Rhythm of the Night—DeBarge	Baci, Baci, Baci —?
Dancing on the Ceiling —Lionel Richie	Roxanne —The Police

Burning Down the House
  —Talking Heads
Dance
  —Van Halen
Straight Up
  —Paula Abdul
Blister in the Sun
  —Violent Femmes
LGBNAF
  —?
Saving All My Love
  —Whitney Houston
YMCA
  —Village People

Girl You Know It's True
  —Milli Vanilli
We Got the Beat
  —Go-Gos
Word Up
  —?
La Isla Bonita
  —Madonna
Smooth Operator
  —Sade
Does Your Mother Know
  —ABBA

"I can't fucking believe it!" Carrie says. "I have no idea how to say that in Italian, by the way."

We have assembled as a group of American students abroad and are seated on the steps of a fountain in some piazza. Carrie nudges me and says, "Bet he's mine by tonight." She motions for me to look at some guy in a polar fleece jacket and jeans whose face is hardly visible from under his baseball cap. I shrug.

"We were like, best friends at summer camp," Carrie explains to everyone throughout the day. "*Our* really good friend, Shana, told me at camp reunions that Italy was, like, *the* place to be! So here I am." On the walking tour, Carrie looks in the shop windows, both at the clothing on offer and at herself. I already begin to wish that the summer camp grapevine didn't exist.

We are told that we will have a week in the dorm to get settled before going to our host family for the first half of the year. After that, we'll be living in small, dark flats near the university. The dorm is an old abbey, complete with arched wooden doors and closets that used to be confessionals, with small notches cut into them. All the American students are assigned rooms and room-mates. These rooms are scattered throughout the large, stone building, mixed in with regular travelers. Carrie switches with my assigned roommate before I even know what's happening.

"This way," Carrie says, "we won't keep some random person up all night!" Carrie goes to a Big Ten school and is cochair of many groups, including Students Against Pollution (SAP) and WART (Woman Are Radical Too), so most of her sentences end in exclamation points. I half expect her to do a cheer and a split as we unpack.

"Isn't this just like camp?" she asks.

"You think?" I ask. Out the tiny window in our room, birds flock to the square below, a bell bongs somewhere and Florence waits. Suddenly, I am a cheerleader, too. I am spunky and fun and able to woo foreign men with my studied languages.

"Let's go!" I say. Carrie's thrilled to have me pull her by the arm and out into the hallway, where one girl cries about her lost luggage and missing home, button-down-shirted boys heave their duffels into their rooms, and the French and German tourists ignore us altogether.

"First stop, shoes!" Carrie says. I was envisioning cappuccino at one of the nearby places, table facing outward, tiny slip of the bill being delivered with the caffeine.

"What about soaking up the local atmosphere?" I ask.

"Bo-ring!" From Carrie as she stares longingly into the window of a clothing store. "I just love that look." She points to a broad-shouldered mannequin wearing leggings and black boots.

"Kind of Third Reich, don't you think?" I say. I imagine the plastic woman marching straight out of the window display and into the square, rounding up the troops.

"Only you would think that," she says.

"I'm not sure about that," a boy clad in a backward baseball cap says from behind our shoulders and we both turn back to look at him. He has the trip nametag like we do.

"You see what I mean, right?" I ask him.

"Oh, totally," he says.

Carrie makes the decision to flirt with him and asks, "We're going to buy shoes. Want to come along?"

"Actually," I manage to fit in, "Carrie is buying shoes. I'm just along for translation purposes."

"Don't you speak Italian?" he asks her.

"Ah, no! That's why I'm here! To learn!" Carrie says. Everyone was supposed to have taken at least a semester of Italian, preferably a year or two before coming to Florence. Carrie had taken Spanish for one year and French for a term, but both of those programs filled up. At the last minute, her father had complained and got her a space on the Italy year abroad through another school.

We follow Carrie as she winds her way back to the store she had seen on our walking tour. For the rest of the year, Carrie will prove to have no recall for directions or addresses and will confuse streets, piazzas, monuments, and names, except when it comes to shopping for apparel. "And accessories!" she will add whenever this comes up.

"What's your name, anyway?" I ask when we fall two paces behind Carrie.

"Hale," he says and actually removes his baseball cap.

"Wow," I say, "a gentleman of Firenze."

"Apologies for the hat head," he says. "Who are you?"

"Laney," I say and then, for kicks, "I'm not really here. I'm just a holographic image."

Of course, part of me isn't—part is back at home, awaiting the latest results of my mother's MRI at Mass General. The tests were conducted in two large trailers positioned at the back of one of the main buildings. Cloistered away, with the dim buzz of the machine, my mother was used to lying there, very still, as her insides were illuminated on MRI films that would be read later, by people who knew the misery that lay beneath each spot, who understood the whitewash of anxious sweat we all had waiting to hear the word *normal.*

Normal is also what I want to be on this trip, I think, as Hale and I sit in the shoe shop while Carrie tries on three different pairs and buys two.

"I figure, may as well buy them *now,*" Carrie tells us. "My mom's always saying, buy shoes at the beginning of your trip, that way they're broken in sooner!"

I feel broken in already, worn-out before the year's even begun.

That night, after dinner at the long communal tables in the basement of the abbey, the program leaders give us a list of activity suggestions. A couple of people head off to the movies to see the Italian-dubbed *Weird Science*. Some go to a concert at a local church. I hate moments like this when I feel I am about to define my year by the first night's choice of activity.

"Come on!" Carrie says, the leader of the bar crowd. There's a group of people standing, waiting for Carrie to start walking.

"Go on ahead," I say to Carrie. "I'll catch up with you."

"You won't know where we are, Laney." My not joining her is interpreted as a deliberate slight. Slowly, the crowd moves to the door. Soon, I am alone in a stone cave, no Americans, no peers, not even a monk to tell me what to do.

With my door key in my pocket, I go into the Italian night. People are just sitting down to dine, women still sell leather briefcases from street stalls, lean young men in khaki pants head off to cool parties with slinky girls in tight dresses.

I watch all this from my perch at a cafe. I try to find the name of the place somewhere so I can record it, the delicious dessert I had, and the nice waiter who smiled at me and told me I spoke beautiful Italian. Partly, this was true. I had a knack for languages and tones, and often the words came out sounding so smooth. I was asked more than I knew how to say. The other part of the waiter's kindness was just that. Alone and writing postcards, he could do no more for me than compliment my attempts at jokes.

Maybe the white-haired waiter has a son who will come in and pay his dear dad a visit, I think, when I watch a couple walk by with fingers laced, her face burrowed into his neck. I think about meeting an Italian artist, youngish, gorgeous, who only knows American expressions like my friend Maggie did—dated ones like, *far out, groovy,* and *what's shaking?* This would be good, I think, since my Italian slang is probably just as dated.

"Vorrei un' altro," I say to the waiter and know that the second cup will keep me awake. I try to think how to say *decaffeinated,* but can't remember.

"Bella, bella." This from the striking boys who walk by my table and offer me a cigarette. I shake my head but smile, too.

I say, "Force . . ." Maybe. I wonder what the hell that conveys.

"What's *maybe?* What might you do later?" Hale asks when he appears and sits down with me. The Italian boys cheekily blow me a kiss and walk away. One of them turns around after a stride or two and waves. *Gorgeous,* I think.

"What?" I ask.

"What were those guys saying to you?" Hale asks.

"Do you want this?" I ask him and push the coffee toward him.

"Sure," he says. "It'll counteract the beer."

"How was it?"

"I'm sure you can guess," Hale says. He's showered and capless, American handsome and warm in his polar fleece and worn jeans.

"Loud Americans drinking too much and throwing what looks like play money around?" I say this but part of me wishes I could do it and that I'd have a good time, but nights like that are only fun when you are absorbed in them all the way, not wondering what the hell you're doing there.

"Pretty much."

"Sorry I missed it," I say and build a log cabin out of sugar stick packets. I love the way sugar comes in a tube here, rather than a flat rectangle of paper.

"Architecture major?" Hale asks when I complete the structure.

"Art history. Theory, technique, all of it," I say.

"Do you draw or anything?"

"I attempt painting. Really, I like to look at other people's paintings. I think I might want to do restoration."

"Cool," Hale says. "I guess this is the place to figure that out. I look at this as my only chance to do something different, you know, creative. Since I'm going into business, probably venture cap or maybe trading."

We pay and walk along a dim street toward the abbey. Our steps echo and scuff. I am just about to comment on how peaceful it is, how far away from home I feel, how nice, when there are shrieks of laughter and moped horns.

"So much for our quiet night," Hale says. I want to be put off by the fact that he used the word *our,* but I'm not.

Ahead of us, two mopeds stop. Carrie, her arms around the driver's waist, leans forward and kisses him on the cheek.

"Thanks for the ride!" she says. "Gracie!" Everyone laughs like saying *thank you* is a funny thing, and the mopeds zip past us. The group of students with Carrie waves good-bye, fans of some sort. I watch, too. The other driver, the one who'd been without a passenger, stops and turns around, waving. He's the gorgeous one from the café.

"Looks like Marco likes you!" Carrie says. "You should go for him. He's really hot. Not as hot as Francesco, my guy, but what can you do? Nothing!" Carrie is loaded and stumbles her way back to the abbey with us.

Hale looks at me and raises his eyebrows. We share a noiseless laugh. Then we're all back in the entryway.

"These fucking shoes are killing me!" Carrie says.

She's drunk enough for some girl to say, "Serves you right for wearing them the first day!"

Carrie makes a face at the girl and then says, "Okay! Post-bar party in our room, pronto!" And then, "Hey, pronto is, like, Italian. I so never knew that before."

In our room, I try to bunk in like I'm one of the gang. I sit cross-legged on my bed until someone says, "I want to lie down."

"It's my bed," I say. And then, with my first-grade manners, "Can we share?"

"Whatever."

I move to the floor and listen to bits of conversation, unable to pick out a whole one or join in, since it's all jokes from earlier in the evening or from the plane. I had flown in from Boston, while most of the other students had come from New York and Cleveland, a couple from Dallas, so I had missed the in-flight humor.

"And then, the guy's like, no, we don't have that in this country!" Everyone laughs.

"Remember the tray table incident? You were pulling it and then, suddenly, *bam!* It was out and then that lady in front was all pissed at you. Oh man, classic."

From next to me, "So, do you think he likes me or what? Should I invite myself back to his room?"

"Definitely."

Don't do it, I think. I look at the two discussing possible hook-ups and think that they seem like the kind of friends who will try to set each other up to fail. The guy doesn't like her, and the friend knows this. She just wants to watch a drama unfold—either she'll go back to the guy's room and then deal with the aftermath the next day, or she'll invite herself and be turned down, but either way the friend will be able to comfort her and look like the nice one.

I hardly notice that Hale's not in the room until he motions to me to come out to the hallway. I squeeze past people who grunt so much I think I must be treading on their toes or something.

"Hey," I say.

We sit near the room and lean against the stone of the walls, facing each other. The corridor is so narrow, Hale can stretch his legs out and rest his feet on the wall in front of him, next to my waist. He does this.

"It'll all be different once we get moved in to our host families," he says.

"I know," I say. "Then they'll all have to arrange to meet at a bar instead of just moving in a herd."

What I find out about Hale in the next two hours: he's a comparative lit/business dual major, he goes to Columbia, and is a senior, not a junior. Less funny than he is appreciative of humor, he does have a terrific laugh and incredible eyes. I tell him this and it comes out far flirtier than I mean it to.

"I'm sorry," I say. "Sometimes I think I should edit myself more than I do."

"If you edited yourself more than you do," he says, "I think you might be mute."

I consider this for a second and then I say, "Isn't it funny how people say stuff like that the first night they meet someone? How do you know what I'm really like?"

"Every time there's a pressured or unreal situation like this trip, people get close really fast or hate each other right away for no good reason."

"You think it's because people are not in their day-to-day lives?"

"Yeah," Hale says, "I do. It's like none of what we do here matters in the real world, in our lives back home."

"Been reading Dante?" I ask. But what I think about is how I wish life was just here, that it didn't connect to my home life, how easy it would be to just exist moment to moment.

"How can you tell?" Hale pushes his hair out of his eyes and rubs his face.

We are tired and done talking, so we sit and say little else until, slowly, people trickle out of my room and into their own and I can lie down on the thin mattress and sleep.

It's months later, after Carrie and her new best friend, Kerry, manage to be assigned host families that live next door to each other. I live with cousins of Kerry's host family, so every once in a while, like before Christmas, I am invited over for a meal. My actual host family doesn't join me, due to some falling out from a long time ago that nobody bothered to explain.

Our lectures are finished for this term. I help my host mother cook a dish made of noodles whose name translates into *"telephone wires";* truffle oil, cheeses, and slivers of fresh tomatoes all go into a dish. I have tried to teach my host family some English, but there's just the parents, no kids, and they have little interest.

"No, no," the mother says. She knows only this word and a couple of other negative orders. The father just says, "Good, good," all the time to tell me my Italian is improving. He's never there, anyway. Usually, he comes to the house at lunchtime, eats, goes to work, and doesn't return until after eleven at night. I still don't know what exactly he does—I know he works in a building that is made of brick, that the work involves writing, but not numbers, and he uses no computer, but sometimes a phone. This much I have understood from our advanced beginner conversations that involve as much gesturing as they do words. Beyond that, I do not know and they won't say.

The pasta dish goes in the oven and I leave the house to meet Hale. He's leaving the next day to meet his parents in Milan, where they'll stay for a couple of days before going to Madrid and Barcelona.

On the way, I stop and buy a postcard for him and write the address where I'll be for the next month. I am leaving for London in two days and going to meet my family at my aunt's house. My mother's been given clearance to travel from her oncologist, so long as she doesn't tire herself out. She will rarely leave my aunt's house during the visit, but enjoys herself nonetheless, watching the rest of us suck up London's pre-Christmas swirl of lights and wrapping papers and cooked chestnuts. Jamie and I have exchanged letters and I can't wait to see him, can't wait to have him show me his world again—the last time was right before Ben died.

"This is for you," I say and hand the postcard to Hale. He looks at it and then at me.

"How lovely, Laney, a bridge and a sunset. And it looks so real! Not airbrushed at all."

Our hug is a little too long and I am the one to break away. It's not that I don't enjoy our hugs. I do. Hale is the male equivalent to flannel, warm and sturdy. Also, I think, when I make the analogy, he'll be better when he's more worn.

"What are you thinking about?" he asks.

"Sheets," I say. He raises his eyebrows.

"Lucky them," he says and then he leaves.

Alone in Florence, I remember I need to pack. Back at the house, in my small room, I take out a suitcase and put some clothes in a bag. Later, I'll be going for dinner with Carrie and Kerry and their families, since my host family appears to be the only Italian family ever not to celebrate Christmas. It is with irony that I make note of this. I call Casey on the phone. She's studying at UCLA for the year, learning about animation and puppetry. We've written long letters across six thousand miles, sometimes with photos enclosed. She is a touch point, a reminder of my life outside of Italy, a tether to my college self.

"My whole life I wanted to find somewhere that didn't flood me with Christmas *stuff*," I say.

"Christmas *shit* sounds better," Casey says. I've caught her early in the morning and she's not fully awake.

"But I got to the point where I kind of liked some of it. You know, songs and ruddy cheeks and good food. And the lights are pretty."

"Yes, Laney, the lights *are* pretty. Did you get together with that boy yet?"

"Hale is just my friend and no, we haven't—even though I'm sure my host parents think Hale is my lover or something sinful. God, this host family is just not what I pictured."

"Not everyone can find the Italian Brady Brunch," Casey says. But she hasn't seen Carrie's life here. Assigned at first to a family that claimed to be well-off and well-situated in the center of town, Carrie's original family ended up being a lone, sleazy man in his late forties who wanted to have a not-so-cultural exchange.

Upset and frightened, Carrie took a taxi to the abbey and stayed there with the group leaders for a week while they figured out an alternate plan. Meanwhile, Carrie had no curfew, no language barriers to contend with, and no bulking up due to being force-fed pasta. It was at this point that Kerry introduced Carrie to her host brother, Giorgio.

"I was going to go for him myself, but it's way too weird with us being fake siblings and all," Kerry said one day when a group of us happened to have lunch together after class.

"You are so right! It's way too weird to fool around with your Italian brother!" Carrie agreed and proceeded to make a date with Giorgio for that night. Kerry and Carrie treated men the way they did clothing; it was all right to get attached, but good friends could always borrow.

Carrie wore Giorgio like the cashmere blend that he was, good-looking, refined, with perfect English from his British boarding school days. Together they were a stunning couple. In turn, Carrie loaned Kerry her first-night date guy, Francesco, and they all went out.

"We don't mind the Americans like her," Lucia, my one Italian female friend from my painting class, had told me.

"She always has a group of girls around her," I said. "It seems like even the young Italian women think a lot of Carrie."

"No, they don't," Lucia said and showed me to a small café in a section of town we hardly went to.

In plain view, Francesco and Giorgio sat with two Italian women who wore suits and drank demurely from their espressos. Neither of the women screamed or laughed loudly or sang along with the Lionel Richie song that played on the speakers on the wall. Lionel Richie's music was everywhere in Italy. Most days, I had "Easy" stuck in my head. But my Sunday mornings weren't easy at all, they were cleaning days for my host family, and we spent the morning scouring the counters and floors with bleachy water that made my eyes burn.

"How come they don't go to church?" Hale wanted to know when he stopped by one Sunday.

"I live with the Anomalies," I said.

Lucia told me that during the holidays, the Americans would leave and the Italian women would get their men back full time. She explained the Italian women we saw were busy in new careers and finally being taken seriously, so they didn't have time for full-on relationships, but they liked the men and wanted them for some-day. So the arrangement worked perfectly, with men like Giorgio dating the Americans, who were fun and loved sex, and who would later leave. A long kiss, a cassette tape, and an inky letter filled with Italian phrases and the men were free to go.

At Carrie's host family's house, it's a huge Marconi gathering. Kerry and Carrie bring around trays of appetizers, small onions stuffed with pancetta and mushrooms and artichoke *sformati*. It occurs to me that our cultural exchange maybe provides our hosts with cheap, live-in help. Carrie lucked out and was offered a room by Giorgio's mother's best friend, who lived next door, and moved in shortly thereafter. Carrie had her own section of the house, complete with its own set of stairs and small kitchen. "It used to be the servant's quarters," she said when we'd all been roped into helping lug her bags over. "In the olden days," she'd added.

"You have to try these," Carrie says.

"Yum," I say, trying to be pleasant, when all I really want to do is leave, to free myself from Italy and go to London. Then I think how maybe I should stop moving onto the next phase, the next place, and just be where I am. So I pick up a stuffed mushroom and smile at Carrie. "You're right, Carrie, these are good!" I mean it to come out enthusiastically, but somehow there's sarcasm, too.

"Look," Carrie says and hands her tray knowingly to Kerry, who brings it back to the kitchen for a refill, "I know we aren't exactly the best of friends here, but the least we can do is enjoy tonight."

"Sure thing," I say and make the smile my mom does when she's offered food she doesn't care for at someone's house. My mother always takes one of something, even if it's got cilantro in it, which she says tastes like metal.

The Marconis' house is large and filled with elegant furniture, lighted candles, and mirrors that run the length of the drawing room walls. The rooms are all painted in pale tones, salmon, a light beige, the aquamarine green that looks terrible as a T-shirt but is removed, cool, and fancy in a town house. I wander from the drawing room to a sitting parlor, to a large powder room. I go in and close the door, even though I don't need to use it. The mirror is gilt-framed and glowing, since even in here the light is from giant dripping candles.

When I see a dark shadow move behind me, I scream.

"*Shh*—you'll ruin our hiding spot," says the shadow. Then he comes over to the mirror and shows himself to me. We stand there in the flickering glow for a second until he says, "I'm Marco. We met when you first arrived here, I think."

"Tonight?" I wonder how I could forget such an attractive face.

"Not tonight, when you first arrived in Firenze."

"I don't remember, I'm sorry," I say.

"I was the one on that motorbike, waving to you while your friend, the screaming girl, Carrie, scolded you for not going out with her or something to that effect."

"Now I remember," I say and blush, though he probably doesn't see it.

"So, hello."

"Hello," I say and wonder what he's waiting for. Maybe to kiss me, I suddenly think.

"I am waiting to know your name," Marco says.

"Laney," I say and spell it for him the way I have to all the time in Italy, since it's not a name here. "You don't sound like you need me to spell it for you."

"Not really, no. Oxford educated, I'm afraid. And I was just escaping for a moment in here, in case you think I'm mad or antisocial."

"I'm actually just about to leave for England," I say. "Not this minute, but, you know, soon."

"Me, too," he says.

When it turns out we are due to be on the same flight, we can't believe it.

"Should we leave the bathroom?" I ask.

"Someday, we'll leave the bathroom," Marco says. "But now? We have so much to catch up on. And how unusual to have a first date in a bathroom, no?"

"I guess," I say and think how he called this a date. I shake my head at all Italian men. I sit on the lid of the toilet while Marco sits across from me, straddling the bidet.

"This is very rude, isn't it?" he asks of his position.

"Let's just say it's not the most proper." I smile.

The next day, Marco and I meet up at the museum for the Bonnard exhibit.

"Look at this," he says by one of the paintings. Behind Marco, a canvas of a large, pale woman in the bath dwarfs him.

"I like this one," I say and read out loud, "Balcony at the Vernonnet, circa 1920." There's a reaching figure in the painting and the colors are incredible. Marco comments on this.

"Sometimes," he says, "I wish I could just drag my hands through the paint itself."

"I've always thought about that," I say. "It's like I want to feel the texture of the paint in my fingers so much, I want to eat it."

Thankfully, Marco doesn't laugh, he just nods and we move on to the next painting.

"Do you have family in England?" I ask.

"No, just friends," he says.

"Won't your family miss you for the holidays?" I ask.

We stop in front of *Pears, or Lunch at Le Grand-Lemps.* Marco turns to me and says, "They won't actually, because my family is Jewish, so we don't celebrate Christmas."

"Oh," I say and look at the painted fruit, feeling an ease spread over me when I think about Marco—did he have memories of family Passovers? Did he feel a bit left out with all the Christmas festivities? He would be an ally of sorts.

He goes on to explain to me as if I'm part of the non-Jewish masses, "There's Hanukah, but it's not really—"

"I'm Jewish, too," I say.

"Then I don't have to explain the lights to you, I guess," Marco says.

"Not unless you're going to give me some chocolate-covered gold coins in return," I say.

"They don't do those here," he says. "You get chocolate-covered slices of orange."

On the plane, Christmas music pipes in from speakers we can't see. Marco trades his seat to be near me and we spend the flight playing cards and talking about movies.

After a game of crazy eights, Marco slides his hand over mine while I am in midshuffle.

"Meet me in the back left loo in two minutes," he says.

It takes me a minute to figure out what he means, but then I stand up, ultracasually, stretch my arms up like I've been sitting for hours, and walk to the back of the plane. Through the scattered readers, sleepers, and eaters, I go toward the door on the left where the occupied bubble is alight. I knock and the door slides open.

"I know," Marco says when I can't stop laughing. "You think this isn't romantic."

The green-hued lights need to be on or the door won't lock, and there are no candles or gold mirrors anywhere, just two people squeezed into each other.

"I think you're romantic," I say.

I sit on the sink counter and Marco stands as we share our first kiss. He puts his hands under me and lifts me to him, kissing me the whole time until all my thoughts have melted into engine noise and mouths, hands, and lips.

At Heathrow, we wait for our luggage to appear and swap local phone numbers.

"Let's meet tomorrow," he suggests.

"Call me tonight and let me see what my family is doing," I say. "But, of course, let's get together as soon as we can." I picture introducing Marco to my mom, taking him to see my father's ceramic exhibit at the new gallery in Notting Hill, where it's billed as "American Stone Ware." Danny could take Marco out, no doubt jokingly calling him Polo, or something equally horrific, and Jamie—well, Jamie would be able to interpret Marco's speech and actions for me, translating them into American from Britalian.

We kiss good-bye in our shared taxi and I hop out near the Holland Park tube stop, which is just near my aunt's house. I stop to get flowers for her and a tube of Smarties candies for Jamie, which we will later use to play Smarties poker, our private version left over from his summer with us, when Ben still laughed and breathed.

"You have the glow of love about you!" Aunt Jemima sighs as she finishes hugging me and pulls me out at arm's length to have a look. I put my bags down and shake off the plane flight.

"Are you shagging an Italian?" Jamie asks and pops a Smartie into his mouth.

"She won't tell you anything here," Jemima says. "Take her to the pub, for God's sake, and let me get some dinner ready before the rest of the crowd gets here."

After a glass of wine, I tell Jamie, "This guy Marco is delicious."

"Oh, dear," Jamie says and takes a drink, "once a woman uses food terms, the relationship is doomed."

The next day at lunch, Marco greets me with a full make-out kiss.

I say, "Marco, you are something."

"You are everything," he says, wooing me and knowing it.

After lunch, we sit in the cold. The park is empty except for one old lady walking a small dog.

"I hope she has someone to go home to," I say as we watch the woman linger near the frost-covered shrubs.

"She probably does," Marco says.

From his pocket, he takes out a small parcel wrapped in waxed paper.

"For you," he says.

The crinkling and unwrapping reveal a crescent of orange dipped in chocolate. I smile at Marco.

"You may not be used to eating the rind. It's a bit bitter. But with the chocolate, it tastes sweet. Better than those plastic-tasting gold coins."

I take my first bite and Marco says, "By the way, Laney, I'd rather you didn't mention to your friend, Carrie, that I'm Jewish."

"She is, too," I say and swallow.

"I know that. But Giorgio doesn't. Neither does Francesco, though I doubt he'd care. But the Marconi family—they're anti-Semites from way back, serious ones, if you understand me. Your host family, they hid during the war, lost their only child to one of the camps. It's well known in town that their own relatives, the Marconis, bartered them in exchange for their own."

He pauses and then, wagging a finger back and forth, "*Alora.* Jews? No. Not in that house."

"No one knows what religion you are?"

"I don't see that it's anyone's business but mine," he says. Then, trying to take my hand, "Or ours." He smiles at me. His hands are cold and red, the knuckles slightly chapped.

"So we can be secret Jews together?" I ask. Marco snags the bit of chocolate from the corner of my mouth and licks his fingertip.

"If that's how you choose to see it, yes."

I wrap up the slice of orange and keep it in the waxed paper, in my hand. I know what I need to do, so I do it. I give the tiny waxed parcel back to Marco, press it into his hand like Zadie handed the necklace to me.

Our last kiss tastes like chocolate and orange, rind and all. Back over the crisped iced grass, alone, I think about the colors of the Bonnard paintings. On the balcony in one of them, something hung, boneless on the rail, arcing toward the blossomed trees on the ground below. And I realize what I like so much about Bonnard's work—that he paints from an odd point of view, always looking elsewhere, moving on to the next thing instead of being where he is.

*   *   *

Looking at the hotel where my mother lies sleeping, I think about when I'd returned to the States from Florence, feeling empty despite a year's worth of experiences. I had opened the parcel my mother made me promise to keep closed until back on home soil. Inside was a leather-bound journal and a card that read: "Write the past to move into the future." I'd filled the pages with descriptions of scenery, a tape, silk ribbon the color of clotted blood that I'd tied in a bow around my ponytail when I painted, and index cards filled with facts about various pieces of art.

The journal is packed up somewhere in my parents' house, in the stack of things I can't get rid of, but don't want to drag around with me. Looking at the Florence mix again, I remember other songs that went with that time. Songs that found a home on another tape that came into existence the August after returning from Italy.

SIWIW (Songs I Wish I Wrote)

SIDE A	SIDE B
Slip Slidin' Away	I'll Follow the Sun
—Paul Simon	—Beatles
Summer, Highland Falls	Mona Lisas and Mad
—Billy Joel	Hatters—Elton John
Fountain of Sorrow	A Case of You
—Jackson Browne	—Joni Mitchell
Under Pressure	I Hope That I Don't Fall in
—Queen and Bowie	Love with You—Tom Waits
Baby, Can I Hold you	Jungle Land
—Tracy Chapman	—Bruce Springsteen
Our Love Is Here to Stay	Anticipation
—Cole Porter	—Carly Simon
Straight to My Heart	Forever Young
—Sting	—Bob Dylan

Any World   No Myth
  —Steely Dan   —M. Penn
September Morn
  —Streisand and Diamond

Sitting on the floor of my senior year room, Marcus—who'd come to visit before he left to start his new job in Florida—had wanted to know who the tape was for. When I shrugged he had said, "Maybe it's just for you."

I think now that he was right, although at the time I tried to say it was for Jamie or Casey or Danny. Someone who'd help me feel present.

I remember that when Marcus said it was time for him to go, I didn't watch him. Maybe it was too hard for me—it only empha-sized my empty room, empty self, emptiness. My window over-looked the driveway and lamp-lighted street that lead toward town. I sat on my bed, drank water from the cup that had been there since the night before, and wondered what I was going to do.

Just as Marcus's form disappeared from sight out my window, my father called to say that Grandma Zadie had died. Outside, the thermometer that had rusted to the window frame registered nearly one hundred degrees and I sat sweating and crying.

"What small words," my father had said when we both could say nothing else.

"It's so sad," I'd whispered, hating that I couldn't come up with any other words.

On the way home for the funeral, I'd film-reeled my memories of Grandma Zadie. The star of David, slices of pie, her yellow bathrobe, the way she stroked my hair as I cried, saying good-bye to her for the last time—"Don't cry for me," she had said and held my hand, "I'm just an old woman."

Somehow Zadie's death reinforced my feeling that at any minute your whole world could change. I don't even remember how my mother was at the time—was she well? Sick? In the mid-dle? Maybe that was when the MRIs kept producing results that involved "gray patches," and when my father retreated to his pottery and clay, something he could mold and design.

In the midst of lymphoma, my parents had grown accustomed to eating meals in the hospital cafeteria; my mom liked the peach cobbler, my dad favored the key lime pie. They called their outings dates at first, until the regularity and persisting fluorescent glow of the overhead lights got to them. The cashiers knew my parents by sight, nurses said hello as they spooned Jell-O cubes into their mouths, and other patients gave knowing glances to my mother's bruised IV-spots.

Outside, the hot air makes the trees seem to sway in slow motion. This is what guidebooks mean when they talk about the Deep South—the thickness of the warmth and humidity is stifling. I stay in the air-conditioned car for another minute before heading into the hotel. I think how well my mother is now, how wide her smile is, how sad and taut her face had been after Zadie's funeral. She'd gone to lie down upstairs while my father retreated to his shed, spinning the water-slicked wheel. He'd pressed his hands into a clay mound until they flattened it into a plate or low-lipped bowl. I thought of Zadie, of her flowered housedresses, her cake, of her watching her own daughter wither, of clay muck, and of lemons.

And it's obvious to me now that all of the disconnect—my mother's sickness, an empty year abroad with my romantic ideals dashed, with Zadie's death and my whole family retreating away—that I would have done anything to feel some click. That all I wanted was to find someone who got it. Unfortunately, that someone ended up being Jeremy.

CHAPTER
sixteen

Since she never made it there with her girlfriends in college, I decide that my mother must see Graceland. I tell myself it's not so much backtracking as detouring. I'm starting to feel like we both deserve it. We head out of Columbus and into Tennessee. Along with the other half a million visitors this year, we will see the gold-leaf piano, the King's basement entertainment system where he reportedly watched three televisions at once, a framed photo of the famous fried peanut butter sandwiches Elvis loved.

"I'm inside Elvis's house!" my mother says, like she's surprised to be there even after paying the admission fee. Under the green shag of the carpeted ceiling, she begins to giggle. Between the zebra sofa and leopard lampshades and the shooting gallery, we are strange birds amid an even odder safari of stuffed creatures.

"Quick," my mother says and pulls me away from the rest of the tour group. "Let's get back to the real world." I think she means the world where we are on our own tour, our winding, nonlinear road trip. Our mother-daughter world.

We try to escape, but the security guard informs us that we must finish the tour, and we do, but we hang back now from the rest of the bulb-flashing cameras and tourists sweating in the heat and glare of Elvis's trophy collection.

Outside, we bypass the Elvis-themed McDonald's and head out of Memphis.

"I'm glad I saw all this with you," my mother says, fanning herself with a visor. On the brim is a miniature Elvis, his tiny lips in a snarl, his thimble head cocked at an angle, his arms threaten to poke my mother in the eye with each wave of her hand. I watch her as we stop at an intersection. In the sideview mirror, Graceland recedes, slips out of sight, shrinking until it is to scale with the baby Elvis on her hat.

We follow Route 78 east. Past the Tupelo of Elvis's birthplace and of the Van Morrison song that used to make me think of Lady Godiva naked on her horse just because of the album cover, but now makes me think of Jeremy thinking of his girlfriend before me. Making the trip across North America, I have come to know there's no telling what might pop up in front of you; the most incredible ocean view, a pitch-forked cactus prickling into the dry air, a bizarre monument like the Praying Hands, or the ball of string set into the expanse of a cornfield somewhere. So I am not totally surprised, then, when we drive into Marietta and past a fifty-five-foot-tall chicken.

"Hold on, Laney, go back to that!" my mother shrieks, reaching for the camera before we've even stopped. She tries to lean out the window to get the shot, but then says, "No, wait, you go stand near it, so we can tell how little you are next to it."

I stand near the thing, not touching it since it's made of sheet metal and it's ninety degrees outside.

"I'm roasting!" I yell to my mother, who fiddles with the camera's panoramic view box.

"Ha-ha!" she says. "Flip over!" She mimes basting me.

Behind me, the chicken looks off into the distance as if it has somewhere more important to be. I don't. I smile when I realize this. This is where I am. Where I should be.

Satisfied with her photos, my mother motions for me to come back. We swing by a fried chicken stand nearby and pick up cheese grits in small cardboard cups, fried wings and thighs, and biscuits with gravy. As we nibble and peck, my mother takes a greasy finger and points to three tapes held together, coverless, with a rubber band.

"I'm too greasy to touch them," she says, her mouth outlined in oil, her lips slick.

I wipe my hands on the paper napkins and look at the cassettes. There's an order to them, so I put in the first one and find the covers shoved into the side door pocket. I show them to my mother. The inserts are made of photographs, one of me and Maggie when we were little, spliced with one where we are grown, kid arms linked over grown ones.

"Tell me about Maggie," my mother says. "In my mind, she's got braces and braids, but I know she's all glamour and poise now, right?"

I put in Maggie's old mix. She'd only made me two tapes during our whole time of knowing each other; the other one in the stack was Danny's, but I'd always kept these three tapes together, like they were one long, extended mix. This first one she'd given to me back in New York, right after college when just listening to the thing—sides A and B with her commentary and then dancing, and pausing again—took all afternoon.

This period with Maggie was all tied up with Jeremy, with New York, and the gray days I'd spent there after college. Maggie was magic and her life proved it, and I think being with her then was my attempt to have her stardust rub off on me.

*   *   *

Favorite Songs from the Womb and Before: Maggie's Mix

A SIDE	B SIDE
If Loving You Is Wrong, I Don't Want to Be Right —Isaac Hayes	Shaft —Hayes
Funky Broadway —Wilson Picket	Freddy's Dead —Curtis Mayfield
Grits Ain't Grocery (All Around the World) —Titus Turner as Performed by Little Milton	Mama Tried —Merle Haggard
Que Será, Será —Sly and the Family Stone	If That Ain't country —D. Allan Coe
Drinkin' and Dreamin' —Waylon Jennings	Parlez-Moi d'Amour —Piaf
Mamas Don't Let Your Babies Grow Up to Be Cowboys —Waylon and Willie Nelson	My Hero, Zero —Schoolhouse Rock
Streets of Laredo —Willie Nelson	Ring of Fire —J. Cash
A Boy Named Sue —Johnny Cash	Girl You Know It's True —Milli V.
	Blame It on the Rain —Milli V.
	Black —Pearl Jam
	Love Boat Theme —Who Knows?

"This is the weirdest mix I have ever gotten," I tell Maggie when we've listened to both sides.

"Really?" she asks and means it. Maggie's continually surprised by her own funkiness because it's accidental.

"Edith Piaf's the only woman on here," I say and show her the tape cover in case she's forgotten.

"I know," she says and frowns. "I just don't like girl singers very much."

"Love, exciting and new," I say along with the *Love Boat* guy.

"Come aboard . . ." Maggie gives me a silly welcome and I mime checking her off of my passenger list like a cabin attendant.

Maggie likes soul and funk, country and foreign, but not female singers. We joke that she'll fall in love and then obsess over Streisand, but it's doubtful. She adores Milli Vanilli, so it's no surprise to find them on the tape.

"Yum," Maggie says, mixing her orange juice with cranberry concentrate from a can. Maggie is the biggest mix of everything. Her mom's half Senegalese and half Native American, her dad's Israeli/Italian by way of Australia. Maggie has skin the color of wet sand and hair that's wild and thick. Her hair has a height of its own and makes a good hiding spot for pens and flowers. She can put a snapdragon bud in the curls at breakfast and it will still be there when she's ready to go to sleep. She's almost a foot taller than I am and together we get eyed up, the seemingly shrunken blonde and the striking model. Maggie modeled as a teenager, she missed school for weeks at a time, traveling to Milan and to Paris, but then she grew bored with it all.

"You know what?" she said the summer before senior year of high school. "Models aren't that bright." This was a shock to her. "No one cares what I think about politics or art—they just like my bouncy boobs."

After that, Maggie studied more and ended up at Columbia for undergraduate. Now she's moved downtown for law school.

"Do you like my apartment?" Maggie asks and flips the tape back to side one.

"You're the only person I know with a mezuzah on the door, a cross over your bed, and a dream catcher in the window," I say.

"I like all of that stuff, you know. Why leave everything to chance? And isn't that pillow so pretty? Mummy brought it back from New Delhi for me," Maggie says. Her mother supplies antiques for people in the Back Bay and Beacon Hill who want their homes to reflect world travel while they prefer to go only to Europe. Maggie's language is slightly off even though her English is perfect and her accent mild, so when she calls her mother *Mummy,* no one seems to mind. Her dad moved back to Sweden, and when she comes back from visiting she always brings me licorice bits in a small box with a flip-top lid, pictures of pandas on them for no apparent reason.

"It's so cozy here," I say and lean back on a large circular cushion that's covered in peach-colored silk. I feel tucked in. Maggie's taste is somewhere between streamlined bare wood Swedish and the inside of Jeannie's bottle, with silk throws and multiple pillows on the floor.

"How are things with you and what's-his-name?" Maggie asks. This is her nickname for Jeremy, who is not high on Maggie's like list—a list she actually keeps in her Filofax. I'd called Maggie right after I first got together with Jeremy at college graduation and even then Maggie hadn't been impressed—she thought Jeremy would be my summer fling.

"He's fine," I say because I don't want to tell her I might possibly be unhappy, that I might possibly have moved in too quickly with him, that he might possibly be kind of jerky. Mainly I don't want to say this to her because I don't want to reinforce the ideas to myself.

"How about we get some paint and cover that bare wall?" I ask and make an elaborate gesture to the arched doorway to her bedroom.

"Perfect!" Maggie jumps. "We'll go to Pearl Paint and stay up all night making a mural."

And we do. You can say these things to Maggie as mere slips of ideas and they turn into reality. She will drive all night to Florida on a whim, ask strangers their favorite Beatles song if you dare her, or knock on her neighbors' doors and offer them frozen blended drinks at one in the morning.

Maggie insists on taking public transportation since you never know who or what you might encounter. We both love being on a train, even if that train is a subway and smells bad. She minds the smelling less than I do, and I don't like riding backward; it makes me feel queasy, which is how I feel when we surface from the 9 and emerge downtown. Maybe I just like the *idea* of trains.

"Yuck," I say.

"You look a bit green," Maggie says.

"Spring green?" I ask.

"Yellow green," Maggie says as we walk in the cold air to the store.

In sixth grade, Maggie and I shared a box of sixty-four crayons and would divide them up each afternoon for taking home. Somehow she always managed to get yellow/green and green/yellow, and I had the lighter spring green, which didn't look like spring at all. In fact it barely showed up on that grayish newsprint paper we drew on.

We walk through the aisles of Pearl Paint and move our hands over the tubes of paint. All around are bottled-up ideas and colors. Briefly, Maggie and I plan out a mural for her wall and then we grab some paint and brushes.

"I could go to work and get some from there," I offer. A few stops back uptown, my first post-college job sits waiting for me.

"No way," says Maggie. "I want to get everything here and then go straight back and start."

Maggie is not one for delaying her spontaneity, so we leave Pearl with four kinds of brushes, a craft sponge, a can of clear glaze, and more paint than I'd use in a year. Also, Maggie has bought each of us an artist's palette so we can feel like we're painting at the turn of the century, with our fingers looped through the holes in the middle of the board.

Back uptown, Maggie squirts paint on her palette and moves one of the brushes against her cheek.

"It's so soft," she says. "I wish I could be painted."

"Oh," I say, "you probably will be someday." Maggie is most likely after Demi Moore to be on the cover of a magazine while pregnant and naked except for paint.

I sketch out what I plan to paint until Maggie says, "Stop it, Laney. Just paint, will you?"

Even though it's Saturday and I have all the time I want to be with friends or alone, I'm on slow motion. Jeremy is at work. I think of him while I mix brown and blue, and make a color similar to his eyes.

Maggie cranks up the volume on the tape player, blasting the mix she made as we get to work with our paints. At first, we seem to be only dotting the wall with color, but by the time we've heard "Shaft" again we are well on our way to covering the whole wall. I do landscape and broad stokes while Maggie makes vague outlines of faces or bodies.

"You never make people," she says, just like she said in seventh grade when we had to make cardboard cutouts of Greek gods and goddesses and I chose to just make the armor and swords, and a lightning bolt for Zeus.

"They're hard," I say.

"You see people as hard because you don't give them a chance," Maggie says. "At least not the right ones." I know she means Jeremy as the example of not-right.

"I'm just not as open as you are," I say. "You see the world as a huge canvas that could have any design on it."

"Sometimes," she says. "But mainly I try not to push people away. When you push, you don't get."

Maybe this is some Swedish expression that loses in translation or maybe it's Maggie's way of telling me to stop closing myself off to everything. But I paint instead of talk more about it, and ask her to rewind to the Milli Vanilli songs. After we're finished with the first layer, we soap up at the kitchen sink and watch the swirls of odd tones go into the drain. My hands are usually clean because we wear special gloves at work, but today my hands are the poster children for what I do.

"I work with paint," I say to Maggie and display my hands. "It understands me."

"Yeah," Maggie says dryly, "because you can tell it what to do."

She gives me her I'm-almost-a-lawyer look and we get ready to go to sleep.

The next morning after brunch at a place on Amsterdam that's supposed to look like a Vermont farmhouse, we finish the mural. Over the archway are splotches of blue, the deep kind, just prior to going black, and the purple of borsht before the sour cream. Over the paint, Maggie rubs some gold leaf in jagged strips. It's the night sky in some mythical land. Nothing is as perfect as the wall we've created.

We sit on the floor looking up at what we've made. Sly and the Family Stone belt it out in the background and we sway, just slightly.

"Hey," I say. "We're watching paint dry."

After the Maggie tape ends, my mother gathers all the chicken remains and lunch remnants into a bag and slides her seat back as I slide the next tape in the series into the cassette deck.

"I love hearing about your friends," she says. "I wish we'd exchanged tapes in my generation. Jean Reitz and I always sang together—Mamas and Papas, and then the Simon Sisters after they played up in the Catskills."

"I wish you did, too."

I picture sorting through nonexisting bins of tapes and wish my mother did have them—ones from my dad that would help explain their early love or ones with Jean Reitz, so I could try to think of them at camp together, practicing harmonies in the echoing hollow of the main lodge.

I press play.

"Part two in the Maggie saga," I say. "This is what happens when you're not a closed-off person, when you're not perpetually scared of—of whatever." I stop short and watch my mother's face for signs she's going to press me for more words, but she doesn't.

*   *   *

After passing the bar, Maggie went to Paris for a month and she didn't come back. She'd gone over to visit Brian—a guy she says she dated; but really, we all know they went to exactly one movie, one dance senior year of college, and kissed a handful of times, once, in the big fountain, at night. Very romantic. With this picture in mind, Maggie expected that they would have a European-style relationship. She told me she wasn't even sure what this meant anymore, just that there would be books, bridges, and smoky kisses involved.

Maggie was surprised, then, to find that Brian was gay and very much in love with Jacques, the up-and-coming cinematographer. This was the explanation for the first half of the tape she made me then. But by the time side B was started, Maggie and Jacques were close friends. They bonded over their bizarre fascination with the history of French cheeses, and a mutual twenty-eight by thirty-four-size jeans, which allowed them to all share Brian's trouser collection.

Maggie called me and told me about some café she went to all the time. One afternoon, when she and Brian went for lattes, Jacques wore cream-colored carpenter's pants. Maggie tried her best to explain who or what a carpenter is in English, since her French had not progressed since she arrived at Charles de Gaulle. They laughed as Maggie mimed building bookcases and Jacques thought she was a librarian. Jacques complimented Maggie on how Brian's gray silk harem pants looked on her. Since she's so tall Maggie can wear things like that and not look as if she's in costume.

Maggie ordered coffee and Jacques smiled his American smile, with all his teeth showing. Maggie did her French ingenue. The café itself appeared to be so French, it seemed a facade. The bottles on the rack behind the counter could have been the ones they use in Western movies to whack people on the head; the pastries might have been cardboard and painted foam rubber. Maggie thought the woman who brought the coffee could be Frances McDormand, complete with matter-of-fact manner and kind smile.

"We're in the movie of this moment," Maggie said.

Jacques studied Maggie and then the café door opened as if on cue. Maggie saw the guy walk in and her face opened in one quick motion like a hand fan. She stopped herself before regressing to her arm-grab, oh-my-God stage.

"You need a deep breath, no?" Jacques laughed.

Maggie took his advice before he introduced Pete Mann. Maggie couldn't believe it—*the* Pete Mann. *People* magazine's headlined "Mann of the Year." The supposedly gay actor gave Maggie a look that made her feel they had just had sex. She held back making references to his two Oscars. Jacques left when Pete gave him some code line about "checking on the dailies." In retrospect, Maggie knew that Jacques staged his scene at the perfect place, that he knew the casting would work, that Pete is not only not gay and not in love with any of her ex-boyfriends, but would be interested in her.

Pete canceled his meetings for the day and night and didn't let go of Maggie's hand for the next four days. Not when they brushed their teeth, not when they called me from the payphone with the sound of bells ringing in the distance, not while they slept, not even making omelets in the kitchen. A month later, they bought a flat in the Sixth Arrondissement.

What More Can I Say?

ONE

California
  —Joni Mitchell (a woman!)
Theme from *The Valley of the Dolls*
I Saw Her Again
  —The Mamas and the Papas

DEUX

Tombé Pour La France
  —Etienne Daho
Ne Me Quitte Pas
  —Jacques Brel
Divine Intervention
  —Matthew Sweet

Save It for Me
—4 Seasons
It's Not Unusual
—Tom Jones (Mr. BIG!)
Mirage
—Tommy Simon and the
Shondells
Bird Bath
—from *The Sandpiper*
Standing on the Corner
—Four Lads (?)
Foul Play
—from *Mission Impossible*
What More Can I Say
—Nina Simone

Theme from *What a Way to Go!*
Theme from *Thoroughly Modern Millie*
Where the Boys Are
—Love Is a Many . . .
Quando, Quando, Quando
—Engelbert Humperdink
Don't Give in to Him
—Gary Puckett + Union Gap

Side B was completed on their Bang Olufson stereo. It's Maggie's montage—music played over the romance and falling in love part in the film of her relationship. Neither she nor Pete is French, so they didn't care about whether real Parisians eat crepes from those street vendors or what time of day was the proper time to have café au lait. Pete and Maggie are the genuine article. She and her leading man were to be married in Los Angeles.

At Maggie's bridal shower a couple of months later, I busied myself with chores. In the kitchen, Maggie's metal cafe table and chairs were cool on my bare legs. The counters were white, the floor checkered like bathroom tiles, the room light though not sunny. The single window was frosted, a curiosity—what's so secretive in the kitchen? Maggie had been given things she'd never use: notepads with her name in carefully printed Bloomingdale's-style font, potholders quilted in the shape of roosters, an apron along with the framed *Hello!* magazine from London that shows the inside of Maggie and Pete's Paris digs. Unbeknownst to the other shower guests, Maggie had separated those from some things that she will use: a non-Ceramics Shack lamp base from my dad and a handmade duvet cover from my mom, beaded coasters, assorted candles.

Maggie came in and thanked me for the shower. She put a rooster potholder on her hand and gave me one, so I did the same.

"You are the sister I never had." She fake clucked and pecked my rooster. We made our rooster hands hug.

After her wedding, Maggie still called me—mainly from her car phone as she sped down the 101. She sent pictures of the holiday she took with Pete to Fiji, the house they'd rented in Bath, England, and when they'd come back to Cambridge to visit, we'd all had dinner at the Afghani restaurant near Kendall Square. True, it was odd to see her superstar husband Pete in person, but only for a minute. Once he'd dripped wine onto the table, or coughed, or laughed hard at a story, he was just my friend's husband. He was real.

Back in the car I say to my mother, "I wanted someone real, too," and then point to my T-shirt and pretend it says, *But All I Got Was This Lousy Jeremy.*

"Ugh, Jeremy," my mother says. This time it doesn't bug me. It makes me feel like telling her. Telling her what else she missed out on.

But instead I show my mother one of the photographs I have in the car. In it Danny, Pete, Maggie, and I are all smiling, blushed, flushed, all bundled up in winter gear when the night had actually been quite warm. Danny was a year or so into medical school then, past the stage where he'd walk around smelling his hands; they were the part of him that smelled the least like formaldehyde. Danny had written on the back of the photograph the songs he'd been given on a tape from his old girlfriend, who'd completed side A.

"This tape doesn't really have a B side," I explain to my mother. "Danny was supposed to add songs to it, I think, but he never did."

"I remember the two of you locked away in your room making tapes, sharing music," my mother says. "Danny must have copied nearly all of your tapes. I think that's one of the reasons he loved having you home for the holidays."

"Me, too," I say. I had always looked forward to coming home to have Danny listen to whatever new music I had. Sitting around fast-forwarding and rewinding was part of our holiday-time tradition, particularly the Jewish holidays, which meant good food and hanging out at the house. At Rosh Hashanah my grandparents would come up and we'd record them singing some golden oldie.

"Do you miss having family dinners?" my mother asks.

"I guess," I say.

"We should start up again—you know, plan for them. I assumed you were too old to want to come home, but now that you'll be living so close . . ."

"It's not an age issue," I say. "Danny and I didn't want to cook and gather around the lox tray without you." Imagining her gone from Jewish holidays was like losing all ritual, and the scattered flux of her sickness dispersed the feasts, fasts, and fun until all we could do was try and piece together what we remembered.

"Mom," I say. "I just feel so—"

"I know," she answers, like I've asked her something.

"No—relieved," I say. "And I'm sure Danny does, too."

She nods. "Is this a tape of his?" she asks.

"Mine, Danny's, they'd get mixed up when we'd come home—especially when he and I went out," I say and then feel bad.

"I know you both couldn't spend all your vacation in the house, baby-sitting me. It couldn't have been a fun place," she admits.

"No," I agree, "it wasn't. But the world outside wasn't so great, either. I think this mix is like all the mixes from when you were relapsing again, unfinished and strange. Let me tell you . . ."

*   *   *

Holiday—for Danny in the Snow

SIDE ONE   SIDE TWO

This Woman's Work   Under Pressure
  —Kate Bush   —Queen and Bowie
Cornflake Girl
  —Tori Amos
Borderline
  —Madonna
Even If
  —Karla Bonoff
Thorn in My Side
  —Annie Lenox
Songbird
  —Fleetwood/Christine
Sweet Dreams (of You)
  —Patsy Cline
You Ain't Woman Enough
  —Loretta Lynn
One of a Kind
  —Tammy Wynette

One thing that bugs me in movies is when a character stands in the bluish light of the fridge and smells the supposedly leftover Chinese food boxes before they make a face that says *eww,* and chuck them out. You always know when you ordered the food in the first place, and if you can't remember, then it's obviously too old to eat and what the hell are you doing smelling it. The way it's presented in the movies, it's as if the food magically appeared and the character then has to figure out if it's good or not. Not likely.

This is what I am saying to Danny as we watch some movie on cable that's been edited, so every time someone really says fuck, it comes out as *frig.* "Frig you," we joke.

"Mom," says Danny when my mother appears and blocks the television.

"Are you ready to order?" she asks. She's been dozing off again each time there's too long a pause in the action.

We've been looking at the take-out menu for ages, debating the merits of certain dishes.

"We're stuck," I say.

"Laney frigging wants everything fried," Danny complains.

"Not everything," I say. "Just the crispy sesame beef."

"General Gao's is fried, too," Danny adds. He appeals to Mom, "Now that I am part of the medical world, I don't think I can advise so much of the deep-fried stuff. We should focus on the tofu, the steamed vegetables."

Mom sits between us and circles all the things we mention on the menu. Her writing is shaky, like an old woman's. The menu is the same one we've had since I was in eighth grade, so there are new dishes that didn't even exist then, which we've written in our family code, "B.C. w/s.v." is the tofu dish we always get. All over the menu are obsolete messages and scribbles—"Call Hilda," whoever that is, phone numbers that go to nothing, stars next to dishes no one likes anymore, like chicken wings.

"Nothing too salty," Mom says.

"It's all salty," I say.

Usually, we go for Chinese and a movie on Christmas Eve, but Dad's upstairs, swamped with orders and mergers and legal papers for an official Ceramics Shack mail-order catalogue, and Mom's exhausted and pale.

Danny and I go to pick up the food and he sings along with the first songs on the tape.

"What's with all the girl music?" I ask.

"I have good musical taste. There are some great singer-songwriters out there, Laney," he says.

"This from 'Mr. Clapton-Is-God'?"

"All teenage boys think that. Or Hendrix," he says. "I'm mature now."

"I like this song," I say when the Annie Lenox one comes on.

"The tape's not done. The woman I'm seeing made the first side for me. I want to finish making it with some of your old stuff. Can I look through your tapes later?"

"Sure," I say. "I think the Loretta Lynn might be overstating it just a tad. I don't think you'll ever be woman enough for this one."

"You might be right about that," he says.

Danny's serious and enlightened about his girlfriend, so when I ask, "What's the girl's name?"

He says, "The *woman* I'm seeing is great. Her name is Fiona. She's the one who got me listening to some of this stuff. Maybe this sounds dumb, but I kind of hope she's the one—you know, so if something happens to Mom, at least she'll have met her."

He just says things like this without editing himself. This awes me and annoys me at the same time. I wish I had part of his ease with my mother's sickness and that I could accept life the way he does—that things have a way of working out. Danny tells me about how sweet his current girlfriend is, how she studies seaweed and aquatic life and makes dinner for them.

"Nice," I say.

I picture how Danny's next girlfriend will get the Danny who already knows about Kate Bush and Tori Amos, and how, when she first sees his CD collection, she'll think that she has found a guy who's always been sensitive, always liked these songs.

While we wait for the food, we go next door to the coffee chain place and watch people.

"Check it out," he says. The woman across the room is multi-layered in wool sweaters and socks and reads a local paper called *Politicize This!*

"I'm so glad we're not like that," Danny says.

"Politically active?" I ask.

"No," he says, "like that." The woman has read something and gives a "yes!" out loud to the paper, nodding and furrowing her brow.

"I know it sounds awful," he continues, "but like, what if you did that, spit like she just did. She's indignant about it. Seriously."

"You better not go into psych," I say.

"No shit," Danny says. "But it's worse, somehow, you know? The not-truly nutso, but the fucking freak show side of being human."

"That's because people identify with the weirdos more than freak shows," I say. "So it feels worse."

"Oh my God, you're right. I could be Angry Paper-Reading Guy given the right circumstances."

Danny doesn't go into psychiatry. He does a surgical residency and then, much later, specializes further in reconstructive surgery. On his better days, he is so cheerful in the hospital cafeteria that he'll talk about how he just helped a burn victim regain a whole side of her face. On bad days, he resorts to, "Hey, at least I get to make boobs."

"I think Danny's right," my mother comments as the unfinished, empty side of the mix starts.

"About what?" I say.

"I think a lot of what you kids—even Daddy—did must have been just a reaction. You know, doing things sooner than you might have or dating someone just in case I died, at least you'd have something."

Of course she's right. Of course. If only I could have had the insight then and been able to apply it to myself. Then I'm mad that I didn't. "I wish *you* could have been this insightful back then," I say. It comes out angrier than I wanted.

We listen to the unfinished, empty side of the tape as if it has something to convey.

CHAPTER
seventeen

We cross over state lines into Martinsville, Virginia, self-declared Sweatshirt Capital of the World. I hop out of the car at a roadside stand that sells, of all things, sweatshirts. I buy the ugliest one I can—plaid poly-blend with special beads on the cuffs for Danny.

"For a dollar extra, I can have his name written on it with iron-on letters," the Sweatshirt Lady tells me. I gladly hand over the money and watch her use a cordless iron, and hand her an extra dollar when she spells his name "D-A-N-N-I-E."

"Rock on," I say as if my Sexy Roadtrip Boyfriend is there to hear.

Back in the much-needed air-conditioning, my mother map-reads us to our next destination. There's no music on and no talking as we drive the seventy-nine miles instructed by the map.

"I see it up ahead." My mother points. We've entered Thomasville, North Carolina. What's been great about driving with my mom as opposed to any of my girlfriends, or even Sexy Imaginary Boyfriend, is that she just doesn't care about fastest routes, direct routes. Somehow, Casey would have mapped out the most direct route, and Shana the route with the hottest guys, and Maggie would have only made it as far as Tahoe before realizing she misses her movie star and heading back to L.A.

My mother goes wherever she feels—retracing steps if it means being able to sit in the World's Largest Duncan Phyfe Chair. Not that I know who Duncan was or is, but my mother soon informs me as we sip our bottled lemonade and gaze up at the seat-in-the-sky that he was a Scottish-born New York cabinetmaker. I try to imagine the high-bidding wars that would take place at auction if this chair were really his.

I go to the tourist booth in town and make another purchase, the Tiniest Chair on a Key Ring, a perfect replica of the Phyfe chair outside. Danny will later get back at me by bringing me not one, but two gifts from a weekend trip to Maine—a comb set into a large plastic lobster, bright red ("Yup," Danny would say, "she's cooked!") and slippers shaped like squid—ones that squish and squirt noise when you walk.

"Laney, there you are," my mother says and steps into the dark cool of the tourist room.

"Where to next?" I ask. We haven't called ahead for reservations since we didn't know where we'd wind up.

"I have it all taken care of," my mother says.

Another good part of driving with her—now that she's healthy, she's stepping bit by bit back into her role of organizer, comforter, her role as my mother.

"Thanks," I say and hope it conveys all my meanings.

When we pull up to Chambrington House in Pittsboro, North Carolina, I feel like the ugly sister at the prince's ball—southern gentility is everywhere, the hushed floral garden, the tea service and biscuits lined up on the terrace, the deliberateness of each piece of furniture, and especially, how grimy my own shorts and tank top look in comparison to my mother's crisp white cotton shirt and wide-legged black trousers. I leave her to appreciate the rolling green out back while I go up to shower and change.

In the claw-foot tub, I sit up and look out the windows. The bathroom is as large as my bedroom in San Francisco, and just as bright. Far off, the sway of willows and ease of greenery makes me relax. I practice what my graduate professor suggested—clearing my head by letting a wash of colorful images slide into view, and then how I would explain the picture to a child. By simplifying, I could create an even work of art—one that was accessible but interesting. Immersed in the water, it dawns on me that I don't need to fix other people's work to justify my own art. That the continual cleansing and clearing I'd focused on might give way to something else—a whole new start of creating rather than curing. I float my hands on top of the cool water and when I slide completely down, submerged, all I hear is the water's whale music, the skids of my skin on porcelain, air bubbles that pop like a crush, suddenly, surely. I come up for air and climb out.

I suddenly have a desperate need to talk to Marcus before he is forever part of a Mr.-and-Mrs. team. Maybe it's all this talk of past boyfriends or the past in general, or the fact that his wedding is in a matter of weeks—six and one half weeks exactly, but who's counting? I dial the number at his parents' house where he's staying until his fiancée moves to Boston and they find a house. I'm embarrassed to find that when his parents pick up—his dad on one phone, his mother on another—I call them Mr. and Mrs. and blush like I'm in seventh grade. When they tell me he's not there and call me *dear*, I feel like the loser girl at the dance.

Marcus has been and is my touch point in some ways, though I never would have predicted it. In this memory-lane scenario my mother has created during the car trip, I've thought about him, about how many times he's surfaced and reappeared in my life— high school, college, summers, post-Italy. But then, if he were here he'd probably be looking for southern belles to sleep with, or affecting a southern accent to make me cringe.

Once I'm dressed, I find my mother in the Chambrington

library. We read in silence, our books in different decades, and then play chess. Neither of us is skilled, but we have fun and don't lose patience when the other person takes forever to move a piece.

My mother sleeps in her old plaid shirt. When we say good night I ask her why she's kept the thing for so long.

"It has a lot of memory tied up in it," she says.

"Want to tell me about it?" I ask.

"Not tonight," she says. "Let's just appreciate where we are right now."

That night, away from the garish structures of Vegas, the funny and grotesque roadside wonders, I sleep deeply surrounded by finery, and feeling strangely lovelier than before. My head's only on the pillow for a second or two before I'm asleep—a great change from the sleepless nights I had months before, years ago, miles back.

CHAPTER
eighteen

We're heading home. On some stretch of road between Connecticut and Rhode Island, the ocean comes into view and my mother begins furiously searching through tapes. She knows there's more to hear, more to find out. It occurs to me that we might not talk like this when we get to Cambridge.

The past couple days have been a blur—we seemed to speed up as we approached Massachusetts. Behind us are the pristine white buildings of Washington, D.C, jutting up like bulbous bones from the green of summer lawns. Back, too, is the lunch we'd had at the Soup Tureen Museum in Camden, New Jersey. We'd taken the small plastic packets of salt crackers, my mother with her trial-size clam chowder and me with my cold cucumber soup, and sat on the hood of the car like teenagers.

At dusk, we'd driven over the bridge and into Manhattan, tempted by the constant throb of New York in early summer. It seemed like my mother wanted to freeze us there just for a minute or two, to press pause and just be together amid the taxi horns and sirens. Chatter rose up from the streets—vibrant, the sounds mixed with the candied nut smell on Seventh Avenue as we drove to our hotel—and my mother and I smiled at the simple thought of being among so many people, so much incident. We didn't talk about the next day marking the final segment of our trip. We knew we'd drive up I-95, passing the Largest Insect in the World, which we call the "big blue bug," that perches atop a pest control building in Providence.

Now, we're off the highway, driving in and out of tree shade and sun. I tell my mother of my indiscretion, my listening to a couple tapes without her, and she pretends to scold me. The line of ocean in the distance rises every time we go over a bump, then drops down again. Soon, we will be near Newport, with its yachts and grand houses set back from the road, some notched into the cliffside, just waiting for debauched partiers to go careening into the Atlantic.

"Mom, what are you doing?" I ask as she rummages through the glove compartment and then the box of tapes.

"Looking for something," she says.

"For what?"

"A certain tape," she says. "You know there's more to tell." I know what my mother means, that there are unspoken incidents, secrets we both have still. But emotionally, I am at the end of the road trip. Though we've got one more night before we hear the familiar crush of gravel on the driveway at home, I'm just about ready to end my looking back phase. I'm ready to move forward.

I have tried to reconcile going home to my parents' house—to my old room, files, more tapes, boxes of aged clothes and school papers, shoes with no matching pair, all so untidy. I know how my body will feel sleeping in my old twin bed, how it will feel to see my dad again and watch him with my mother, loving her health as much as he loves her. Part of me will miss explaining myself to my mother. It occurs to me that all the tapes combined will be what makes me think of our trip—and that, for once, the tape I'd made for the trip, Moons and Junes and Ferris Wheels, couldn't possibly sum up our trip, our time together.

As if she can tell what I am thinking as we turn onto the route that will take us to our bed and breakfast in Newport, my mother says, "Now when we get home, I want you to just go about your business and don't feel like you have to move back in all the way. Your dad and I are used to being alone together."

Alone together. I think about this as I look at the tape she's chosen—it's got the letters SYWHK on it—which only I know stands for Songs You Would Have Known.

"Oh, I'd rather not listen to that tape, if you don't mind," I say and try to take it from her grasp.

"I'd like to listen," she says.

"Well, I don't really want to talk about it, so . . ." I let the words stop coming out and drive slowly past the seaside mansions, marbled elegance, clipped lawns, and gated distant charm.

"You know what, Laney?" my mother asks.

"What, Mom?"

"I know that some of these stories, or memories, the tapes, aren't pleasant. Believe me, we all have points in our lives that aren't fun to look back on."

"Yeah, well this one," I take the tape from her, "is one of those, and it's set to music."

My mother says nothing and nods. I know she won't ask again to hear it, but she doesn't let the tape go, either. A few miles later, we've reached the hotel driveway.

"I thought you booked us a night at a quaint B and B," I say to my mother as we step out of the car.

"I wanted the last night of the trip to be special. Memorable," she says, securing her hair into a bun.

In front of us, set back on a sea cliff, is Ocean Bluff, a giant shingled house weathered gray by slanting winds and water, with full wrapping decks and rolling hills dotted with Adirondack chairs. A flag flaps back and forth, welcoming us in.

For some reason, my mother has booked us adjoining rooms, maybe pre-home separating. My room faces the sea directly, with a curved window and small deck. Hers has a fireplace and looks out onto the grass.

My mother phones my dad and as she's describing the fabric that covers the armchairs in her room, I go into my room and get changed. Sneakers on, I gave a half wave to my mother and go down the back stairs and out the door for a run.

With each step, I recite lyrics in my head, let whatever songs come to mind flow against the sound of ocean hitting rocks and think how good it feels to stretch my legs. I'm amazed at the freedom of not having any particular song stuck in my head, that I'm just looking around and thinking about where I am.

When I get back to the hotel an hour later, I knock on my mother's door, but she's not there. First casually, then more frantic, I look for her. She's not in the card parlor, not in the oak-paneled library, not eating oysters, wet and slick from the shell and made vibrant from the cocktail sauce. I imagine for a moment her falling down, unable to rise, sick again, needing me. When I finally see her, hair covered by a scarf she's had since Vermont, she's staring out at the water, sitting in a chair on a hill far from the hotel deck.

"Mom, Jesus Christ. I looked everywhere for you," I say.

"Well, now you found me," she says.

"It's not funny," I say. "I thought . . ."

"You thought I wandered into the ocean and got swept away?"

I sit at her feet. Her sneakers are old but well kept. She never slips them off without untying the laces and after each wearing, she carefully undoes the double bow on each shoe and lets the laces go slack, ready for next time. My laces are permanently tied, and the backs of the sneaker mushed into the ankle, dirty and worn, fringed bits of string pop out of the air holes even when the shoe is close to new. My mother looks at me looking at her shoes and then at mine.

"You and your father, always so hard on your footwear," she says.

I finally tell her I am scared about what might happen, about the continual lurk of illness.

"Well," she says, "let's just deal with that as it comes. But don't take things too seriously. We've seen rough times, just appreciate what we have now. Focus on yourself and what's important to you, Laney."

"I won't worry too much," I say and we both know I am lying.

The waves lap one over the next, bashing into the stone jetty that curves out into the navy blue water.

"I love you, Mom," I say, but I slur and it comes out more like "I live you."

"I live you, too," she says. I don't know whether to laugh or not, so I kneel, reaching up to her. I put my palm flat onto her cheek, like I used to as a small girl, and she leans her face into my hand.

"You know what?" I say. "I never got to tell you about Casey!"

"That's right, you didn't! You did allude to her wonderful love life—tell me about it," my mother says.

"Well, it's more than that," I say. "Casey pretty much figured out the reason her life wasn't working—at least not the relationship side. And after I went to visit her in London this year, I pretty much realized what my problem was, too."

"Well, between Casey's big revelation and yours, I'm certainly curious," my mother says. She walks with me to the car where we sit in the park, looking at the ocean and listening to my very recent past. I show her the tape I sent Casey from graduate school, and the one I made when I saw her in London.

What Did We Do Before Polar Fleece?

EARLY FALL

Everybody Knows Her
  —Jonathan Edwards
Like to Get to Know You Well
  —Howard Jones
Radio Free Europe
  —R.E.M.

LATE FALL

Getting Better
  —Beatles
Last One Standing
  —Finn
#41
  —Dave Matthews

Bleed to Love Her
—Fleetwood Mac
That Is Why
—Jellyfish
Sunporch Cha-cha-cha
—from *The Graduate*
London Rain
—Heather Nova
The Ocean
—Led Z
South Central Rain
—R.E.M.
My Bag
—Lloyd Cole and the
Commotions

Alice Childress
—Ben Folds Five
California
—Rufus Wainwright
Through the Long Night
—B. Joel
Solace of You
—Living Colour
The Salmon Song
—Courage Bros.
This Perfect World
—Freedy Johnston

On the phone I tell Casey about my graduate school apartment—it's the whole first floor of one of those Victorian San Francisco houses that always show up in the opening credits to movies and TV shows.

"Very arty," I say, and then softer, "and very empty now that I'm single—you know, without Jeremy."

Casey tells me how she got the job she wanted—she created a puppet and will be on *Tea Time Travels,* a top-rated British show for kids. Her character, Blupie, comes complete with Mardi Gras beads and top hat and gets to hang out with all the letters of the alphabet.

"I'm going to be totally good friends with Q and R," Casey laughs.

"Don't forget Z—or is that zed?" I ask. Then we both laugh. "Do the people who hired you know your torrid past?"

"Basically," she says. "It's total irony that *I'm* playing a character that's supposed to teach kids a valuable lesson each week."

When we hang up, I feel bad that I haven't admitted to my

own lack of learning—that I have let Mr. Wrong, aka Jeremy, into my life again.

"Don't even fucking tell me scumbag Jeremy is living with you or I'll have to fly out there myself," Casey says and sighs when I call her again a couple days later.

"No, don't worry," I tell her. "It's not like that."

I explain how I'd come back from my Italian master's lecture to find a neighbor's dog, Dante—and yes, I got the hell symbolism—had come in through the screen door and chewed my new paint box and the bulk of the tubes. Vermilion, brown number three, spring green, locust, navy were all paw-printed onto the floor, tiles, and couch. It was like Dr. Suess meets *The Shining*. Dante was frothing green when I walked in the front door and all I could picture was those giant needles they always talk about in reference to rabies. Then Jeremy appeared at my door.

"I swear," I say to Casey, "for a second I felt like you."

"What do you mean?" Casey asks.

"Like how you live in some alterna-universe where Big Bird is considered God," I say and Casey laughs. "Only I'm stuck with the mean puppet." One I hadn't learned how to say good-bye to.

Jeremy was on a break from *Murder She Croaked!*, a frog mystery for kids in which he played the toad. He helped clean Dante the dog and then told me he missed me, that he was sorry about the way everything ended, that he'd come to surprise me.

"Anyway," I whisper to Casey in case Jeremy emerges from the shower and overhears, "he's here for a couple more days while we figure things out. Don't be mad that he's back in my life—I just want to be happy."

All Casey says is, "Ummm, okay." But what I hear in her voice is that I'm a fool. She sends me an email that night that asks what the hell is wrong with me. She says she's sorry if she sounds like a giant bitch, but that she knows Jeremy will never make me happy. Part of me knows she's right, but it takes me another week to be entirely sure.

*   *   *

"Okay, Case," I tell her via long distance in the middle of her night. "You were right." I explain about the night before.

"I like it when you try to win," Jeremy had said when we'd played Scrabble in town and I'd used all my letters.

"Why?" I'd reached into the tile bag while he wrote down the score.

"It makes me feel like you're really here," he said.

That was the one thing he'd said that made sense to me. That I wasn't here, not anywhere. So Jeremy wanted me to understand his hesitation to commit back in NYC, to talk about our relationship while we hiked up the mountain near my house. On the trail toward the sharp peak, he moved like he was being timed. I wandered off the path every now and again to point out a plant or a view, but he wasn't interested. Three miles in, I tripped and twisted something until I heard a snap. Ahead, Jeremy went on, unaware.

"Hey!" I said still grounded. "Jer!"

He didn't rush to me, but calmly came over and asked what happened.

"Well," I said, "obviously, I fell."

"Are you hurt?" he asked.

"I don't know," I say. The sky changed to predusk and it was getting cold. "My foot is sore."

Jeremy played doctor like he had in *Physician Fair,* that off-off-off-Broadway thing he did and asked, "Does this hurt?" I made my wincing sound that I do when something actually hurts a hell of a lot, but I don't want to say.

"Well, it's kind of swollen," Jeremy says. "It doesn't look great. You're definitely going to need an X ray."

I attempted to lace my boot back up over the bloated foot, but couldn't. I turned to head back and said, "Sorry. I know you were looking forward to finishing this hike." It was another four miles up and eight down the other side where a shuttle ran back and forth to the university. Jeremy just looked at me, confused, and asked if I needed him to come with me. There, on that dumb mountain, I realized he was sucking the life force out of me. That all the hopes I kept pinning on him were just a waste. That he would leave me stranded like he had before.

"Jesus," Casey says and even though we're on the phone I know she must be shaking her head—at Jeremy and at me.

"Anyway," I continue, "I told him never to contact me again. To just leave and let me get over it—him—us—whatever."

I listen to Casey breathe. I can hear a London ambulance speed by, siren wailing. While I wait for her to respond, I think about a phone call I had with my mom before Jeremy's surprise visit in which she'd asked me if I'd met anyone in California. When I said *maybe* just to keep her quiet, she'd quipped that she didn't like *maybe*, that I'm the one who *likes maybe*. That I *live in maybe*.

"Casey?" I ask. "Are all the guys I've liked *maybes*—you know, one foot with me and the other out the door?"

"Who are you with these maybes, Annie?" Casey says, then hums a few bars of the "Maybe" song from the musical *Annie* and adds, "Sorry, I meant that to be funny. I forgot it's your mom's name. But as long as you're asking, I think it's not so much the guys, it's you who's *maybe*."

I don't respond, I just sit in the weight of what Casey said.

"Hey!" Casey says. "Why don't you come here for New Year's or something? I don't think I can get the time off to come there, but you're in school—you should use your winter break for a trip to London."

I perk up. "Maybe," I sing.

"Besides." Casey coughs dramatically. "There's a certain someone I want you to meet. A certain special letter of the alphabet. I need you to meet the alphabet love of my life, the letter zed."

We confirm my ticket and schedule my arrival in time to see the taping of *Tea Time's Terrific Holiday Show*. I can meet all the puppets Casey's been telling me about and get to see my cousin Jamie, too.

*　　*　　*

My mother interrupts my story and asks me, "I always got the feeling there was something about Jeremy you never told me." I nod. "Is this it? That he left you on a mountainside?" she asks.

It would be so easy just to say yes, but instead I hint there might be something else. "He did leave me stranded. But not there. Anyway, enough. Listen to my London tape. It's what helped me get to right now."

London, Midwinter

SIDE A

The Day We Caught the Train—Ocean, Colour, Scene
Fake Plastic Trees—Radiohead
It's Only Natural—Crowded House
Theme from *Tea Time Travels*
"C" is for Cookie—Cookie Monster
A New Flame—Simply Red
Thorn in My Side (Acoustic)—Eurythmics
You Got Something—J. J. Cale
I'd Like That—XTC
Nobody's Diary—Yaz
Kayleigh—Marillion

Cousin Jamie meets me at Heathrow. He's not holding a sign or anything, but he's standing with the cab guys and the chauffeurs making chitchat. He throws his arms around me in a decidedly un-English manner and I respond by kissing him on both cheeks.

"Now, look," he says, "I've got it all sorted, you're going to shag my dear friend, Simon. Enough of American guys—they're crap, as far as I can tell. Go for a Brit. Simon's a playwright and he's very good-looking, so no more questions."

                    *   *   *

The day of the night of Jamie's New Year's party, Casey introduces me to the letter Z. We're in one of the costuming rooms near the stage for *Tea Time Travels*. In the corner, Blupie, Casey's puppet, who I met earlier, is slumped against a chair.

"Should he sit like that?" I ask as Blupie faceplants into his own lap.

"He's a puppet, Laney," Casey says.

"I know that. I mean, doesn't he/she need to be protected or something?"

"No, she's fine," Casey says. "Besides, there are doubles of all the creatures."

"So, where's the infamous Z?" I ask.

"Outside," she says. "You'll see everyone later on. I kind of mentioned Jamie's party to some of them, I hope that's okay."

"I guess," I say. And I look at Casey. She looks back at me and lets her shoulders slump down. "You look like Blupie."

"Thanks," she says and then, "Laney, I'm gay. I'm in love with the letter zed and her name is Louise."

My small friend sits next to her puppet, surrounded by bits of feathers and eyeballs made of foam, noses and beaks, antique lampposts made of cardboard, waiting for my reaction.

"I'm really happy for you, Case," I say.

Suddenly, she smiles and leaps up and does her little dance, fingers pointing into the air while she twirls around. We hug.

"You've come to life!" I say.

"That's how I feel!" she says. "I wonder if Blupie's a lesbian?"

I think about all the guys, the flings and semidecent relationships Casey had to go through—Greg, Paul, Richie—sometimes I couldn't keep them straight and we'd give them names—the Russian Guy, the Guy Who Licked Her, Baseball Boy, the Dude. I tell Casey my thoughts.

"Did I leave any out?" I ask when I tell her my list.

"Oh, probably," she says. "It was like I had to check and make sure—like if I dated every guy, then maybe my issues with myself would go away. Then, after the last one—who was he, Crazy Carl?

Or, no, wait—Don't Touch My Forehead Freak—anyway, I realized I was just on automatic. That I wasn't participating in the relationship. I was just going through the motions."

She looks at me pointedly to make it clear she's talking about both of us.

"I'm really proud of you," I say. "It must feel good to be honest. With yourself, I mean."

"It does feel good to be honest." Casey smiles. "With myself, with my parents. But you know what feels great?" I wait for her to continue. "What feels the best is being able to exist in the moment—to not always be thinking about who or what might come next."

At Jamie's flat, I take a bath and kneel to wash my hair under the tap. All around me, sudsy water flows and I let myself float in the tub. Soon I'm out and dry and helping Jamie prepare for his big party by splitting a bottle of Rioja with him.

"Fucking brilliant, the Spanish," Jamie says after his second glass.

"How so?" I ask.

"Good wine, fantastically sexy women, something else, too, I just forget."

We open packets of confetti stars, moons, and multicolored squares and spread them around the hardwood floors and onto the mantel. When we light candles, the whole place feels like the inside of a lantern, sparkling and warm.

On Jamie's bedside table is a photograph of our old friend Ben as a little boy. Even though he was only about three when the picture was taken, it looks just like him. Tom Petty songs swirl into my head. I remember that summer Jamie and Ben came to visit, sitting on the roof with them, how this image somehow merges with my mother's small frame propped up on the bed in the hospital. How she'd watched us play cricket out the window, unable to join in. I think of Ben and imagine him here, think that he'd be lying down and making confetti angels in the middle of the room while we busied ourselves setting up the bar, putting out napkins and platters of food.

"I miss Ben," I say out loud. "I wish I got to know him as a grown-up."

"Me, too!" Jamie says and it comes out cheery.

"How can you say that and sound happy?" I ask.

"Because I am happy," Jamie says and looks at me from across the room. The flicker of lights reflecting red and silver and gold goes over his face as he smiles at me. "It's okay, Laney. Really. Ben's gone, long gone, but we're here. We have to celebrate the fact that we're here. I wish Ben could be, too, but he's not."

Jamie comes over and pushes the sides of my mouth into a smile as he says, "We miss Ben because he was so great. *That's* why you miss people, because they were good or kind or made you laugh so hard you wet yourself all over the tube. Being sad only tells you how much that person meant. Then you just incorporate it into your own life."

"And you can just be happy as you're thinking that? That this person is gone and won't ever come back?"

"Now, yes." Jamie opens another bottle of wine and puts three discs into the changer. "It wasn't always like this, but there's just some level of acceptance you need to . . ." I watch him as his voice trails off and wish that I had that sense, the distance of not over-thinking, of not allowing myself to go straight back to the middle of a memory, the music swirling around, until I am truly sad.

At first, no one's in the flat except for me and Jamie, so we dance around listening to Simply Red, feeling terribly eighties and punc-tuating this by eating tiny quiches Jamie has warmed in the oven. All around, candle flames make the glitter confetti glow and I think that this could be enough as it is. A good New Year's Eve. Then, the doorbell rings and Jamie dashes down the steps two at a time to let people in. I stop dancing by myself and sit on the couch eating Twiglets and licking my fingers.

Soon we leave the door closed, but not locked so we don't have to respond to the buzzer anymore, especially since we can barely hear it over the music. I spend fifteen minutes talking to Louise and Casey, who stand hand in hand under the mistletoe. Other friends and colleagues of theirs have come right from the studio, some in costume, some in plain clothes. When I ask people what they do for a living, I keep getting responses like, "I'm a Jersey cow, you?"

In the kitchen, I make mulled wine. This involves pouring vast quantities of wine into a large pot and adding lots of brown sugar, fruit slices, and cinnamon. As I stir, a vision of English good looks enters the room and rummages in the fridge.

"Don't tell me," he says. "You're a comma or a giant, wooly sheep?" Simon says.

"Just an American," I say.

"An American sheep?" he asks and drops an ice cube into his wineglass.

"Too hot for you?" I ask, blushing and hoping he knows I meant the alcohol, not myself.

"A bit," he says. "My name's Simon, by the way."

"This is my cousin," Jamie interrupts as he passes by with a new tray of snacks.

"Oh, right," says Simon.

We all stand and look at each other until Jamie says, "Okay, I'll fuck off now."

Left to our own devices, Simon and I sit at the kitchen table and drink mulled wine and eat thin crackers with crème fraiche and salmon slivers. I show him how to play table hockey. He puts his fingers on the tabletop in goal position and I shoot a bottle cap hockey puck in and score. We continue like this for ages until Casey comes in and says she and Louise are leaving.

"I'll walk you out," I say to them.

"I'll walk *you* out," Simon says to me, and we all go down the narrow stairs and out onto the street. It's about to be midnight. In the middle of our good-bye, when the minicab is waiting with the back door open, the bells chime and Louise grabs Casey so she tumbles into the car. The driver pulls away and Simon and I stand watching them wave and kiss, kiss out the window to us until we can't see them anymore.

Empty of revelers, the pavement is dark and cold. Upstairs, through the window of Jamie's flat, we see the tall flower puppet bob in conversation and random people embrace as, dimly, the music slides out and down to us.

"Shall we go back inside?" Simon asks.

"Okay," I say.

We share a bunch of cigarettes from a ten-pack Simon has found in the kitchen. He says he doesn't really smoke, that it's just for tonight, and I nod in agreement. On the floor of the living room, we sit with an ashtray between us and talk about dialogue.

"It's terrible, really," he says and exhales. "I feel sometimes like I'm giving stage directions in my head as I move or talk."

Later, I go to the bathroom and wonder if anything will actually happen with Simon. Usually, by this point in the night, I'd know. We were past the leave-and-go-somewhere-else stage of an evening, too deep into conversation for one of us to partner up with someone else. Mainly puppets were left, anyway.

When I reenter the room, I see how gorgeous Simon is, especially when he smiles, which he does when he sees my smile, which at this point is from half of my mouth. My wine-drinking smile.

When the last visitors have gone and it's almost four, we help Jamie pick up debris until he says, "Sod it, I'm going to bed. Alone! Crap."

By now, I am confused and tired myself. I sit on the rug and light another cigarette.

"You're smoking a lot for someone who doesn't smoke," Simon says.

"I know," I say. "It's very bad."

We sit and talk, shoes off, not touching until the conversation has dwindled to the point where Simon says, "So, what's your middle name?"

Then before I know what's happening, I'm on my back and being kissed.

"Sorry that took so long," Simon says from his perfect position above me. Stage left, I think, and we keep on kissing.

The next morning, which is only five hours later, Simon and I wake up and smile politely at each other. This is the time he should get up and slide into his jeans, which I look forward to only because I get to watch his lovely body, the triangle of broad shoulders into taut stomach. But Simon props his head up and says, "I don't like Sundays, do you?"

"The lesser-known Boomtown Rats song," I say and then when Simon doesn't know what I'm talking about I continue with, "No, Sundays are blah days, and very coupley."

"Shall we have a Sunday, then?"

"Yes," I say, and we do. We have the English equivalent of a diner breakfast at a greasy spoon called Lido's up the road from Jamie's flat. I have beans and cheese and eggs on toast, which is what everyone else around me has, too. I have coffee and Simon has tea.

That night, when our Sunday is finished, I say, "Well, this was fun." It was. We watched sports on television, read the Sunday papers, and brought food to Jamie, who was still hungover.

"Would you like to come over to my house?" Simon asks as we're supposedly saying good-bye in the doorway. He asks it like a small English schoolboy, so I say back,

"Oh, yes, please," like I want more dessert.

Simon and I develop a relationship somewhere between admiration and passion. I feel about him the way I once felt when I would look at a Nick Drake album—I wanted Nick to pop out of the pages, to appear lifesize and to love me, but his image stayed flat. The record was one of those double-folded ones, with lots of lyrics and liner notes and pictures. I'd stare at the black-and-white moments from decades earlier—sepia-stained Nick with a boxy kind of camera that doesn't exist anymore, or, in his suede jacket and funny striped scarf sitting under a budding tree, or at Nick's face as he looked out at the view from a building top and feel—if not love—then something. I was sure we could have connected. Through kisses, his odd-metered half rhyme, his sorrow and continual referencing of the moon. And his beautiful mouth.

Simon and I hold each other in the same regard for the five weeks I stay in London. Most of the time I stay at his flat, though every once in a while I have time alone with Casey or with Jamie. We act like we know each other, we make tenderloin and roast potatoes, discuss art and theater, laugh at silly American import sitcoms, and dig through sale bins at our favorite clothing shops, holding articles up to each other, saying, "What about this one?" or "This would look good, don't you think?"

Simon buys me a long, maroon scarf of silk and chenille. It's so long we joke about it getting caught in the escalators or tube doors, but it doesn't. Mostly, it hangs on the wooden peg near the door.

One night, Simon tells me about his father. Each time one of Simon's plays is put on, he sends his father a flier, hoping he'll come. But he doesn't. This detail is in slight disregard of the unspoken affair rules. Really, we should just exist right now, with no explanation as to how or why we got here or where we'll go next.

Aside from that, and the fact that Simon went to a very famous school/university combination, and how he won some theater award, I know little of his life. He knows just about the same of mine, except he envisions everything I have ever done taking place in California, since that's where he imagines I'm from, even when I tell him Massachusetts, Boston, Cambridge.

We have terrific, energetic sex, the kind in movies—each time lasts until we are sweat-slicked and finished, good and tired. Afterward, I fall asleep and wake to Simon writing or cooking eggs and toast for me.

We socialize in the way new lovers do, chatting and gaily recounting stories no one's heard five times already. We leave dinner parties right after the coffee, rush back from lunches out, and head to bed. Simon has a show being produced in the spring, but the meetings he has don't occupy all his days.

One afternoon, walking down Kensington High Street, we notice a sale fare for last-minute trips to Majorca. We board a plane two days later.

The beach land is low and sunny, almost too hot. We sit and drink guava juice and rip off pieces of mango from the pitted halves we buy from the fruit sellers who walk the length of the beaches in the mornings. Later, we hire a car and drive through the mountainous region of the island, where the air is cool enough for sweater wearing and the giant trees are tall, trunks long since hollowed like caves.

I think of the London weather and realize that, together, Simon and I have experienced just about a full year's worth of seasons already. Back at his flat, brown and with obvious tan lines, we glide through the next ten days and never mention my impending departure. We listen to the tape we made, but I'm gone before there's even a B side.

"You see, Mom?" I say. I put the window down to let in ocean air.

"I do, actually," she says. "Casey was finally honest with herself and with you."

"And I just kept doing what I always do—"

"And what is that?" she asks, even though I think she's aware.

"Being with Simon in London—especially with all the Ben stuff, which links to you being sick—I don't know. It's just like I all of a sudden knew I had to make a choice. To either keep having this—I don't know—semi kind of relationship or . . ."

"Or?" My mother stops the tape and puts it back where it belongs, tucked in its case.

"Or stop. And figure out who or what I want. Who my Road Trip Guy is. Or where I want to be."

"And are you there?"

"Nearly," I say. "Getting closer."

I think of what else I have to do still: I have to call Shana and deal with Marcus's wedding, I need to find an apartment and start my new job. Maybe I'd even try to find Josh, my long-lost camp boyfriend and tell him I never got the tape. Who knew what going home had in store for me. But for once, I felt okay about not knowing.

CHAPTER
nineteen

In one last graceful buzz of passing scenery, Rhode Island, the South, the whole country we've seen is behind us and we're back home. In my parents' house, my room is still the same. I notice how even my body acts as if I am still the seventeen-year-old home for a holiday break, legs loose, my whole self floppy and undone from driving so far with my shoulders up around my ears. I've brought the tape-filled shoebox inside and shoved it under the bed. Other bags, boxes, two lamps, and a variety of painted canvases lean against the wall, perched to remind me that my stay here is just until I find an apartment, just one summer.

Visiting my old room is getting to see the stages of myself all at once. Aside from old letters and tapes, there were magazine clippings, pale, pretty faces torn from *Elle*, complete with details on how to pluck eyebrows, how to apply electric blue mascara so it didn't clump, old editions of *Let's Go* wherever, and guides to colleges, ones where they claimed to tell what the school was really like. In the desk drawers were class schedules, obsolete *I like so-and-so* graffiti, a single name barrette with the letters on it spelling

Maggie. Maggie and I had swapped one of each of ours, so the sides of our heads read half her, half me.

I try the barrette in my hair now and I look not like a high schooler being ironic or an indie-cool college student, but like someone's mother—as if I'm in a commercial where the businesswoman can't get it all together, so last minute she shoves her daughter's hair clip in, nails the presentation, and gets the account. Only in the room where you grew up would you find name barrettes next to books of matches from the on- and off-smoking phases and a bracelet filled with glittery gel that oozes around its clear plastic case. And letters, some with addresses and names I couldn't even place.

The house is empty, my father is with my mother, out for a fancy you're-healthy-now-let's-eat-butter dinner at L'Espalier, the classical French place downtown. Suddenly, it's clear what I need to do. I go downstairs, reach under the kitchen sink for a heavy-duty trash bag, and return to my room. Business cards from restaurants long closed up, postcards from people I don't remember, friendship bracelets, yellow, orange, fuchsia, all chucked into the garbage. I don't throw out anything that I'm still attached to—not whole letters, not the tapes. Not yet.

Tucked into sheets of canvases I'd worked on this year, amid the small tubes of paints, I find the invitation to Marcus's wedding. *Please join us for . . . Please celebrate with us as we*—show the world how alone we are? As we lose our backup plan? If Road Trip Guy, the right guy, wasn't Marcus, who could it be? I know I don't need a man, but I'd like to think that out there, somewhere, is a flesh-and-blood person I can connect with. That I could give myself to in ways I never had, forming a true union.

But in the meantime, I have to deal with Marcus's wedding. A wedding day that's fast approaching. I'd met Marcus's bride-to-be, Rachel Block, once before, back when she was just his girlfriend and weddings seemed far off. Now even her name has a sturdy ring to it, and when I think of her with Marcus, I know they'll balance each other out. She'll humble him with her various degrees and smarts and he'll make her laugh. Then, when I think about how

Marcus makes me laugh, how he'll be too busy being the groom to make me laugh at the wedding, I suddenly realize something important: I need to find a very reliable date. One who'll understand what watching Marcus getting married means for me.

I hear my parents' car pull into the driveway and the noise breaks my Marcus trance. I survey the piles in my room—keeping ones, trash bags tied up and knotted, rows of books, essays about the Battle of Hastings, other papers.

"Do you want any of this stuff?" I ask my mom when she comes to stand in the doorway.

"Maybe," she says. When my father comes in, he sits down, using a filled garbage bag like a cushion against the wall.

My mother holds the tape she had wanted to listen to in the car. The tape contains reels of bad times, of things I've never shared with her. She holds it out for me to see, an unspoken question. I motion for her to put it in the stereo.

"Can I stay?" my father asks, looking at both of us.

I look to my mom, who nods at him. "If it's okay with Laney."

Looking around my room, not wanting to rush me, my mother looks at the heap of clothing stashed way in the back of my closet near incomplete board games and a pile of notebooks. She and my father smile at my grade school photograph, the one with the fake-cloud background.

"Remember when you wore scarves nearly every day?" my mother asks, letting the stringy end of metallic gold threads and faded blues slide through her fingers.

"Yes," I say. "I think I wanted them to have the same affect on me that they did on you."

"Which is what, exactly?"

"I don't know. An aura. Some sort of magical, timeless thing. Like those old pictures of you from Vermont, with silver dangling earrings and one of Dad's old shirts."

"I never thought I looked so good then," she says, and sounds like her mother.

"You did. You looked so good in that one shirt of Daddy's—the deep green plaid one, the one with yellow woven in. The one you wore on our trip, you remember?"

"Of course I remember it," she says and looks at her hands in her lap. "It's the softest brushed cotton. So worn."

"Well, it was funny to see you in it this summer. It seems like in my memories of Vermont you wore that shirt all the time."

"I did. At least for a while."

I wait for her to say more, but she doesn't. The tape cues and I begin to tell her and my father about this one—tell myself one last time—before I get rid of it.

Songs You Would Have Known If You Had Been Cooler in High School

SIDE A

The Ghost in You
   —Psychedelic Furs
No More I Love Yous
   —The Lover Speaks
Summer's Cauldron
   —XTC
Hyacinth Girl
   —Winter Hours
Erica's Word
   —Game Theory
All for Leyna
   —Billy Joel
See You
   —Depeche Mode
Hot You're Cool
   —General Public

SIDE B

One More Colour
   —Jane Siberry
Crash
   —The Primitives
Mr. Brown
   —Marley
Backwards and Forwards
   —Aztec Camera
That's All
   —The New Originals
Please, Please, Please, etc.
   —The Smiths
Her Majesty
   —The Beatles
I've Been Loving You Too
   Long—Otis

Solid Rock
  —Dire Straits
End of the Party
  —English Beat

Dreaming of Me
  —Depeche Mode
Adonis Blue—Voice of the
  Beehive

"The fucking violinist gets to murder someone every night!" Jeremy is pissed. He sits down on our futon couch and then gets up again. Then he sits down again. He is an actor in *Orchestra of Evil,* one of those audience-participation shows that's been playing in Manhattan forever. It's one of those plays that actually advertises, "Since 1981!" like it's a steak house or a private school.

Jeremy is the flautist, and even the word is grating. The coveted role, which anyone could have, is that of the accused murderer, and that's what the audience decides. The show goes from there. Another good role is the conductor, since he never gets killed and has the funniest lines. The part you don't want is the person the audience chooses to be knocked off in the first half of the show. That person has to lie sprawled out on the stage and look blankly at the people in the first row for the whole rest of the night until the bow. This is the role that Jeremy fills the most.

"I mean, do people just hate flautists?" he rages, smoking his one after-show cigarette of the night.

"I don't think so," I say and go to hug him until he softens. We stand with our bodies pressing until the traffic lights outside have changed from green to yellow, yellow to red, four times.

We are still in the gentle phase of our relationship, when it doesn't take much to calm each other down. I've made our favorite dinner, risotto with Parmesan, asparagus, and chicken. Jeremy sits on the futon and I bring dinner to him in one of our bowls. Actually, they are the bowls my dad made for me for college graduation. Wide with a low lip, yellow the color of eggnog, they are perfect.

Jeremy lifts a leg and puts it on mine. We eat like this for a while until I put one of my legs over his. Then he does the same with his other leg. We are Lincoln Log cuddling.

"I'm almost done with her arm," I say when Jeremy asks what I've been working on this week. I work in art restoration for a small museum filled with paintings and sculptures on loan from private collections. My team has the assignment of cleaning and restoring *Angel Mourning,* a canvas the size of a lap pool, in total disrepair. I'd been working on it ever since.

I'd met Jeremy in New York, at college graduation. He was there, leaning up against one of the tent poles you're not meant to lean on, talking to some pretty girls I didn't know. In a vague way, I knew who he was—the brother of a campus-goddess-woman in my class, but I knew nothing of him, really, even though he was a sometimes-figure on campus. Jeremy's hair was like his sister's, flat, cut close to his head, but soft looking. We noticed each other briefly before he resumed his conversation with his admirers and right before I stepped in dog crap. Holding my folded graduation gown in one hand, the tasseled hat in the other, I made my way over to a pole far away from Jeremy and began scraping my shoe bottom off on the rope that secured the line to the ground.

Later, gowns dropped in black rippled puddles on the floor, Casey and I made for the outdoor party. It had only taken four years, but finally I felt like I had made a space for myself at the place I was now leaving. With the flicker of stars against the backdrop of blaring music, beer spilled onto the lawn from the kegs tucked against the stone walls. The grass sucked up the liquid as if it were fresh water, and it occurred to me that the grass couldn't tell the difference between what it longed for, water, and something else; it just drank it in, glad for anything.

When the crowds moved across the grass to watch a Beatles movie being projected on a giant, flat rock, I stayed. Next to me, a couple of people spaces over, Jeremy sat on a stuffed frog someone had brought out to enjoy the festivities.

"What is it," he'd said, "about these kinds of end-of-the-year parties that make it completely reasonable for me to be sitting on a frog the size of a toaster?" He'd made no reference to my stepping in shit earlier and this had impressed me at the time.

We'd moved in together fairly quickly, since he was looking for a
new place anyway, and I needed, if not a roommate, the company—
to grasp onto something now that college, friends, my mother—
probably—were all leaving me. Casey was headed to her puppetry
program, and Maggie—who had gone to NYU—had her set of
friends in the city from college. I knew I'd meet people at work, but
generally art restoration was a lonely process. At the internship I'd
done, while there were teams of people assigned to particular pieces,
they might all do different jobs, so there wasn't a time to connect. In
the apartment Jeremy and I shared, there was *only* space to connect
since we had a tiny bedroom that fit the double bed, a standing
lamp, and some books propped on the windowsill.

I can still think of those beginning months and feel a trace of
warmth. Only for a couple of seconds, though, before the rest of
that time slips in and takes over. As an adult, I am annoyed that
there's still emotion there—that time and maturity should mellow
everything. And I guess only traces of hurt are left and much of
what I feel is toward myself for allowing myself to be dragged in,
held down. And that it's all accessible by tape.

In the car with Jeremy on the way to see my parents one weekend,
I ask, "Do you like it?"

Jeremy flips over the tape case, studies it, and says, "Yeah." He
digs around in the side pockets of the passenger side door and
clicks a pen into the write position.

"What are you doing?" I ask. The sun visor is loose, so we've
put adhesive Velcro on it to keep it up, and I have to yank it down.
It tears with the sound of skin being ripped from an orange, one of
the big ones with a thick outer layer.

"Changing the title," Jeremy says. I downshift and slow to a
stop while Jeremy crosses out Songs I Knew in High School.

"What's it called now?" I ask.

"Songs you would have known if you had been cooler in high
school," he says, satisfied and sleepy, balling his jacket up and tilting his head onto it.

"That's not what I meant it to be," I say. "I don't know if I like the sound of that."

"I do," he says and holds his hand over mine on the gearshift. He's asleep before we're even in Hartford and I listen to the tape myself, hearing the songs as I meant them. They were just songs I knew. Not anything else.

I read somewhere that the truly considerate traveling companion never sleeps while the other person drives, unless there's a third person to keep the driver company. Partly this is for safety, but mainly it's about being polite. This is what I think to myself as we get onto the Massachusetts Turnpike with all the other cars heading home for Thanksgiving: *We need another person to travel with.* Or maybe I just need a new passenger.

During the family dinner, Jeremy talks about film as a medium, how no one should see any film in translation.

"So we should only see movies in languages that we speak?" my father asks.

"Right," Jeremy says and I know he'll argue about anything just to hear himself talk. All the world is his personal stage.

"I mean, does it really matter if you see the Chaplin film as *Dan Les Temps Moderne* or as *Modern Times?*" I ask.

"Yes, of course it does," he says. Then I point out that it's a silent film and he sulks.

I say, "I'd rather see *Spinal Tap* or *When Harry Met Sally* again," just to annoy Jeremy further. I'd seen it in Florence and enjoyed the Italian-Jewish New Yorker voice they'd used for dubbing Billy Crystal's. It was almost as good as the ATM card advertisements on TelItalia with the Italian Woody Allen. Jeremy reminds us all again that his uncle is the Spanish Tom Cruise. This makes Jeremy feel that he and Nicole Kidman are in-laws of some kind, the kind of in-law he'd like to sleep with. Now, of course, he'd have lost the connection, what with the divorce and all.

This, and the fact that Jeremy was the first in his school to wear Vans and skateboard to class, are things I don't want to hear about anymore. Everything we did felt like a contest, who'd been the most different, the innovative one, and Jeremy had a tendency to discredit many of the stories I told, picking apart what I'd say. In August, we'd rented sailboats and I'd shown him how to steer. Later, when he told the story of that time, he'd commented on mistakes I'd made, how I'd dropped a line, forgot the way to tie off the dock line, so the knot went in the wrong direction.

"And you said you taught sailing . . ." He'd shake his head.

"I never said I taught it, I would never say that. I said I did a lot of it growing up, at camp, and on the Cape."

"Well, still, you're pretty rusty, Camp Girl." But all this he'd say with the right inflections, the actor knowing his delivery, and who-ever was around seemed to think him funny. Danny adored him and my parents were amused, if not thrilled. They liked some of what they saw, the way he helped me with my coat, offered to refill my ginger ale, and helped my father rearrange the living room for the hundredth time. But now during that weekend, my mother knows something is up. She watches Jeremy, hardly says anything to him, and lets me nap in her bed.

Later on Sunday afternoon I'm in my own blue period. Danny plays Blind Operation, his version of the board game.

"It's the *very* wacky doctor's game," Danny says with his eyes shut tight. Jeremy watches as my brother removes water on the knee without touching the sides and setting off the buzzer. Then he removes the funny bone.

"She had hers removed, too," Danny says and points to me.

Back in New York, I still listened to the tape Jeremy had retitled. Jeremy didn't want to recall his high school experience, so he had no interest in hearing my stories. He never knew that I had played "Erica's Word" nonstop the months I'd been a mother's helper on Nantucket. How, in the evenings, when the parents went out and I'd tucked the kids into their beds, I'd go out into the sandy garden and listen to the song, the lyrics slowly becoming familiar, repeat-ing each night like the waves that seemed louder in the dark.

The next morning, outside our apartment window, the sky is

the color of milk after the Fruit Loops are gone. It's the February during which I grow even worse at sleeping, so I stay up at night alternating between *Bosom Buddies* reruns and *Scooby-Doo*. I like watching Tom Hanks and the other guy dance around to "My Life" and dress up for classy about-to-be-the-eighties living, deep tan hosiery and all. And it's *Scooby-Doo* the original series, so there's no annoying little dog to contend with, just Shaggy and Scooby in their drugged-out frenzy. Just like Velma, I start to say, "Jinkies!"

The tape I make but never give to Jeremy gets only a couple of songs on it before I wonder what the hell I'm doing and stop. I title it Which Will.

Which Will

SIDE A

Which Will—Lucinda Williams's cover of a Nick Drake song
Ricochet in Time—Shawn Colvin
Love Keep Us Together—Martin Sexton
Losing Our Job—The Roches

"What're you doing?" Jeremy asks and drops his coat by the door.

"I was making a tape," I say and stare at the jacket.

"I'll pick it up later. I assume it's for me. Sweet."

"By the way," I say, "the girl you fucked called for you today. Just thought you'd want to know."

This is the only time I ever get to see Jeremy surprised. Not his birthday party two months earlier, when I drove us to the airport, passports in hand, and surprised him with a trip to Madrid, not even when I told him that I was accepted into a graduate program in California and thinking of leaving soon.

Jinkies! I think, and put the tapes away. It's a mix that never gets made or sent. It occurs to me that I don't know who it was for, anyway. Our relationship turns out to be like a bottle of medicine that's meant to be child-proof, but turns out to be just child-resistant, only with

Jeremy, fidelity's the issue. I'd found a note from the French horn player in his show and it was signed with her initial, S, and a large, XO. At the time I thought, *Jinkies! I'm being cheated on!* Trapped in my own crazy cartoon of what I imagined security felt like. I imagined that with the help of Daphne and Fred, and possibly Scooby, we could get to the bottom of this. I remember Zan and Jana, the Wonder Twins, cartoon siblings who lived at the Hall of Justice.

"Wonder Twin powers, *activate!*" they'd say.

"Form of, a bucket of water," one would say.

"Shape of, a falcon," from the other, and the bird one would pick up the bucket with its beak. I picture a sopping-wet Jeremy, an enemy, defeated, melting so that only the good, regular person underneath was left.

Back in the true safety of my girlhood room, my mother says, "I never liked him."

"Oh, Mom," I say and take the tape out of the player.

"I didn't!" she insists. "Danny thought he was funny, but I just thought he was mean."

"Well, so much for that trip down Jeremy lane," I say, trying to wrap it up.

"But what about . . . ?" My mother looks at me with her Mom expression.

"What?" I ask.

"You know what," she says with a look that tells me she was more in touch than I gave her credit for. My dad sits quietly, afraid, it occurs to me, that if he speaks he will be cast out of this explaining process.

"Give me the tapes. Hang on." I sort through and find the other tapes from then and I show her the covers, how they are not decorated, just songs listed with artists, no frills. She knows there's more. More that happened with Jeremy, more that she wasn't there for.

"Well," I say and show my parents another tape. "Marcus taped these songs for me. He was there when . . ." I stop. I have to tell them.

CHAPTER
twenty

My mother tilts her head to let me know she's concerned, interested. My father shifts around, preparing himself. "Remember that time I went to visit Marcus? In Florida? Right before that family bris?" I ask. "Well, it wasn't just for the weather." I press play and start to explain.

200,000 Miles

61,000–150,000	150 ONWARDS
Crash into June	Come Down in Time
—Game Theory	—Sting
Different for Girls	Knock You Out (unplugged)
—Joe Jackson	—L.L. Cool J
Real Love	Water of Love
—Mary J. Blige	—Dire Straits
Killer Queen	Love Rears Up Its Ugly Head
—Queen	—Living Colour
Sometimes	Love Is a Stranger
—Erasure	—Euryhthmics

This Must Be the Place
  —Talking Heads
Ojala Que Llueve Cafe
  en el Campo—?
The Ocean
  —Led Zep
Drive My Car
  —Beatles
Dreams
  —Gabrielle

The Beautiful Ones
  —Prince
Someday, Some Way
  —Marshall Crenshaw
Jennifer, Oh Jenny
  —De La Soul
Handsworth Revolution
  —Steel Pulse
D-I-V-O-R-C-E
  —Tammy Wynette

I hadn't known right away that I was pregnant. Looking back, it seems clear, of course—the fatigue, the bra that didn't fit. But I wasn't queasy yet. I had found out several days later by fluke, after I'd told Jeremy that I was leaving for good and going to California for grad school.

Shana—who'd moved to the city around Labor Day—had called with her own pregnancy scare and pleaded with me to go with her to the drugstore and buy a test. It felt like camp, like when she'd wanted to try Sun-In, to see if it would really lighten her hair *naturally*, like the package said. She'd dunked her head in the sink, sprayed on the stuff, and panicked. "You do it, too!" So I had, and my already blonde hair became see-through. Shana's turned a shade of orange, just lighter than a life preserver, and it took a year to grow it out.

Shana was still looking for work, temping until something permanent came along. Back at her place, we'd both peed and then not looked at our test sticks until three minutes had passed. Relieved, Shana smiled. I hugged her, glad for her, and then looked at mine. We'd said nothing. I left with the pregnancy test in my purse.

When I went back to my soon-to-be-vacant apartment and started packing up my stuff, I was amazed at the noises outside. Cabs slurred by, brakes high and loud, fragments of passing conversation drifted in from the hallway, pausing for a moment, stories I'd never know wholly, and then were gone. The world outside my apartment was continuing on while my whole life felt stuck on pause.

I'd wanted to call my mother, to have her come get me and make everything okay again, but I couldn't. She was home, laying low after her bone marrow transplant and I couldn't even bring myself to tell her that the only reason I'd thought about not terminating the pregnancy was so that she could hold a grandchild. I wanted her to be the Grandma Zadie I had.

So I called Marcus instead. He flew up, arranged for movers to come and collect my boxes, storing them until I went out to California. I never spoke to Jeremy, but I assume Marcus found him at the theater. Jeremy had left for work like it was a regular day, leaving me a simple note. His show would go on tour and I would go to Marcus's place in Florida and then I'd go to the family bris and then out to California for school. Jeremy would find the used EPT in the trash and say nothing.

Marcus taught at a private school in Coral Gables, and was just about outgrowing his fondness for the warm climate. A teacher friend of his there had recommended a private clinic where her father worked and I had an appointment for several days after I arrived.

"I'm almost ready for the seasons again," Marcus said when we sat outside his apartment. The sun was just sliding down into the skyline of distant condominiums and high-rises across the bay. Marcus zipped up his windbreaker.

"You're cold now?" I said more than asked. "Better toughen up." Marcus never said the same to me, and I was grateful.

Marcus and I are zooming around the loops on the Florida Turnpike, waiting for the odometer to flip. Even though the car's not the cruising kind, we've been acting like we're in a David Lee Roth video and reclining in the Volvo 260 like it's a giant limo with a pool in back. He's had the car since 61,000 miles, so we're commemorating the day by guessing what he was doing at the big mileage points, listening to the mix he made the whole time, letting it flip back over when the B side's finished.

"Well, I know at seventy-five thou' I was in Idaho, skiing and smoking too much weed," he says. "So glad those days are over."

Marcus does Ashtanga yoga now and eats a high-fiber diet. It's all part of his "get on track" approach to living out his personal ideals in his day-to-day life. He fixes the outside and then works his way in.

"It's working," I say when he asks if he looks like he's in the best shape ever.

"I know," he says. "Okay, so, eighty, eighty-five, maybe on the Cape?"

"No," I say, "that was later, because I remember we commented about being so close to one hundred when your sister visited."

"Right," he says. I can fill in the blanks of his memory date book just like Maggie can do for me. "I know for sure I had sex with Luna at ninety-three thousand."

"Charming," I say. "Why do you remember that?"

"You don't want to know," he says. He's right, I don't want the details.

"Oh," I say, "at one-ten, your parents had their anniversary party."

"Yeah," Marcus says and signals left. We're near 200,000 miles, so we head to the overpass. In the sunlight on the ramp, I can't see anything. Maybe Marcus can or maybe he can't, but it's a rush, not knowing where we're heading.

It's been two days since I've left New York. With palms and sand, it feels longer. I've been tired, though. Tan from sleeping in the sun, but my appetite has faded. I eat only ripe tomatoes sprinkled with salt. Marcus grows them in his rooftop garden along with basil, which smells so strong it makes me feel sick.

Tomorrow Marcus will drive me to the clinic. He will wait for me like the patient, sorry boyfriend and comfort me the way my real one never did. We're doing all this zooming and funny talk to avoid more tears and sallowness on my part, more anger at Jeremy from both of us, more questioning about maybe why he and I never got together for real.

After the "procedure," as we've been dubbing the abortion, Marcus has agreed to come back to Boston. He'll see his folks and meet my mother's cousin's kid's new baby at the bris I have to go to. Marcus looks forward to going north since it's home base for him.

"I'm always checking in on myself," he says. "You know, making sure to remind myself where I come from, just in case I get too into the palm tree lifestyle."

That night, we sit in the roof garden eating tomatoes like they are apples. We pass the salt shaker back and forth as needed. Seeds slip from my chin onto my bare thighs.

"I think," Marcus says, "that Jeremy was a fucking idiot."

"Was he?" I ask. "Or is he still?"

"Forever to dwell in the land of the idiots. And assholes."

"Thank you," I say.

"Hey," Marcus says when we're walking to the beach in the dark, "I just remembered where I was at one hundred sixty thousand."

"I'm ready," I say.

"So, Prince is playing, 'The Beautiful Ones.' *Baby, baby, bayyy-bee!* Anyway, and I was at this whacked-out party. Picture it—me, a hot tub, and two girls."

"Marcus, that's the song. You know, Prince says, 'Is the water ready?' Or 'Yes, Nikki,' or whatever. He takes a hot tub or a bath with Darling Nikki or something."

"Crap," Marcus says. "I think you're right. Somehow, that became *my* memory for that song. Bummer."

"Isn't that funny? It's like I knew this girl, Carrie Lowenstein, and she told me this story of how she lost her virginity on New Year's Eve to this jerky guy. Afterward, the U2 song 'New Year's Day' was playing. Now, whenever I hear that song, I think of *her* thinking of that."

"And what makes you think of me?" Marcus asks. He takes my

hand at this point and we sit on the cool sand. It would be dark around us, but the lights from the restaurants and bars and nearby boat launches make the waves glow.

" 'Babylon Sisters,' I guess," I say. "But I don't know why."

"Maybe it's better not to know why," he says. Marcus's hand slips naturally into mine. We're not romantic, not platonic—we've just always been. A couple walks by and nods at us in that communal coupley way. How settled and happy we must look, the tall guy, the tan, blonde girl, cross-legged on the sand at night. How disparate image and reality can be. Like at my grandmother's funeral, people kept coming up to my mother and commenting on how lovely my mother looked. I try to get into that other couple's frame of reference, but cannot.

Back at Marcus's is when in another lifetime we would have kissed. I'm lying on my pregnant stomach, sad, on his bed. He's propped up against the bed. We look at each other, letting our noses touch. If only we had it—the *thing*, the song that makes everything fit between two people—maybe it would turn out differently. But it doesn't. The wind knocks over one of the tomato plants on the deck, dirt spills onto the terracotta tiles, and the moment is gone, gone, gone, carried out the screen door, over the balcony, and out to the ocean forever.

Songs for Sad Jews

SIDE ONE

Jamaica Say You Will
—Jackson Browne
Same Old Lang Syne
—Dan Fogelberg
The Lost Children
—The Samples
I Loves You, Porgy
—*Porgy and Bess*

SIDE TWO

Stranger in a Strange Land
—Leon Russell
Someone Saved My Life
Tonight—Elton John
An American Tune
—Simon and Garfunkel
At a Better Time (You
Couldn't Have Come)—?

Songs to Aging Children
  Come—Joni
Scandinavia
  —Van Morrison
Don't Let Him Steal Your
  Heart Away—Phil Collins
Emma's Theme—from *Terms*
  of Endearment
Cello Sonata in G Minor
  —Beethoven

April Come She Will
  —S and G
Dogs in the Yard
  —from *Fame*
Empty Pages
  —Traffic
Wish I Could Stand or
  Have—Game Theory
C'est Le Vent, Betty—
  From *Betty Blue*
Ocean Drive
  —Lighthouse Family

Just before the circumcision, Marcus leans in and whispers, "Love Shack." The scent of Manischewitz puffs from his mouth, indistinguishable from the actual taste in mine. I laugh as I picture the mohel, the baby, everyone in a film image as the B-52s "bang, bang, bang" in the background.

Since we were fifteen—okay, he was fifteen, I was almost fourteen—Marcus and I have tried to pick the least appropriate song to match the moment. No time is exempt. High school graduation, "I Shot the Sheriff." Barfing into the coolest senior girl's L.L. Bean blucher shoe, "Band on the Run." Gruesome news report of a train wreck, "Mary Had a Little Lamb." His sister's wedding, "Mister Bojangles." The song isn't just the opposite of what's happening—it's not like your first kiss set to the tune of "Keep Your Hands to Yourself" or "Lips Like Sugar"—you want actual non sequitur, nonsensical, the *huh?* Like, your first sex while Kermit's twanging "Being Green." Pretty soon, any song can pick up irony, so you make the connection between ironing a shirt and "I Still Haven't Found What I'm Looking For."

The baby is placated with wine dripped from his father's finger and the random cousin I hardly know comes over to offer delicate triangle cookies. Marcus smiles as he bites into one—I know he's got the inevitable penis jokes stored up in his head, but even he can hold back.

"So, what are you up to nowadays? Isn't that a good cookie? Oh, the baby's crying, but isn't Lauren so lucky to have such a handsome man?" The cousin I hardly know because she's not my cousin, but my father's cousin's kid, asks so many questions at once that I can pick the easiest and reply without seeming to dodge the others. This could be the worst day of my life—aside from the day I found out my mother was sick.

"These cookies are *so* good," I say with the emphasis on *so* that we would have had in seventh grade, with extra *o*'s, possibly underlined. I hope that no one but Marcus can tell that I am riddled with pain and sad enough to want to fall to the ground, to curl up my empty self, my empty abdomen, and just wail. But I don't.

"Especially with the Mani," Marcus kicks in, taking a sip, always able to abbreviate the unabbreviatable without annoying people. With a look from me, he goes on, a rapid blather to facilitate my silence:

"Cookies and wine. You don't get to do that very often, you know? Maybe in Italy, with biscotti, but not here, really. You don't mix Toll House with Pinot Grigio. But you could. We could play a game—which cookie suggests which liquor or wine—Mallomars and Cabernet Sauvignon. Milanos with . . . something crisp."

Marcus can fill any gap with words or music. No weird times at introductions, no unused moments during his haircuts. He doesn't tire of small talk and makes lists, games, and songs with whatever he wants. Most of the time this is good. When we bumped into the girl who was so mean to me in fifth grade, Marcus was right there with some anecdote about getting stuck in the clothes drier with his niece. At his uncle's commitment ceremony, he had no loss of clever things to talk about. But when my Grandmother Zadie finally died of pancreatic cancer, in the midst of her own daughter's radiation therapy, I called Marcus, unable to say more than, "I'm still sad. Just so sad." Marcus proceeded to launch into his mystical crystals-and-light crap, with talk of spir-

its and everything for a reason and she's better off—I had to cut
him off with:

"Marcus, that's such bullshit."

"Yeah. I know." And then he went on and said how nice my
grandma was and how he loved her kugel and how she taught him
to dry roses once and then he cried.

When I tune back in, Marcus is saying, "Well, Prince is clearly the
Mozart of our generation."

The cousin tries to ask pertinent questions of me while Marcus
finishes his cup of wine. They're the clear plastic ones that come in
two parts, one stem, one cup. Marcus has taken the base off from
his and holds the rest like it's a baseball.

"Oops, all gone," he says and, smiling at the cousin, pulls me
past the table of bagels and lox, past my father, and into the powder room. All in all, a good move since, when the cousin asked me
what I had been up to recently, all I could come up with in my
head was, *Well, I got an abortion two days ago. That's something.*
What song went unheard there?

Marcus locks the door and hefts himself onto the counter.

"Hey," he says, "my ass is almost exactly the size of this sink."

I manage a laugh and then start bawling.

"I can't go out there again," I say and I don't know whether I
mean to the bris or into the world, into the world of love and
muck and rejection and loss. Marcus tries to hug me with his
knees. His arms reach partway around my back, but Marcus is
wedged into the sink, so I lean farther in.

"Okay, now?"

"Better." I nod.

He's so strong and wide, Marcus can envelop me until I feel
like a marble.

Marcus was built differently than Jeremy. Jeremy is five foot eight,
but wiry, so he seems smaller. Lean and strong, yes—comforting,
not really. He made me feel big. Jeremy and I fit better when I was

around him, his back to my chest. In the movie, I was the guy. He fell asleep first, always. I was stuck there, half pleased by the way his smooth shoulder felt on my lower lip, the other half wanting to get out of bed to read or watch *Family Ties* reruns.

I picture Jeremy on the road. By now he's probably in Atlanta, the one "real" city on the tour. *Orchestra of Evil* was hitting all the places you'd expect: Hartford, Bangor, Yonkers, Somewhere in Delaware—the list goes on. The cast would probably stay in a Comfort Inn or its rival. Jeremy wavers between thinking this is the height of cool—"I mean, I am an employed actor! I get food vouchers!"—and telling me how strong he will be for surviving life on the road—"I mean, eighteen cities in six weeks—and no one intelligent to talk to—no one even knows who wrote *Look Back in Anger!*"

Jeremy was forever bringing up that play. When we first met, I thought his casual reference suggested that this was one of the many plays he had studied. Later, it became clear that it was like his guitar playing. He knew exactly three and one half songs. The half was so that he could try to play and say, "I'm working on getting this one down" to whoever happened to be listening. He'd play the blues version of "Bye-bye, Blackbird," which made me swirl inside, filled with longing, the melancholy that comes when you just want to go home.

Jeremy would bring up Osbourne's *Look Back in Anger* because the play allowed him to say to people who haven't heard of the play, "Really? I'm surprised you're not familiar with it. It's *the* 1950s British 'kitchen sink' drama—without it, there'd be no theater as we know it today."

Jeremy hadn't been genuine, I knew that, but I'd loved Zelda, Jeremy's mother. Shaped like an enlarged raisin, she was so warm, slightly detached from Jeremy as if aware of Jeremy's half-learned songs, of his smugness. With her long, thick braid undone, her curls had spilled over her batik T-shirt, the brown coils draping over her clear green eyes until she'd gather up a mass of it and rope it off, knotting it back onto itself. Zelda had been a corporate lawyer who'd left Manhattan for small-town Rhode Island. She seemed at once out of place and part of it all. She'd taken me to the abandoned winter beach to collect driftwood that we'd later painted and put hooks in for a makeshift coat rack I still owned.

I'd brought the piece back to Cambridge to show my father after a weekend with Jeremy and his parents, and when my mother had seen it, she'd gone quietly upstairs to her room. I'd watched the tiny bounce of my mother's curls as she walked away. Her hair had been long enough only for one trim when she relapsed for the third time, and upstairs, I am sure now that she waited both for a stranger's bone marrow to replace her own and for me to return to her.

Look Back in Anger ends with the main character, Alison, saying to Jimmy, "Poor bears." This is how I became "Beary" to Jeremy. Sometimes, just B. I got cozy with the nickname until right after he shouted for me, "Hey, Beary!" right into the ear of the New Stage's respected director. I made my way back through the sweaty actorfest near the bar, only to find Jeremy in animated mode, telling the story of the name to the director, who was busy looking at some understudy in leather pants.

But the name continued, even on the last note he left for me before I left the apartment and his life for good:

> B—
>   *Hope this note finds you well and happy when you wake up. I'll think of you and miss you.*
>   *I love you to pieces, Jer.*
>   *PS If anyone calls for me, can you give them the itinerary for the show? They probably will want to meet up with us wherever we are. Thanks.*

I think Jeremy has the idea that he will be tracked like the Grateful Dead, that the word is out and his nonfamous days are over. I don't know what's ahead for him—all I'm sure of is the part of him that really did, as his note said, love me to pieces.

*   *   *

In the bathroom at the bris, Marcus begins to hum "Eye of the Tiger"—or, more accurately, not hum, but do the "buh, duhduh-duh, bumbum-BAH" part at the beginning. I back up and pretend to box his hands. Out the window, there are small drifts of snow scattered, collections of what will most likely be the last snowfall of the season. The late March muck just around the corner.

While Marcus pees, I rummage through the medicine chest for Advil. The pills are found and swallowed. The skin around my hairline is flaking and itchy and is now a jagged line of pink, the sunrise around my still-tanned face. Marcus washes his hands with a soap in the shape of a scallop shell. In his palm, the soap is dwarfed, embryonic.

Back in the bris crowds, I stand by my mother's side while Marcus heads for the lox and bagels. Talking to my mother are old friends of the family, Dr. and Mrs. Reitz, better known to us as Harry and Jean.

As my mother speaks to Jean, I watch her animated movements. Jean and Harry always make my mother seem more Jewish. More Jewish in the way my parents are not. Somehow, with a good mix of atheism, shyness, and my mother's European sensibilities, we are all Jewish-in-the-WASPy tradition. In college, this seemed sophisticated to me, the Elegant Jew. But today, it doesn't seem fair.

Jean Reitz doesn't take even one bite of her knish, as though this will distract from the fact that she is giantly overweight. My mother's small frame seems ridiculous next to Jean's, as if they come from separate species. Harry meets my gaze and says, "Hey, kiddo, you okay?"

Harry still gets away with expressions like "kiddo." I nod. Harry takes a closer look at my face and tilts his head like that dog on the RCA label.

"What's going on, Laney?"

And I almost lose it. It's like people from my past can see right inside the tiniest lint speck of longing or loss. I'm so close to letting myself cry in the middle of the laughing and talking around us. But I lick my lips and bite a bit of dry skin on the bottom one and do that face where I raise my eyebrows and turn the corners of my mouth down.

"Not too much, really." I cope. Harry doesn't push for more, but I feel that he knows. But that's most likely just me, and really he couldn't have less of a clue, be further from the twisting that's going on in my gut.

My mother and I go to congratulate the parents and kiss the baby. On the way over, my mother refers to the mohel as "the butcher" and it's hard to tell if she's made a joke or being forgetful, the ongoing side effects of her radiation seem to be memory loss and a cough that cracks out of her chest every couple of minutes. There's a side to my mother that comes out when she's around old friends that makes it easier to imagine her at camp, sleeping in a bunk, with no duvet and no special moisturizer to slather on at night.

My mother holds the random cousin's cousin's baby. And then insists on arranging the baby's head in the crook of my arm. I stare at the tiny chin and mouth as he does his baby yawn. I watch my mother watching me.

Then I say, too loud, "No. No—Mom—take it. Take him." And hand the baby over to its rightful owner.

Later, my mother steps aside to freshen her lipstick. Using the hallway mirror, out of sight from the gathering, my mother shapes her mouth like a slice of melon and draws it shimmery brown. I seem to be clinging to her side, but unable to tell her why.

"What do you think?" she asks. "It's new. Bobbi Brown."

"Nice," I say. And count the seconds until my mother asks if I want to have it.

Instead my mother holds my shoulders and says, "You *will* have a baby someday." She pauses and I wonder if this is just her response to me and Jeremy breaking up or if she knows about the abortion. "And when you do, you will have everything to give."

I am annoyed in the way you can only be when what you hear is right. But it is too soon for stating what I know, and have known—that *Angel Mourning,* the painting I have been working on at the museum, is completely cleaned and rehabbed, that Jeremy is gone, that I am empty-wombd and ready for otherness.

My father, who missed that interchange, stands near the bathroom. He wipes his eyes and leaves his arms at his side, asking mutely for a hug. He misses his father, who has been gone now for just over two months. Unlike Zadie, who had suffered and withered, shrinking in her slim cotton dresses until the belt hung like a hula hoop, Papa Hen had gone in an instant, right on the dock in town on the Cape, fishing line already set up and baited. When my dad and I had gone to collect the rod and drop lines, the town official had given us not only Papa Hen's rod and drop lines, but the fish Papa Hen had hooked minutes before. I held it, the firm slippery ooze of it, and then gave it to my dad, who slicked his hands on the thing's scales as if it were clay, as if he could make it into something new.

In the hallway my dad cries softly to me, "He won't get to know your babies." He's mushed together Papa Hen's death and my mother's nearness to it. His words resonate too much for me, so I cry, too. There's such ferocious sadness here, the walls don't seem able to hold it all. I picture them falling flat, like they're a set, facades we can change at will.

Out in front of the house, Marcus makes a big, flat handprint on his snowy windshield.

"Don't even think of putting that down my back," I say as he gathers some snow and forms it into a miniature snowball. I tell him how I'm glad he came, how much it means to me, that I'm feeling better.

"Laney," he says, "I'm better just because you're in this world." At another time I would have made some joke about crystals and New Age spells, but today I give in. He says just what I want to hear. He drives away into the soft already-dark afternoon and I stand rubbing my arms for warmth, which only leaves me colder when I stop. Then I make my own hard snowball. The snow is so wet and heavy that the small ball molds to the shape of my curled fist, shows each line of my palm, each of the ridges between my fingers. I have no one to throw it to.

Back in my room, the digital clock reads nearly 1:00 A.M. I am exhausted, I realize, and my mom and dad must be, too. The tape is nearly finished, at the tiny place with no music, just scratchy unrecordedness. When I look at my mother, she is crying.

"I knew at Thanksgiving," she said. "You already looked different—and I wanted to tell you that I knew, but I was too scared—and I'd missed so much already, I thought you'd be more angry if I'd tried to help you. You weren't exactly open with me at that time."

"I really needed you then. More than ever, I think." I cry, too. But not for what I went through, but that I went through it unmothered.

"Well, I had no clue," my father says, twisting so his back cracks. He means this in a serious way, but it strikes me as funny. We all start laughing and then I wind up wheezing from my guffaw.

"What else did I miss on this cross-country trip?" my father asks. He stands up. "I'll leave you girls to it." Halfway out he adds, "Love you, Lanes."

"Mom," I say, now that the story's out. "I do really look forward to being pregnant someday. And having you as a part of it."

I quickly picture shopping for oversize T-shirts with her, hearing how salty crackers help with the nausea, or my mother buying tiny white all-in-ones for whoever would grow inside me.

"You know, Laney," she says, sighing, "I'm just glad you got through that time without building up so much scar tissue that you couldn't move on."

We hug and she moves her arm across my back.

"Thanks, Mom," I say.

"You know that shirt you were talking about before? The one

from Vermont that you remember so well?" she asks. "The reason you have it in your mind as one I wore all the time is because I did wear it, almost every day for about five months. When I was pregnant in Vermont." She pauses and waits for my mind to catch up to her words.

"When was this?" I ask.

"That winter with the blizzard. You and Danny jumped off the barn and into those snow piles. I worried you'd get stuck in there, but you didn't."

The barn had a low, sloping side that lead right into the snow heaves. After we'd jump, we'd free our legs, do a half roll, half fall down the rest of the pile, and walk back into the barn to come out the hay door and start over again. I think about the rustle of my snowpants, my legs rubbing against each other, and the mugs of snow we'd taken inside so my mother could drizzle maple syrup on for a treat. My dad loaded up the wood-burning stove and we'd sat around in long underwear talking about weather. Meanwhile, I had no idea that under the soft shirt my mother was growing a whole other person.

"Anyway," she continues, "it was obviously a totally different situation from yours. But your father was very happy with just you and Danny. And me, of course. We all were happy. And so when I found out I was pregnant, very much by surprise, I got excited."

"And Dad?"

"He was . . . less so. In fact, he wasn't thrilled. His pottery was beginning to do well—you remember that award and the newspaper thing—so he wasn't up for another round of changing diapers and feedings at all hours, not to mention babyproofing the house and his shed."

"Did he want you to get—"

"No. He never mentioned abortion and neither did I. It was just something he had to get used to. Except, then we did, and we got a little excited. And then I miscarried. Quite late. I never knew why exactly. I'm sure now they'd know more, but this was the local hospital and a long time ago."

"And you wore Daddy's shirt as a maternity shirt."

"Yes."

"Oh, Mom. I am so sorry."

"We never told you kids because Danny was too young, and you were . . ."

"What?"

"You were just so sensitive. I worried you wouldn't get over it. And then we moved and things just changed."

I think about how what she's said is true, but maybe instead of not getting over bad events, I've just breezed past them, pushing them into the past. Maybe if my parents hadn't tried to protect me early on, I would have been clear about what or how to feel.

"I don't want to be so sensitive now," I say. "I want you to tell me things when they happen."

"We will, we do," she says. "I know now you can handle it."

My mother stands up and brushes herself off as if we've been weeding. She is ready for bed. When she leaves, I picture her watching us out the window in Vermont, watching her children jump, soar like unwinged angels into the whitest snow.

CHAPTER
twenty-one

A week or so later, I find an apartment that's cheap enough to buy. It's the first floor of a three-story row house in West Cambridge, far enough from my parents, but close enough, too.

While I pack up the rest of my things at home, my father comes into my room and seems taller than I remember. I say this to him.

"Well, that makes a certain degree of sense, since you're sitting on the floor. Or maybe you're just smaller than you realize." He sits near me, looking at the various piles I've constructed of my paintings.

"More summer cleaning?" he asks.

"I guess," I say. "It's the second phase of trying to get my things in order here." I can't decide how to categorize them—chronologically, or by color or theme, by size, even. It's the end of summer. The days have blended, a mix of reading, of using thick Magic Markers to label things for the short move over to my new place, of painting the living room of my about-to-be-lived-in apartment while the rest of the apartment gets fixed up—no big renovation, just basics, like plumbing.

I got a good deal on a place that needed to be updated. The orange tiles in the kitchen were rimmed in a green sludge, the bathroom didn't work at all, and there hadn't been a door to the bedroom except from the outside. Soon I know it will be ready and then I can retrieve my boxes from storage and unpack for good.

My dad and I spend most of a weekend in his shed, painting square tiles to take the place of the 1960s remnants in my new kitchen and bathroom. He mixes glazes and comes up with a brand-new color, a nonexistent fruit color we call blasberry for its blue core and bright red edging. Later, I add tiles painted with bright lemon and lime colors, and my dad's vision grows as he imagines tiling more and more. Of course, in a couple of years, the tiles will be available in the Ceramics Shack summer catalogue, but I don't mind.

"Want me to take a load of stuff over for you?" my dad asks. I nod. Dad says, "I have some papers to look at, but I'll take a run over with you in an hour or so."

"Sure," I say. I look at my watch and do the time change—too early to call Maggie in Los Angeles. Too late to call Casey in London. I haven't told them yet about how well my mom is. I knew they'd be so happy, so relieved. So amazed at all the stuff I'd told her on the trip and after being home. I know who would be happiest, though. Shana.

After we move boxes, my dad and I sit in his pickup truck, and he asks me about work, if I am looking forward to it, about dating and who I could meet, and how I feel about Mom.

"Good," I say.

"She loved your trip, you know."

I nod, watching my dad fiddle with the various switches and clickers on the truck's dash.

"I think part of me is jealous of your time together. It's like she knows all these things about you that I don't."

"Don't be jealous, Dad. Think how much she missed out on— college graduation, shopping for that ugly prom dress . . ."

"It really was ugly, wasn't it?" My dad laughs.

"Terribly," I say.

"But I thought you looked beautiful," he says.

In the fading afternoon light, I think what a balance my parents are, but how unbalanced they must have become with her illness, how being away from it I couldn't imagine the damages and reparations they had to get through.

Two days later, when the plasterers are patching up my apartment, I'm sitting at my parents' breakfast table.

"Are you still living here?" Danny asks me when he comes in the kitchen screen door and takes a bite of my toast without asking.

"Are you still a doofus?" I ask.

"Are you?" he says.

"Great comeback," I say. "Are you sure you're an actual doctor?"

"Only just," he says. His residency has started, so he's a walking mess of sleep-deprived nerves, but in the Danny way. If you ask him if things are difficult, he says, "Nah. Not really. Challenging, maybe, but not hard."

Outside, our parents pull weeds from the muddy rows of soon-to-sprout flowers. Danny watches them, my mother particularly, and he asks me, "How's she doing, do you think?"

"Really great," I say. "Have you heard the latest? They're thinking of building a pool here."

"Hey," Danny says, "that'd be great! I could be, like, the young doctor with a swinging pad."

"Um, yeah, until you lure some other young, sleep-deprived person back here and they find Mom and Dad making out in the shallow end or something."

"Gross," Danny says, instantly fifteen.

"Anyway," I continue, "the last of my plumbing issues should be fixed this week."

"Hey—I don't want to know about your *plumbing* issues, ha-ha," Danny interrupts.

"Anyway," I say as if I hadn't heard his attempts at ten-year-old boy humor, "work started, and I'm kind of ready to settle in at my place. You think you might—"

"Sure," Danny says, interrupting. "I have no social life and I'm all about heavy lifting. How is work, anyway? You've hardly mentioned it."

"Yeah," I say. We're in the cleaning phase of restoring a large oil, a shipwreck. And though I've loved refurbishing before, loved using tiny brushes to clear away debris and dirt, I find myself distracted. I say, "Maybe I'm just in summer mode, Danny, but I feel a little—I don't know—bored?"

He nods and shrugs. "Maybe it's not enough anymore."

"But I only just started," I say. "I just finished my degree."

"Nah." Danny shakes his head. "You've been trying to repair things forever." We smile. He looks at a wedding photograph of my parents that sits in the middle of the table. "What's this doing here?" It's usually in the study.

"They're getting things reframed—you know—part of the life celebration or whatever," I say.

"Speaking of weddings," Danny says, "isn't it time for your friend Marcus to walk down the aisle?" He raises his eyebrows at me, like his question will inspire me to admit I'm freaked out. Which maybe I am.

"Two weeks," I say. "And by the way, I'm totally fine about it, if that's what you mean to imply."

"I'm not implying anything," Danny says. "You were inferring." He taps his temple to show me. "Brains. That's right, folks, I gots the brains."

"You gots nothing," I say.

"At least I have a date for the wedding," he says. And when I'm surprised he adds, "What? You didn't think your dork-ass brother could get a date or you didn't know Marcus invited me? He always thought I was cool. Or at least he pretended to."

I don't say anything, I just shake my head and dramatically mope, putting my head in my hands. Even my brother will have

someone to dance with while I'll be the one all alone at the ceremony, staring at a girl who got one of the best guys around.
Suddenly it occurs to me that maybe Marcus invited Danny to the
wedding so I'd have some company, some support, my brother as
my escort, even.

"You gotta get a date, dude," Danny says and shoves a piece of
bread into his mouth.

"Yeah, dude, you're right," I say imitating his frat-boy tone, but
I know what I need to do.

I FedEx Shana a mix and make the cover out of an old camp photo
I'd dug up in my cleaning. In the picture, she has her arm around
my shoulder. It's the Sun-In summer and very blonde-orange, very
smiley, very young. I use a pen to draw in one of those cheesy broken friendship heart necklaces—half a heart for her, half for me. I
figure it's the only symbol she won't resent, that she might find
funny, like the way we'd once tried on the ugliest prom dresses we
could find and complimented each other as we paraded around
the store, inventing boyfriends for prom dates with names like
Blair and Chase Morgananofovitz III. I write, *I miss you Shana—
pretty one—Love, Laney (aka the tattletale).* Then I wait.

It's Your Tape—You Name It

SIDE A	SIDE B
The Sun's Gonna Shine—	I'm Down
Ray Charles	—The Beatles
Sooner or Later (One of Us	Rock 'n' Roll
Must Know)—Dylan	—VU
Walkin' After Midnight	No Surprises
—Patsy Cline	—Radiohead
Broken Arrow	Life: How to Live It
—Neil Young	—R.E.M.

Dear Old Stockholm
  —Coltrane
Any World
  —Steely Dan
If You Ever Did Believe
  —Stevie Nicks
  & Sheryl Crow
Take Five
  —Dave Brubeck
Suzanne
  —Leonard Cohen
I'm Just a Lucky So and So
  —Louis and Duke

Positively 4th Street
  —Dylan
Gypsy
  —Suzanne Vega
Circles
  —Soul Coughing
Mother
  —John Lennon
Cedar Hill
  —David Grisman
Ain't Life a Brook
  —Ferron

Late August moves in, kicking deep green into the wide leaves, bringing halter tops and sandals out from my still-unpacked boxes. I go to work and let my gloved hands wave in the muck and cleaning fluid while I think about my summer. I feel released, freed from my tape-and-snapshot–filled past, the lurk of memories and distance. My days feel fuller now than before, even though I'm not doing all that much, even though I'm alone.

The museum doors are so grand, I'm surprised most mornings on my way to work that there's not a giant metal lion to guard them, or at least one of those Beefeater Gin guys, dressed in ballooning knickers, ready to say, "Halt." Sometimes the lions make me think of Trafalgar Square and the way Ben and Jamie had posed on them. For the first time ever since his death, since my mom got sick, I can think of Ben and smile. Maybe it's not just my mom who has a decent prognosis. Maybe I do, too.

I hold the phone to my ear and hear, "You suck!" and this makes me happy because I know only Shana would start this way.

"Yup," I say. I think about feeling the need to defend Shana to Kyle and think now, as my adult self, that I only acted out of my own discomfort. That had I stepped back and thought about it, Shana was just experimenting—only instead of drugs or sleeping with her teacher, she was lying about where she came from to see if it might change where she wound up. And maybe that's just what I'd done with my mother's illness. I'd used it as the reason not to do things, to push away what I wanted, what I needed.

"So do I." Shana is crying, softly, but I can tell. I know she's probably using her sleeve as a tissue, sticking a finger into the hem of whatever shirt she's wearing to wipe at smearing eyeliner. Then I remember it's summer and hot and maybe she's in a tank top and I get sad thinking of her sitting dripping goop with nothing to wipe on.

"Are you raccoon-eyeing?" I ask.

"It's okay," Shana says, "I have air-conditioning and long sleeves." We sigh a minute and then Shana says, "I love the tape."

"You don't think I'm a total freak show loser for mailing you a tape when I'm thirty years old?"

"Actually, it's what got me to open the package. I might have waited on a regular letter, but how can you resist that rectangle shape, you know? I'm so glad about your mom. She's so lucky."

"What do you mean?" I ask. "I'm so lucky."

"No, she is. She gets to hang out with you for years to come. I was beginning to wonder if I'd lost my chance."

We talk for an hour more about my mother, about the trip, about Shana's most recent breakup, about camp and being sorry. And then:

"You know I need you now, right?" I ask. "I mean, I'll always need you, but—listen, you understand that I need the best date ever for Marcus's wedding . . ." I trail off, but Shana doesn't say anything. I begin to panic. "So will you do it?" I ask. "Please?"

"Of course," she says finally. "But only on the condition that you come to New York this weekend and help me celebrate the end of another bad dating situation. Oh—and help me figure out what to wear!" She laughs. "If I'm going to be your date for this guy's wedding, I'm damn well going to look incredible."

"I'll take a shuttle on Friday," I say.

"I'll be a good date," she says. "Besides, you never know who you might meet at a wedding."

"Whom," I correct.

"You need help." Shana laughs.

In New York City, Shana's just been dumped, so we listen to her breakup mix as we get ready to go out. She hands me the case and I can't help but shake my head and laugh at her title and the fact she still can't accurately identify bands or song titles. Rarely does Shana remember who sings what, but she loves all kinds of music, so she's always open to new stuff.

Screw You and the Horse You Rode in On

SIDE ONE	SIDE TWO
Sleep to Dream —Fiona Apple	I'm So Happy I Can't Stop Crying—Sting
Outta Me, Onto You —Ani DiFranco	That's Just What You Are —Aimee Mann
Jane Says —Jane's Addiction	Sweet Ride —(can't remember)
Return to Innocence —Enigma	The House that Jack Built —Aretha
Ain't So Easy —David and David	Who Are You —The Who
When We Found Love —(A band in L.A. whose name escapes me now)	Ladder —Joan Osbourne

Fuck and Run
  —Liz Phair
Sort-of Fairy Tale
  —Tori Amos
Flying Cowboys
  —Ricki Lee Jones (live)

Jimi Thing
  —Dave Matthews
Love Her Madly
  —The Doors
Back to Life
  —Soul to Soul
Never Going Back Again
  —Fleet. Mac
Reverie—DeBussey (that looks
  so wrong, is that how you
  spell his name?)

Some eighties band that used to sell out stadiums is playing in a small bar downtown, and we're going, even though it's kind of depressing.

"Every breakup comes with it's own music, so I just make the tape for it," Shana explains for the hundredth time in our friendship as she presses play.

"I really missed you!" I say.

Shana makes a little girl sad face and says, "Me, too. But—we're back!" She holds her arms up like Bette Midler doing a show and grabs mine like we're doing an encore and we bow. Shana shows me a picture of the latest and not-greatest breakup. Shana likes to date the less-cool identical twin from a set. This breakup is her third twin.

"Maybe that's enough," I say, looking at the photo.

"Enough what?" she asks.

"Twins," I say. "Maybe you'll meet some hot nontwin at Marcus's wedding."

Shana's theory is that there's always a less-cool twin in identical sets. Shana's best friend from Shaker Heights is the cool girl twin, who backs her up on this. With relationships, Shana's explained to me, people want to be with someone who knows themselves. And twins are with a reflection of themselves all the time. But the not-as-cool one knows that they're the odd one out, that their smile's not as straight, that the cowlick doesn't make their hair do that neat thing like it does on the other one.

"You dated a twin," Shana reminds me.

"True," I say. I smile. He was so sweet. A swimmer, with the smoothest skin ever and a lovely laugh I can still hear when I try.

"So, was he the cool one or the uncool?" Shana asks, squirting a mound of mousse into her hair. "Look, it has glitter!" She rubs the foam in.

"I'll never tell," I say. "You know, you look more like you did at camp right now than you did when you were at camp."

She's going for it with the 1980s aesthetic tonight, wearing electric blue mascara and mousse. She works in retail and uses her in-store discount each month. It's hard to tell, sometimes, if what she's wearing really is from the past, like her floral three-tiered Laura Ashley skirts, or new retro.

"I know!" She shrieks. "And I still love Wham!" Antithetically, she sings a line from the Jane's Addiction song and then interrupts herself with, "Hey, maybe I should wear a fedora to the wedding? Very Carly Simon, no?" She's wearing a black zip-up boot on one foot and a shoe that looks like it comes with an orthopedic prescription on the other.

"Sure," I say and give a thumbs-up to the booted foot. "That way Marcus can make jokes about you to Rachel before they've even said their *I dos.*"

"Hey—Rachel seems cool enough, she might be able to appreciate my style," Shana says. Then she looks at herself in the mirror and pulls at her bangs so they cover one eye. "Or—maybe *you'll* meet someone at Marcus's wedding! You must be panicked, though," she says. "Or are you just resigned to the fact that your backup boy won't be yours anymore."

"I guess I'm okay about it. I feel weird—not sad exactly, but something. It's not like we ever dated, it's not like he's an ex," I say, fiddling with the tape case. "Which is maybe why it's so bizarre. He's still going to be my friend, but he's not exactly who I'd call in the middle of the night if I needed someone."

"Well, you'll always have me," Shana says. "Even if you tell everyone I'm the biggest Jew that roamed the earth. The elephant Jewess. The wooly mammoth of the chosen people."

"I get it," I say and smile.

"And I promise, promise, promise—I will never take a tape of yours again. And I won't get in the way of your true love next time. I'll only help!"

In the cab, Shana digs through her big purse to find lip gloss and I watch the whizzing red of the just-turning lights.

Shana's recently read an article or seen a talk show, she can't remember which, about body language. She tells me how the expert said you're supposed to mimic the body language of the person you're attracted to, breathe when they breathe, hold your head to the side, if that's what they're doing.

"And this would accomplish what, exactly?" I ask.

"It makes the person like you more," she says.

"Oh," I say.

We go into the bar and order drinks. After we've been talking to the two guys sitting to our left for a while, the band starts. We sway and listen to songs that make me think of Shana, which is convenient since she's next to me. She watches Smiths T-Shirt Guy, the one she clearly likes. I know this not because we're old friends and I know her type, or because Smiths T-Shirt Guy is so stunning anyone would be interested, but because Shana mirrors his every move. First, she times in with his breathing, then when STS Guy touches his face, she does the same; his hand through his hair, she slips hers through her sticky moussed hair, too. Soon, they are a secretly synchronized swim performance.

But it works, or something does, and they make out while "Crazy for You" plays on the speakers during the band's break. Shana leaves with Jack's (STS Guy's) number on her hand. In the cab, he watches us go and Shana puts her palm against the window, so Jack sees his own number showing back at him and Shana blows him a kiss.

"Great," I say, "that's a wrap."

"I know!" Shana says. "I just made my own music video."

CHAPTER
twenty-two

The rabbi is under the huppa and I think, *"Cool Rider" from Grease 2.* Maybe that's the song that doesn't go with this. For a minute, I imagine Michelle Pfeiffer decked out in her tight satin ensemble, waiting for her Motorcycle Guy to come get her.

"I wish I could dance with John Travolta in that tilty box," I whisper to Shana, suddenly switching myself to the classier Olivia Newton-John as Sandy in *Grease.*

"Totally." She knows just what I mean. "Maybe there's a looka-like on the bride's side."

"She went to Penn," I say and this clarifies the situation, thinking that it's ironic that Marcus is marrying someone from the school he claimed more than once had the "least attractive women ever. Except Yale."

"But Marcus went to Brown, so that should even it out, right?" We take turns being not very subtle as we look to find cute wedding guests. I catch my brother Danny's eye and he gives me a giant exaggerated wave and gasps like we haven't seen each other in years. An old joke of ours, but one I find both embarrassing and endearing on this occasion.

"Hey," I say and grin at Shana, "there appears to be a plethora of dashing men I vaguely recognize from my one drunken visit to Brown, though it is hard to see from here."

We're near the front, so we have to crane around to see everyone in back. We can only pretend to look for the bride or other guests for so long before we have to sit frontways and be mature. Then the music starts and I start to cry. Shana hands me a tissue before the first tear's even out.

"You're the best date ever," I say as the bride and groom meet under the huppa. I realize what it is that I feel—not sad about losing Marcus, because I know we'll always have our shared history—but confused, like if it's not Marcus that I end up with, who else could it be? Who could I possibly meet that I'd have enough in common with, who could make me laugh, who knew music and would understand me? Maybe I spent so long—too long—assuming the rug would be pulled out from under me that I never bothered to consider the other side. That I might find happiness or fun or security. That maybe I'd find myself under the huppa, under the tallis my grandfather had worn, and stand saying vows with my mother there to witness.

The wedding music starts and Rachel Block, soon to be Mrs. Marcus Feldberg-Block, does the snail ooze bride walk down the aisle.

"Dum-dum-da-dum!" Shana hums along.

"Shh!" I say and nudge her. And then I consider for a second. "If you change the beat a little, this music could sound like the theme to *Jaws.*" Shana bears her teeth and puts her hand to her head like she's sprouted a fin.

"Do you wish you were up there with him?" Shana asks before the rabbi starts.

I don't say anything.

Each wedding table is given a name rather than a number. Since Marcus and Rachel met at a ballroom class, the names are dances—Waltz, Tango, Foxtrot.

"Oh, look, we're at Rumba," I say. I start to try an imitation of a professional rumba-er, but then I realize I have no clue how to do it.

"We should totally be at Lambada," Shana says. "Unless it's truly forbidden."

"Why can't we all just dance like we did in seventh grade?" I ask as we take our seats at the linen-draped table. Sprinkled across the top around the glasses are tiny silver hearts. "You know, where you do the Frankenstein sway." I remember arms on shoulders, looking anywhere but in your dance partner's eyes, rocking back and forth like you might tip each other over.

Danny appears and sits for a moment in the chair Shana's left between us—just in case an eligible Brown man should wander by.

"I'm at the Lindy Hop table," Danny says, acknowledging that the name is dorky. "It rocks."

I look around for his date. "She's back at the table," Danny says. "All the way across the room. You can't see it from here, but you should visit if you get a chance. There's a couple guys you might like."

I blush then soft-punch him. "Is this what my life is now? My brother finding me dates?"

Shana says, "I'll be over after the salad course!" She turns to me. "You'll come, too, right?"

"I don't think so," I say. "You go and have fun. If my Imaginary Road Trip Guy is there, get his number for me. Right now, I think I'd like to congratulate Marcus."

I find him looking at himself in the giant mirrors that flank the hallway near the bathroom. He's straightening his tie and yarmulke and watching his new gold band catch the light, winking at both of us.

"Can you believe it?" he asks to my reflection.

"Marcus, Marcus, Marcus," I say.

"Laney, Laney, Laney," he replies. We stand still, staring at our mirrored selves, and then he turns so he's facing the real me.

"I'm happy for you," I say. "You and Rachel looked so peaceful up there."

"Did you see me almost loose it?" Marcus asks. "Twice?"

I had. He'd nearly exploded with giggles when some old aunt of his had asked rather loudly if her flatulence had been heard, and then almost cried when he'd repeated the vows. "It's surreal—the whole thing. You watch so many movies about weddings and throw the *I do* stuff around, but then when you're there—it's . . ."

We hug. In my whole body I can feel all the years between us: the way we'd met through my high school flame, Eric, the kiss Marcus and I had had by the glow of his fish tank, the way he'd visited me everywhere I'd lived, the way he'd helped me during my mom's sickness, how he'd been the one to sit waiting for me at the clinic in Miami.

"You're a really good friend, Marcus," I say.

"Right back at you," he says. It's all we are, friends, but we're old friends. And that's enough.

Back at Rumba, I am alone. Everyone's either mingling or dancing or inspecting the gift table, counting how many light blue Tiffany boxes Rachel can have the pleasure of opening later. Shana bounds back from across the room and grabs my shoulders.

"Oh my God!" she says. She's speaking fast and out of breath. "Oh. My. God! You are never going to believe—you just have to— just can you . . ."

"Spit it out, woman." I laugh. She pulls me up.

"I really am the best date ever!" Shana says and pulls me along toward the other side of the room. "I have someone I want you to meet."

We go to cross over the dance floor. "Who?" I shout over the big band music and chatter. Shana says something, but I can't hear her. She pulls me farther along, but then suddenly the bandleader announces that it's time for the hora. I wonder for a moment if there's a table with that name and before I can move, I am nearly trampled by wedding guests. Soon, Rachel's up in a chair and Marcus, too, and I am in a sea of happiness and suits, little black dresses and love. And I never find Shana or the person she wanted me to meet.

*   *   *

Danny finds me later, outside where the stragglers mill around on the dropped confetti we threw an hour ago as Marcus and Rachel headed off for their honeymoon.

"Too bad no one uses rice anymore," Danny says.

"Yeah," I say, "too bad it makes pigeons explode."

"Where's Shana?" he asks.

"Oh, you know, I lost her somewhere around the hora—speaking of which, I think she might have gone home with a groomsman. She knows how to find me." I point to my cell phone.

"Good for her," Danny says. "By the way, I gave your number to some guy."

"Some guy?" I roll my eyes at my meaning-well brother. "He better not be that guy with the shiny suit. Or the one who gave that boring toast."

"Would I do that to you?" he considers. "Okay, at another point, maybe I would have. But this guy—he's cool. I think you'll like him. I think—if you play your cards right—I'll be giving the speech at your wedding."

"Slow down, doofus," I say.

I watch Danny make patterns and swirls in the fallen confetti.

"What'd you tell him about me?" I ask. "He could be some crazy stalker—I hope you didn't give out too much information."

"Don't worry," Danny says, "all I told him was that I thought he'd get along with my sister. My sister Elaine!"

"Elaine? Are you nuts?" My name is just Laney—it's not short for anything—but when junk mail comes it's often addressed to Elaine.

"What—I thought it was a good cover-up in case you end up thinking he's a loser or something," Danny explains.

"Loser? Two minutes ago you had us walking down the aisle."

"Whatever—Elaaaaiiinnne." Danny laughs. Then his date comes out and we all get in the car to drive home.

The next morning, I get a message on my cell phone from Shana. "Hey Laney—I'm calling from—well, I'll tell you about my night later. But I wanted to let you know that I have a surprise for you—you just won't believe who I . . ." She pauses here and laughs as some guy tells her to put the phone down. "Look, I gave your number to . . ." And then just silence as the call cuts out. I hate cell phones.

CHAPTER
twenty-three

All my mother really wants to do these days is swim. She longs to wake up and slide right into water, immerse herself and move. I meet her at the local Y after work and we take the long lap lengths together. The kick of her legs creates the perfect swirl of water, her slim arms dip and rise, and I follow in her wake.

At home for brunch on Sunday, Danny studies for his medical boards while eating a bagel and I fix my dad one with lox and a speckle of capers, no onion.

"What's that?" My mother points to a photograph in Danny's textbook.

"Neutrophil cells," he says.

"Neat!" she says and pulls a chair close to him. Danny watches our mother's face, how her mouth curls up as her eyes squint when she's excited.

"You still like this stuff?" Danny gestures to his USMLE books, the tight pages of medical facts and procedures highlighted in pink and yellow.

"Oh, yes, I do," she says. Danny hands her a book. They look together at the flimsy pages, reading the same paragraphs, pointing to the same vivid pictures. Danny has always been good about having people read over his shoulder, something that, no matter how I try, still annoys me. I watch them. Danny looks up at me.

"What?" he says. "She likes it."

He shrugs his left shoulder and they continue in their new roles, doctor and former patient, fascinated mother and calmed son.

In the yard, the crocuses, once bright yellow and bright purple—the color of those marshmallow sugarcoated birds that crowd store shelves at Easter—are wilting to rust. Across the muddy patches of lawn the slate pathway is leaf-scattered. My father sits in his shed. I shield the bagel from drips of water coming off the trees, but some hit. The bagel's pocked and cratered, its own page in the dermatology textbook of baked goods.

My father's back is to me when I open the door and put down the plate. He's wearing a nice sweater, one not really suitable for potting, and his hands are in the clay bucket. I go over and look at him.

"Dad?" I say. "I brought you a bagel."

"Thank you," he returns. He stays with his hands shoved deep in the clay, water up to his elbows. He is a potted plant, rooted, with his eyes cast down into the murk, as if he's waiting to unfurl a new bit of fern or leaf.

"Daddy," I say and it's a whole sentence. He smiles into the bucket and I allow myself to do the same.

"What are we smiling about?" I ask.

"You fix things," he says. "You, your mother, Danny, you fix things. I just make them. But, now—I don't know, Lane. I was watching you guys eat breakfast in there and thinking, *This is what I wanted.*"

There is a big pause where my head is clouded with the oddest assortment of things: puppets and clouds, toast and rolls of birthday ribbons, moments of memory or flashcard images. I don't know what to say, but I think of something. I go to the sink basin and turn on the warm tap. I fill a watering can and bring it to my dad. Wordlessly, he lifts his hands from their clay mess and into the new water.

"I might not want to fix things anymore," I say. "Over the summer—you know, during the car trip with Mom—I just thought that maybe I should put my energy into something else for a change. Maybe make things. Like you."

"You mean maybe now that things don't *need* to be fixed?" he asks.

"None us could have fixed Mom, Dad," I say, more for my own benefit than his. I tighten my whole self to stay tearless. "But she's better. All better." Somehow, when I say it, the relief is so great I am overwhelmed. I wonder if it will ever go away completely, if I will ever think of my mom as just Mom, not well-Mom.

My dad stands up and with dripping hands hugs me like I've just gotten up from falling on the ice, unbruised. His sweater is warm and itchy and what I want to do is scratch my face, but I just hug.

"I think you can do whatever you set out to," he says. "Whatever comes naturally."

Later, we call my mother into the kitchen.

"What's all this?" she asks and lets herself be treated as the game show contestant, shuttled into a chair and surrounded by faces.

"We're building you a swimming pool," my father says and smiles.

"Fantastic!" My mother smiles, as if she's not at all surprised. Shock and anxiety have left her these days, though calmness has increased tenfold. She used to follow me around the house, swiping at my muffin crumbs before they'd even landed on the counter. Then, with the lymphoma she'd eventually receded into the upholstery. Now she's all about ease and every action seems to carry with it a soothing quality. She's gentle with her quilts, with repainting an old armoire for my new apartment, gentle about the house cleaning, bills, if we've mistakenly put one of the antique linen napkins in the dryer to have it emerge gauze pad-size, useless.

"It won't be huge or anything," says Danny. He mimes the crawl stroke, giving my mother the thumbs-up.

"But it will be good for laps," I say.

"Where? Where will it go?" she asks and stands up and turns around, like the pool might suddenly appear right there in the middle of the kitchen table.

"In the living room," my father tells her. We have spoken with the construction contracting group and they approve of the placement since the living room is part of an addition the prior owners put on before we moved from Vermont—there's no basement underneath. We tell ourselves that it's the most convenient place; that room's hardly used anymore, and that year-round swimming will please Mom. Really, I think that we don't want to have the chore of cleaning an outdoor pool, collecting the fall leaves and dirt, mucking out the emptied pit of it.

"Can it be yellow?" my mother asks while we move the furniture to see what the room will look like.

"The pool?" my father asks.

"Yes," she says. "People always like to swim in blue. Water isn't really blue, though, it's clear, like cellophane. And I would prefer to swim in something brighter."

Maybe she remembers the blue tiles and sterility of the hospital bathrooms, the toilets complete with metal rails, as if she were trying to wade into something. Once I'd visited with her and kept the door partway open, the sound of my urine hitting the toilet water echoed up, illuminating the fluorescent-lighted room with sad noises. The squares of blue tiles rimmed the white bathroom, boxing me in. I had been embarrassed, somehow, even though my mother was too weak to use the bathroom herself, and relied on a pink plastic bedpan curved like an amplified U, shouting incompetence and humiliation.

I hated the hospital, but I think I'm only admitting that now. It's funny how I wound up far from it and Danny wound up comforting himself by immersing himself there. I couldn't deal with the medicine, the supposed cures that made her well by making her sicker. I looked toward everyone—the chemotherapy nurse, the medical resident who kept checking back, the medical student who studied her with great remove—I saw them all as protectors, lifelines, people who had a responsibility to get her well, since I couldn't do it myself.

As she stands now, at the edge of the uncreated swimming pool, I imagine her toes curling around where the first steps will be. I think of her wading into the clear liquid, or standing waist high in the shallow end and letting her hands graze the water's surface. I remember her taking my hands as a young girl and flying my weightless body around in a circle, until everything, past, present, sunlight and water, became one blurred, fun mass. Then I think about our road trip here, about the swirl of music and water and highway.

We drive to Tile World and my mother roams around, feeling the fragments of ceramic. My father will glaze large triangles for the center of the pool and arrange them like a bursting sun, but my mother likes the idea of us all choosing and going through this together, rather than cloistering my dad away in his shed.

"Any phone calls yet?" Danny questions as he flips through pages of tile patterns. He dramatically clears his throat.

"No, Dr. Love, none yet," I say. Could I really go on a blind date? And who was Shana setting me up with? Maybe I'd wind up with two dates—or none.

My mother lines up tiny squares of duckling yellows and big squares of the color of outer daffodil petals until she finds the color she likes best. She used to do the same with fabrics for a room, a house, a chair—she'd line them up in her own mystical order and see the way it should be.

That night, inspired by the thought of an in-house pool and a mother who's well enough to use it, I make my mother a tape.

Songs that Sound Like Water

Heaven or Las Vegas
  —Cocteau Twins
Let the Rain Come Down
  —Toni Childs
Spoon
  —Dave Matthews and
  Alanis
Rubber Duckie
  —Ernie and Bert
The Salmon Song
  —Courage Brothers
Harry's Theme
  —Enya
First Circle
  —Pat Metheny
Down to the Waterline
  —Dire Straits
Answering Bell
  —Ryan Adams

Here Comes the Flood
  —Peter Gabriel
Judith Dancing
  —Josh Dodes Band
Ballet for a Rainy Day
  —XTC
You Had Time
  —Ani DiFranco
Bad
  —U2
Pink Moon
  —Nick Drake
Morning Dance
  —Spyro Gyra
Swimming Song
  —Kate and Anna
  McGarrigle

When the pool's all in except for the tiling and final sealing, I find my mother walking inside the empty rectangle of it. She looks beautiful. Her hair is long and soft now. White and gray-lined, it flows in a way it probably hasn't since the Vermont days, and often she'll wear a scarf on her head, the blue and white kind or the red and white. I love her like this, even though I catch myself thinking that it's back then and we're the wacky artists in the converted barn, now with a pool right in the living room.

"Come on in, Laney, the water's yellow," she says, doing that ridiculous dance from the sixties where you hold your nose and shimmy.

We sit on the concrete steps and she maps out the tile flow for me, which size where, which color on what surface.

"It's so sunny," I say when I am imagining it.

My mother turns to me. "We like color a lot in this family, don't we?"

"We do," I say. I think about how I've been painting more, trying to let the pictures out onto canvases. When I do, I feel free somehow, like creating makes me more present.

And then, "I look forward to swimming in here with your kids," she says. "Not too soon after they eat, of course."

We each have a hand on the metal rail that runs the length of the stairs and my mother watches my grip tighten.

"You sound like a Jewish mother," I say.

"I am a Jewish mother." She laughs. And then, like she's been practicing this part, "It's good you're back here in Boston, Laney, but I think you need to do your own thing. You know, I don't need you to take care of me. I'm not going anywhere."

I nod. Her words are elementary, but I know they are true. It's easy to stay in one place, fixed. I look out at the empty white in front of us and will it to flood. She pries my hand from the railing and holds it in both of hers. I think about love, how I am ready for it again.

"How did you know it was meant to be with Dad?" I ask.

"Oh, I don't know if I think certain things are just meant to be. I think you need to be a bit more proactive sometimes—maybe decide what you want and make moves to get them. But I do think you just know with *that* person when the fit is there." She takes a handkerchief from her pocket. The cloth is edged with rickrack, tiny hills of violet that my mother touches with the tip of her pinky.

"You know what it's like?" she says. "It's like water. It's like water draining from a bath and then refilling, slowly until you are buoyed up by this feeling of love."

"And that's where you feel like you are now?" I ask.

"Some days it's that romantic—other days, less so—but that

buoyancy doesn't change," she says. "I wanted to ask you—do you see yourself marrying someone Jewish? I just wondered, after the talks we had on the road . . ."

"I never did before—but now I've sort of realized that it means a lot," I try to explain to her. "This might sound silly, but finding someone who's Jewish—where the fit is natural—would be ideal, like when you look at someone's music collection and there's a big overlap. I know religion and music aren't the same, but they're both my faith, I think." My mother nods, takes my hand, and smiles; proud.

In my apartment—filled with its empty canvases, its half-squeezed paints tubes, feather brushes waiting to be used—I start something new for myself. Not a big deal, I tell myself, just a small project, painting small worlds in vivid hues—solar systems or unseen night skies—on palm-size canvases. I make a mix for myself to listen to as I paint—a reward somehow, for branching out from just fixing. My mother hears it when she comes for tea and asks for a copy. She listens to it over and over, as if it's one song.

Little Planets

SIDE A

Fisherman's Blues
    —The Waterboys
I've Been Waiting
    —Matthew Sweet
Skateaway
    —Dire Straits
Little Wing
    —Hendrix
74/75
    —The Connells

SIDE B

I'm Lucky
    —Joan Armatrading
Bittersweet
    —Big Head Todd
Last Chance on the
    Stairway—Duran Duran
Knife Edge
    —Brooks Williams
Almost Hear You Sigh
    —Rolling Stones

Little Wing
  —Sting
She Makes My Day
  —Robert Palmer
Baby, Now That I've Found
  You—A. Kraus
When You Were Mine
  —Prince

Overkill
  —Men at Work
Crystal Flame
  —Blues Traveler
I Will Survive
  —Cake
I'm One
  —Pete Townsend
Bachelorette
  —Björk

As the songs play on my Walkman, I think about why I chose them, about how they blend or don't, how I can choose color and texture, whether to splotch or dot. It's a bit like how I used to picture characters jumping from book to book, becoming friends or not. These songs feel like mine, the paintings feel like mine, my life feels like mine.

My father comes over to look at what I've done.

"Someday," my father says as he looks at the different ones, some as small as a thumbnail, some long and narrow, the length of a forearm. He holds one up. "You always wanted to do a children's book, remember? Look at the lines here, how uplifting they are, how that red tone makes you want to smile."

I remember sitting in his shed in Vermont while my mother was inside the house wearing her plaid shirt, helping Danny with a puzzle or something. I'd announced to my father that I'd be a musician-illustrator. Now it was sort of coming true. Music would always fill me up in some way, swirl inside and mix with lyrics from my past, but I felt a new kind of letting go. Maybe being closer with my mother had freed a part of me—the creating part— or maybe my mom had just put me back in touch with all the bits of my life I'd tried to leave behind, and now I was able to put myself—and my art—out there.

"I'd need someone to do the words," I say while I nod at my dad.

"You can handle more than color," he says.

That night I remember lying in the bath at that fancy bed and breakfast during the road trip. Just like I did then, I try to explain my paintings to some nonexistent child audience. The simplicity of the exercise makes the words come out of me—I don't need someone else to fill in where I lack—I don't need music to express what I'm feeling.

Little by little, I begin to gather phrases—a word here and there—and match it with the small frames I have done. One canvas is a storm, circles of color and metallic light, with a small figure in the corner, waiting for a spark.

CHAPTER
twenty-four

Danny and I are sitting on the porch handing out candy. We don't want the house to be one of the dark ones that are passed by on Halloween. Upstairs, my parents are asleep already, while down here small witches, tomatoes, gypsies, and politicians trot from door to door, casually ringing bells in search of sweets. I am no longer an employee of the museum—I have taken the plunge and am painting for a living. The *Boston Voice* accepted one print for publication—a watercolor for their upcoming holiday issue—and I'm getting ready to shop my children's book illustrations around to the publishing world.

Faintly, music from the short CD mix Danny burned for me as artwork inspiration swirls up like genie smoke from under the door. He hadn't made me a mix in a long time, years maybe, and he told me how much he liked piecing the songs together.

"I labeled a side A and B just for old time's sake," Danny says when we're looking at the cover, "even though obviously there's just one side. You gotta get with the program, Lane, and make some CDs instead of tapes."

"Hey, I like tapes—they're what I know."

"Yeah." Danny nods at me and reaches for a piece of candy. "Sounds like the Laney I know and love—one foot in the past the other . . ." He pauses to chew. "In her mouth."

Danny can always make me laugh, even when he's pointing out some personal flaw. I realize he might be right—that my cassette-making days might be over, and that it's time to learn about making mixes that don't have B sides—that are just one long, continual stretch of uninterrupted music.

A Little Light, 12 Songs (Not) to Sleep to:
Love, Danny

FIRST
(IF THERE WERE A SIDE A)

SECOND
(FAKE SIDE B)

Divided Sky	Sun Tan
—Phish	—String Cheese Incident
Tightrope	Holiday
—Leon Russell	—Madonna
Tonight's the Night	Lawyers, Guns, and Money
—Styx	—Warren Zevon
See a Little Light	Miles from Nowhere
—Bob Mould	—Cat Stevens
Love Goes On	Love Over Gold
—The Go-Betweens	—Dire Straits
Na Laetha Geal M'Oige	Flight of the Cosmic Hippo
—Enya	—Bela Fleck

"What if people handed out something else entirely on Halloween?" I ask.

"Like?"

"Like bath products. Can you imagine? Mom would dress up just to collect the Kiehl's packets." I laugh, thinking of grown-ups looking through their pillowcases of goodies.

"I'd want books," Danny says.

"Bummer to lug around, though," I say. He nods.

"What would you want?"

I think for a bit and then say, "I'd like to be handed a copy of the best letter the person answering the doorbell had ever received."

"Cool. Do you know yours?" Danny asks.

"Yeah," I say. "It starts with, 'Dear Laney—The bad news is that I didn't win the lottery and so cannot quit my job and fly to meet you for a romantic journey. The good news is that I think you're the Eighth Wonder of the World.' "

"Not bad," says Danny.

"Yeah, although it was from this guy, Simon, a playwright, so he had the writer's advantage. What's your best letter?" I ask and open a small box of Junior Mints.

"Well, I was thinking about that when you said it. I guess it's a letter I got from a girl on that bike trip I did."

"Melissa?" I ask.

"No. God, how do you remember all that stuff, anyway? It's not your job, you know," Danny says and shakes his head. "But it was the other one. Not Melissa. Psycho Hose Beast. Man, that was a good letter. I should look her up—she's probably married by now or still hates me."

"Actually, you know what?" I say. "I should qualify and say that the letter I told you about was the best beginning to a love letter."

"That's different," Danny says.

"I have some good ones from Mom and Dad," I say.

"Me, too," Danny says. Dropped leaves blow and rustle along the curbside. We watch small ghosts walk under the lamplight and Danny puts his head down onto his arm.

"So, did you happen to get that guy's number?" I ask.

"What guy?" Danny looks at me. "You mean the guy from Marcus's wedding?"

"Yes," I say. "I'm woman enough to call."

"Oh—now you've changed your tune. A month goes by, you

quit your fancy museum job, and now that you're a real—artiste—
you have the guts?"

"Did you get it or not?"

"Sorry," Danny says, "I only gave him yours. I didn't get his.
What about that guy Shana met for you? Can't she fix you up?"

"I left her a message today, asking her to figure something out,"
I say, "though I hesitate to think what."

"Long time no nothing," Marcus says when I pick him up after a
couple of days of post-Halloween sugar-rush painting. He's a history
teacher at Greyson Academy now, the place where we went years ago,
just over the bridge on the other side of town. He's also the lacrosse
coach, so he's got a whistle around his neck, as well as a mesh bag
filled with sticks and balls that he shoves in the trunk. He and Rachel
returned from their three-week honeymoon and then he started
teaching, so he was busy. Then I was caught up in my pictures and
wrapping up my position at the museum, so we'd been out of touch.

"No kidding," I say. "You're a sight for sore eyes."

"How 'bout a sight for sore thighs." Marcus cracks himself up.

"Either way." I smile. I was busy finding words for the children's book. And seeing family—catching Danny for coffee in the
hospital cafeteria for three minutes before he's paged away, busy
helping Dad plan his days now that he's cut back working on the
catalogue, trying to return to his roots and make fine, one-off
pieces for his lymphoma research fund show. And seeing Maggie,
who'd come to town toting her daughter and famous husband,
both in jeans and cashmere. I am the godmother, but have yet to
be photographed for *People* magazine.

"We look good," he says, looking at my slightly disheveled
self—paint-splattered jeans and wool sweater—and then at himself. Marcus'll probably always look great, his dark hair will accept
willingly the grays that sprout, his olive skin won't wrinkle. I met
his grandfather once, and the man looked like a graduate student,
except for the cane and the way he seemed shrunken when he sat
behind the wheel of his Cadillac Seville.

We're on our way to meet Rachel to finish packing up Marcus's parents' house so they can live in Florida year-round. The living room is its own cardboard city with box buildings and bubble wrap towers. We put the pizza on the coffee table and Marcus hands me a compact disc.

"This is for you." Marcus grins. I look at it for a minute and then twist my face up, confused, when I notice it's in Shana's handwriting.

"What's going on, Marcus?" I ask and look at the songs.

The Last First Kiss

FIRST	LAST
Fly —Nick Drake	Nightswimming —R.E.M
We Belong Together —Ricki Lee Jones	Love Reign O'er Me —Pete Townsend
I Want You —Tom Waits	And So It Goes —Billy Joel
Here Comes the Flood —Peter Gabriel	Hold Me —Fleetwood Mac
You Can Close Your Eyes —James Taylor	It's Always You —Chet Baker
Last Train Home —Pat Metheny	Blue Eyes —Elton John
Shelter from the Storm —Bob Dylan	On Tuesday —Men Without Hats
Just You 'n' Me —Chicago	I Can't Help Falling in Love —Lick the Tins
For the Asking —Simon and Garfunkel	Magic —Ben Folds Five

"Tell me!" I say, like the sixteen-year-old who guesses her surprise party is waiting for her.

"I don't know what you mean," Marcus says, grinning. "Shana

sent this to me—for you." Marcus winks. "You'll just have to wait."

I join Rachel near the kitchen, where she's rolling up glasses in newspaper and boxing them. Then the doorbell rings.

"Who's that?" I ask.

"Oh," says Marcus and turns to me, "it's your husband. The future love of your life."

"Huh?" I ask with the roll of tape in my mouth. I flip a box around and continue taping until it's steady enough to be filled.

"A friend from Brown," he says and gives me a wink and opens the door. "Shana met him at the wedding and thought you might—ah—have something in common. But then, because of the honeymoon and whatever, this whole thing just took longer to arrange than I—"

"What whole thing?" I ask, but Marcus doesn't answer, he just opens the front door. When the friend first walks in, I am behind a stack of boxes, so all I hear is the voice, which is only a little familiar.

"You can't really see her," says Marcus, "but there's a woman back there."

I step out from behind my wall of boxes and say, "Hi—I'm Laney."

"I'm Josh," Josh says. For one second, I am back at camp with him, wanting to stay on the lake's shore forever. I half expect rays of morning sunlight to halo around him. He is grown up but still the same.

"Ah, here's our moment," Marcus says, proud. Josh and I stare at each other and then laugh.

From his pocket, Josh takes out his keys.

"Leaving so soon?" I ask and have a fleeting thought that he might be. But what he's showing me is the key chain, which is a wire loop through a Turk's head knot.

"The same one we made that day," Josh says before I can ask. Instantly, I want to know all the places the knot I made has traveled, all the conversations, hands, keys it has held.

*　　　*　　　*

When the pizza's done and the downstairs rooms are bare but for boxes and crumpled newspapers, Josh and I kiss. Marcus and Rachel have gone upstairs, leaving the music on. Josh and I are spidered on the couch, leg over leg, and arms everywhere. We keep stopping to look at each other or laugh or ask something like, "And then, where did you go after that?"

This is it, I think. Love, key rings, and my last first kiss ever. We hold tight and listen to the James Taylor song playing: *Well, the sun is slowly sinking down/And the moon is slowly rising/And this old world must still be spinning 'round/And I still love you/Close your eyes/You can close your eyes, it's all right.*

A week later, Josh says, "This was the best first date in the history of dating."

"That's a lot of confidence to have since we haven't gone on it yet," I say.

"I just have a feeling," he says.

Josh hands the tickets to the usher and we are led to our seats. The theater's warm and gilt-edged, as if we're inside a tea caddy with the dome closed above us.

Josh helps me off with my coat. "I like the seasonal feel of Christmas, even though growing up I couldn't stand how there was this insistence on the Christianity of it. Now it just feels quaint and cheery."

We point out the heavy velvet curtain that pleats over the stage, the ancient box ashtrays that have not been removed from the seat backs, and the opera-style glasses that we can use by dropping a dime into a slot, freeing the binoculars from their holder.

Josh hasn't told me what we're seeing, but I imagine it's a Handelesque performance, something that comes with the season and calls to mind trumpets or pine-scented air. He'd hidden the ticket stubs in his inside jacket pocket and kept me away from the programs the usher gave us to keep the performance a surprise. Since we're in one of those private box seats on the side of the balcony, I can't read over someone's shoulder.

"Have you ever been in a seat like this before?" Josh asks.

"I've always wanted to," I say.

"It's very *Dangerous Liaisons*," he says and puts his hand on my knee and we pretend to be shocked.

"How dare you!" I say and then put my hand on his knee, too. Then I remember something. "Wait, you know what? I have been in this kind of seat. But it was when *Cats* first opened and I was with Danny and Maggie. I'm not sure that counts."

"Oh, it counts." He takes my hand. "But at least it's new in the dating context."

"I can't believe we didn't find each other at the wedding," I say while we wait for the show to start.

"Well, I wasn't exactly looking for you—well, in my mind, maybe." Josh grins. "Besides, I thought Shana—who I didn't recognize by the way—could've been some drunken wedding weirdo saying I just *had* to follow her and then some guy sitting at my table swearing he was going to fix me up with his sister." Josh takes a breath, looks at me, and holds my hand as if he's trying to keep me from floating away. I give him a squeeze to let him know I'm not going anywhere. "Anyway," Josh says, "then I had to walk Marcus's ancient, flatulent aunt around until she found her hat. All in all, it was an odd wedding."

"Wait a minute," I say. "That guy who was going to fix you up with his sister. Was the sister Elaine?"

"Um, yeah, I think so—why? You know her?" Josh rummages in his wallet for something.

"I'm Elaine! I'm Elaine!" I'm nearly shouting this.

"Okay! Okay! You're Elaine." Josh shows me the slip of paper in Danny's handwriting that has my number.

"That's me—that's my cell," I say and point.

Josh smiles. "So it is," he says. "So the fixer-upper was your brother—the Doctor Danny?"

"Yes," I say and think that my whole life was leading up to right now.

The lights dim and then come on again to tell people to take their seats.

"Can I call you Elaine?" Josh whispers.

"You can call me anything," I say and lean into him.

And then the lights dim for good. The curtain opens and men in suits take their places.

"So, tell me," I say. "What is this performance?"

"This is the Mieskuro Huutajat," Josh explains.

"Who?" I ask.

"Wait," he says. I do. And when they begin, I am amazed.

The men don't sing, they shout at the top of their lungs. Josh hands me a program. They are the Finnish Choir of Shouters. They go on in harmonic yelling. A national anthem, some traditional Finnish songs, all in moans, grunts, and howls.

The night will be my answer forever to the question, "When did you laugh the hardest?"

Josh and I are wheezing and coughing and laughing, but no one can hear us because of the onstage screaming—a bellowing harmonized version of "Yesterday" by the Beatles.

On the way to the car, Josh and I yell at each other, mouths open wide like the professional screamers.

"This was great!" I yell.

"I'm so glad you liked it!" Josh screams at me.

We imagine what kind of dancing could accompany tonight's performance and then try to yell-sing Fleetwood Mac's "Hold Me," which plays on the car's CD player. It comes out more like an order.

"If you insist," Josh says.

We hold each other and try to stop laughing. In the middle of a kiss, I laugh into Josh's mouth. He puts his hands in my hair and we just look at each other until my old image of him from the sun-rayed dock one summer long ago is the same as the one right now.

CHAPTER
twenty-five

The day comes, of course, when there isn't much time to make tapes anymore, and there's Josh's MP3 player which holds it all, our entire collection plus downloads, but we decide to make one more mix, just because, and save it as a play list on his Arcos. Together, we mourn the lack of side breaks, but realize how much easier it is not to try to figure out the timing of songs, how to squeeze all the ones we want onto one mix.

Just Joshin' with You

SIDE ONE

Do That to Me One More
    Time—Captain and Tennille
Trials
    —Jackopierce
You Make My Dreams
    —Hall and Oates

SIDE TWO

A Problem Like Maria?
    —*Sound of Music*
To Reach Me
    —The Go-Betweens
Forever Young
    —Bob Dylan

Sweet Melissa
  —Allman Brothers
(Keep Feeling) Fascination
  —Human League
What a Wonderful World
  —Louis Armstrong
Second That Emotion
  —Smokey Robinson
Dreams
  —Gabrielle
For You
  —Springsteen
He's Got the Whole World
  —Odetta

I Have a Song
  —Lucy Simon
Always Something There
  —Burt Bachrach
Once in a Lifetime
  —Talking Heads
On a Clear Day
  —Streisand
Well, All Right
  —Buddy Holly

Sometimes when Josh and I show up at my parents' place unannounced, my mother will insist on us making use of the pool. Secretly I wonder if my mother just enjoys Josh's technique for getting chlorine out of my hair with Joy.

"Old camp trick," he said the first time he squirted the yellow goop into his palm and rubbed it onto my head.

Josh will lean my head back over the sink, make a visor with his hand so the soap doesn't get in my eyes, and I think my mother likes watching this. She likes watching me be taken care of properly.

My father was the one who washed our hair when we were little, though. Downstairs, my mother would set something on the stove to simmer and come up to help with the final stages of our bath. She'd sit on the toilet with the lid down while my father squeezed shampoo onto his big palm.

"Too much," she'd say to him. She was right, of course, and he'd have to triple rinse us to get the last of the suds out. This was before conditioner, so we'd get out, tangles and all, and wait to be dried off. Dad took the dropcloth approach and covered you from the head so you were draped like a ghost. I reached out for my mother, who wrapped the towel around my back and shoulders and then used another towel for my hair, first wiping away the drips from my forehead and then from under my chin. As Josh sweeps the water back from my ears, I think about babies, about shampooing tiny fingers and rinsing barely there hair.

It's spring again. The muddy driveway, the gravel pushed aside in postwinter piles, Passover seder. I work on scrubbing the brisket pot without taking off my wedding ring while Josh and Danny clear and dry. Josh's parents are off in the study with mine, talking about mutual finds or art or Europe, or their becoming grandparents in the not-too-distant future. I'm already the proud mom of a kid's book, *Annie's Magic Roadway,* that's due out next winter.

I think about good hiding places for the *afikomen* when the next generation comes along, which it will by year's end. Once my father kept the matzo in plain view, but on the edge of a painting and no one found it. We were so busy looking in the usual places, under the couch cushions, between the big coffee table books. This year, my mother reads from the Haggadah more than she ever has in my memory. Instead of skipping through, she insists on going through each page, questions, answers, and Hebrew. Danny and I didn't even know she could read it so well, since my dad used to do that part, if it was done at all.

Josh's parents, more formal than mine, nod with approval. Josh squeezes my hand and whispers, "I'm so hungry!"

Papa Hen, my dad's dad, had been of the mind that no seder could be short enough. He'd whiz through the prayers, give a short talk about freedom from oppression for all peoples, and then get on to the eating part, which was his favorite. Meals with him were fun and simple, unlike they were for my dad growing up, when Papa Hen had to host diplomats and Dad's mother would have to write out place cards that fit into sterling silver art deco placeholders. Guests would be a mix of Jewish and non, and aside from displaying the lamb shank, a sprig of parsley, and a glossy, white egg on a Limoge dish, no one could tell the meal was important or sacred.

I liked it when the meals had become our own. There was a sense of passage, of choice. We could finally have kugel the way we liked it, with no crushed pineapple, the way my dad's family made it, and no bloated yellow raisins as Zadie had done.

"Everyone likes their noodle pudding done a little differently," Zadie had said the last time she came to our house. It was Rosh Hashanah, and the cooking started early.

"Don't you want to add raisins?" she asked my mother.

"No, Mom, I don't," my mother had answered. And then, worrying she had sounded curt, "We love your recipe. We just don't like the texture of raisins in such a wonderful, smooth dish."

"I never did, either," Zadie had said.

"Then why on earth would you keep adding them?" my mother asked. I waited for her answer.

"It was how you made it then," she said. My mother nodded and added the cooked waves of noodles to the bowl. I waited for more of a reason, but none came.

"Laney, come here," says Danny, motioning from the doorway into the dining room. I go to where he watches my parents and Josh's. My father twirls my mother around and around while she sings the wrong words to "A Problem Like Maria." She's got the melody, but sings the words to "Doe, a Deer." It doesn't sound bad. My mother's arms grace the back of my father's neck as he leads her, navigating the table, chairs, and into the living room.

By the pool he says, "This is where I dip you!"

"Ha-ha!" my mother says, getting it.

Josh's mother and father do the twist and then the Charleston.

"What are they—dancing through the decades?" Josh laughs.

Danny, Josh, and I watch until we are the proud parents. I remember walking into a classroom in seventh grade and reading what some teacher had written on the board about kids dancing around to everything—sirens, songs, the hum of an outdoor bug zapper—since they don't know what constitutes music. I feel that way now.

Back in the kitchen, I sit and watch Danny do the cleanup. Even his counter-wiping skills seem doctorly these days.

"You are such a doctor," I say.

"I am such a guy who worked at Subway and cleaned up the lettuce shavings," he says.

Josh sits next to me. I put my feet on the rung of his chair.

"How're you feeling?" he asks.

"Tired, but less nauseous," I say. "My ring's starting to get tight." I turn the wedding diamond around and around the way I used to do with my mother's ring on her finger, watching the stone appear and vanish.

"Sweetie." He kisses my palms and makes it look like I'm keeping him from saying something.

"You know what?" asks Danny from his own little world.

"What?" I say.

"That girl in *The Sound of Music*—"

"Maria?" Josh asks.

"No, Lisl. The I'm-sixteen-years-old-and-I-don't-need-a-governess one."

"Yeah," I say. "What about her?"

"She must have been pretty screwed-up about relationships. I mean, she likes this guy, who sings her this song about growing up and how he'll take care of her, but then he's actually part of this evil force."

"And you're just getting this?" I ask.

"Well, sure, it's always on TV this time of year—I saw it last night," Danny says. "Mom and Dad never let me see the end. When the littlest girl sings the *so long* song, I had to go to bed, too."

"Really?" I ask.

"Yeah," he says, "I had no clue what the movie was about until like three years ago, when I saw it all the way through for the first time. Heavy shit. Tell your kids everything—don't let them be surprised later on."

"I suppose," Josh says.

"So, how come I got to see the whole thing? What does that mean?" I ask Josh when he sits down with us.

"Who knows," he says. "Dating advice for you?"

"Charming," I say.

Danny says, "No—I think Mom and Dad figured that whatever you saw or went through, that you'd be okay. That you'd understand it and make sense of it all."

"They didn't tell me everything," I say. "It probably just seemed that way because I'm older—you know, like I knew the grown-up secrets of the universe."

"Don't you?" Danny winks.

One Sunday we go to my parents' house to look through the attic. Josh and I go through boxes marked *Maternity, Layette,* and *Other.* In the maternity box, my mother's Marimekko dresses are neatly folded and separated by tissue paper. I hold up a sundress and ask Josh what he thinks.

"Very cool." The dress is floor-length and sleeveless with a black, fuchsia, and white bull's-eye design. Another has green and blue fish all over it, like some Escher print.

"This is for you guys," my dad says from the top of the attic stairs. He pushes a box toward us and stays until we look inside. Under bubble wrap and yellow tissue paper, we find a mobile made from smoothed driftwood. From each section hangs a planet or a sun, a star or a moon.

"Mom made this when you were born," Dad says. "I think she sewed it by hand." He points to the different parts. "She added the satin around the edges to make it seem like it was glowing."

Josh smiles and says to my dad, "Thanks. This'll be great."

"Yeah, Dad," I say. "Thank you." I get up with the mobile and give my dad a kiss on the top of his head since it's the only part of him I can reach while leaning down over the railing. We hug with all the planets and stars between us.

*　　*　　*

Since I am antsy waiting for the baby to make its way, I go back on my original decision to stop making mixes. I can't help it. I call Shana and tell her to expect me to be sending those cushioned envelopes with antiqued cassettes to her for her ninetieth birthday. Josh thinks its sweet, how I will still make such a process out of it, but I can only roll my eyes and laugh when he suggests taking the finished product into the delivery room with us. There's a poignancy to the most recent mix, and I can't figure out what part of me is sad until I realize that I am about to split into two people, literally push out a person to make my small family three. Addition—the math of the whole process—suddenly seems so large that it looms ahead like a blank sky, a canvas that needs filling. I spend an hour or so feeling glum until I see Josh folding the smallest white T-shirt, placing a palm-size baby cap into our hospital bag, at which point, even though my belly aches and my feet don't fit into my shoes, I can't stop grinning.

The Sad Hour

Once in a Very Blue Moon
 —Nanci Griffith
Old Man
 —Neil Young
Tell Me on a Sunday
 —Sarah Brightman
Every Time
 —The Samples
Perhaps Love
 —Domingo and Denver
You're Gonna Make Me
 Lonesome When You Go
 —Bob Dylan
Going Fishing
 —David Knopfler

The Water Is Wide
 —Karla Bonoff
Over the Rainbow
 —Judy Garland
Stranger in a Strange Land
 —Russell
Home Again
 —Carole King
Suite for Two Violins
 —Bach
The Things We've Handed
 Down
 —Marc Cohn
The Circle Game
 —Joni Mitchell

The Rainbow Connection
—Kermit
Gardening at Night
—R.E.M.
Fountain of Sorrow
—Jackson Browne

You Can Close Your Eyes
—J.T.
Long and Winding Road
—Beatles
When Ye Go Away
—Waterboys

All over my parents' bed are spread fabric pieces, swatches from my mother's archives and sample books. My mother is seated in the middle of the floor, laying out more bits of cloth, some overlapping like clusters of leaves. My mother senses me there, though I didn't knock. She says, "Daddy's old potting shed had a bench cushion made out of this."

Now that I have given birth to her first grandchild, she says her project for me is ready. Outside, it has snowed again. The empty trees break up the dull of the milk-tea sky. She's called me over to her house for some event.

"I have something for you," I say.

"I have something for you," she counters.

I hand her the shoebox filled with all my tapes. "I thought you might want to keep these here," I say. "You might want to listen sometime. We don't have room for everything at our place."

She nods. I put the cassettes in the hallway, knowing she will keep them safe, stashed away for sometime.

"And for you." My mother holds out a large square of pale red corduroy and keeps holding it out until I reach over and feel it.

"Oh," I say, "this was in Dad's shed in Vermont. What exactly are you doing, Mom?" I look around. She is collaging herself into one corner of the room.

"Seeing all the fabrics together," she says. I nod. I see how at peace she is in her skin, in this room, with the cloth around her. "Do you see?" she asks.

When I don't and it's clear from my expression, my mother stands up and walks over the now-blanketed rug to where I am. She takes my hand and we start at the bed where the deepest colors are, the ruby silks and assorted navies cover the pillows and gradually turn to periwinkle toile, pink organza, pale green dupioni, melon- and lime-splotched cotton that drips in one long piece onto the dust ruffle.

"Pretty, isn't it," my mother says, and then we turn to look at the rest of the room. "Shoes off, Laney," she says and waits for me to slip my sneakers off and put them neatly together by the door. "And socks."

I get rid of those and walk in the path my mother does, over the creamy section, all winter whites, pearls, laces, sateens, and more silk. Our bare feet rustle and slide. Between my toes and all around me are years of fabric—the daisied flannel from my old sundress, poplin squares from Papa Hen's shirts, an untouched bolt of silk my mother bought in Paris and never used after her second relapse. Terrible polyester plaids from bell-bottom slacks. So many years of collecting, all of it in front of me.

"So you do see!" she says with her bright smile.

She sits next to me and for these minutes we are just mother and daughter, the simplest link, kneeling on fabric. Systematically, she lists all the fabrics, all the names she has running around her beautiful head. She is trying to tell me, to show me that she remembers or knows things, too. That all this is her story. Suddenly, I remember I had a teacher who grew up in a funeral home. He had written a story that started, "I know a little about death."

"You know about fabric," I say to my mother.

"I know about knowing," she says to me. "I know about weaving everything together." I collapse in her lap, flooding her with tears I am surprised to find I still have left and let her cover my hair with her hands. I don't raise my head, but look at the bits of fabric from a side angle. This is her mix, her tape for me, some unwritten, uncharted song I will have in my head forever.

"All together," she says, "doesn't it look like one big piece? Something solid?"

later on

I always get sad in the fall. Maybe it's the mottled light, the autumn red-hued maples, or the fact that my calendar says September and I'm not rushing out to buy school supplies or starting somewhere new. But somehow in the morning my feet find their way out from under the duvet and my body feels weighted. Josh calls my mood MelanFallia.

"You're so punny," I say while he's changing our son's diaper.

He smiles at me and blows me a kiss, before coming over to the bed where I'm snuggled under the quilt my mother gave me. The collage of fabric in her room that day covers our bed, blankets us in all the scraps and moments I can recall just by looking at them. I love how Josh will point to a square and ask about it, or how he'll read in bed, tucking the quilt around his legs. And I love how our son likes to roll around, making snowless angels on top of the blanket.

Our son's book of *Diggers and Dump Trucks* shows photos of all the different vehicles and describes their parts and functions. The tunneling loader, the imposing giant dump truck, the backhoe. Fascinated, he still wants the book read at least four times a day.

He is impressed with the size and strength of the trucks—he holds his hands above his head with closed fists and says, "Ohhh." This is how he shows *strong*. He doesn't realize that the trucks in the photos are miniatures, lifelike Tonkas.

As he moved his small fingers over the picture of the bulldozer yesterday, I heard myself describing the truck again, pointing out the steel blade, the crawler tracks that keep the thing from sinking into the mud, the rich soil piled up around. And then I looked closer. Not closer, differently, and I saw that the dirt wasn't really dirt, but instant coffee. A tiny truck pushing granules of Sanka, or maybe it was caffeinated, I don't know.

I think about San Francisco, about sitting on the steps of my rented house with my mother just before our road trip home and how she waved to the moving truck as it grew tiny in the distance. How something so massive and concrete can appear tiny enough to fit entirely into a palm.

While our son naps, Josh and I talk about songs we'd put on a mix for him. His own mix of early days songs. But the songs I suggest are essentially the ones from the first tape I made, when my mother's tape recorder was new to me. It occurs to me that the songs on that tape were my parents' songs, the albums the ones they shared with me and with Danny. And that no matter how much those songs seemed like they were just mine, they were really ours. Now I will hand that music to my son and he'll have his own song preferences. I remember the box of tapes my mother and I shared, all my pasts gathered up, that will sit in my old room until possibly my children find them.

I think about how my last first kiss with Josh was really our second and how it felt like music. The way our lips felt together, the way I still feel around him—is the relief, the love you suddenly feel throughout your whole being when a song you'd absolutely loved but forgotten about comes on the radio. How the heart races, the fingers go to turn up the volume, and you're amazed that you'd lost the song in the first place and you swear to keep it now forever.

For my birthday, Josh makes a tape of the baby talking. He calls it 0 to 18 in Ninety Minutes.

"Five minutes of talking or talking and singing for each year until he's eighteen," Josh explains.

"It's perfect," I say. "It's just what I wanted."

"Freezing time?" Josh pokes gently.

"Replaying it, I guess," I say.

"Yeah." Josh flattens his palm on the bedspread and I cover his hand with mine. Our son's hand goes on top of mine. I look at our layers of fingers, the staggered ridges and knuckles, our baby's tiny nails, each with a clear crescent moon of white, just like my mother's.

"And then what?" I ask.

Three of us sit and press play, listening to the small giggles and not-quite-words. "And then more," Josh says. Our son stretches all thirty-two inches of himself out along our big bed and laughs.

"Lala," he says. It's a word he uses to mean many things: laundry, water, yellow, love. I think about all the ways words change and re-form to mean other words, to show what somehow seems impossible. How I know what he means by the chords it strikes in me. How it's all about context.

Up Close and Personal with the Author

WHY DID YOU CHOOSE *LINER NOTES* AS THE TITLE OF THIS BOOK?

When I set out to write this book I wanted to try to tell the story of one woman's life through her tapes. Recording artists use liner notes (which are on CD inserts and in the insides of tape covers) to tell the story behind the making of the album—the where, when, and who of how the songs came to be. For Laney each mix tape brings her back to a specific time in her life. In essence, the stories she shares with her mother are the "liner notes" to her life.

LINER NOTES IS ESSENTIALLY A NOVEL WITH A BUILT-IN SOUNDTRACK—IS THAT HOW YOU LIVE YOUR LIFE?

Well it's true in that music is definitely an important and emotional part of my everyday experience. Like Laney, I use music as a kind of time-travel device whereby I choose songs sometimes just to think about the times that go with them. But in terms of a "built-in soundtrack" I don't spend every minute of the day thinking *what song goes with this moment?* I mean, much of my day is spent changing diapers and finger-painting.

HAVE YOU TRIED EXPLAINING THE MIX-TAPE CONCEPT TO YOUR CHILDREN?

Actually, my oldest who is three and a half has already burned his first mix of a CD! It's an eclectic mix of songs ranging from "Twinkle, Twinkle Little Star" to Dave Brubeck's "Blue Rondo a la Turk" to Bob Dylan. He's ready to create a second one!

SOME OF THE SONGS IN LANEY'S MIXES APPEAR MORE THAN ONCE. WAS THIS INTENTIONAL?

Of course! I've always been fascinated with the life of a song—how maybe you first "got" a song from a friend, and then later put it on a mix for someone you dated, then got it back on another tape from your sister. The context shifts the meaning—and that's the beauty of the mix; you interpret songs based on who created the tape or CD.

LINER NOTES IS VERY MOVING BUT FUNNY AT THE SAME TIME. WAS IT DIFFICULT TO ACHIEVE THIS BALANCE?

I guess I see the world as both sad and funny all the time so in some ways, the telling of this story came naturally. I did feel, though, that it was important not to exclude the reader from Laney and her mother's emotional reconnecting by using too much humor—and that at the same time, I didn't want this to be a "cancer" story, with attention paid only to the illness. And I didn't want it to be a "girl finds a guy and makes everything okay" story, either. I guess I wanted to feel that all the characters were well-rounded, that they had lived through a variety of experiences, incorporating Laney's mother's non-Hodgkin's lymphoma as only a part. In this way, just as in real life, Laney could tell her mother about a funny day she'd had in high school while still being aware that the sickness lurked in the background.

WHAT IS THE SIGNIFICANCE OF THE ROAD TRIP? IS THE JOURNEY METAPHORIC IN SOME WAY?

I intentionally had Laney and her mother take a roundabout route home—I wanted the road to run parallel to Laney's memories—fast in some places and slower in others. I thought putting Laney and Annie in the car together, basically trapping them for three-thousand miles, would force them to confront the past. At the start of the book, Laney has years of defenses up—she won't let her mother in and yet knows she has to figure out why she's so closed off. Plus, the car's the ideal place for the music to play a role.

THE IDEA OF CONNECTING THE PAST WITH THE PRESENT IS A CENTRAL THEME IN *LINER NOTES*. CAN YOU TALK ABOUT WHY THIS MIGHT BE AND WHAT IT MEANS IN THE NOVEL?

As we all move forward in this incredible age of electronics and discovery, the idea of keeping hold to where we come from strikes me as very meaningful. I think sometimes my generation focuses on whatever's next—but it's during times of reflection and piecing together of our pasts that we best move forward. Somehow if you make sense of what *has* been, moving forward can be freeing instead of overwhelming. I used music to convey a link between the past and the present, a bond for Laney that allows her to communicate better with her mom and explain herself.

CAN YOU TELL US WHAT YOUR NEXT BOOK IS ABOUT? ANY MUSIC INVOLVED?

I'm excited about my next project—it's a novel about sisters, marital affairs, and the general craziness surrounding the week between Christmas and New Year's. Set in a quirky small town, the novel uses humor to get to the heart of big life choices—marriage, career, kids. Music isn't a central force this time, but it's perpetually the backdrop.

CRITICS HAVE NOTED THAT *LINER NOTES* IS A GREAT CHOICE FOR A BOOK GROUP OR THAT IT'S THE KIND OF BOOK THAT MAKES ITS WAY THROUGH WHOLE CIRCLES OF FRIENDS— WHY DO YOU THINK THIS IS?

First of all, that's such a nice thing to hear. I think that *Liner Notes* has broad appeal based on the fact that at its core, it's a mother-daughter book—and whether you had a close or rocky relationship with your mother or daughter, there's a story there. Plus, the music makes for a lot of conversational sharing. One book group wrote to me and told me that the book inspired each member to bring a tape from their own pasts and tell the "liner notes"—a kind of personal "Behind the Music." One of the ways people my age communicated was through tapes, so talking about their importance comes naturally. *Liner Notes* tells Laney's story, but maybe book groups or friends relate to it because we all have an internal soundtrack—we just have to choose to share it.

Like what you just read?

IRISH GIRLS ABOUT TOWN
Maeve Binchy, Marian Keyes, Cathy Kelly, et al.
Get ready to paint the town green. . . .

THE MAN I SHOULD HAVE MARRIED
Pamela Redmond Satran
Love him. Leave him. Lure him back.

GETTING OVER JACK WAGNER
Elise Juska
Love is nothing like an '80s song.

THE SONG READER
Lisa Tucker
Can the lyrics to a song reveal the secrets of the heart?

THE HEAT SEEKERS
Zane
Real love can be measured by degrees. . . .

I DO (BUT I DON'T)
Cara Lockwood
She has everyone's love life under control . . . except her own.
(Available June 2003)

doWn tOwn press

Great storytelling just got a new address.
Published by Pocket Books

Then don't miss these other great books from Downtown Press!

HOW TO PEE STANDING UP
Anna Skinner
Survival Tips for Hip Chicks.
(Available June 2003)

WHY GIRLS ARE WEIRD
Pamela Ribon
Sometimes life is stranger than you are.
(Available July 2003)

LARGER THAN LIFE
Adele Parks
She's got the perfect man. But real love is predictably unpredictable. . . .
(Available August 2003)

ELIOT'S BANANA
Heather Swain
She's tempted by the fruit of another . . . literally.
(Available September 2003)

BITE
C.J. Tosh
Life is short. Bite off more than you can chew.
(Hardcover available September 2003)

Look for them wherever books are sold
or visit us online at **www.downtownpress.com**.